The Loveday Scandals

Kate Tremayne

headline

First published in 2003
by HEADLINE BOOK PUBLISHING

First published in paperback in 2003
by HEADLINE BOOK PUBLISHING

10 9 8 7 6 5 4 3 2 1

ISBN 0 7472 6591 7

Typeset in Plantin by
Letterpart Limited, Reigate, Surrey

Printed and bound in Great Britain by
Mackays of Chatham plc, Chatham, Kent

Papers and cover board used by Headline are natural, recyclable
products made from wood grown in sustainable forests. The
manufacturing processes conform to the environmental
regulations of the county of origin.

HEADLINE BOOK PUBLISHING
A division of Hodder Headline
338 Euston Road
LONDON NW1 3BH

www.headline.co.uk
www.hodderheadline.com

To all my friends for their support and encouragement and especially to Linda Acaster and Audrey Reimann for some great times and sight-seeing tours which made the research for this book such fun.

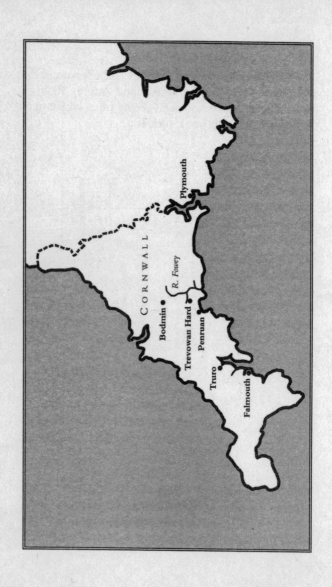

THE LOVEDAY FAMILY

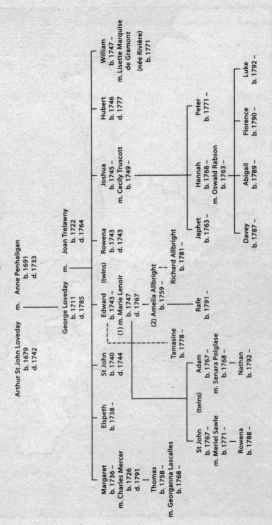

Arthur St John Loveday   m.   Anne Penhaligan
b. 1679   b. 1691
d. 1742   d. 1733

George Loveday   m.   Joan Trelawny
b. 1711   b. 1722
d. 1785   d. 1764

Margaret
b. 1736 –
m. Charles Mercer
d. 1791

Elspeth
b. 1738 –

St John
b. 1740
d. 1744

Edward   (twins)
b. 1743 –
(1) m. Marie Lenoir
b. 1747
d. 1767
(2) Amelia Allbright
b. 1759 –

Rowena
b. 1743
d. 1743

Joshua
b. 1745 –
m. Cecily Truscott
b. 1749 –

Hubert
b. 1746
d. 1777

William
b. 1747 –
m. Lisette Marquise
de Gramont
(née Rivière)
b. 1771

Thomas
b. 1758 –
m. Georganna Lascalles
b. 1768 –

Richard Allbright
b. 1781 –

Tamasine
b. 1778 –

St John   (twins)
b. 1767 –
m. Meriel Sawle
b. 1771 –

Adam
b. 1767 –
m. Senara Polglase
b. 1768 –

Rafe
b. 1791 –

Japhet
b. 1763 –

Hannah
b. 1768 –
m. Oswald Rabson
b. 1763 –

Peter
b. 1771 –

Rowena
b. 1788 –

Nathan
b. 1792 –

Davey
b. 1787 –

Abigail
b. 1789 –

Florence
b. 1790 –

Luke
b. 1792 –

Chapter One

1793

It was an hour before noon and Senara Loveday was enjoying what had become her daily walk around the grounds of the estate that would one day be her home. The land that had been neglected for decades was overgrown and the healing herbs that she used for her remedies grew in abundance. Boscabel, as its name suggested, had a magic of its own, and the wildness of nature reclaiming the once-formal flowerbeds and knot gardens held its own beauty for Senara.

Senara tilted her face towards the sun, her skin the colour of palest amber from her long hours in the open air, her hair the warm brown of freshly tilled earth. She breathed in the scent of roses and honeysuckle, which climbed unrestrained amongst the ivy-covered walls of the outbuildings, hiding the scars of crumbling wattle-and-daub walls, broken windowpanes and disintegrating thatch. Through an archway leading to the garden, marigolds and marguerites had self-seeded to form a white and golden carpet around the borders. In the stable yard, brambles laden with dark, succulent fruit twisted around a rusted plough and harrow, and spread across the flagstones.

Her wicker pannier filled with blackberries for preserving, Senara turned to study the Elizabethan manor house. The stone cladding around the porch was cracked and mottled with lichen. No one had lived here for over twenty years, and winter storms had taken their toll on the beautiful house. The stonework was broken on the upper storey of the turret. Tall brick chimneys rose above the long gallery whose lattice windows ran the entire length of the upper floor of the house. From a bonfire in the courtyard rose blue spirals of smoke as the flames consumed old timbers riddled with woodworm and deathwatch beetle. One of the apprentices from the Loveday shipyard threw more wood on the fire, and two carpenters unloaded a wagon of cut timber.

As the wife of Adam Loveday, Senara had accepted that the heir to a shipyard owned by one of the oldest families in Cornwall would wish to raise his family in style. Yet a grand mansion with immaculate gardens would have stifled Senara's gypsy blood. Adam had promised that the grounds of Boscabel would be her domain and should be landscaped as she desired. The renovation of the old house would be his creation and responsibility, for she knew nothing of grand mansions and she felt uncomfortable in large buildings.

Senara hummed softly as she walked to the wood at the edge of the gardens to collect the herbs she needed to attend her patients. Boscabel Wood was purpled in places by deep shadows. The late summer sun was low in a cloudless sky, its rays piercing the canopy of foliage to cast golden spears of light against the gnarled tree trunks. Senara paused to collect some lady's mantle, a herb that was effective in treating wounds, vomiting and the bloody flux. Engrossed in her work, she could push to the back of her mind the duty expected of her that evening. She had been invited to the end-of-harvest feast at Trevowan.

Trevowan was the home of Adam's family and this was the first time she had been invited to visit without her husband. She should be delighted that the Lovedays were holding out an olive branch and finally seemed to be accepting her as Adam's wife. Yet with Adam at sea it would be a traumatic ordeal, especially since the family expected her to stay the night at Trevowan. At least the harvest feast was a simple celebration for the tenants and farm workers, and she would not be forced to mix with the local gentry who she knew disapproved of Adam's choice of bride.

Senara was under no illusions that the Lovedays approved of her. They simply wanted to present a united front to their neighbours following the trial of Adam's twin brother, St John, accused of murder. St John had been declared innocent but the scandal had been the gossip of the county and it had harmed the reputation of the shipyard.

Senara rubbed the tender spot at the base of her spine. She was carrying her second child, though little evidence showed as yet in her slim figure. She pushed

3

aside her misgivings about the visit to Trevowan as she
walked to the grass slopes on the far side of the wood
in search of horehound to ease cases of consumption
or rheum of the lungs. As she worked, raucous cries
from pheasants in the undergrowth and magpies and
rooks in the treetops were accompanied by the songs
of linnets and blackbirds. A fox carrying a dead rabbit
peered at Senara through a lace fretwork of meadow-
sweet and tansy before continuing to his lair.

Senara gathered a bunch of comfrey and laid it in
her basket, enjoying the tranquillity and solitude of
Boscabel. Here she could savour the peace that only
nature could bring her. The constant hammering and
shouts of the shipyard, which was her current home,
were the sounds of an alien world where she still felt ill
at ease.

A distant shout made her look towards the crest of
the next hill, which sloped down towards an inlet of
the River Fowey. A woman in a blue riding habit
galloped at a dangerous pace over the rough ground
dappled with granite boulders. Recognising the sable
Arab mare belonging to Gwendolyn Druce, Senara
frowned. It was not like Gwen to be so reckless. Then
a second rider appeared – a man, in pursuit of Gwen.
Was the second rider another suitor encouraged by
Gwendolyn's mother, the Lady Anne? How galling
that must be for Gwen. She would love only one man
and he was as feckless as he was charming. Gwen had
been in love with Japhet Loveday for years, but Japhet
relished his freedom far too much to consider marriage. Unfortunately, whilst Gwen steadfastly refused

all alternative suitors, the Lady Anne Druce was equally resolved that her daughter would marry any man except Japhet Loveday.

Senara shook her head as she stooped to slice the sharp blade of her dagger through the stems of a bunch of St Peter's wort that she would use in a purge to ease the sciatica of a shipwright's wife. Dew from the morning mist still clung to its leaves. Unaccountably, the hairs at the back of Senara's neck tingled, a sign that forewarned her something was amiss.

Her eyes narrowed as she straightened to study the two riders once more. Gwen's mare had stumbled and her companion was gaining on her. The man was dressed as a gentleman and, as there was no accompanying groom, Senara surmised he was known to the family. But the grim determination in his posture increased Senara's unease and she could not dispel the feeling that Gwen was in danger. Her intuition was rarely wrong.

Senara ran to where she had tethered her mare, Hera. Abandoning her herb basket, she called to Scamp, her husband's dog. As she swung into the saddle, the liver and white crossbred spaniel appeared out of the undergrowth where he had been chasing squirrels.

Senara had covered less than half a mile when she heard a scream, which was abruptly cut off. Her unease turned to a sickening dread and she urged Hera faster. She was a fearless horsewoman, raised by her gypsy father to ride bareback as a child, but a fast-running inlet of the River Fowey cut her off from the direction of the scream. The two riders would have crossed by the stone bridge further upstream but Senara, fearing for the safety of Gwendolyn Druce, plunged Hera into the reed bed at the edge of the bank. Startled moorhens and coots squawked and flapped their wings noisily as they flew away from feeding in the reeds. The water was several yards wide but not so deep that Hera would lose her footing.

Scamp loved water and shot like an arrow into the water at her side. The cold water swirled around Senara's legs, drenching her green riding habit, but she did not falter.

A horse whinnied in the trees on the opposite bank, followed by the sound of scuffling and a muffled cry. There was a flash of blue through the branches and waist-high bracken, then silence. The wood was too thick to ride through so Senara dismounted, staggering under the weight of her sodden gown, which wrapped around her legs, making walking difficult.

Fear churned her stomach. 'Is that you, Gwen?'

A loud growl was her only reply. Senara pushed through the bracken into a small clearing to discover Gwen pressed against a tree trunk, striving to push away a man who held her tightly and was forcing his kisses upon reluctant lips. The pins had fallen from her chestnut hair and it was in disarray about her shoulders, while her lace stock and lapel of her jacket had been ripped in the struggle.

'Stand away from Miss Druce, or the dog will attack,' Senara commanded. 'Are you unharmed, Gwen?'

Gwen nodded, too shaken to speak as she struggled to regain her composure.

The man turned and pulled a pistol from inside his jacket. 'Set that cur on me and I shall shoot it.'

The arrogance of his tone roused Senara's anger. She recognised the thin figure and haughty features of Lieutenant Francis Beaumont. All summer Lady Anne Druce had encouraged him to call upon Gwendolyn.

'Sir, how dare you force yourself upon Miss Druce in such a despicable manner?'

Senara summoned Scamp to her side and ordered him to lie down before moving forward to confront the man. As she approached, his expression became sullen at her intrusion. He viewed her wet skirts with chilling derision and Senara could feel his scorn for her gypsy blood. But if he intended to intimidate her he failed. Senara despised such men.

'You mistake the matter, Mrs Loveday.' The words were a venomous hiss. 'I hold Miss Druce in the highest regard. We are to be betrothed. I have the blessings of her family.'

The colour was returning to Gwendolyn's cheeks and she shook her head. She was not an established beauty but when animated the soft lines of her oval face and almond-shaped eyes were striking. Her voice shook with outrage. 'You lie. I never agreed to wed you. You do not have my blessing, sir. Neither shall you. You sought to compromise me this day. I will not be browbeaten into a marriage that is repugnant to me.'

He rounded on Gwendolyn, his thin lips twisting

into a sneer. 'Your conceit astounds me, mistress. You should be grateful that a man of my position and family would consider you as his wife. Your reputation has been tarnished this summer by consorting with that rakehell Japhet Loveday.'

Gwendolyn flushed but the anger continued to spark in her eyes. 'It is your conduct which is reprehensible, sir. Japhet Loveday is a man of honour. He would never give false evidence in a court of law as you did at the last assizes. Your lies could have hanged St John Loveday. You sicken me.'

He squared his shoulders and stuck out his narrow chest. 'I was carrying out my duty as an officer of His Majesty's Excise Office. St John Loveday is a smuggler and murderer. I spoke the truth.'

Senara had heard enough. 'Mercifully, your evidence did not hold up in court. St John was acquitted. There was no evidence that he murdered Thadeous Lanyon. Lanyon had won many enemies as a smuggler and he killed anyone who crossed him.' She strode to Gwendolyn's side, the two angry women flanking the officer. Senara bristled. 'No gentleman would force their unwanted attentions upon a lady of Miss Druce's position as you have done.'

'What would a gypsy brat know of gentlemanly conduct?' Beaumont sneered.

The insult had no power to hurt Senara for she felt no shame in her heritage. Pride lifted her head. This man had been her husband's enemy for years – since the days that Beaumont and Adam had served together as midshipmen in the navy. After instigating a duel with Adam, Beaumont had been dismissed from the navy to serve upon an excise cutter. Unable to get his revenge upon Adam, Beaumont had taken up a vendetta against Adam's twin, St John. Again he had failed. Beaumont had abused his position as an excise officer, taking bribes from Thadeous Lanyon to turn a blind eye to the smuggler's trade.

'A true gentleman is a man of honour and integrity both in word and deed.' Her tone was scathing. 'I see no evidence of that in yourself.'

There was hatred in his eyes as he glared at Senara. He clearly held her responsible for thwarting his plans to damage Gwendolyn's honour in such a way that she would be forced to marry him. It was not love that drove him but greed for her substantial inheritance.

Beaumont grabbed Gwen's arm. 'You will marry me.'

She cried out at the pain he was inflicting and wrenched her arm free to slap his face. 'I will marry the man I love or no man at all. And certainly not an arrogant blackguard as you have shown yourself to be this day.'

Beaumont did not move and his face was rigid with fury. 'I will have you as my bride.'

Senara's flesh prickled in fear for the heiress at the menace of his threat. Scamp growled, his fangs barred as he edged closer to the lieutenant.

'You are on private land, Lieutenant Beaumont,' Senara informed him. 'My husband's land. Leave now or I shall be forced to summon the gamekeeper and bailiff to arrest you for trespass. I will also bear witness if Miss Druce presses charges of assault. That would ensure that you are never accepted within polite society again.'

His belligerence was frightening but Senara refused to back down. She had lied, for there was no game-keeper or bailiff at Boscabel – Adam had acquired the property in recent months and they could not afford servants to work here while they continued to live at Mariner's House.

Gwendolyn added her vehemence. 'If you present yourself at Traherne Hall again I shall inform my mother and Sir Henry of your conduct today.'

Lieutenant Beaumont smirked. 'The Lady Anne said you would be difficult. She has already placed an announcement in the *Sherborne Mercury* and informed the Reverend Mr Snell that the ceremony will take place in the old chapel at Traherne Hall in one month's time.'

'Mama, would never—'

Beaumont's cruel laughter cut across her words. 'It is all arranged. Unless you wish to create a scandal and be shunned by society, you have no choice but to marry me.' He turned on Senara. 'The Lovedays think that they are invincible. But they are not. They had better stay out of my affairs in the future.' He bowed mockingly to the women and marched away.

'I will never marry you, Lieutenant Beaumont.' Gwendolyn sagged against the trunk of a beech tree, her legs stripped of the strength to support her.

He whirled and flung out his arm in an intimidating manner. 'Marry me you will, or you and anyone who crosses me will live to regret it.'

Gwendolyn put a shaking hand to her temple. 'Does Mama hate me so much to wish me to wed that monster?'

The heiress's pain was heartrending to witness. Gwendolyn had been one of the few people of her class to accept Senara as Adam's bride. Putting a comforting arm around Gwen, Senara was fearful. Lieutenant Beaumont was a vindictive man and his threat was no idle one.

Gwendolyn ripped off the torn stock and crumpled it in disgust. 'I love Japhet. He is the only man I will marry.'

Senara shivered, chilled by the premonition that if Gwendolyn continued in her infatuation with Japhet against the wishes of her family, it would bring further retribution to the Lovedays.

Senara did not want to be unkind but she felt the need to be truthful. 'I can understand you not wishing to marry such an unpleasant man as Lieutenant Beaumont. Yet as Japhet has left Cornwall again you must realise that it is unlikely he will marry you.'

Gwendolyn shook her head and looked around to locate her mare, which had wandered to the river to drink. As they walked back to the horses, Gwendolyn continued, 'I believe that Japhet loves me. Mama said such dreadful things to him after St John's trial. She caught Japhet kissing me.' For a moment Gwendolyn closed her eyes as though hugging that memory close to her heart. She sighed and her throat worked as she struggled against her anguish. 'Mama called him a

11

scurrilous knave, a lecher and a blackguard. She accused him of corrupting me and declared he was the worst reprobate in all Cornwall. That was so unjust.'

'Your mother spoke in the heat of the moment.'

They had reached the horses and Gwendolyn rested her head against her mare's neck. 'Mama will not have Japhet's name mentioned in the house. She told him that she would never allow her daughter to marry a profligate, a man who shames the Loveday name by his base living and gaming.'

Senara was shocked. Japhet did have a wild streak but he was no worse than many other young gentlemen of his class. He was loyal to his family and had spent many weeks this summer helping his sister, Hannah, on her farm when Hannah's husband, Oswald, had been ill. Japhet was a complex man, but if he dallied with a woman's affections, he would never sway them with false promises. Women adored Japhet and welcomed the handsome rogue into their beds.

'Mama wanted to drive Japhet away and she succeeded. But only because Japhet had convinced himself that I would be happier without him.' The pain was stark in Gwendolyn's eyes as they pleaded with Senara to support her faith in Adam's cousin. She gripped Senara's hands as she spoke with passion. 'You love Adam no less than I love Japhet and many said that your relationship was doomed. I know Japhet's faults, but I adore him. I can accept that if it means I am part of his life. He makes me feel alive, gives me confidence to be myself. I used to be such a timid mouse. He made me see that I can stand up against my domineering mother.'

Gwendolyn tipped back her chestnut ringlets, her eyes fierce with determination. 'I will not marry Lieutenant Beaumont. I am of age and I am in command of my own fortune. I am going to London, for eventually Japhet will visit there. He never stays away from the capital for long.' She hoisted herself into the saddle and gathered up the reins. 'Mama will learn that I will no longer be bullied by her, or anyone.'

The tremor of her lower lip showed the vulnerability beneath her bravado.

Senara mounted Hera, and as they turned the horses towards the stone bridge Senara did not doubt that Gwendolyn would carry out her scheme. That took courage, for by such an act Gwendolyn's reputation would be damaged. The heiress could find herself cast out from society and shunned by her friends.

Caution prompted Senara to reason with the distraught woman. 'Lieutenant Beaumont could be bluffing. Your mother would not have announced your betrothal without your consent.'

'Mama wants me wed. And he is desperate to get his hands on my fortune, for if he is not wed before his cousin has a child, his grandfather will disinherit Beaumont in favour of his cousin. The baby is due in two months.'

The greed of people never failed to astound Senara. Providing that her family had a roof over their heads and enough food to eat, money had never been important to her, although poverty was not something she willingly embraced, for there had been too many nights in the past when she had gone to bed hungry. Senara could sympathise with a woman who was desperate to marry the man she loved, but she found it hard to understand the reasoning of gentry who would bully a wealthy woman into an unhappy marriage.

'Gwen, surely your family would not tolerate such underhand tricks from Beaumont? From the way Adam speaks of Sir Henry, he is a man of honour. He never would allow you to be forced into such a marriage. Beaumont is a fortune-hunter.' When Gwendolyn continued to look distressed, Senara added, 'You must go to Sir Henry and explain how you feel, but it would be prudent to keep your feelings for Japhet from him. His friendship with Japhet does not mean that he would see a man without a profession, or the means to support a wife, as a suitable husband for you.'

The tension in Gwendolyn's shoulders relaxed. 'You are so wise, Senara. Sir Henry will help me. I will be free of Mama's tyranny. But I mean to marry Japhet.'

Chapter Two

A late summer haze hung over the wheat field on a slope of the hills at the northern part of the Trevowan estate. The air was spangled with a fine powder of dust and straw, stirred by the long-handled scythes, as a score of men in loose linen smocks worked in a line across the land. The rhythmic swish of the scythes was accompanied by the song of skylarks that were no more than specks against the cobalt sky. Sweat ran down the ruddy faces of the workers and flattened their hair to their skulls.

Harvest time banded together the estate labourers, living in their tied cottages, and the local villagers of Penruan and Trewenna. All able-bodied men worked to cut the wheat – a competition running between them as they vied to cut the most. Edward Loveday rewarded the winner with an extra silver crown in his wages.

There was a flow of banter from the men as they teased or encouraged their companions. While the women tied each sheaf and stacked them in rows, they gossiped, laughed and reminisced over the events of past years. Babies were laid on shawls in the shade and were watched over by an arthritic grandmother. The older children worked with the women, while the younger ones carried water to the workers to drink, or separated weeds and wildflowers from the cut wheat. Most of the children regarded the harvest as a time of play and not of work. They were easily diverted from their tasks to give chase to each other and hide amongst the stooks, or run after a rabbit or pheasant that had been startled from its hiding place.

Everyone had been working since daylight. Now, as the sun skimmed over the hills to the west, the folk songs and ribaldry faded and the workers concentrated on cutting and stacking the final sheaves before dark.

The field had turned to the warm gold of honey in the evening light and Edward Loveday leaned on the handle of his scythe to watch the last sheaf stacked. He wiped the sweat from his brow with a coloured kerchief, weary from his work but filled with a deep contentment. He had been working in his shirtsleeves since early morning, putting in as many hours as the labourers. For thirty years he had worked on his land and also laboured as a master shipwright on the vessels built in the Loveday shipyard. Born with the privileges of money and land, he was no stranger to back-straining work, and calluses and blisters roughened his hands. The crop had been a good one and some of the tension that had beset him in recent weeks eased. The harvest would pay off a substantial part of the debts that had mounted on the estate.

The workers cheered as the last sheaf was placed with its companions. Nora Tonkin, whose family worked on the estate and lived in one of the four tied cottages, rose from where she had been sitting amongst the stooks and held up the woven corn dolly. It was presented to Edward with a curtsy.

'May the spirit of this prosperous harvest bless Trevowan's fields in the coming year, sir.' Nora Tonkin blushed as Edward's fingers brushed hers as he took the offering. She was ten years younger than Edward and had borne seven children, the youngest still a babe in arms. She was plump and pretty and like many of the local women was affected by Edward's still handsome looks.

Edward smiled and bowed graciously to Nora. 'Thank you, you have made a fine corn god.' He handed it to Isaac Nance, the estate bailiff, to place in the barn for safekeeping. Next spring it would be cast into the field with the sowing of the seed to bless the field with fertility and abundance. It was an old and revered tradition, and one that any farmer would no more fail to honour than to leave his tools out to rust through winter. Tradition and folklore were an integral part of a farmer's year, and when the harvest was good you gave thanks to the realms of nature and also to God in his church.

Edward was a tall and imposing figure as he addressed the workers. 'Well done to get the crop harvested before nightfall. There will be drink and a feast to mark the end of the harvest. Make your way

17

to the field behind the barn where refreshments have been laid out for you.'

He turned to Isaac Nance, who had collected the scythes and placed them in a cart to be stored in the barn. 'I have much for which to thank you, Isaac. You reaped most of the harvest whilst we were in Bodmin for St John's trial. If the weather had not held we would have stood no chance to ease our debts.'

''Twern't nothing, master. I but did my job.' The stocky bailiff was muscular and strong; his eyes, creased into walnut folds, were vigilant as he surveyed their work. 'It be a goodly yield. Master St John has done you proud with his hard work on the estate this year.'

Edward nodded. He was saddened that St John was not here to receive his gratitude. The elder twin had now proved his worthiness to inherit the estate in a transformation from the wastrel ways of his early manhood, when Edward had feared that his heir would squander his fortune on gambling.

Not that St John had become the respectable citizen Edward would wish. His involvement with smugglers had led to the charges of murder and St John's trial. Though his son had been found innocent it had been agreed that he must leave the country for a year or two until speculation and the gossip surrounding the trial died down. Gossip could wreck the family's rickety finances. Edward needed customers to regain their confidence in the integrity of the Loveday shipyard. The family had been the centre of too many scandals in recent years. Respectability and stability were needed to bring them back from the brink of financial ruin. Whilst St John stayed with their cousins in Virginia, Edward hoped his son would reform and cast off the wilder, dissolute side of his nature.

Edward returned to the house, walking with a long assured stride through his fields. There was still warmth in the evening air and he breathed deeply. There had been so many financial problems in recent years that he had forgotten the simple joy of walking over his estate and being at peace with his accomplishments and home. The prospect of the harvest cancelling many of his debts lightened his step.

As he entered the grounds of the house he could detect the song of the sea as it broke over the beach of Trevowan Cove. The three gables of the house were in shadow; the ivy recently trimmed back from the stonework had left a tracery of black lines where the stems had clung to the wall. The glass walls of the orangery had been added as a wedding present to Edward's first wife, Marie, when they had wed twenty-seven years ago. Marie was French, and Edward had built the orangery to remind his wife of her French home. Marie had died a year after their marriage, giving birth to the twins.

Through the windows of the orangery he saw his second wife, Amelia, whom he had married five years ago. He raised his hand in greeting to her, but the gesture was not acknowledged as she sat staring out across the gardens.

He hesitated before entering the house. The trials and scandals of the last two years had been difficult for Amelia to accept. She had led an unworldly life in London before her first husband died, and her upbringing had been puritanical by the general standards of the day. The Lovedays were by nature wild and reckless, and Amelia had struggled to accept her new family, but St John's trial had been too much for her to bear and it had put a strain on their marriage.

He entered the house by the side door and was met in the entrance hall by Amelia, the sound of her heels agitated on the black and white marble floor. He smiled in greeting, conscious of the sweat and dirt on his clothing.

'The last of the wheat is cut. It is the best harvest for several years. I am proud of St John.'

He was disheartened that Amelia remained aloof, almost guarded, as though she was bracing herself against an unseen attack. The worries of this summer had slimmed her figure, brought hollows to her cheeks and a heightened prominence to her fine cheekbones. Her auburn hair, worn high in a chignon and covered by a square of lace, had lost its brightness and was threaded through with recent streaks of grey.

'Our luck is changing, my dear,' he added to cheer her.

The effort it took Amelia to return his smile was obvious. 'Let us pray that is so. But we still must live through the scandal that has been thrust upon us. Have you seen how the villagers look askance at Rowena and whisper behind their hands?'

The laughter of the five-year-old child in question

carried to them as Bernie Tonkin, Nora's eight-year-old son, chased her in the courtyard.

Amelia put a trembling hand to her mouth and shook her head. 'The county gossips that Rowena has been deserted by her scapegrace father. And as for her trollop of a mother . . .'

'We have only hearsay that Meriel did not sail with St John.'

'Lady Traherne lost no time in informing us that Meriel *had* run off with Lord Wycham after St John's trial.' Amelia kept her voice low but there was anger in her eyes. 'The way Rowena was left without explanation is something I will never forgive. Your son and his wife have a great deal to answer for. I love Rowena dearly, but she has been crying herself to sleep every night since her parents abandoned her.'

'Abandoned is a harsh word, my dear.' Edward curbed his annoyance at Amelia's condemnation. 'You wanted St John and Meriel away from Trevowan until the gossip of the trial died down.'

Amelia stiffened with affront. She adjusted the placement of a Chinese vase on a carved Jacobean chest. 'As any self-respecting woman would wish her family free from gossip. Meriel's flight and Rowena's presence here but adds to the scandal which has hung over us since St John's trial. How will we live with the shame of it all?'

'St John was judged innocent. I never believed him capable of murder, nor would anyone who knew him.' Edward's patience was wearing thin at his wife's obsession with appearances. It was a trait that had not

been apparent when he had first met her. He rolled his shoulders to erase the pain from the hours bent over a scythe. 'I see no reason to be ashamed of anything my family has done. Rowena is a resilient child. St John will be away a year or two, but she has the love of her family and the friendship of her cousins to sustain her. Rowena will come to no harm.'

'I pray that will be so.' Amelia's voice rose to echo around the high ceiling of the hall, its curved staircase lined with ancestral portraits.

'Is everything in readiness for the feast tonight?' Edward deliberately changed the subject.

Amelia turned away. 'I will check with Winnie Fraddon that the food has been laid out in the barn. With everyone involved in the harvest Winnie had only one maid to help her. I spent two hours working in the kitchen myself.'

Amelia looked so pale and drawn that Edward wanted to make amends for the pain she had suffered through the behaviour of his sons. He did not like dissension within his home. Amelia had never complained of the economies that he had enforced, neither did she balk at taking on a servant's task if the situation required it. He tenderly cupped her chin with his forefinger and turned her face towards him.

'Now that our fortunes are looking brighter, you must employ another maid to help with the running of the house. You have made many sacrifices in the last two years. All will now be well. These last years have been far from the life of entertainment and luxury you left behind in London. Our luck is changing. St John's

time in Virginia will be the making of him. Adam is married and settled now.'

Amelia gave a strained laugh. 'I would not describe Adam's life as settled. He is roving the seas in his ship, seeking his fortune. Now we are at war with France and Adam has been granted letters of marque, he is no better than a government-approved pirate. Adam should be helping you in the shipyard, not putting his life in danger.'

'He needs the money from his voyage to rebuild Boscabel. The loans we have to repay, which were raised to sustain the shipyard, leave little in our coffers to spare for Adam. We also have to recover our reputation after Thadeous Lanyon claimed that the wreck of the *Sea Sprite*, which was built in our yard, was caused by her unseaworthiness. Our name was cleared but we lost orders and it takes time to re-establish the trust of our customers.'

'All the more reason for Adam to take on the responsibility of the yard which will one day be his.' Amelia remained unsympathetic.

Edward tried again to reason with her. 'If Adam returns successful from his voyage, it will prove that the speed of *Pegasus* puts her ahead of anything in her class. *Pegasus* and the cutter that Adam designed are the way forward for the yard to recoup our fortune. Otherwise we return to constructing fishing smacks. For three generations our family has worked to build the prestige of the Loveday yard and I will not allow it to go under.'

'I still do not approve of piracy,' Amelia returned.

Edward shrugged and allowed his hand to drop to his side. 'It was how my grandfather made the fortune, which enabled us to start the yard. Our family is not without skeletons in its cupboards. But I suspect that few families are without secrets which they would prefer left buried.'

Amelia laid a hand against her heart. 'I pray there will be no further scandals in my lifetime. St John and Adam are in their mid-twenties and have responsibilities. It is time to put their wildness behind them. And as for their cousin Japhet . . . Again, I can only pray that he brings no further shame upon us. It is time he married and settled down to a respectable life.'

As he washed and changed from his work clothes Edward's thoughts echoed some of his wife's. Surely the trial would have shaken St John enough to curb the wildness that had made him join a band of smugglers. Adam had a wife, a child, and a new home to work for.

Edward would have preferred that Adam had sailed with a valuable cargo and made his fortune as a merchant adventurer, instead of intending to prey upon any enemy ship now they were at war with France. Life at sea was dangerous enough without Adam becoming involved with the war. But a privateer could reap high rewards. The sea had been in the blood of many of his family and Edward did not condemn his son's quest for riches and adventure. One of his brothers had lost his life whilst blockading the American ports when the colony had fought for its independence from England. And Edward's youngest brother, William, was a naval captain and commanded a ship that had sailed with the English fleet.

The pressure of the last few years was making Edward feel his age. He wanted to reap the rewards of his years of hard work expanding the yard. It was the heritage of his children. St John, as the elder twin, would one day inherit Trevowan, and Adam the shipyard. There was now also two-year-old Rafe, the son Amelia had borne him, to provide for.

Edward looked out of the window of his dressing room. The apple and pear orchard contained the beehives tended by Amelia, and beyond that a few hardy blooms covered the wall of the rose garden. In the distance the sea was dotted with a handful of sailing ships heading either for Fowey or Falmouth harbours. As he pulled on his navy broadcloth jacket Edward hoped that all his family skeletons were securely buried and peace would return to his home life.

Even as the thought surfaced, his conscience mocked him. There was one recent secret from his own past that could threaten the very foundation of his marriage if Amelia ever discovered it.

The young woman pulled her weary body over a stile and paused on its wooden step to survey her surroundings. No more than a mile ahead the peak of a cliff showed the line of the coast. Tamasine closed her eyes in relief. An hour ago an old woman gathering early blackberries had told her that

Trevowan lay four miles along the coast.

Tamasine shielded her eyes from the evening sun, the breeze snaking her long, dark hair around her face. Three gables of a house were visible through the trees. Could that be Trevowan? She glanced self-consciously at her attire. Her cloak and plain grey school dress were dusty from a week walking from Bodmin. It was ten days since she had run away from the Mertle Moxon Ladies' Academy in Salisbury, refusing any longer to tolerate the strict regime.

There were grass stains on her skirt. Her feet were swollen and raw with blisters and she had removed her shoes and hose, tying her sturdy shoes by their laces and hanging them around her neck.

Her initial confidence at presenting herself to her guardian, Edward Loveday, had begun to fade when she arrived in Bodmin to witness the end of St John Loveday's trial. Following immediately upon the trauma of the trial was not the right moment to approach her guardian's family.

Now she was worried that Mertle Moxon would have contacted Mr Loveday about her disappearance. She had not expected to be received with open arms by her guardian, but she hoped that the surprise of her arrival would prevail upon his mercy. Her stomach growled with hunger. She had not eaten since waking in the deserted charcoal burners' hut yesterday morning where she had spent the night.

Tamasine climbed from the stile and pulled from her pocket a small cube of cheese. It was all she had left of the food she had purchased in Bodmin to sustain her on her journey. She was light-headed from lack of nourishment, and the urge to lie down on the grass and sleep was almost irresistible.

When she'd run away from the academy she had viewed the escapade as an adventure. The mail coach she had taken to Bodmin had been an exciting journey and she had been idealist and enthusiastic that all would be well. Although she had had to fend off the unwanted attentions of a man who had tried to seduce her when the coach stopped overnight at an inn, she had avoided any further molestation from strangers after she left Bodmin.

The nights alone on the road had been frightening, and several times she had hidden behind hedgerows when she heard riders approaching after dark. Neither had she risked asking any wagon driver for a ride.

The excitement of her journey had faded to become an ordeal and a battle against hunger and exhaustion. Twice she had woken chilled and on the point of despair when she was drenched from a night shower of rain. Her determination had kept her going. She would not arrive weak and broken. She would be strong and succeed. The idealism of youth and naivety bolstered her strength. She must be close to her goal. To sleep now would delay her and, weak from hunger as she was, would only make the final stage of her journey even harder.

Tamasine lifted her skirts to tramp over long tussocks of grass, but halfway across the field she swayed and fell to her knees. She dragged herself upright. What if they did not welcome her? It had been presumptuous of her to assume that after one meeting with his ward Edward Loveday would open his home to her. Was it not more likely that he would have kept her identity a secret from his family?

Tamasine tossed back her dark hair, a determined fire returning to her azure eyes. She had come too far to turn back now.

Chapter Three

On the same night as the harvest feast at Trevowan, Japhet Loveday sat with his arm resting on his bent knee under the canopy of an ancient chestnut tree. The branches were as thick as a woman's thigh and curved in shielding arches around him. He was as motionless as the air, and his stare was brooding as he studied the moonlit road across the heath. On the horizon the lights of London hovered like sparks from a bonfire. Since late afternoon he had sat waiting but the highway across the heath remained deserted.

His stomach growled at not receiving food for two days. It was not the first time he had faced deprivation, for Madame Fortune was a fickle mistress and, while he chose to live by his wits, he doubted it would be the last time hunger was his companion. The sourness in his stomach matched his mood. He was nine-and-twenty and until now he had prided himself on being master of his own fortune and freedom.

Japhet narrowed his stare. He loved life and women in equal measure, and for years he had shied away from any relationship once his precious freedom was threatened. But suddenly that complacency had been stripped from him and from the most unexpected quarter – Gwendolyn Druce.

Japhet rubbed his long slender fingers across his brow. For years he had enjoyed Gwendolyn's friendship. Gwendolyn was an heiress who would one day marry well. Japhet had always known she was not for him. Yet to have his own reputation and unsuitability as a husband thrown in his face by Gwendolyn's mother had struck him more forcefully than he would have deemed possible. He had chosen to leave Cornwall to safeguard Gwen's reputation. So why did his conscience bray as stubbornly as an ass that he had failed Gwen?

The feeling of discontent intensified. The Lady Anne had been justified in her accusations when she had discovered Gwen in his arms. The woman's fury had been vitriolic.

Japhet had been born a gentleman, though as the son of a parson he had no fortune of his own, and had to make his own way in the world. He had been a womaniser and a gambler – as were many men of his generation and background. Also, when financial necessity drove him, he had even been a rogue who had stepped too often and too close to the wrong side of the law.

He picked up his sword belt that lay on the ground at his side. There was a pistol in his belt, another in his saddle holster and a dagger secreted in his boot. Japhet never ventured anywhere unarmed. The sword was the weapon of a gentleman and he was an expert swordsman. He had needed that skill to save his life on several occasions. His rakehell existence was not something he was proud of. Gwendolyn was not like his other women – who were usually neglected wives looking for the love and excitement a man like Japhet could provide. Gwen was an innocent and that had always been the greatest problem between them.

It had been as much to push Gwendolyn from his thoughts as to re-establish his finances that he had chosen the reckless path of highway robbery. Danger brought its own excitement. A restless wildness had driven Japhet since he left Cornwall. It needed to be dissipated if he was to find peace. As though sensing his master's sombre mood Japhet's Arab mare, Sheba, nuzzled his shoulder. He absently stroked her nose. 'My beauty, you are the only female who does not complicate my life.'

Sheba snorted, blowing the long tendrils of Japhet's ebony hair, which was tied back with a black ribbon. Japhet grimaced. 'Do you also doubt my integrity?' Sheba shook her ebony head, rattling her harness as she turned away to tear at the long grass. At least his mare was not starving from his current lack of funds.

At a stirring on the heath that was louder than the song of the nightjars, Japhet tensed. The distant pounding of galloping horses and rumble of an approaching coach were unmistakable.

He rose and gathered Sheba's reins. 'So my beauty, it seems that fate decrees that I become a highwayman this night. I was about to abandon the notion as ill-conceived.'

Japhet pulled a black silk kerchief over his lower face and jerked the wide brim of his hat low over his eyes before mounting Sheba. They trotted out of the cover of the trees to stand across the road. In the moonlight, the track ahead curved in a silvery arc as it skirted a coppice and he would be hidden from the coachmen's view. When the coach, pulled by four grey horses, rounded the curve, Japhet drew two pistols and cocked them in readiness.

'Halt, or I shoot.' Japhet adopted a rough accent to aid his disguise.

Apart from an ageing driver there was a burly liveried postillion whose close-set eyes and heavy brow were those of a man who used brawn before brains. Another liveried servant stood on the footplate at the rear of the vehicle but he had raised his hands and looked too terrified to move.

Sheba stood without moving as she had been trained. Nerves tightened Japhet's stomach and he began to sweat. He had picked many a pocket when driven by need, but this was the first time he had taken to highway robbery. The idea had been born out of anger and a desire to get back at society for Gwen's mother's condemnation.

As the coach slowed the postillion raised a pistol. Japhet reacted by firing his own weapon as a warning. At the same moment the horses pulled to the left and Japhet was aghast to see the postillion clutch his shoulder, his weapon clattering to the ground. Japhet's throat dried and his heart raced with growing fear. The hold-up was not going to plan. He could have killed the postillion. No robbery was worth taking another's life.

It was too late for him to back down. Even if he rode away, he would be pursued and hunted. 'That was foolish. The next man who draws a weapon against me dies.'

He replaced the spent pistol in the saddle holster, his stare fixed on the coachman and footman as he guided Sheba with his legs to the side of the coach. He leaned forward to wrench open the door to address the passengers: 'No one inside is going to do anything foolish, I trust.'

A middle-aged and still beautiful blonde-haired woman glared at him with defiance. There were jewels sparkling at her throat, wrist and ears. The man beside her was some years younger. He was dressed in a yellow and black striped cut-away coat and a profusion of lace was at his throat and wrists.

'Get out of the coach,' Japhet ordered, easing Sheba back as the two passengers stepped to the ground. 'Hand over your valuables and no one will be hurt.'

'Damn your eyes!' The man was rigid with anger and his hand went to his jacket as he alighted.

'Put your hands in the air,' Japhet commanded. 'If that's a pistol you are reaching for, you'll be dead before you draw it.'

The man raised his hands. 'You err gravely if you think to rob us.' His eyes glittered in the moonlight and there was suppressed fury in the set of his jaw as he found himself helpless to retaliate.

Japhet recognised him as Sir Pettigrew Osgood, a profligate and gambler. Japhet had sat at cards with

Osgood on several occasions. He had never liked the baronet, who had a country seat in Berkshire and houses in London and Bath. He was reputedly mean with his money and a poor loser at cards.

Japhet trusted that his mask and altered voice would disguise his identity. It was cursed ill luck to hold up someone who knew him. Japhet was glad that he had taken the precaution of rubbing soot over Sheba's white markings so that his horse could not be identified.

'You will live to regret this night,' Sir Pettigrew Osgood warned. 'You'll hang for this infamy.'

Japhet ignored the taunt but was aware that his position was precarious. Danger had always excited him and overriding his fear was a rush of exhilaration. 'That remains to be seen. In the meantime I would relieve you of your purse and jewels.'

At any moment the driver or footman could draw a hidden pistol and shoot him. Japhet could not keep his eyes on them all. He brought his riding whip down on the lead horse's rump and shouted, 'Ride on! Get up there, my beauties!'

The horses plunged forward, forcing the driver to haul on the reins to control them as they bolted into the night. It would be some minutes before the driver had them under control and he could return to his master.

The thrill of the moment heated Japhet's blood and he began to enjoy the escapade. 'Now, sir, your gold hunter watch, purse and jewels, if you would be so kind.'

'Devil take you for a lily-livered knave! Put down that pistol and face me like a man, then we will see how brave you are.' Sir Pettigrew pulled out his money pouch.

'No tricks!' Japhet took the heavy pouch and dropped it into a bag that hung from the pommel of his saddle.

Osgood glared at him with impotent fury as he withdrew the hunter chain from his waistcoat and removed three rings with large gemstones from his fingers. 'You may hide behind a mask but you will not escape justice. My uncle is a magistrate.'

'They have to catch me before they can hang me. And I'll have your diamond stock pin,' Japhet mocked, then bowed to the woman. 'Now, madam, your jewels, if you please.'

'If you want what is mine you must take them for yourself,' she challenged. 'What cur steals from a defenceless woman? These jewels were my mother's and she but recently died. They are all I have to remember her by.'

Japhet chuckled as the woman placed a hand theatrically to her heart. He recognised her as an actress who was famous for her bawdy roles. She claimed to be in her late twenties but, close to, Japhet guessed that she must be a decade older. Even so, she was a voluptuous temptress and possessed a sexual allure few women could match.

'The world knows that Celestine Yorke was a penniless orphan. Those trinkets were gifts from your paramours. They can be easily replaced.'

'Insolent knave!' Celestine Yorke's eyes narrowed. Her hands clasped her hips and she thrust out her breasts in provocative defiance. 'So, cur that you are, you recognise me. I am fêted as "the Darling of London". There will be an uproar and a price on your head for this outrage.'

Japhet unclasped the necklace and bracelet. He was close enough to smell her heady perfume and was intrigued by the brazenness of her stare. She showed no fear, but then the woman was notorious for her audacity. Her talent as an actress was debatable, but her amours over the last fifteen or so years had made her infamous. 'Are these not the diamonds which you insisted Lord Egerton paid you for a single night of your company? The story was the talk of London for weeks. Those jewels were all that remained of Egerton's wife's legacy that he had gambled away. He shot himself a week later when you spurned his further advances.'

Celestine Yorke tilted her head to appraise Japhet. 'Egerton was weak and dissolute. If I had not taken the necklace it would have been his next gaming stake. I've never underestimated my value. Do you truly intend to deprive me of my jewels? I am but a poorly paid actress.'

She stepped forward, her manner coquettish in a bid to save her finery. Japhet allowed his finger to trail along her neck but he was too worldly to be tricked by her duplicity. 'Stand back, Mistress Yorke.' His natural gallantry made it hard for him to steal from a woman. The bracelet would fetch fifty guineas and the money pouch had been heavy enough to contain another hundred in gold. Tonight he would be generous.

'Dear lady, your bravery moves me. I shall take only the bracelet, a trifling trinket compared to the diamond necklace. It will be something for me to remember you by – a memento from London's most alluring actress.'

'Damn your insolence!' Sir Pettigrew Osgood choked, having given her the bracelet last week.

The actress smiled at Japhet. 'Oh, I am sure the trinket will be replaced by one of far greater value if my admirer wishes to retain my favours.'

The ruthless streak in Japhet admired her audacity. He raised her hand to his lips. 'It has been a pleasure meeting you, dear lady.'

She ran the tip of her tongue across her lips. 'Under other circumstances I am sure the pleasure would have been all mine, sir.'

Japhet backed Sheba away from the couple and bowed to Celestine Yorke. 'Your pardon for delaying your journey.' He handed her the necklace. 'The driver will soon have the horses under control and by then I shall be far from here. Your servant, madam.'

He rode off to the sound of Sir Pettigrew Osgood's curses.

Celestine rounded on her lover. 'Fool! What use to stand there damning the knave? Why did you not challenge him?'

'He would have shot me before I could fire.' Osgood's eyes narrowed as he watched the rider disappear into the night. It had been too dark to see his face clearly even if he had not been wearing a mask. The villain may have dressed like a gentleman but his accent was that of a common man. If the heath was the vagabond's haunt, Sir Osgood would pay ruffians to lie in wait for his next attempt to rob his betters. He would be caught. 'Highwaymen rarely escape the gallows and I shall enjoy watching that rogue dance at Tyburn. That knave shall pay for his infamy this night. I shall remember that voice and I shall personally post a reward of twenty guineas for his capture.'

'Twenty guineas! You would place so paltry a sum upon my safety, or the gift you gave me, which you presented with your undying love.' Celestine poured out her scorn. Sir Pettigrew had been her paramour for less than a month and the bracelet had been his only gift. A clutchfist of a lover was no use to her. 'All highwaymen should be hounded by the law. Make it one hundred guineas.'

Sir Pettigrew Osgood winced at such extravagance. Celestine was too free with her demands on his money, but she was a sensuous and exciting mistress and he had no intention of losing her. The money pouch was a trifling amount compared to his monthly income from his vast estate and investments, but he was an innately greedy man, and to lose any possession to a common thief was something he could never forgive or forget.

The carriage returned, and as he assisted Celestine inside, he said, 'It will be as you say and your ruby bracelet will be replaced by one of diamonds.'

When the carriage set off he pulled her down on to the seat. After the ordeal of the robbery he needed to make love to her.

Celestine laughed at his ardour and eagerly accommodated him. But even as she responded to his lovemaking her thoughts were on the bold highwayman. She had always admired the exploits of the gentlemen of the road and had visited several of the most notorious in Newgate Prison before they were hanged. The highwayman who had robbed them tonight was no common thief. The devil-may-care twinkle in his eye sent a shiver of anticipation through her. He would be a deliciously wicked and exciting lover . . .

The last six months had been difficult. Celestine saw a rival in every young actress who appeared on the London stage. Recently the playhouses had not been filled to capacity, and she had begun to fear that she was losing her appeal to the public. That must be recaptured, and how better than for it to be known that she had faced near death from a highwayman? She wove a story where the rogue had only spared her and her companion because of her fame and favour with the people.

Celestine warmed to her ruse. She would engage a pamphleteer to pen her ordeal. Her courage would win the hearts of the people and she would retain her place as 'the Darling of London'.

Celestine had no intention of losing her popularity and returning to obscurity. For seventeen years she had been the mistress of any man who could further her career, or provide her with jewels and riches. Born Mary Grey, she had spent her first thirteen years as the favoured child of a major in the King's Hussars. Her mother, Lily, had been indifferent to her existence, but basking in the love of her father, the young Mary Grey had been content. Unfortunately, the major had a wife who was not Celestine's mother. When her father was killed in a duel, shot by Lily's latest lover, Celestine learned the cruelty the world could inflict upon a bastard child.

A year after her father's death, Celestine awoke to the sound of creditors banging on the door. She found herself alone in the rented house that had overnight been stripped of furniture. Later she learned that Lily Grey had left with a new officer lover when his regiment sailed to India. Lily had taken all her possessions except the daughter whose blossoming beauty she viewed as a rival to her own. Celestine was penniless, homeless and alone.

There followed a year of fear and nightly terrors that she chose to forget. She thieved and whored to survive, until an ageing actor heard her singing in a tavern for any coppers the men would throw at her. He made her his mistress, changed her name to Celestine Yorke and schooled her in acting. At sixteen she made her first appearance in a play. Her voice thrilled the audience, and her beauty and hourglass figure became her fortune.

Within a month she left the actor and was set up in rooms paid for by a young and handsome nobleman.

She became the toast of the playhouse, courted by the wealthiest men in England.

Gradually in the last two years, the royal lovers and politicians who vied for her favours became less eager for her company. She had amassed a large house and a fortune in jewellery, and a thousand pounds was lodged in her account at Mercer and Lascalles Bank.

Celestine had a voracious appetite for new lovers and was rarely faithful to any, no matter how wealthy or important.

In the darkness of the carriage Celestine's lips curved into a smile. Sir Pettigrew dozed after their lovemaking when he should have been attentive and admiring of her charms. She was becoming bored with him.

The interior lantern in the coach had briefly revealed the highwayman's greenish hazel eyes and fine-shaped black brows. He was a bold, dashing adventurer with a self-possession and commanding air that marked him as a gentleman. If they ever met again Celestine would certainly recognise him.

Chapter Four

Gwendolyn was in a rebellious mood and her thoughts were in turmoil. She had not returned to Traherne Hall after leaving Senara but had ridden to the moor where she had spent hours trying to devise how she would escape her mother's schemes to wed her to Beaumont.

Even when darkness fell she remained too angry to reason coherently. The mare had been ridden hard and needed rest and water. When the sun had vanished behind the hills to the west Gwendolyn had dismounted by a stream and sat on the grassy bank. When darkness fell it was a protective cloak around her and gradually the soothing sound of the water began to calm her. It became easier to think more rationally how best to deal with the situation, for she knew that her mother would do everything in her power to force this abhorrent marriage upon her.

The evening was warm but the heat of her anger would have kept away any chill in the air. Her timidity, which had always made her shy away from confrontations with her family, was blasted away by her fury.

Always she had been meek and mild, controlled by her domineering mother and sister, Roslyn. From childhood her confidence had been crushed by their overbearing wills. The constant criticism by her mother for her lack of social graces had increased her shyness in the company of others. Gwendolyn had come to accept that she lacked the qualities of many women of her class. Used to her mother and sister talking over her, she had also lost her sense of worth in her ability to be witty or to charm others.

Yet that attitude had changed in the last two years. Gwendolyn had loved Japhet for as long as she could remember and had blushed and stammered like a callow schoolgirl whenever they met. Throughout their teenage years he had barely noted her existence, nor did she expect such a handsome man to look her way. But she had cherished every word or glance he had casually thrown her when they mixed at social gatherings.

Her change of outlook had come from an unlikely source: Meriel Loveday, who had been newly wed to St John and was striving for acceptance amongst their friends and neighbours. Meriel had teased Gwendolyn about her infatuation for St John's cousin, and then unexpectedly helped Gwendolyn to win his attention. Meriel had suggested that Gwen change her hairstyle, styling her thick rich chestnut hair in a more flattering manner. She also insisted that Gwendolyn rid herself of the demure, old-maidish gowns that Lady Anne insisted her daughter wear. Meriel had chosen several stylish gowns that flattered Gwendolyn's rounded, feminine curves.

Gwendolyn knew that Meriel was not acting out of kindness, for the young woman had always been too self-centred for that. St John's wife could not forget that she had been the daughter of a tavern-keeper before her brothers had forced St John at gunpoint to marry her, after he had got her with child. Meriel resented that Gwen's sister, Roslyn, who was married to Sir Henry Traherne, had never accepted her as an equal and had patronised Meriel and belittled her in public.

It was to spite Roslyn that Meriel, who never forgave an insult, had helped Gwendolyn – for once Roslyn had been infatuated with Japhet. After Japhet spurned Roslyn, she tried to hide her pain behind vitriolic condemnation of his lifestyle and behaviour. If Meriel could assist Gwendolyn to capture Japhet's interest Roslyn would be jealous that her sister had succeeded where she had failed. Roslyn's marriage to Sir Henry had been one of convenience and there was no great affection between the couple.

After the transformation to Gwendolyn's appearance no one had been more surprised than herself when Japhet began to compliment her looks. Gwendolyn gained confidence when she realised her natural wit made him laugh, and she never condemned him for his wayward life. When Japhet was in Cornwall and they attended the same hunt dances or soirées, he frequently sought her out. Yet despite his wicked reputation he had never attempted to seduce her.

Once she had been hurt enough to challenge him that he found her too unattractive. His shocked response had heartened her: 'I respect you as I respect no other woman.'

It had been a bitter-edged compliment. The few occasions that Japhet had kissed her, he had roused Gwendolyn's sensuality.

Now the memory of those kisses bathed her body in a hot flush and her flesh tingled with excitement. She lifted her face to the gold-tinged harvest moon. Her voice was impassioned. 'If I cannot marry Japhet I vow now that I shall wed no man. I can love no other man and I will not accept second best. Better to live alone with dignity and pride than with a man who could never fill the ache in my heart.'

The hoot of an owl in a tree overhead startled her, reminding her how late the hour had become. She remounted her mare and as they trotted home her resolve strengthened. It was time to fly free of the constraints placed on her by her mother and discover her destiny.

To reach Traherne Hall Gwendolyn skirted Trevowan and could hear the fiddler playing at the harvest feast. The music seemed to be celebrating her resolution.

When Gwendolyn arrived at Traherne Hall the first maid she encountered burst into tears. 'Thank God you be safe, Miss Gwendolyn. I were afeared some dreadful mishap had befallen you. Though Lady Anne kept informing the family that no harm would come to you with Lieutenant Beaumont as your companion.'

Gwendolyn ran up the stairs to the grand salon to confront her family. When she entered the room her sister stopped playing the harpsichord and looked expectantly towards her. Lady Anne, who was seated at her writing desk, put down her quill, her expression equally excited. Sir Henry put aside the newssheet he was reading but did not meet her gaze.

'There you are, my dear child,' Lady Anne giggled. 'Such a long ride you two lovers have taken.'

The gilded and ornate plasterwork on the ceiling with its central panel painted with cherubs seemed to swoop down to smother Gwendolyn. Even the pattern of the red and blue Persian carpet danced chaotically before her eyes. Gwen had left Traherne Hall seven hours ago. On her return she had expected to find her family distraught that she had been away so long. Her mother's words confirmed her fears. She was expecting Gwendolyn to announce her betrothal to Lieutenant Beaumont.

When Gwendolyn did not respond, Lady Anne stared past her daughter. She frowned and two circles of red on her fleshy cheeks showed her displeasure. 'Where is Lieutenant Beaumont?'

'As far away as possible, if he has any decency,' Gwen retorted.

Lady Anne threw up her hands in horror and the flesh around her eyes puckered, their depths glittering with contempt. 'You refused him. You stupid, inconsiderate woman. Your reputation will be in tatters.'

'If it is, it will be your doing, Mama, not mine.' Gwen faced her mother without flinching. 'Beaumont forced his attention on me in the basest manner to shame me into accepting him as my husband. He was foiled by the appearance of Senara Loveday. Your scheming plans have all been in vain.'

Sir Henry shot from his chair with an exclamation of anger. His cinnamon hair flopped over his brow and his slim figure strode to tower over Gwendolyn. 'Are you saying the man tried to force himself upon you?'

'Yes.'

'Then he must be called to account,' Sir Henry declared.

'Oh, nonsense. You know nothing of this matter, Henry,' Lady Anne defended. 'Gwendolyn has over-reacted and is being foolish.'

'I did not imagine his attack, Mama.'

Gwen's fierce glare made her mother grow pale but Lady Anne was never daunted for long. 'I am sure you mistook his ardour. This match is for your own good. You have brought shame upon yourself by your disgraceful conduct with that ne'er-do-well Japhet Loveday. Marriage with Lieutenant Beaumont will save your reputation.'

'And condemn me to a life of misery. I will not marry him and that is an end to the matter.' Gwen felt the control on her emotions slipping. Her gaze fell upon the cluster of Sèvres figurines on a walnut table, and in her frustration she had to grip her hands together to prevent herself sweeping all the porcelain to the floor.

'Gwen, you are overwrought.' Lady Anne bore down on her daughter, elbowing Sir Henry aside. 'I know what is best for you. This shame you have brought upon us—'

Gwendolyn's head jerked back. 'No, Mama, I will no longer allow you to dictate my life. You talk of shame. The shame is yours. Beaumont told me you had announced our betrothal in the *Mercury*. I will not be bullied or browbeaten. I am of age. I have my inheritance. I will never marry the odious Beaumont.'

Lady Anne turned to Sir Henry. 'Talk to her, Henry. Make her see reason.'

Sir Henry was pacing the floor by the window, his freckled face tight with fury as he repeated, 'If Beaumont acted as he did, he should be called to account.'

'Gwen exaggerates,' Roslyn placated, but her thin countenance was pinched with disapproval. 'She is so innocent.'

'Your sister is not a fool.' Sir Henry glared at his wife. 'I was informed that this betrothal was what Gwendolyn desired. Did you lie to me, Ros?'

Roslyn shrugged. 'For years Gwendolyn has made a fool of herself over Japhet Loveday. It is time she was married. Beaumont is from a good family.'

'He is a better match than Gwen deserves, given the way she has thrown herself at Japhet,' Lady Anne proclaimed. 'The wedding invitations are engraved. The marriage will be in a month.'

'No, Mama. I will not wed—' Her mother's slap halted her words. Gwen reeled back from the blow, her hand holding her stinging cheek.

'Ungrateful wretch! How dare you speak to me in that manner! I know who is behind this . . . Japhet Loveday.' Lady Anne spat the name in disgust. 'You shall never marry him. You will come to your senses and marry Lieutenant Beaumont.'

Sir Henry stepped between the two incensed women. 'Lady Anne, you have said enough. While Gwendolyn is under the protection of my home I will not condone you treating her in this manner.'

Gwendolyn was grateful for Sir Henry's intervention but was determined to fight her own battle. 'Beaumont does not care for me. He is only interested in my fortune.'

'It is all you have . . . You have no beauty . . . no graces . . .' her mother continued her tirade. 'Is not Japhet Loveday after your money? What else would he see in you?'

Once Gwendolyn would have been devastated by such insults; now they strengthened her determination. She was fighting for her happiness. 'Mama, you wrong Japhet. I know you caught him kissing me, but that is no great sin. Not compared to what I nearly suffered today at the hands of Beaumont. Japhet cares for me. Lieutenant Beaumont lied at St John's trial because he hates the Lovedays. He is without honour. How can you even consider him as my suitor?'

'Family and lineage are everything, child.' Lady Anne was at her most scathing.

Roslyn rose to stand by her mother and sneered, 'The Beaumonts are an old and revered family.

Francis's grandfather is an admiral and his uncle is a lord.'

'The Lovedays are gentlemen,' Gwen protested.

'Edward may have achieved that status,' Lady Anne continued venomously, 'but Japhet is not fit for decent society. And what of Edward's grandfather? Arthur Loveday was a rogue and many suspected he was a pirate in his youth before he established the shipyard. Had he not married a Penhaligan, for her land at Trevowan and her money, they would be nothing more than shipwrights. My dear, that is *trade*.'

Gwendolyn refused to be intimidated. 'Mama, since lineage is so important to you, it is convenient that you have forgotten that my father's grandfather made his fortune importing cocoa. He was in trade, which you so despise. Your own grandfather was created an earl only because he was the illegitimate son of King William of Orange by an actress.'

Lady Anne shuddered with horror. 'You graceless, unholy child. Japhet Loveday has been an evil influence upon you. You used to be a perfect daughter, obedient and respectful of your mama.'

'No, Mama, I allowed myself to be bullied by you because you made me feel dowdy and unattractive. I will not marry Lieutenant Beaumont. I intend to wed Japhet.'

Roslyn gasped with shock.

'Has he asked you?' Lady Anne gripped Gwendolyn's shoulders and shook her.

Gwendolyn shrugged off her mother's bruising grip and stepped back. Her statement had been rash, but she would not back down. 'Japhet has not asked me yet. But he will.'

'You are a fool,' Roslyn laughed.

'You will forget that reprobate,' Lady Anne ordered, 'and you *will* marry Lieutenant Beaumont.'

'I will not renounce Japhet.'

Gwen faced Sir Henry. She had never seen him so angry. 'Did you agree to the announcement in the *Mercury*, Sir Henry?'

'I believed it was as you wished. I am shocked to find that it is not so. I never liked Beaumont nor trusted him. This is your mischief, Lady Anne. I suggest you put it to rights. I will deal with Beaumont. He will answer to me for his conduct towards Gwen.' He strode from the room.

'There is no need for that, Sir Henry. The announcement will appear in the paper tomorrow.' Lady Anne called after him. She regarded her daughter with triumph. 'We will make the best of it or face a scandal.'

There was no response from Sir Henry, only the sound of him descending the stairs.

Gwen stared at her mother and sister with disgust. 'I suggest you pen another announcement for the *Sherborne Mercury*, proclaiming no betrothal took place between myself and Lieutenant Beaumont. As to any scandal . . . I will not be here to face it. I intend to go to London and make a new life for myself.'

As she walked towards the door, her mother continued to rage: 'You will do no such thing, Gwendolyn. How dare you walk out while I am talking?'

Gwendolyn continued to her room, her ears buffeted by the sound of her mother's threats.

'Disobey me and I shall wash my hands of you. You will be no daughter of mine.'

Gwen knew her life would be ruined and miserable if she gave in to Lady Anne's demands. Her mother had lied. Japhet did care for her and she would prove it to them all.

In a day or two Margaret and Thomas Mercer would return to London. Margaret had often extended an invitation to Gwendolyn to stay with her throughout the Season. Margaret was a born matchmaker; she had introduced Edward Loveday to Amelia. And Margaret adored Japhet. She would be her ally.

Gwendolyn had no misgivings about deserting her family. Her mother had only herself to blame when she must face the explanations as to why Gwendolyn had left Cornwall.

Chapter Five

It was dark when Senara arrived at Trevowan for the harvest celebrations, in the carriage sent by Edward Loveday. She had left it as late as possible to arrive and stepped self-consciously from the carriage, holding her nine-month-old son, Nathan. Apprehension caused her to take a steadying breath.

'Don't you be fretting, madam.' Jasper Fraddon touched his wrinkled brow in salute. The coachman hobbled on stiff, bow legs to hold the lead horse's bridle. 'Master Adam would be right proud of you this day. Family will be gathered in the orangery. You go on through.'

Senara hesitated. Her maid, Carrie Jensen, who had accompanied her, picked at the adolescent spots on her chin and jaw. Carrie was the daughter of Pru and Toby Jensen who ran the Ship kiddley, the alehouse and provision store at Trevowan Hard, which was stocked by Adam for the shipwrights' families.

'I bain't never bin inside the big house afore, Mrs Loveday.' Carrie looked worried. She was plump due to an overfondness of her mother's delicious pasties. Clearly she felt as out of place as Senara did in such grand surroundings. 'That Miss Elspeth, she do scare me.'

'Her bark is usually worse than her bite.' Senara had similar reservations concerning Edward Loveday's elder sister. She had faced Elspeth's sour tongue too often not to find the company of the formidable woman daunting.

'You are here to assist in Nathan's care,' she reassured her maid. 'You will have a truckle bed in my room tonight. There is nothing to fear.'

Senara also felt an outsider in this house but Nathan was a true Loveday. Trevowan was part of his heritage. This was only the second time she had attended at Trevowan since her marriage to Adam. The last time had been for a farewell meal for Adam and St John on the eve before they sailed to Virginia.

At the sound of her footsteps on the black and white marble floor of the hall, Jenna Biddick, the Lovedays' maid, appeared. She was a plain woman whose family were tenant farmers on the estate.

'Family be expecting you.' She gave a scant curtsy to Senara and kept her eyes lowered. Senara could feel her resentment at having to wait upon a woman from her own class. There was no warmth in Jenna's voice as she informed them, 'Your servant should go through to the kitchen; Winnie Fraddon will deal with her. A servant's got no right coming in by front door. That be for gentry.'

'Carrie is nursemaid to Mr Loveday's grandson,'

Senara was stung to remind Jenna. Carrie was gazing up in wonder at the curved staircase hung with family portraits. Senara gave her a gentle nudge and smiled encouragement. 'The kitchen is through the corridor over there. Winnie Fraddon is a kindly soul. Offer your services to her, as she will be busy with preparation for the feast. I will tend to Nathan.'

Senara followed Jenna to the orangery at the rear of the house. One side of the room was almost entirely glass and the rising moon painted the white marble floor with a silvery-gold glow. Four orange trees were planted in huge urns. The family were seated upon padded wooden chairs. When the maid announced her, Senara held herself stiffly, unsure of her reception. She kissed Nathan's cheek to still her nerves. 'Good day to you all.'

Edward Loveday, who had been lighting the candles in the wall sconces with a taper, stepped forward. 'Welcome to Trevowan, my dear. The feast is an informal affair for our workers. I hope you will enjoy yourself.'

'Thank you, sir.' She glanced at Amelia and Elspeth, who were seated by the window. These two women had been the most virulent in their opposition to Adam's marriage. Both now bowed their heads in silent greeting to her. Margaret Mercer, Edward's eldest sister, who was visiting from London, rose from her seat with her arms outstretched to take Nathan.

'The child is the image of Adam,' Margaret chuckled as she held Nathan and he clutched her finger in his tiny fist. 'But then I suppose your family see you in

55

him, Senara. That is the way with relatives.'

Senara nodded and a mischievous sparkle brightened her eyes. Her mother had often commented that Nathan's dark hair showed his Romany blood. That would never be acceptable to the Lovedays, but Nathan had his father's blue eyes and Adam's hair was as dark as that of any of Senara's gypsy relatives.

There was an excited squeal from behind Senara and she turned to see Georganna Mercer hurrying into the room. Her husband, Thomas, followed her. Unlike his Loveday cousins, Thomas was blond-haired and pale-complexioned. He was wearing a green cutaway tailcoat and ruby waistcoat that would be the envy of any Court dandy.

'Good gracious, Georganna! What is that you are wearing?' Elspeth frowned and peered over the top of her pince-nez at the tall, slender woman dressed in a satin gown of red, green and yellow stripes. 'You look like a maypole.'

'I think my wife looks very well, aunt,' Thomas loyally defended. 'The style is quite the thing in London.'

'You have always been a peacock, Thomas,' Elspeth responded, but her voice was mellow and she chuckled. 'Thank heavens you do not hunt. You would scare all the foxes to earth from half a mile away.'

Georganna greeted Senara with obvious pleasure. 'Thomas and I have been walking on the beach at Trevowan Cove, where he was inspired to write a poem. It is so moving he must read it to you.'

Thomas waved his hand in any airy gesture of dismissal. 'You are too kind in your praise, my dear. It is but a trifling piece and not worthy of attention.'

'A reading would be enjoyable but at a later time,' Edward interceded with an edge of disapproval in his tone. He did not condone his nephew's preference for poetry and writing plays over his partnership in Mercer and Lascalles Bank in London. 'Thomas, have you seen Lisette upstairs? I sent word for her to join us in the orangery.' Edward took out his timepiece from the fob pocket in his waistcoat. 'That was over half an hour ago.'

Thomas raised a manicured hand to adjust the elaborate folds of his cravat. 'From our bedchamber window I saw Lisette leave the house for the field where the workers are dancing, uncle.'

Elspeth stood up and rapped her walking cane on the floor. Constant pain from her injured hip had hardened her features. She was as lean as the foxes she loved to hunt and her stare was as sharp and rapacious. 'That young woman will be up to no good. I shall never understand what possessed my brother William to wed the baggage. Since William had kept himself a bachelor for so long, you would have thought him wiser and more sensible in his choice of a bride. Worst thing you ever did was to give a home to that French minx, Edward. Niece, or no niece, I would have thrown her out. Her tantrums and wild behaviour make her little better than a strumpet.'

'It was Lisette who chose William,' Amelia observed

with frost in her voice. 'I pray the twenty-year difference in their ages will bring stability and a greater sense of decorum to Lisette's life.'

'I know that she has been a trial to you, Amelia,' Margaret added, 'yet the poor girl suffered greatly in her last years in France. William has always been a calming influence on her.'

'But William is no longer here to control her,' Elspeth remarked. 'He has sailed with the English fleet. Lisette found many excuses to visit the fields during the harvest and flirts with the male workers in an unseemly fashion.' Elspeth peered over her pince-nez at Edward. 'You keep an eye on her, brother. That scheming minx will bring shame upon William.'

Amelia groaned, her mouth compressed in her distress. 'Lisette pays no heed to my advice. She is as shameless as Meriel. I cannot hold my head up in church or in the village with the gossip rife that Meriel ran off with Lord Wycham.'

'Good riddance to the scheming baggage,' Elspeth snapped. 'Meriel was a fortune-huntress. Always was and always will be. She tricked St John into marriage and influenced him to become her brother's partner in smuggling. She was greedy for the money it would bring them and had no care for St John's safety. I blame that uppity madam for all St John's troubles.'

Senara was appalled by the family's virulence. The atmosphere in the orangery was sharp with recriminations, and she felt out of place in this forbidding, uncompromising world. The intolerance shown was a sign of the strain that the family had been under in

58

recent months, and Senara was uncomfortably aware that her marriage to Adam had been responsible for some of that strain.

Edward let out a harsh breath. 'Meriel has gone. There is nothing we can do about it. Let us not allow the matter to spoil the harvest feast.' He offered his arm to Senara. 'We will, as always, present a united front. The Lovedays have never permitted idle gossip to govern their lives.'

Senara took Edward's arm and was relieved his words had deflected the tension. She cast an anxious glance towards Nathan, wishing that she still had him in her arms to give her confidence.

Margaret Mercer smiled at her. 'Permit me to indulge my fancies that soon it will be my own grandchild I hold in my arms.'

Senara saw Georganna turn pale and Thomas put a protective arm around his wife's shoulders.

'You are impatient, Mama,' he said. 'We are not yet wed a year. We are in no rush for children.'

'But they are such a blessing. I will never understand you, Thomas.' Margaret looked at her son in exasperation.

'Children come in God's own time,' Amelia reassured. 'I have prayed that Edward and I will be blessed with another child. Rafe is two and a half and I am getting no younger.'

Again Senara could feel the undercurrents of tension swirling around her new family. Edward was tense, clearly worried about his elder sons, and also the task of recovering the reputation and fortunes of the shipyard. Amelia was pale, looking thinner, with a haunted air about her. The financial and personal troubles that the family had endured in the last year had taken their greatest toll upon Edward's wife.

Thomas and Georganna exchanged glances that spoke of a bond and also a secret between them. When Mercer's Bank faced closure and ruin, Thomas had married Georganna Lascalles, whose family owned a rival bank in London. The couple seemed happy but in the way of a close friendship rather than as lovers, and it was obvious to all but Margaret Mercer that men would hold a greater sway over Thomas's emotions than any woman. His relationship with the poet Lucien Greene remained as strong as ever after his marriage. Fortunately, Georganna seemed content, and even encouraged Lucien to be part of their family circle.

'You look lovely, my dear,' Edward interrupted Senara's thoughts as they left the house. 'You have been visiting Boscabel daily, so I hear. Yet the place is not much more than a ruin. Are you not content at Mariner's House?'

'More than content,' Senara was quick to reassure him, 'but Adam left plans for some renovation work to be carried out to Boscabel house, though there is little money to spare for such improvements at present. Seth Wakeley and his son are repairing the roof on their day off from working in the yard. Other shipwrights are willing to help during what little free time they have. Adam has inspired much loyalty from the men in your shipyard.'

Edward nodded. 'Many owe Adam their jobs. Without his ship designs the yard would be bankrupt by now. Also you will take no payment when you heal the families of our workers. They could not afford a physician's fees and they see this as a way of repaying your generosity.' He frowned. 'I wish I was in a position to release more of the men to work at Boscabel instead of the yard, but we need every man at present to meet a current order.'

His generosity touched Senara. They were passing the courtyard of outbuildings and stables behind the house. The paintwork around the windowpanes and on the doors was flaking in places; the stables were half empty – signs of the economies forced upon the family in recent years.

'The yard must always come first. Adam would not expect otherwise,' she replied. 'Neither do we wish the families at the yard to feel indebted for what little aid I can give them. Though such gratitude is heart-warming.' She became pensive. 'I spend each morning doing what I can at Boscabel. Even overgrown, the gardens are a great source of useful plants. Inside, some of the furniture left by the previous owners can be renovated. But the years of neglect means timbers and furnishings have rotted and Adam left instructions for the repairs. There is mould everywhere. All the curtains, mattresses and bed hangings had to be burned. They will be replaced in time.'

'There is some old furniture and chests packed with household wares in the attic here. I am sure that

61

Amelia will go through the chests with you so that you can choose what is needed at Boscabel.' He gave her a sideways glance. 'Or perhaps you would prefer everything to be new.'

Senara shook her head. 'You are very generous, sir. I realise that your wife has many duties at Trevowan, but I would appreciate her advice on the matters of furnishings at some later time. My tastes are simple and unlikely to be appropriate. Though it will be some months before the repairs to the roof and walls are completed.'

'Do not underestimate yourself, Senara. I have seen the improvements you have made to Mariner's House. They incorporate both style and comfort. Ostentation is not Adam's taste.'

Senara began to relax, aware that in his kindness Edward was trying to make amends for the censure she had suffered from his family. 'Adam's first concern will always be the survival of the shipyard. There are still outstanding debts, I believe. Boscabel is our home for the future.' She hesitated, not sure if she should go on. Edward was watching her closely and she confided in a soft voice, 'Adam will never have the home he loves – Trevowan. His pride must create its equal in Boscabel and that is the work of a lifetime.'

Edward did not answer as they crossed the meadow at the side of the barn where the workers were dancing or sitting on the grass drinking ale and cider. The smell of a pig roasting on a spit was tantalising, reminding Senara that she had been too nervous to eat anything that day. Winnie Fraddon, strong and sturdy as an oak cask, was carving slices from its side on to wooden platters. Her round cheeks were rosy from the heat of the fire and her fleshy arms dimpled as she worked.

Eventually Edward said, 'Now that the harvest is over, I can spare a man or two for a day a week to clear some of the land and to help Seth Wakeley with the roof and replacing any damaged windows at Boscabel. That will keep the ravages of another winter at bay.'

He paused for the rest of the party to catch up with them. The sound of a fiddler playing a jig lightened the atmosphere. The evening was still warm and the workers laughed and sang as they danced. A petite dark-haired woman dressed in pink silk was talking to Baz and Bob Tonkin, whose family lived in a tied cottage on the estate. She spoke animatedly, her hands expressive as she leaned closer to the young farmers. Her face was flushed with heat.

'Lisette!' Edward hailed her. 'You have come early to the feast.'

'I heard the music and wanted to dance.'

Edward moved away from Senara to remonstrate with the Frenchwoman. 'The feast and dancing is for the workers. We make but a token appearance for our presence puts a restraint upon their merriment.'

Lisette folded her arms and tapped her foot. 'I restrain no one. I intend to enjoy myself.'

'Your husband has placed you under my protection whilst he is at sea. You will act as befits a matron but recently wed, or you will face the consequences of my anger.'

'You no longer have the right to curtail my pleasure.' The delicate beauty was stripped from Lisette's face by her temper. 'I will do as I please.'

Edward took her elbow and led her out of the hearing of others. His expression was glacial. 'We have suffered your tantrums since you arrived from France because of the horrors you endured during the revolution. We have shown you love and tried to be understanding, even though at times your behaviour has been disgraceful. Such conduct will no longer be tolerated.'

'I will do as I please.' She wriggled to free his hold on her arm. Her petite figure and her delicate beauty were deceptive. She looked so helpless and fragile but when thwarted, she would scream and wreak havoc until she collapsed from exhaustion.

Edward was in no mood for one of her tantrums. Because she was the niece of his first wife, Edward felt responsible for her. Lisette had been orphaned during the revolution in France and deserted by her brother. On her arrival in England it seemed that she had been a cruel victim of fate, who needed love and understanding. But now Edward was not so sure. She could be a scheming minx with no thought but for her own gratification and pleasure. William had been gulled into marrying her.

Edward had been lenient with her for too long. Lisette clearly needed medical help, for her actions were not those of a normal woman.

'I have long promised Amelia a visit to London,' Edward said. 'We will accompany Margaret and

Thomas on their return and you will come with us. There the King's own physician shall assess your health.'

'But your king is mad.' Lisette's eyes rounded with terror. 'I am not insane. Why will you not accept that the French temperament is different from your own?'

'I am not saying that you are insane, merely that your mind has been disturbed by your ordeal in France. The King's physician will know how to cure you. You were never like this as a child.'

She put her hands to her head. 'No one understands me. Everyone betrays me.'

Edward sighed. 'How are we betraying you if all we want is for you to be well and happy?'

Lisette began to tremble and then burst into loud sobs. Amelia hurried to her side. 'Now what has upset you? Can you not control these wayward emotions?' Her own patience with the volatile and spoiled young woman had been tested past its limit. 'Go back to the house until you have calmed down. This is no way to deport yourself in public.'

'You hate me. You have always hated me,' Lisette screamed, and raised her hand as though to slap Amelia.

There was a shocked gasp from the onlookers, but before Lisette could strike, Margaret, who had left Nathan in the care of Carrie, stepped forward to grab Lisette's wrist.

'Is this how you repay the goodness of our family?'

Lisette stamped her foot and fought to free her hand. Margaret jerked her closer, her voice low with warning. 'One more word . . . one single action of defiance, young lady, and I personally will start proceedings to have you committed to an asylum. Edward has been lenient because you are his dead wife's niece. I have no such constraints. I see you as a wilful, spoiled, and disruptive woman who has no thoughts for anyone but herself. Tantrums only confirm my belief that your mind has been deranged by your experiences in France. Your dear father would turn in his grave in disgust at your ingratitude.'

Lisette stared at her with horror. She shook her head as her eyes filled with tears. 'Papa loved me. Papa said I was an angel.'

'And where is that Lisette who your father adored?' Margaret flared, then continued in a more reasonable tone. 'No one wants to send you away. Show us the Lisette your father loved. Show us the sweet woman we remember.'

Lisette hung her head. 'That Lisette is dead. She died in Auvergne in a château of fear and terror . . . long before the revolution. My first husband was a monster.'

Margaret pitied the once-innocent child who had been so cruelly corrupted. She sighed. 'With help that sweet Lisette can return. If you wish her to. William adores you.'

Lisette shut her eyes and a tremor rocked her body. Her defiance crumpled and she threw herself into Margaret's arms. 'William hates me. We quarrelled before he sailed. I said such dreadful things. Lisette is not always kind. Lisette is not always good.'

Margaret glanced over the Frenchwoman's head. Elspeth was making scathing comments and Amelia was waving her fan in agitation, mortified by Lisette's behaviour. Edward had walked away, ordering the fiddler to play a lively reel and distract the workers from the family drama.

Margaret had seen and heard enough about the young Frenchwoman's conduct in the last days to know that she was seriously disturbed and needed help.

She began to lead Lisette back to the house, saying to Senara as she passed, 'Have you a potion to calm her?'

Senara nodded, surprised that Lisette had responded so easily to Margaret's care.

All Margaret's maternal instincts were aroused as she smoothed Lisette's hair. 'Your tears are spoiling your pretty looks. You must be aware that these wild moods are not normal. A few months in London taking the cure prescribed by an eminent physician will bring back to us the old Lisette whom we all adore. On his return from sea you will enchant William. You have not been to London and will enjoy the entertainments. And, of course, many French émigrés will be there.'

Edward watched Margaret, Senara and Lisette as they walked back to the house, and rejoined his wife. 'Margaret coped with that well. I shall make arrangements that we leave Cornwall next week. Lisette needs treatment. With Adam and St John away I can spare little time in London, but you must stay on for several weeks to see your old friends, Amelia.' He squeezed her hand. 'You have been my mainstay through the trials of the last months, but it has been a strain on you. Now it is time for you to enjoy yourself, my love.'

Amelia nodded. 'To get away from the gossip which surrounds us at the moment will be a relief. Lisette needs professional help and where better than London?'

The fiddler struck up a more sedate dance and Edward escorted his wife into the centre of the dancers. 'Tonight we shall forget our troubles and enjoy ourselves. There is so much that is good in our lives, we must put the bad times behind us and give thanks for our blessings.'

Edward raised his wife's hand to his lips and for the first time in weeks Amelia relaxed and smiled. 'You are right. We have been through so much, things can only get better.'

Chapter Six

The harvest feast lightened the mood of the family, their laughter mingling with that of the labourers as the drinking and dancing progressed. Edward danced with Margaret when she returned from the house with Senara.

'Senara gave Lisette a potion and she has fallen asleep,' Margaret explained.

'You defused a difficult situation. A few weeks in London will benefit Amelia – she deserves a rest from the tribulations we have undergone these last months. It is difficult for me to leave the yard for long at this time but Lisette must have treatment.'

The family drew together, talking about other London visits. Feeling excluded, Senara stood self-consciously to one side until Isaac Nance approached her.

''Appen with Master Adam away, you would honour me with a dance, ma'am.'

She smiled at the bailiff. 'Thank you, Isaac.'

He grinned, showing two missing front teeth. His

greying hair had receded to the top of his crown and it was pulled back into a leather band. 'You'll not be without a partner for any dance this night. The men be eager to dance with you.'

To Senara's surprise Isaac was proved right. She was also partnered by Thomas and by Edward to show her acceptance into the family. A fire had been lit, and a score of flaming torches were set in the ground as it grew dark. As the labourers became inebriated Edward gestured to the family that it was time for them to leave.

'Fiddler, continue with your playing, and eat and drink, good people, for you have earned your feast.'

As they began to walk towards the house a commotion broke out on the outskirts of the gathering and a frightened woman's voice called out, 'I am here to see Mr Loveday.'

Senara glanced in Edward's direction and saw a young dark-haired woman pushing her way through the crowd towards him. Her hair was tangled and flowing to her waist and her plain grey gown was smeared with dirt. She was pale and looked close to exhaustion. Senara was immediately concerned that the woman would collapse.

'Thomas, take the women back to the house,' Edward unexpectedly commanded. His body was rigid with tension as he moved to intercept her approach. Before he could reach her, she stumbled and fell on her knees at his feet.

'I am so sorry. I never meant . . . never meant to arrive like this.' Her voice was cultured, though tiredness slurred her words. She reached out to Edward, but he recoiled from her. Momentarily his composure deserted him and guilt was stark in his eyes. The expression rapidly vanished, replaced by a cold and lethal fury.

'I do despise women who cannot take their drink,' Elspeth retorted.

Amelia agreed, but something about the intruder's manner held her attention. Edward looked as though he had seen a ghost, whilst Senara had run to help the woman to her feet.

'You are ill, let me help you.' Senara was surprised that Edward's impeccable manners had deserted him and he had not helped the woman. Senara could feel the newcomer trembling as she steadied her, but the young woman's eyes remained locked upon Edward.

'Forgive me, sir. I couldn't stay at the academy . . .' She fell against Senara, who braced herself to stop her stumbling to the ground.

'She's fainted,' Senara declared.

Amelia was at her husband's side. 'Who is this young woman. Edward?'

Edward did not move and seemed incapable of speaking. The young woman stirred in Senara's arms.

'Who are you?' Amelia demanded.

'Tamasine . . . Tamasine Loveday . . .' Her eyes closed as she again fainted.

Elspeth hobbled forward. 'A Loveday, did she say? Good heavens, she's got the Loveday looks. But what is one of our family doing arriving in such a state? Must be one of cousin Sandy's brood from over St

Ives way, but we haven't heard from them for years. Not since Sandy fell out with our father.'

'If she is kin, we had better take her into the house,' Amelia's puzzled stare settled on her husband, 'though from her appearance she looks like a beggar. Perhaps she should be seen in the kitchen. Dick Nance should carry her into the house. You had better attend her, Senara—'

'Take her into my study,' Edward cut through his wife's orders. 'Senara will attend her there. Then I will speak to the girl.' He strode towards the house.

Amelia was disturbed by his strange behaviour, but ordered the fiddler to continue playing. It would help to distract the gathering from this new drama unfolding around the family. She then addressed the curious onlookers. 'There is nothing to concern yourselves over. We will leave you to enjoy the evening.'

She groaned to Margaret, 'First Lisette and now this. Would it be too much to expect that a member of your family will act as convention demands?'

'I think you exaggerate, Amelia,' Margaret was stung to reply, but her gaze was curious as Dick Nance picked up the unconscious young woman.

Senara hurried ahead to fetch her bag of potions and herbs for the second time that evening. When she entered Edward's study the young woman was sitting on a chair with her head in her hands and Amelia was bent over her, waving a bottle of smelling salts under her nose. The book-lined room with its large leather-topped desk was lit only by a three-sconce candelabra, which threw the corners of the room into deep shadow.

'She had just fainted,' Amelia announced. 'From the way her stomach is rumbling, she has not eaten for some time. Well, young lady, perhaps now you would be good enough to inform us who exactly you are? And why you have presented yourself at Trevowan in such a fashion?'

Tamasine scanned the room for Edward and her eyes were round and pleading. In the light of the study she looked more of a child than a woman, and very vulnerable and helpless. 'I am sorry . . . I could not bear it any longer. I thought you would help me . . .'

She swayed in the chair and Senara put her arm around her and took her pulse. It was strong but when Senara stared into Tamasine's eyes they were not entirely focused.

Senara looked up at Edward, who was standing in the shadows, rubbing his chin with his thumb and forefinger. 'Sir, she is exhausted. She needs some broth and rest. I am sure that she will be fine in the morning.'

Elspeth sniffed in disapproval, demanding, 'What happened to you, young lady? If you are kin to Sandy Loveday why were we not informed of your arrival?'

Senara felt Tamasine flinch at Elspeth's strident tone, but she ignored the older woman, her gaze beseeching upon Edward. There was a strained anger to the tightness of his features.

'The girl is my ward and should be at school,' he coldly informed the women.

Senara had only ever known Edward to be completely in control of a situation, even when he was angry. The stiffness of his manner betrayed an inner fear that was puzzling.

'You have never mentioned a ward,' Amelia accused.

Edward stood to attention with his hands clasped behind his back. 'She had but recently come under my protection. With all the trouble this summer, I saw no need to add to your worries. Tamasine was attending school in Salisbury and is due to remain there for another year.'

'I could not stay at the academy. You saw how dreadful the place was.' Tamasine jerked upright, her figure straight and defiant. 'I ran away. I saw in a journal a report on the forthcoming trial of a St John Loveday in Bodmin. I guessed it was your family from what little I knew.'

'The girl is ranting,' Elspeth snapped. 'Her wits have gone begging.'

Tamasine ignored the outburst, her words spilling out in a torrent. 'Sir, I saw you in Bodmin at the end of the trial, but it did not seem right to approach you there. I had a little money and have been on the road ever since to come to you at Trevowan. Please, sir, do not send me back.'

Amelia was breathing heavily and had difficulty controlling her anger. She was staring at Edward as though he had betrayed her in the grossest manner.

The growing tension in the room filled Senara with dread. This was a family of high passions, and she was slowly learning that they hid many secrets behind their façade of gentility and respectability.

'How can you take on the responsibilities of a ward and not tell me, Edward?' Amelia demanded.

'And whose child is she?' Elspeth was frowning. 'We should all have been told. She is a Loveday, after all.'

'Not exactly.' Edward turned his back on the group to stare out of the window to the distant fire and dancers. 'It is complicated.'

'Then you had better explain, husband.' Amelia sat down on the other free chair and gripped her hands together in her lap. There was a challenging light in her eyes. 'I find it insulting that you did not discuss so serious a matter with me at the time.'

Tamasine put her hands to her cheeks and tears sprinkled down her face. 'Why are you all so angry at each other? I am to blame. I should not have come. But who else could I turn to but my guardian?'

'Indeed you should have stayed where you were,' Edward rapped out. 'Conditions were harsh at the academy but your previous guardian would not have kept you in a school if they ill-treated you.'

'Lady Keyne told me that she had no power over where I was to be educated. Her husband chose the school. He wanted me to be hidden away and forgotten.'

Senara shifted uncomfortably. 'This seems to be a private matter. I shall leave. Call me if Tamasine needs any medication to help her to recover.'

'You may as well stay, Senara,' Edward clipped out. 'The harm is done.' He then turned to his wife, and a vein pulsing at his temple showed that he was fighting an inner battle with his emotions. 'Of course I would have told you, Amelia. Tamasine became my ward shortly before St John's trial. You had enough to contend with at the time.'

'What is it about this ward you fear would upset me, Edward?' Amelia put a hand to her throat, suspicion narrowing her eyes. 'Is she not then a distant cousin?'

Elspeth regarded Edward over the top of her pince-nez with condemnation. 'If Lady Keyne was her guardian, and by that I presume you referred to Lady Eleanor and not the young Lady Barbara Keyne, why did not the Keyne family assume responsibility for the girl?'

'This is not something which I wish to discuss in front of my ward.' Edward glanced at Senara. 'Perhaps it would be best if you took Tamasine upstairs. Have Jenna make up a bed in the gable room overlooking the stables. She needs food and rest before she is returned to the academy.'

Tamasine swayed to her feet. 'I will not go back there, sir. I was wrong to come here. I thought you meant what you said when you told me that you would take care of me.'

'Do not add impertinence to your disobedience, young lady.'

Tamasine held his angry glare, the defiant tilt of her chin mirroring Edward's own stance. 'I have the right to know what my fate will be.'

'You are fifteen and as such have no rights, young

lady. You will do as I say. We will speak of this tomorrow. If you were at Bodmin and have taken nearly a week to get here, how long have you been absent from your school? And why the devil was I not informed of your disappearance by Mrs Moxon?'

'Let the girl stay in the room,' Amelia ordered. Her knuckles were white with tension and she stared at her husband as though the man before her was a stranger. 'I want the truth, Edward. Elspeth has raised a relevant point – why did not Lord Keyne take on the guardianship of one of his family?'

'Good heavens, is the child yours, brother?' Elspeth gasped. 'She is your image. I always thought that you and the Lady Eleanor were too often in each other's company to be just friends. Her husband was in London for two years, leaving her on her own in Cornwall. That would be fifteen or so years ago.'

'You have a twisted mind, sister.' Edward glared at Elspeth but the candlelight revealed a coating of sweat on his brow.

Amelia emitted a tortured groan. 'Tell me that it is not so, Edward.'

'Of course Edward is not the girl's father,' Margaret defended her brother.

Edward did not look at any of the women but stared at a fixed point above their heads.

Elspeth tutted. 'My assumption is not so preposterous is it, brother?'

'I knew you were my father,' Tamasine burst out. 'That means Lady Keyne was my mother.'

'It means nothing of the kind,' Edward snapped. He

paced the room, still refusing to look at Amelia, who had become deathly pale.

She rose to her feet with a rustle of petticoats. 'You have not denied it, though, have you, Edward?' She left the room with a silent and regal dignity.

'Amelia!' Edward strode after her.

Margaret nodded to Senara. 'This is all most unfortunate. Would you be so kind as to tend to Tamasine? I'll have Winnie Fraddon prepare some food for the child to eat in her room. The family is best discussing this matter after we have all slept on it.'

Elspeth eyed Tamasine with a sour expression. 'This wilful act of yours is disgraceful, young lady. Edward would do well to send you straight back to your school. You are in sore need of lessons on the correct behaviour of a gentlewoman.'

'I should not have come,' Tamasine remained defiant, 'but I will not go back. You know nothing of the place. They stifle you with petty rules and punishments. I shall go on the stage. I have a friend whose mother is an actress.'

'That is enough of your impudence,' Elspeth warned.

To avoid further dissension Senara put her arm around the young girl's shoulders and ushered her from the room.

Once the two sisters were alone Elspeth shook her head and gave a dry laugh. 'She's a Loveday through and through – God help us. What Amelia will make of this I shudder to consider.'

'Edward certainly looked guilty.' Margaret cast a

worried look to the door as she heard her brother returning.

'Amelia has locked herself in her room and will not listen to me,' he announced.

'Is the child yours?' Elspeth confronted him.

He nodded. 'I only learned of her existence a few weeks before Lady Eleanor died. I visited Tamasine before St John's trial. Her school is in Salisbury. Heaven knows how she made the journey here without harm coming to her.'

'She is headstrong and courageous – traits she will need to survive in this world, unless you accept her as part of this family.' Margaret spread her hands in a gesture of resignation. 'That is too much to expect Amelia to tolerate.'

Elspeth agreed, adding, 'Such wilful behaviour cannot be countenanced. The girl needs a good thrashing before she is sent packing.'

Edward left Trevowan the next morning in the family coach for Salisbury. A tearful Tamasine was with him. Margaret had offered to accompany him as they would need to stay at inns overnight and Edward did not trust his ward not to run away again.

Thomas and Georganna were returning to London the following day, for this morning Thomas had a business meeting with Squire Penwithick on behalf of a French émigré aristocrat. The Frenchman was an important customer of Mercer and Lascalles Bank. The count was desperate for news of his daughter, whom he believed had managed to escape with her lover from prison, when so many of his friends and family had been guillotined. The squire worked for the Prime Minister, Mr Pitt, and had a network of spies in France who might be able to locate his daughter and bring her to England. As Edward could not afford to spend time away from the yard with Adam and St John absent, Thomas had agreed to Lisette travelling with them and undergoing treatment for her unstable moods in London. Margaret would join them at the coaching inn in Salisbury to continue her own journey home.

Edward had already spent an hour with his ward before they left, leaving Tamasine in no doubt of his anger, and no expectations that he would relent in his decision. The girl's tears left him unmoved. His anger was so great that he no longer trusted himself to be civil to her.

To make matters worse, this morning Amelia had not unlocked her door to him and refused to listen to reason. She had not even said goodbye when he informed her through her closed door that he would be away from Trevowan for several days. He could understand that his wife was upset. The scandal following St John's trial had barely had time to die down; now Tamasine's arrival would cause more speculation and upheaval.

Chapter Seven

Adam Loveday stood on the quarterdeck of his ship, *Pegasus*, and stared up at the night sky. The constellation of Orion was overhead, distinguished by the three stars that formed the belt of the figure of a hunter carrying a bow. Below Orion shone Sirius, the brightest star in the sky. After ten days of intermittent storms and heavy seas, *Pegasus* was under full sail, the canvas taut arcs against the ebony sky lit with diamond-bright stars.

The brigantine cut cleanly through the waves. It was a mild night, and as Adam strolled the length of the main deck the breeze teased his long black hair, unrestrained by any ribbon.

After so many months on land, he'd missed life at sea. He loved to be on deck with the vast horizon of the ocean spread before him. For him nothing on land could touch the freedom of spirit that the sea offered. Here he felt at one with his God and the universe. It made him understand how Senara, a true child of nature, had an even deeper empathy with the elements. Though Adam could not abide the confinement of his small cabin for long, he never felt restrained by the boundaries of the ship once he was on deck. The swell of the sea and the whisper of the waves as they broke over *Pegasus'* bow resonated in Adam's veins. The rhythm of the waves merged with his heartbeat and it was at times like this, when only a few seamen were on deck, that Adam felt most at one with the mighty ocean.

He breathed deeply, drawing in the smell and taste of the salt spray, and in the distance he heard a whale blow through its air hole.

He scanned the inky seas for sight of the great leviathan and in the moon's reflection he saw six whales surface. These were the true masters of the seas, their only predator man, who hunted the gentle creatures for their oil and blubber. There was a majesty about the whales that never failed to captivate Adam. They circumnavigated the globe in harmony with the turbulence of the oceans, which could destroy men and ships in its fury. Their slaughter had always disturbed him, for Adam had witnessed how closely the mothers protected and nurtured their calves.

Other sounds, as familiar as his breath, were part of life at sea. Alongside the flap of canvas and creak of rigging, the sound of a mouth organ rose from below decks, where the sailors rested in their hammocks before the next watch. Distant voices rose and fell in an argument, somewhere a man sang of his lost love, and a bare-foot cabin boy padded across the deck to throw the slops from the last meal over the side.

A footfall alerted Adam to the presence of another and he glanced over his shoulder as his friend Long Tom joined him at the ship's rail.

'Your brother is still skulking in his cabin,' Long Tom informed him, 'and he's bellowing for more rum.' Long Tom leaned his short figure against a gun carriage and interlocked his stubby hands. Like Adam he was dressed in leather breeches and a thigh-length leather jacket, but whilst his were new, the leather barely creased, Adam's black breeches bore the scuffs of countless voyages, and his brown jacket was stained from battles against the storms.

Adam frowned. 'I will speak with St John. His behaviour cannot continue throughout the voyage. It will affect the morale of the men, who only have a daily tot of rum.'

'Seems to me that he is riled over something. Was it not a last-minute decision that his wife and child did not accompany him?' Long Tom scratched his curly, sandy hair, the lines scoring his face making him appear older than his thirty years. His brown eyes were bright with a keen intelligence and he shook his head and gave a derisive laugh. 'I never could understand families. And they do not get more bizarre than my own.'

Adam regarded his friend with affection. He had met Long Tom earlier in the year whilst working for Squire Penwithick. The squire, who ran a network of spies for the British Government, had sent Adam to France. His task had been to rescue Long Tom, who had been captured by the French. Adam had been amazed to discover that one of Britain's most notable secret agents was a dwarf.

Long Tom was in reality Sir Gregory Kilmarthen, who had been sent abroad as a young teenager by a family who found his stature an embarrassment and regarded him as an oddity. Long Tom had inherited his title from his father three years ago, but his relationship with his mother and sister was so strained that he could not abide to live on his estate. His capture by the French had meant the end of his spying for England, for his height would now betray him. He had been delighted at Adam's offer to join him on *Pegasus* when he sailed as a privateer.

Though Adam was annoyed at St John's strange behaviour since coming on board, he felt the need to defend his twin. 'St John and Meriel had their differences but he idolised his daughter. He will not discuss the matter. I've tried.'

Long Tom groaned and clutched his round stomach. His eyes closed and he shuddered. 'You said this sickness would pass in a few days.' He jumped up to hoist his upper body over the ship's rail and deposited what little he had eaten that day into the waves. When he recovered, he wiped his flushed brow. 'I was always ill on the Channel crossings to France but that took no more than a day or so in good weather. Will I ever be able to eat anything at sea again?'

'You'll get your sea legs soon enough,' Adam sympathised, though he had been fortunate never to suffer with the malady. He had first sailed with his grandfather when the yard put a newly built ship through her sea-trials, and then at the age of eleven he had become a midshipman in the navy.

There was a roar from the companionway leading to the passengers' quarters. St John emerged, his brown hair loose and matted, and his shirt crumpled. Throughout their time at sea St John had kept to his cabin, refusing to join Adam and Long Tom for meals. St John was also drunk most of the time. There had been no explanation as to why Meriel had not accompanied him other than he wanted this chance to be free of her nagging company. Adam knew his brother's marriage was not a happy one. But if St John had gained a year or two of freedom, why was he in such a foul mood? Twice when Adam had knocked on St John's locked cabin door, his twin had been abusive, refusing to talk to him.

The rough seas since they had left Fowey had kept Adam on deck, but with the sea again calm he was concerned by his brother's behaviour. He was not about to tolerate several weeks at sea with St John in a surly and disagreeable mood.

'What sort of shambles do you run on this ship?' St John scowled. 'I asked for rum an hour past. Your men need better discipline, Adam.'

'You have been drunk since your first night on board. I thought you wanted to make this voyage to Virginia.'

'Father wanted the scandal of my trial to die down.

I was an encumbrance to the reputation of his precious shipyard.' St John weaved from the motion of the ship as he strode towards Adam and banged his hip against a cannon. 'Damned ships! No sane man would want to spend his life being pitched and tossed about like flotsam. And the boredom could drive a man insane.' He turned to Adam's friend. 'Kilmarthen, how about a hand or two of cards to pass the time?'

Long Tom clutched his stomach. 'I am away to my cabin. Adam, I should have asked your wife for a remedy to keep my food from the fishes.'

Adam turned to St John once they were alone. 'You look appalling. Morale is important on a ship. Seeing you drunk and dishevelled is a bad example to the men.'

'And you would be the perfect example?' St John snarled. 'My perfect brother . . . Father's perfect son.'

The rivalry between the twins had been strong since childhood but Adam was taken aback by St John's vehemence now. He felt no rancour towards his brother on a personal level, though he had never fully come to terms with the fact that St John, as the elder twin, would inherit Trevowan, the home Adam loved.

'If you are feeling guilty over the scandal incurred by your trial, there is no need. You were declared innocent. Father is proud of all you have achieved by your management of the estate. The harvest will pay many of our debts.'

'Shipyard debts. My sweat went into that harvest and do I see a penny of it? Your damned shipyard takes it all.'

'The yard is Father's and will be, God willing, for many years to come. How easily you forget that for years the yard has been the stable income of our family,' Adam reminded him with sharpness. 'You only think of your needs. Once the yard is again financially secure, Father will use the profits to improve the stock of the home farm to ensure Trevowan will prosper.'

St John remained sullen. 'I have been packed off to the New World because I am an embarrassment to Father and his prim wife. I lost Father's respect when I married that scheming baggage.'

'So your quarrel with Meriel is behind your conduct on board? But I thought you were glad to be free of her nagging. Though you must miss Rowena.'

Adam was unprepared for the blow to his brow from his brother that rocked him back on his heels and slammed him against the ship's rail. His eye throbbed and the wind was knocked from his lungs. Adam pushed himself upright and sidestepped to avoid a second swing from St John's fist.

'What the devil is the matter with you?' Adam was puzzled by his brother's attack. Seeing no reason for a brawl he had no wish to retaliate. Fighting on board was a punishable offence and would set a bad example to his men.

'Meriel. Rowena. My accursed marriage! That is what is the matter with me.' St John was breathing heavily and lashed out again, catching Adam in the stomach.

Adam leaped aside. St John's face was twisted with fury as he vented his rage. 'I was forced at gunpoint to wed that whore. Your whore . . . carrying your child . . . a child born eight months after I first slept with your cast-off whore. Only I was unaware that you had used and spurned the strumpet when she seduced me.'

'Your wits are addled, man,' Adam returned, but there was a sinking feeling in his gut. He had believed himself in love with Meriel at that time. And he and St John had been rivals for her favours. Adam had made love to Meriel a few days before he had rejoined his naval ship after shore leave. Meriel had been a virgin when he had taken her. When he had returned from his voyage it was to find Meriel heavy with child and wed to his twin. He had assumed that she had chosen the heir to Trevowan for the wealth St John would bring her. Adam, as a mere naval lieutenant, could never have afforded to buy her the gowns and jewels she demanded.

With a drunken roar of rage St John again sprang at Adam and they both fell as they wrestled on the deck.

'Rowena was an eight-month child. Meriel fell down the stairs,' Adam gritted out as he was forced to return his brother's blows to defend himself.

'Except no one saw her fall. That scheming wench is a damned fine actress when needs must. She even professed to love me . . .'

Fists slammed into gut and sinew as the fight

became fiercer. Adam was squinting at his brother through a half-closed eye, and as St John rolled on top of him, blood dripped on to his face from the elder twin's nose. Adam brought up his knee and managed to throw St John's heavier weight to one side, then rolled away and staggered upright.

St John kicked out, catching Adam behind the knees just as the ship reared on a heavy swell and dipped abruptly. Adam was caught off balance and fell sideways, catching his head against the side of a gun carriage. Pain exploded through his skull and he lay dazed, unable to move.

A hand clamped over his throat, squeezing his windpipe. St John's face was contorted with fury, the moonlight revealing the manic glitter in his eyes. 'Meriel told me Rowena was your child just before she left to become Lord Wycham's whore. And she said she had never wanted to marry me. It was you she wanted. She tricked me into marriage. Do you expect me to bring up your bastard and own her as my child?'

Another blow to his head and the tightness of the hand robbing him of breath stripped the power from Adam's struggles. He had suspected that Rowena could be his child, and had even challenged Meriel, but she had denied it.

'Rowena is yours! She loves you. Adores you!' he forced out in a strangulated whisper before he passed out.

St John tightened his fingers over his twin's throat. Years of resentment and anger flared into hatred for Adam. He hated Adam for siring Rowena. He hated

Adam for being their father's favourite. And he hated Adam for stealing the shipyard from him that should be part of his birthright, together with Trevowan.

His fingers were locked tight around Adam's throat. His twin was getting weaker. St John glanced up and saw that no one appeared to have heard their scuffle. He could kill Adam and toss his body over the side. Then both Trevowan and the yard would one day be his.

Adam was choking, his eyes bulging as the pressure increased. It would all be over in a few moments . . . Yet even as St John stared down at his twin's unconscious face the pressure in his fingers relaxed. He hated Adam for having won Meriel first to his bed and that it was Adam who Meriel loved. St John had rescued his pride from his enforced marriage by believing that he had triumphed over Adam because Meriel was his wife. All the time he had been duped. But the pain that cut deepest was that his beautiful Rowena, whom he adored, was not of his flesh but his brother's.

His fingers tightened again. With Adam dead his honour would be redeemed. But despite his hatred, he found he could not continue. His brain was foggy with drink but a glimmer of reason roused his conscience. Adam was his twin. How could he kill him and not kill part of himself?

St John was breathing heavily and sat back on his heels. It was then he heard the click of a pistol being cocked.

'Step away from him.' Long Tom held the barrel to

the back of St John's head.

'The fight is over.' St John raised his hands in submission. 'I wanted to kill him but I could not. I thought I hated him . . .' He put his hands to his head, his emotion so raw he felt his brain would explode. 'I could not kill him.'

St John rose and found that he was shaking. 'I'll fetch the surgeon. Adam hit his head on the gun carriage. It knocked him out. I have never bested him in a fight.'

After summoning the surgeon St John collected a brandy bottle from the store and shut himself in his room to get drunk. He bathed the cuts on his brows; one eye was beginning to close. He carefully touched his swelling nose and was relieved to find that it was not broken. His hands were throbbing, the skin scraped from the knuckles.

The brandy bottle was half empty and he was still achingly sober when the door opened. Adam leaned against the frame, his thumb stuck into his belt. Apart from his purple and swollen eye, his lip was split and there was a deep cut on his cheek. The blood congealed upon a long gash on his temple where he had hit his head on the gun carriage.

'What do you want?' St John scowled. 'I've got nothing more to say to you.'

'You could have killed me but you did not.'

St John shrugged and stared at the brandy bottle.

'Meriel spoke out of spite. Do not doubt that Rowena is your daughter. We have feuded for too long. It solves nothing and only brings pain to us both. I resented that Trevowan would one day be yours. You have the one thing I hold almost sacred.'

'You have Boscabel now. The land matches Trevowan for size. Though the house is a near ruin, you can build a magnificent mansion in its place. And you will get the yard and the wealth that will bring. The yard should by rights be mine. Father never shared his inheritance with his brothers.'

'Boscabel will never be Trevowan. As for the yard . . . what is that truly to you? You've never shown any interest in how ships were built. It is its wealth alone which you resent losing.'

'No little thing.' St John tipped back the bottle and drank deeply.

'No. But Trevowan brings in riches enough under your management. Is it not time for this foolish rivalry to end? We all feared for your life when you were put on trial for murder. I discovered then that for all our petty squabbling, there would be a vast gap in my life if you were not there to fill it.'

St John pointed the bottle at Adam, his tone bitter. 'Have you been truthful about Meriel? She said she loved you; that you had been lovers.'

Adam disliked deceit but the pain in St John's eyes was too acute for him to add to it. St John loved Rowena – his love for Meriel had died long ago.

'Meriel knew what would hurt you most. She is an accomplished liar.' Adam held his brother's accusing stare. 'I had not realised that she had run off with Lord Wycham. I'm sorry.'

St John dropped his gaze first. 'I am well rid of her.

I hope she rots in hell.' He held out the brandy bottle to Adam. 'A drink to her damnation!'

Adam took the bottle. 'I would not drink to anyone's damnation, but I will drink to brotherhood. The Lovedays strength is through their being united in adversity.'

St John nodded. Adam put the bottle to his lips and winced as the brandy ran into the cut.

St John reclaimed the bottle and lifted it in salute to his twin. 'United in adversity – I can accept that. But twins or not, rivalry is inevitable between us. It is too long established.' There was a sly light in St John's eyes as he added, 'You will choke with envy the day I take possession of Trevowan. You made as poor a choice of a bride as I did. Father will never accept a gypsy's brat as master of Trevowan. If I have no son, Trevowan goes to our baby brother, Rafe.'

When Adam returned to his cabin, his mood was reflective. St John was right. There would always be rivalry between them, but Adam hoped that it would never again break out with such intensity that it threatened to destroy them both. But that it *would* break out was as inevitable as St John had declared.

Chapter Eight

Japhet had sold the goods from his highway robbery and could now afford to relax and enjoy his stay in London. He moved out of the cheap inn in the backstreets of Covent Garden and rented lodgings in Brook Street.

Yet the usual excitement of London was missing. The thrill of high gaming stakes at White's or Brooks's had lost its edge. The restlessness that had been with him since leaving Cornwall continued to plague him. He had spent the afternoon at Tattersalls, where the finest horses were auctioned. In recent years, Japhet had established a reputation as a discerning horse dealer. Lord Dashwood had approached him at the last race meeting at Newmarket to look out for a colt with the breeding and potential to win the Derby, the most prestigious flat race, established, thirteen years ago in 1780.

Japhet had purchased a bay colt for his Lordship. He was tempted to keep him for himself, for he would dearly love a horse of his own, one day to win the

Derby. Sheba had won many races at smaller meetings but did not have the form of the more expensive racehorses. Reluctantly, Japhet knew he had to part with the colt. The investment had cut into his finances but he would make a large profit when he sold the colt. Horse dealing was a good life, which he enjoyed, especially since his foray into highway robbery had left him with an uneasy feeling.

The exhilaration of the auction soon faded as he stabled the colt and sent a letter to Lord Dashwood for his Lordship to arrange a convenient time to attend upon him.

It was late afternoon and several hours before the gaming rooms opened. He decided to dine at a chophouse, and as he walked through the deepening shadows of the narrow, crowded and noisy streets with their tall gabled houses, his head turned suddenly as he thought he recognised Gwendolyn Druce driving past in a carriage.

On closer glance he saw the woman was not Gwen, and that apart from her build and hair colouring there was little resemblance. The similarity stirred confusing emotions. He was unexpectedly disappointed that Gwen was not in London. He had grown used to her company this summer.

Yet he could not understand why he could not shake her from his mind. They were no more than friends. She had changed in recent years into a lovely confident woman, and her wit never failed to amuse him. Though he had been tempted to make love to her, he had always resisted. He respected her too much to ruin her reputation. But Gwen was no young maid but a woman, who should by now be married and raising a family. Despite numerous suitors she remained unwed. She was an heiress and would one day marry well, but Japhet had always known she was not for him. He cared for her too much to break her heart, for he doubted he would be faithful to any woman.

At his turn of thoughts Japhet became angry. He needed a new and exciting mistress. He reasoned that Gwen continued to fascinate him because he had made her unobtainable. And Japhet had never denied himself a woman he desired.

On entering the chophouse he paused to adjust his gaze to the dim interior. The eating-house was filled with diners, and there was a haze of tobacco smoke from many long-stemmed clay pipes.

'Japhet, dear man, I insist you join us,' called out a fop with short, elaborately curled blond hair and wearing a waistcoat embroidered with flowers of dazzling rainbow hues.

'Lucien!' He returned the man's wave and Lucien Greene moved along the pew-style seat to allow Japhet to join his friends. Lucien's indulgent lifestyle was thickening his once slender body but he still had the grace and beauty of an Adonis. A renowned poet and scintillating wit, no London ball or entertainment was complete without his presence.

Japhet did not hesitate to join Lucien and his companions, although the theatrical entourage was not the company he would normally seek. For several years Lucien had been more than just a friend of his cousin Thomas. That Georganna so easily accepted Thomas's lover into her own circle of friends mystified Japhet. Wives were not usually so accommodating, and Lucien also seemed to adore Georganna. If the strange *ménage à trois* worked, then Thomas had been wise in his choice of bride.

The chophouse was long and narrow, and candle wax dripped on to the walls from the iron sconces. The heaped pewter platters were served with copious tankards of ale or wine. Buxom maids with dimpled arms the size of hams from carrying heavy trays, or several quart tankards of ale in both hands at a time, giggled and flirted with the customers. Lucien and his companions ignored them, but Japhet flicked a silver coin into the generous cleavage of the maid serving him.

She brushed her hip against his shoulder and with a laugh he pulled her on to his lap. She giggled and gave him a playful slap as she wriggled free.

'Shame on you, bold sir. I've work to do. There's a dozen gentlemen need serving. I can't afford to lose me job.' Despite her rebuke, her eyes were bright and admiring. 'A poor girl like me 'as to work hard for a living.'

'Then what time do you finish?'

'Leave the wench, Japhet, my dear fellow.' Lucien waved the woman away. 'You must join us at the playhouse. It will be hugely diverting. Celestine Yorke is playing the virginal maiden in a new play. Have you ever heard anything so absurd? When will the Yorke woman admit she is past her prime? There are a half-dozen young actresses who are more talented than she.'

A short fop, his face a whitened mask of rice powder, guffawed. He was an adoring acolyte who constantly wrote down any quote from Lucien to impress his friends. 'What was it you said but yesterday, Lucien? "Yorke plays the role of virginal innocence with the panache of a bellicose sow. Her fluttering eyelids and blushes of a naive innocent hold the allure of a gargoyle assessing its prey." ' He giggled inanely. 'Her performance is too amusing to be missed.'

Japhet was not amused but he was intrigued that the woman he had robbed was performing that night. 'You are too cruel, Lucien, and worthier of less spiteful wit. Celestine Yorke still has charm and beauty.'

There was a shocked gasp from two of the poet's companions. Lucien was never criticised by his entourage.

'Oh, I say, my dear fellow, it simply is not done to ridicule Lucien that way,' the short fop remonstrated.

Lucien regarded Japhet without rancour. 'Japhet is right. A fit of the megrims soured my judgement.' He waved airily in the direction of the short fop. 'And I would prefer it, my friend, if you were more selective in repeating my less worthy comments. But in justification, I have to say that the woman has an overblown opinion of her talents. She is no longer celebrated as "the Darling of London" by anyone of discernment or repute. And she knows it.'

'The old girl is desperate for acclaim,' another fop declared, and leaned towards Japhet to speak in a loud stage whisper: 'Have you seen the latest broadsheet, dear fellow? The Yorke woman claims she was robbed and left near to death by a villainous highwayman. There are a hundred guineas on his head.'

Japhet went deathly cold, the image of a gallows chilling his mind. Such a reward could make him notorious if his identity was ever discovered. He had not sought such infamy. He cleared his throat, his neck cloth suddenly tight and rough as the hemp of a noose. 'I had not heard. What highwayman is this?'

The short fop chortled in glee. 'She claims he is a Gentleman James, a black-hearted, devilish rogue who showed her no mercy. Can't say I have ever heard of a Gentleman James. Celestine Yorke claims she feared for her virtue, don't you know.'

Lucien guffawed. 'What virtue? Her paramour, Sir Pettigrew Osgood, has put up the reward. He declared the man would have murdered Yorke and himself. Apparently he spared their lives when he recognised the great actress. The man was supposed to be besotted with her. Claimed a kiss and returned her jewels – though he robbed Osgood blind.'

Ill at ease at the information, Japhet attempted a lighter note. 'A tale worthy of the stage.'

'Contrived to restore her popularity,' Lucien tutted. 'She rode through London this morning in an open carriage and was cheered. The public have no discernment. She'll play to the hilt her role of victim. The playhouse will be full tonight.'

'Celestine Yorke snubbed your poetry and you have never forgiven her,' Japhet responded.

'I can never forgive her lack of talent.' Lucien stood up. 'Will you join us, Japhet? At the very least it will be diverting to witness if the fêted "Darling" has a new lover in tow. She walked out on Osgood two days ago, but rumour has it that he is desperate to get her back.'

Japhet was about to refuse but in his restless mood he felt a perverse need to court danger and that made him accept.

As Lucien had predicted, the theatre was full and they took a second-tier box on the edge of the stage. The pit in front of the stage was filled with the lower orders, and here, prostitutes openly solicited clients. In the boxes lovers were more discreet, and some were masked to hide their identities, or the women partially hid their faces behind their fans or nosegays.

The candles along the floor beneath the proscenium arch lit the faces of the audience in the adjoining boxes. Japhet took a seat at the rear of the box. When Celestine came on stage to applause and catcalls from the pit, he leaned forward to study her.

Lucien and his guests whispered and sniggered at her most dramatic scenes. In their position so close to the stage her heavy makeup could not hide the lines around her mouth and eyes, which made her unsuitable to play a young virginal heroine, but Japhet saw no need to mock her for she was still a great beauty. Celestine was voluptuous as a Siren and moved as sinuously as a prowling cat, weaving a seductive spell over his senses. He did not hear her words for he was absorbed by the alluring way she played to the audience, wooing and enticing, her voice sultry and beguiling.

When the play was over and she came downstage to receive the applause and shouts of adulation, Japhet moved to the front of the box and clapped roundly. As she turned to exit beneath him, her glance lifted and he could not resist blowing her a kiss and bowing to her. Briefly her eyes widened as she regarded his handsome countenance. She ran the tip of her tongue over her lips before they lifted in an inviting and predatory smile.

Lucien clapped him on the back. 'Shall we process to the green room? Osgood is here and I saw a young nobleman looking very eager to make our "Darling's" acquaintance. It will be more diverting than the play, which was too dreary and mediocre for words.'

'I have business elsewhere.' Japhet bowed. 'It has been an enjoyable evening, Lucien.'

As Japhet left the theatre the danger Celestine Yorke presented to him was a potent lure. Would she recognise him as the highwayman? He had been masked and his voice carefully disguised. If he had any sense he would avoid her. The temptation she offered was spurred by his restless mood and the need for excitement. He had not found the satisfaction he had sought in the London gaming houses, the cockpit or any of his usual pleasure haunts.

Celestine presented a new and bold challenge. To win her would be exciting, for unlike her usual lovers he was not a rich man and had no intention of buying

her favours. Celestine was all that Gwendolyn was not
– mercenary, scheming, without a single moral and
totally unscrupulous. Celestine Yorke was the very
mistress he needed.

Japhet felt his blood quicken. He would not play the
established role that she demanded of her admirers.
He had no intention of relinquishing his hard-won
money into her avaricious hands. She could continue
to amass the riches she desired from nobles and
wealthy merchants and bankers. Nevertheless Japhet
was resolved that the actress would find him irresistible. To win her from those who would pay dearly for
her charms was the fascination of the challenge.

After that first time, Japhet regularly attended every
matinée and evening performance given by Celestine
Yorke. Outside the theatre a reward poster offered a
hundred guineas for information to bring the highwayman Gentleman James to justice for his foul
robbery and molestation of the actress. The printed
lies fuelled Japhet's need to conquer her and make a
liaison as dangerous as it was fascinating.

At the theatre he always took the same box by the
side of the stage. At the end of each performance he
would bow and blow the actress a kiss, but he held
back from visiting the green room.

Throughout the first week Celestine's gaze during
her performance sought his figure in the box. At the
end of the fifth performance she blew him a kiss, her
eyes bright with invitation. Still Japhet did not seek
her out. The next evening she addressed any innuendo within the play directly at him. He smiled and

applauded her but again did not visit the green room. The next three performances she ignored him but as she left the stage, Japhet called out, 'Bravo, Madonna, your loveliness lights our hearts.'

He then did not visit the playhouse for three days and when he returned he knew that she was aware of his presence the moment that she walked on the stage. Her glance was constantly upon his box, her mood alternating between irritation and fascination. That evening, at the end of the play he sauntered into the green room. Even then he stood against a wall without approaching the actress.

The room was filled with men vying for Celestine Yorke's favours. The noise of their excited voices was as deafening as any race meeting. There was a musty smell of greasepaint, face and hair powder and stale sweat. Gaudily coloured costumes spilled out of wicker baskets or wooden coffers, some were hung around the walls, and a row of wigs and elaborate feathered headdresses sat upon wooden heads on a dressing table.

Japhet stood a head taller than most of the men clamouring for the actress's attention, and from the moment he walked into the room Celestine's gaze was upon him, her brow lifting in an unspoken invitation for him to approach her. Still he held back. He wanted to ensure that he intrigued her when so many others made their intentions so obvious.

Celestine was given several gifts as men vied to be her next lover. She removed her stage makeup and carefully reapplied her face powder and rouge, while she teased and flirted with her companions, playing one against another. She rose from her chair to move behind a Japanese lacquered screen to change from her costume into a low-cut saffron silk gown.

'And which of my dashing friends shall I permit to lace my gown?' Celestine held the bodice to her breasts as she slowly twirled to show the men her smooth shoulders and back. A half-dozen men begged her to choose them. She picked up a long rope of pearls presented to her earlier. 'These are magnificent. Pearls are so flattering. I do love them so. It was dear Lawrence who gave me these. Such a generous gift. He must be the one to lace my gown.'

There were loud protests from the others. Japhet watched the proceedings with amusement. She was an expert at ensuring the next time any of these men wanted to win a favour, they would buy a more lavish gift. Japhet noted that Sir Pettigrew Osgood was scowling in a corner and was ignored by Celestine, even though it was rumoured that he was again her protector. As the men began to file away, Celestine's stare again searched for Japhet. He placed a hand over his heart and bowed, but he made no attempt to move towards her.

She frowned. 'Good sir, what is your business here?'

'To pay tribute to the most talented and beautiful actress in London,' he replied.

'The man speaks,' Celestine taunted. 'I had begun to think you had lost your tongue . . . or perhaps your nerve.'

'I have nerves of steel, dear lady. What need have

you of my compliments when you receive so many?'

'A woman can never have too many compliments.'
She offered her hand, glittering with rings, to him and
he raised it to his lips with a broad smile.

'Or gifts,' he parried, noting the array of trinkets on
her dressing table.

Her eyes hardened with speculation, clearly waiting
for him to present her with something special. As her
gaze pierced his hazel stare he saw his reflection in her
eyes and for a moment fear of recognition quickened
his heartbeat. But it was not recognition that glowed
in her eyes but the hunger of desire.

He placed in her hands a thin parcel tied with an
emerald ribbon. She snatched it from him and tore
the ribbon away with avaricious delight. Her smile
faded as she saw the single white rose sealed within a
wand-shaped glass vial.

'A rose! You would give the Darling of London a
paltry rose, sir? You insult me.'

'A white rose of purity and such perfection to
match your own beauty – a humble gift and I can see
now that it is indeed unworthy of you. Your beauty
outshines even its perfection.'

Her eyes narrowed and for a moment Japhet wondered if he had misjudged her. Would her greed be
more important than his compliments? There was a
long moment of silence while she continued to hold
his bold stare.

'You are very sure of yourself,' she observed in a
challenging voice.

'I sought to match perfection with perfection. Any

fool can buy a trinket. How much more exciting is a lover who proves to be unpredictable?'

Celestine pressed the vial against the corner of her mouth and continued to appraise him for several moments. When she spoke her voice was deep and throaty. 'You have a wickedly persuasive tongue, sir. I shall be at home tomorrow afternoon when I receive callers.'

He again bowed over her hand and whispered, 'Then I shall call when you are alone tomorrow evening for you have no performance.'

'You take much for granted.' Her pulse was rapid beneath his fingers.

He smiled. 'If you do not wish to receive me you may send me away.'

Her smile told him that Celestine would be alone and only too willing to receive him when he called.

On arrival at Mertle Moxon's Ladies' Academy, Edward left Tamasine in the carriage with Jasper Fraddon and Margaret to watch over her. Tamasine was hunched in a corner with her arms folded across her chest. She was close to tears but her expression was mutinous.

Margaret watched her brother stride through the entrance hall of the bleak grey stone building. It was a mild, cloudy morning but as Margaret appraised the dour building and the pristine formal grounds she shivered. The hedges and lawns were clipped into precise lines and there was not a single weed amongst the gravel of the drive. Every window in the building was tightly closed as though the place was blockaded against the outside world. It was so quiet the school could have been deserted instead of the home of some forty girls.

'I shall run away again.' Tamasine glared at Margaret. 'I will not stay. They will lock me in the cellar for a week and make me scrub the floors for a month, but they cannot keep me locked up all the time.'

'My dear, do you not exaggerate? This is a respected and civilised establishment. You are surely taught how to deal with servants, not to be treated as one.'

'So the old crow Moxon would have our guardians believe. Have you ever been inside a school like this, Mrs Mercer? Our guardians rarely visit and we are not allowed to write to them unless Moxon stands over us scrutinising every word. She is too mean to employ more than two servants and a cook. Any misdemeanour, no matter how small, and we are given servants' tasks.'

At Margaret's shocked expression, Tamasine added with bitterness, 'We are not permitted to talk to each other during lessons, mealtimes or the hour before bedtime. In any free time we must read the Bible or sew our samplers. Neither can we talk in the dormitories after bedtime. A teacher sleeps in each dormitory to ensure that rule is observed.'

'Obedience and decorum are not easily instilled upon young women,' Margaret observed with a frown, 'though the rules of silence are excessive. This is not a nunnery. I shall ask Edward to interview the servants and check that you are not exaggerating.'

'Why should I lie? The truth is there for all to see – if they look closely enough. To people of your class servants are the invisible masses, are they not?'

'Servants have their place – as do we all. You repeatedly forget yours, young lady.'

'I will not stay here.' Tamasine sat up straight, her fists clenched and her gaze fierce. 'I did not ask Mr Loveday to be my guardian. I shall become an actress. I do not need charity. I can look after myself.'

Margaret sighed. 'Such rash sentiments have been the downfall of many a foolish woman. Your manner is ungrateful, for my brother does not take his responsibilities lightly. He will ensure that your future is secure.'

'He wants me out of sight and out of mind. Just like my mother's family.'

Tamasine fell silent but her eyes were narrowed and calculating. Margaret was stirred to pity for the lovely girl who showed such spirit, but saw no alternative to the life Edward had proposed for her.

Edward marched through the foyer of the school and almost stopped in his tracks with shock. A girl not much younger than Tamasine was standing precariously on a high stool with a gag tied around her mouth. Her face was twisted in pain and mottled with cold from the icy temperature within the building. To add to this disgraceful sight, the girl was holding a slate in outstretched arms, a position that must have been excruciatingly painful. Printed in large letters on

the slate were the words: 'I AM AN INSIGNIFI-
CANT WRETCH. I MUST BE GRATEFUL AND
HUMBLE FOR ALL I RECEIVE.'

If that sight was not appalling enough, two younger
girls were struggling to carry an overfull slops pail
down the staircase. Both of them were sobbing as it
splashed over their skirts and hands. The stench from
it made Edward put a handkerchief to his nose.

With only a single rap on Mrs Moxon's study
door, he opened it to find the woman sprawled in
an ungainly manner in a chair in front of a fire.
Her skirt was crumpled up over her knees, display-
ing an expanse of purple-veined thigh above her
hose and garters. The thick veil of her widow's
weeds was thrown back from her face and hung
loose from its pins over one ear. The room stank of
gin and an empty bottle lay on its side on the floor
by her feet.

'I think I have seen enough to get this place closed
down,' Edward raged. 'This so-called ladies' academy
is worse than any bridewell.'

Mrs Moxon opened an eye to glare blearily at
him. Recognising Edward, she pushed down her
skirts and staggered as she came to her feet. The
dark-panelled room was as austere as an army
barracks, with no personal adornments except for
the discarded gin bottle. 'How dare you burst into
my study unannounced?'

'I have brought my ward back from Cornwall to
demand why I was not informed that she had run
away. I thought the girl was exaggerating when she

told me how you treated your charges. Clearly she did not.'

'Tamasine Keyne is nothing but a troublemaker.' Mrs Moxon tried vainly to straighten the cap of her widow's black veil, her mood belligerent at being caught at such a disadvantage. 'The little bastard has no respect for her betters. She will come to a nasty end. It will cost you double if you want her kept out of the way here in future.'

'My ward will not return here and the authorities will be informed of your conduct and treatment of your charges.'

Mrs Moxon gripped the edge of the table to support her swaying figure. 'This academy is no worse than others of its kind. It's a place for by-blows to be bundled away out of sight of decent folk. The authorities don't care what happens to such brats, as long as they're not a burden on the parish.'

Edward hated to admit it but the harridan was probably right. But from what he had seen today, he was not surprised that Tamasine had run away, though that did not lessen his anger at the trouble the girl's arrival at Trevowan had caused to his marriage. He turned on his heel and strode from the building. Once outside he glared towards the coach. What was he now to do with Tamasine?

Edward got into the coach and ordered Fraddon to ride on to the coaching inn in the town. Briefly, he told his sister what had happened.

'I told you the place was dreadful. I don't tell lies,' Tamasine cut in before Margaret could respond.

'So what do you intend to do with the girl?' Margaret sat forward in her seat. 'You could find her a school elsewhere but most girls are not educated past the age of fourteen. It will take time to find her employment or a suitable husband, if that is what you had in mind. In the meantime, where will she stay?'

'I hate it when adults talk about you as though you are not present,' Tamasine informed them. Her arms were folded across her chest, and she was fighting against the pain of their rejection. She had been an idiot to think she could be part of the Loveday family. But she would not let them see her hurt. Blinking back her tears, she jutted her chin at a stubborn angle. 'You do not have to worry about me. I have a friend in London who will take me in. I intend to go on the stage, anyway.'

'I will have no daughter of mine parading herself on the stage,' Edward fumed.

'So I am your daughter, you admit it now?' Tamasine seized on his statement.

Edward groaned; his anger had stripped away his usual discretion, making him blurt out the truth. He looked at Margaret and for once was at a loss as to how to deal with a situation. There was compassion in his sister's eyes.

'The news that Tamasine is your daughter has been a shock to us all, Edward. But what is done cannot be undone, and the best must be made of it.'

'Tamasine's existence came as a shock to me.' Edward rubbed a hand across his brow and his voice was strained. He stared at his daughter. 'I will not abandon my duty to you.'

'But I will forever be a charity case and never part of your family, you made that clear enough.'

'In the circumstances, young lady, you are being dealt with very fairly. I will hear no more of such talk.' Margaret, ever practical, had been weighing up the situation. 'It is important to avoid a scandal, Edward. Tamasine cannot return to Trevowan – not for a while. Amelia would not stand for it. It has been a difficult year for her. Neither are you a man to abandon your responsibilities, my dear brother. The situation is not easy. Many men of your position do not acknowledge such children—'

'You are ashamed of me. I did not ask to be born, did I?' Tamasine declared, her pain and vulnerability making her voice shrill. 'You will not acknowledge me as your own, therefore you have no rights to dictate how I shall lead my life.' She drew a sharp breath, demanding, 'What is wrong with the stage? I can make my fortune.'

'Actresses are no better than courtesans. Is that how you would shame your mother – by becoming a whore?' Edward barked with such fierceness that Tamasine burst into tears.

Margaret rapped her brother on the knee with her hand. 'Edward, the girl has gone through enough. Heaven knows what ordeals she suffered getting to Trevowan. That took courage.' She passed a handkerchief to Tamasine. 'We are all over-wrought. Edward, would you truly have wanted your daughter to stay in such a school?'

'Of course not.'

'Then what choice did the girl have but to run away? That monster of a woman would never have allowed her to write to you to ask to be taken out of there.'

He turned to Tamasine. 'Why did you not say how bad it was when I visited in the summer?'

'Would you have believed me?' Tamasine held his glare without flinching. Her tears had dried and her defiance had returned. 'Lady Keyne became upset if I said anything. I learned not to speak of such things for I was frightened she would not come to see me if I did. I am not a child any more. I am fifteen and a woman. I have no intention of being married off at sixteen to salve your conscience that by such an act I am provided for.'

'Did I say that was my intent?' Edward clipped out in a glacial voice.

His tone broke through Tamasine's defiance. He had been so friendly on his first visit that she could not believe her good fortune at having him as a guardian. She had acted thoughtlessly and had ruined everything. She hung her head. 'I ask your pardon, sir. I was wrong to approach you as I did. I could think of no other way. The crow Moxon would never have allowed me to write to your lawyer as you suggested.'

Edward studied her in grave silence.

'Please forgive me, Mr Loveday. I never meant to embarrass you or cause pain to you or any of your family.'

Margaret shook her head, her voice wistful. 'How like Adam and Japhet she sounds. This ward of yours will be a handful, Edward. Could Tamasine not stay with Senara until you arrange what is best for her future?'

Edward spread his hands. 'I am not sure that it would be fair to place such a responsibility upon Senara.'

'It will be company for her while Adam is at sea.' Margaret was enthusiastic. 'And is not Senara's sister, Bridie, of the same age as Tamasine? Since this minx announced to all at the harvest feast that she is Tamasine Loveday, her arrival at Trevowan will be the butt of much gossip. Her disappearance will only add to it.'

'I had meant to say that I was Tamasine Loveday Keyne.' Tamasine looked guilty, despite her protestation. 'But I want nothing to do with the Keyne family. They were unkind to my mother.'

Margaret raised a brow as she regarded her brother. 'If Tamasine stays with Senara it will give you time to consider how best to serve her interests. You would want the best for your daughter, would you not, Edward?'

'Of course I do. It is just that Amelia—' He broke off, unwilling to be disloyal to his wife.

Margaret nodded. 'Amelia needs time to come to terms with Tamasine's existence. But out of respect for all she has coped with in the last two years, Amelia should not be rushed. She will do what is right.'

Tamasine brightened and turned the full impact of

her smile and charm upon her father. 'Sir, you have been most generous and kind. I do not want to cause dissension within your family. I thought you would introduce me as a cousin and everyone would accept that.'

Edward did not return her smile. 'So you have plotted this escapade in some detail?'

'I would have been foolish not to have thought it through,' she returned, and kept her gaze firmly locked with his challenging stare.

'Friends and neighbours may be told such a story, but I would not lie to my wife.'

'I would not expect you to, sir. Senara seemed a very kind woman. I would be happy to stay with her. I heard in Bodmin about her marriage to your son and how it had caused a rift between the two of you. You have now accepted her or she would not have been at Trevowan.'

At seeing Edward Loveday's eyes harden, Tamasine realised she had spoken out of turn and hastily amended, 'I would welcome the chance to get to know some of my family, if even from a distance. I never really knew my mother. Are you also to remain distant from me?'

The anguish in her voice broke through Edward's resolve. Her wilfulness had placed a further strain upon his marriage, but a girl as spirited as Tamasine deserved better than the misery she would endure at that hideous school.

He studied her for some moments in silence. Her dark hair, although unruly, was thick and lustrous.

Both his sisters had said that she resembled him; but as Edward gazed into her face, he could see only Eleanor – the woman he had once loved so passionately. To deny Tamasine made him no better than Eleanor's cruel husband. Also such a denial would be a betrayal of his love for Eleanor, which had been so ill-fated because of her marriage.

'I shall talk with Senara,' he declared to the two women waiting expectantly for his response. 'And Tamasine will be introduced as the orphaned child of a cousin. People can make of that what they will.'

Tamasine gave a whoop of delight. 'Thank you, sir. You will not regret it.'

Edward remained wary. 'There is one condition you must agree to. You are never to reveal to anyone that I am your father. That would cause my wife too much pain.' A flaring of pain in Tamasine's eyes showed how deeply his words had wounded her. To reassure her, he added, 'But you will be known as Tamasine Loveday. For all concerned it is better if there is no link with the Keyne family.'

The coach pulled up outside the coaching inn and Edward suggested to Margaret, 'We will wait with you until Thomas and Georganna arrive.'

Margaret shook her head as she gathered up her skirts to alight. 'Unless you wish to take refreshments, or rest the horses, that would be foolish. I know how important it is for you to return to the shipyard as soon as possible. If you leave now, you will make good time and cover many miles before nightfall.'

Edward hesitated but was clearly eager to return to

116

Cornwall. Margaret was adamant. 'I shall take a room at the inn and rest until Thomas arrives. All the drama of the last weeks has left me quite exhausted.'

The luggage was unloaded, and as the coach rolled out of the courtyard, Tamasine plucked up courage to speak about a matter that troubled her. 'Sir, I truly regret being such a burden to you. And, as I told you this morning, I had to pawn the ruby brooch from the set you gave me that my mother had bequeathed to me. It was the only way I could pay for the post chaise to Bodmin. The man robbed me by giving me but fifteen shillings. Could we not redeem the pledge? I kept the ticket. I will pay the money back to you when I can.'

'Eleanor would wish you to have the brooch, which matches the necklace and earrings she left you. But they will in future be kept locked away at Trevowan. I was unwise to give them to you when you are so young. There will be no further temptation for you to sell them if you take it into your head to run away from Cornwall.'

They stopped at the pawnbroker's and the wizened Jew reluctantly handed over the brooch upon which he had hoped to make a generous profit. As the Loveday coach finally pulled back on to the highway for Cornwall they had missed passing the Mercer coach by a few minutes.

To silence Tamasine's excited chatter Edward closed his eyes and pretended to doze. Sleep proved impossible. He was worried about the financial affairs of the shipyard and wondered how he was going to make amends to Amelia for bringing his daughter back to Cornwall.

Chapter Nine

Gradually Edward relaxed in Tamasine's company. Obviously overjoyed that she would be allowed to live in Cornwall, she chattered incessantly. She bombarded Edward with questions and by the time they had dined and retired to their rooms for the night, Edward was amazed at her intelligence and wit. He found that he enjoyed her company, and only when he was alone in his room did he feel remorse at this new indignity that Amelia must suffer.

By the time they arrived in Cornwall Edward was captivated by his daughter. Tamasine was beautiful and vivacious in a way of which any man could not fail to be proud. She had shown herself to be a woman of courage to run away from the tyranny of the academy. If he had reservations about Tamasine being headstrong and wilful, they were all too familiar Loveday traits for him to condemn them too strongly. He also saw the joy of life in Tamasine that had been so abundant in her mother, and it was that vivaciousness that had first attracted him to Eleanor Keyne.

Nevertheless, it was with some trepidation when, three days later, they stopped first at Mariner's House at Trevowan Hard before he returned to Trevowan.

Mariner's House was the largest dwelling within the yard community. Over the years, as the business expanded, a dozen cottages had been built to house the shipwrights and their families. There was also the Ship kiddley, which was an alehouse and general store for the workers, and the schoolhouse, which Amelia had paid to be built for the children.

Senara saw the carriage draw up and, holding Nathan in her arms, she opened the door. It was the first time she had seen Edward looking discountenanced. Tamasine was at his side and the young woman's excitement radiated from her.

'I need somewhere for Tamasine to stay,' Edward said without preamble as he tipped his hat to Senara. 'Would you allow her to remain here with you?'

'It will be my pleasure.' Senara stood back for Edward and Tamasine to enter, and then followed Edward into the parlour with its bow window overlooking the shipyard and river inlet.

'The school proved unsuitable,' he explained. 'But, as you can appreciate, the situation at Trevowan is somewhat delicate. My wife . . .' he hesitated and spread his hands in a helpless gesture.

Senara shifted the weight of Nathan on to her other hip. 'You do not need to explain, sir. Mrs Loveday will need time to come to terms with your having a daughter. I am sure in time your wife will accept Tamasine into your home.' She could not

119

resist adding, 'Mrs Loveday eventually accepted me. And in the meantime I shall be delighted to have Tamasine here. We will get on famously together. Do you like to ride, Tamasine?'

The young woman had been looking out the window at the shipwrights working on a partly built brigantine in its wooden supporting cradle, her eyes bright with interest. When she turned her attention to Senara, she burst out, 'I would love to be able to ride. We were not taught at school. The crow, Moxon, had an aversion to animals of any kind.'

There was a spate of barking and Scamp tore into the room through the garden and kitchen, his paws slithering on the floor. He ran round Edward and Tamasine's legs, his whole body wriggling as he wagged his tail. Senara ordered Scamp outside.

'No, please let him stay.' Tamasine threw her arms around the dog, who rolled on his back to have his stomach rubbed. 'He is adorable. I've always wanted a dog. Can I take him for a walk? I've been cooped up in the carriage for days.'

Edward nodded. 'Stay within the yard and do not go near any of the workmen. A shipyard is a dangerous place.'

Senara eyed the girl's drab and shapeless grey school dress. 'Sir, I think your daughter will need more fitting attire. I have some material that Adam brought for me before he sailed. I could ask Martha Wakeley to sew a dress for her out of it.'

'Tamasine will need more than one dress and a riding habit if she is to learn to ride. Take her to the

dressmakers in Fowey and have her fitted out. She will
need three dresses at least as she has no clothes other
than what she is standing in. Nothing fancy – they
must be practical. Tamasine will be known as my ward
– her presence explained that she was recently
orphaned, and that her parents were cousins of mine
in Wiltshire.'

'Oh, thank you, sir.' Tamasine abandoned Scamp to
throw her arms around Edward. 'You will not regret
your kindness. You are so generous and wonderful.
Thank you.'

Gently, Edward put her from him. He looked both
embarrassed and pleased at his daughter's show of
affection.

Senara said, 'Will such a story not be questioned?
My observations of local society has shown me that
they seem to know the relations of all their peers.'

'My word will not be questioned amongst my
friends. A simple story of Tamasine's background is
necessary to stifle gossip. It will be said that she has
come to Trevowan now that she has finished her
schooling and is here as your companion while Adam
is at sea. Once it is time for Tamasine to marry her
dowry will be sufficient to silence any speculation
about her ancestry.'

Senara nodded and smiled at Tamasine, who ran
outside with Scamp. Edward walked to the door. 'I
dare say there will be other necessities: under-
garments, stockings, a cloak, shoes and the like. The
dressmaker may send the account to the yard office
for settlement. And you must select something for

yourself, Senara. I would not have you do so much for Tamasine and you not be rewarded by a new dress.'

'I need no reward. I am honoured that you would place the welfare of your daughter in my hands. But would it not be more practical if Tamasine were to stay with Hannah or Cecily?'

'Amelia would find that harder to accept. She frequently calls upon Hannah and Cecily and it is rare that she visits the yard. Though I hope that will change in the future. For now I would spare my wife the embarrassment of meeting Tamasine.' He realised he had confirmed Amelia's reluctance to accept Senara into the family and was quick to reassure Senara. 'A woman alone is in need of a companion. No one will question Tamasine's presence here. And I will be offended if you do not accept my gift.'

Senara was disturbed by Edward's words. 'Sir, are you not aware that Mrs Loveday left with Mr and Mrs Mercer? She informed the servants that she intended to spend the winter in London. Are you sure you would not prefer Tamasine to stay with Hannah?'

Edward stiffened at the news. He had expected Amelia to be angry at learning of Tamasine's existence, but he had not thought she would leave him in this manner. This cold judgemental side of Amelia made her a stranger: their marriage was not the idyll he had believed. His pride was wounded that his wife had not stayed to listen to his explanations. If she preferred London to his company in Cornwall, then she could cool her heels there. Amelia knew that he could not afford to leave the yard without Adam or St

John to supervise the work here or on the estate.

He spoke tersely. 'Tamasine will remain here.'

He left Mariner's House to spend an hour pacing the converted cottage that served as his office at the yard. He had a dozen problems to deal with that had arisen in his absence, yet his mind could settle upon none of them. Even when Ben Mumford, the yard overseer, came to him distraught over a recent spate of thefts from the yard, Edward dismissed him, ordering him to return in an hour.

Edward paused in his pacing to stare out over the darkening yard. Work had finished on the keel of the new brigantine in its cradle, but within the workshops lanterns had been lit and the sound of handsaws and adzes shaping the wooden ribs carried on the evening wind. A dull red glow came from the door of the forge where the blacksmith worked over his furnace, producing nails.

Edward witnessed the workings of the yard through blind eyes, his mind centred upon what he viewed as his wife's betrayal. Amelia's disloyalty was a painful shock. He was not proud of having presented his wife with his illegitimate child, yet had not Tamasine been conceived years ago? He had been a widower in his twenties and had the misfortune to fall in love with an incredible woman who was not free to be his wife. Before he married Amelia, he had been a widower for twenty years and over that time other women had occasionally brought comfort to his life.

Why had Amelia so harshly condemned him for his past? He had been no womaniser. Even his affair with

Lady Eleanor Keyne had been conducted discreetly. He had looked with interest at no other woman than his wife since they had met.

The pain of Amelia's disloyalty seared deeper. His pride rose in defence of his affair as a widower. Many of his neighbours were openly unfaithful to their wives, but that had never been Edward's way.

His anger intensified. He had come to rely upon his elder two sons. It was an added burden that they were not here when the yard needed to recover its reputation after St John's trial, and also from the lies spread by Thadeous Lanyon before the man's murder. The yard brought in the main income for the family – if the business failed he could even lose Trevowan, which was heavily mortgaged. It was difficult enough without the support of the twins, but now that Amelia had gone, undoubtedly taking their infant son, Rafe, with her, he felt deserted in his time of need. Especially as Amelia had been the one to insist that St John spend a year away so that the gossip about their family could subside.

Personally, Edward believed that if St John worked hard and lived in a sober fashion he would soon receive approval from their neighbours. It had been to appease Amelia that he had agreed for his son to leave – and this was how his wife had repaid him.

To Edward, who would never turn his back on any member of his family, loyalty was as necessary as breathing. Amelia had failed him. He wondered if their marriage could ever be the same again.

124

Gwendolyn paced the upper salon of Margaret Mercer's house in the Strand. Margaret put aside her pen and the letter she was writing and shook her head as she watched the younger woman. With the fortunes of the family restored after Thomas had married Georganna, the room had been redecorated and some paintings purchased to replace the ones they had been forced to sell when the bank had been on the verge of ruin. Flowers filled the vases and the air was heavy with the scent of roses and lilies.

'Gwen, my dear, you should have accompanied Georganna to visit the shops at the Royal Exchange. There are so many diversions that London has to offer.'

'I did not come to London for the diversions, Mrs Mercer. I came to escape Mama's plans for my future.'

Margaret smiled, but she still felt uneasy about allowing Gwendolyn to accompany them. She could not resist matchmaking. For years she had yearned to see her nephew Japhet settled in a marriage that would calm the wild streak that could so easily be his undoing. Gwendolyn would be the perfect wife for him. Yet Japhet was his own man, and no one could make him do anything he did not wish to.

The far away look in Gwendolyn's eye showed the young woman's unhappiness. Margaret hoped that Gwendolyn had not seen more into Japhet's regard for her than was really there. 'Japhet will call upon us when he is ready,' she advised. 'He may not even be in

London. In the meantime you should be enjoying yourself.'

'Was it madness for me to come to London? I could not stay at Traherne Hall, not after the way Mama would have forced me into that odious marriage.'

'I dare say your mama thought only of your best interests. But, I admit, Lieutenant Beaumont was not the man for you.'

Gwendolyn clasped her hands together. 'Mrs Mercer, do you believe that Japhet is the right man for me? You have been so kind to allow me to stay here.'

Margaret regarded her fondly. Gwendolyn not only adored Japhet but she had a fortune, which Japhet sadly lacked.

'You are exactly right for Japhet, my dear,' Margaret assured her. 'But are you sure he will make you happy? That is also important. You have risked so much for his sake. Yet he has not made his intentions clear as to how he feels about you. He does so value his freedom.'

Gwendolyn hugged her arms closely around her. 'I know Japhet cares for me. I am also aware of his faults, and his penchant for gambling and beautiful women – all of which I long ago accepted. We both have a passion for Arab horses. My fortune will allow us to set up a stud farm. That is something Japhet has often spoken about. He is wild and reckless because he has no real purpose in life.'

'Many women have tried to tame gamblers and reprobates. Can a leopard change its spots?' Margaret studied Gwen intently. 'Japhet is almost thirty. He is used to living his life without restraint.'

Gwen picked a pink rose from a vase and absently shredded its petals. 'I have to try. Mama and Roslyn have disowned me for refusing to wed Lieutenant Beaumont. It will be the talk of the county by now. The announcement was posted in the *Sherborne Mercury* without consulting me.'

'Lady Anne will forgive you in time. At least while you live with me, there can be no question that your reputation has been damaged.'

Gwendolyn stooped to kiss Margaret's cheek. 'Your kindness is more than I deserve. I have been a wicked daughter.' She sighed. 'I wish I did not love Japhet so much. If I am wrong and he will have none of me, what shall I do? I will not return to Traherne Hall. Even if Mama took me back, she would never let me forget how I have shamed her.'

Margaret smiled into Gwen's impassioned face. 'You have shown great courage. I will do all I can to aid this match with Japhet. And you are welcome to stay here for as long as you wish.' A scheming light brightened her eyes. 'And there are other handsome and suitable men, a dozen times more worthy than Lieutenant Beaumont, to whom I could introduce you if Japhet proves stubborn. But let us hope that it does not come to that. Thomas is making enquiries at Japhet's usual haunts. My son will flush his cousin from his lair.'

Henderson, the ancient and wizened major domo, hobbled into the salon. 'Mrs Edward Loveday and

Mrs William Loveday to see you, ma'am.'

Gwendolyn became flustered. 'I had better go to my room. Amelia does not approve of me pursuing Japhet. She made that plain throughout our journey to London.'

'Stay. I find my old friend's company difficult at the moment, for my loyalty is to Edward. I owe him so much. Without his help when my husband, Charles, killed himself when the bank was about to fail, I should be penniless—' She broke off as Amelia and Lisette entered the salon.

A frigid atmosphere was apparent between Amelia and Lisette, and Amelia's greeting was without warmth as she seated herself beside Margaret on the padded settle. Gwendolyn retreated to a window seat while Lisette proceeded to saunter around the room in a bored and sullen manner.

'It is too bad that Thomas and Georganna are not here,' Lisette said with a dramatic sigh. 'They could have taken me to the play. I thought London would be as exciting as Paris but little happens here.' She sighed again. 'Though, of course, Versailles was the place for entertainments. I loved it so. But then I was married to the Marquis de Gramont and fêted as a court beauty.'

'Versailles, as you knew it, is no more,' Amelia snapped. 'And you are married to a naval captain now, not a member of the French nobility. It is time you learned to appreciate the benefits and privileges of your life in England.'

Lisette flounced to a chair on the far side of the

salon. 'You *Anglais* are so stiff in the lip you forget how to have pleasure.'

Concerned that Amelia looked tired and tense, Margaret suggested, 'Would it help if Lisette stayed here? I am sure she would benefit from the company of the younger members of the family.'

'Lisette is here for treatment by Dr Claver, not to attend frivolous pursuits. It is time she behaved in the manner fitting a young wife. Her behaviour in Cornwall left much to be desired. Unfortunately, Dr Claver is out of London until next week.'

The sharpness of Amelia's tone annoyed Margaret, for her offer had been well meaning.

'I do not need treatment,' Lisette shouted and stood up. 'You hate me. You would make my life miserable.'

'And you would make our lives less trying if you remembered that you are the daughter of a wine merchant and no longer a marquise.' Amelia spoke sharply. 'We are not impressed by your haughty air, madam. The marquis treated you abominably before he was murdered. I thought you would want to put that distressing part of your life behind you.'

Lisette burst into tears. 'You are mean and nasty. You are jealous that I was an aristocrat in France. I give all that up to marry William and he deserts me for his silly ship.'

'We are at war, Lisette. William is doing his duty.'

'He deserted me. We were wed but one day. I was to have a lovely house where I would entertain my friends. Instead I was ordered to stay at Trevowan where everyone hates me.'

Amelia glared at her. 'William married you to protect your reputation when you followed him to Plymouth, knowing the fleet was about to sail. He wanted you safe within the protection of his family.'

'You treat me like a prisoner. I am allowed no friends of my own.'

Margaret cut in. 'You exaggerate, Lisette. We all want to help you. You suffered terribly in France.' She turned to Gwen. 'Perhaps you and Lisette could take a stroll in the park. The weather is pleasant.'

'I would rather stay here,' Gwendolyn protested. She was so desperate to be reunited with Japhet she did not want to risk being away from the house if he called.

'No one wants to spend time with me.' Lisette burst into tears. 'Why does everyone hate me?'

Appalled at the reaction from the Frenchwoman, Gwendolyn overcame her own desires. 'Lisette, must you make such a drama out of everything? Of course I do not hate you. If we hurry there is a marionette show in the park. Georganna told me that it is delightful.'

Lisette stopped crying with remarkable suddenness and was all smiles. 'It will be amusing, yes.'

As the two younger women left the room, watching them, Amelia shook her head. 'Lisette is a trial. Though her presence at my house stops any gossip that I am in London without Edward. I am supposedly here for Lisette's welfare, whilst Edward has business to attend at the yard. But the woman is a thorn in my flesh with her volatile moods. And she is getting worse. Her behaviour is—' Amelia broke off and raised her eyes to the ceiling. 'I find her conduct too distressing to discuss. Edward cannot be responsible for every single member of his family.'

'Edward is an exceptional man and he believed you to be his equal or he would not have married you. I do not understand you, Amelia. You have always upheld the importance of families supporting each other.'

Amelia closed her eyes and visibly shuddered. 'Edward expects too much from me.'

It was an argument they had covered many times and since Amelia was in no mood to be reasonable, Margaret changed the subject. 'How are you settling into your house, Amelia?'

'I had to sack the housekeeper and a maid. The place had not been cleaned properly since I married Edward and went to live in Cornwall. This is my first visit to London since that time.' Her voice was strident as she deflected her anger on to this new problem. 'I thought renting out my home to French émigrés would ease our financial burdens, but the tenants who were in the house until the last quarter day had no consideration for another's property. The furniture is scuffed where they had put their feet on it and the panelling in the dining room is pitted where someone has repeatedly thrown a dagger into it.'

'It is regrettable, but the damage can be repaired when your finances improve. The bank is doing well and Thomas is recovering the Loveday money which was lost when it almost failed.' Margaret lost patience with Amelia, who in the last year had changed from the stalwart she had admired, to a prim and contentious woman. She did not like to hear her brother so harshly judged, and Amelia could not have forgotten that Margaret's husband had taken his life at the shame he felt when his failed investments had brought the bank to ruin. Without Edward's support, she and Thomas would now be in a debtors' prison, their name reviled by the investors who had lost their savings. Edward had helped Thomas save the bank.

Her manner became stiff and challenging. 'Will you be returning to Cornwall when you have seen Dr Claver next week?'

'That will not be possible. Lisette will need treatment and that will take time.' Amelia could not meet her friend's gaze. 'Besides, I refuse to be the butt of gossip in Cornwall. I have endured enough. First Adam's wedding to a gypsy. Then I had to endure the shame of St John's trial and Meriel deserting him. Now there is bound to be a scandal at the appearance of that child . . .' Tears sparkled in her eyes as she battled to retain her composure.

'You have added fuel to that gossip by leaving Cornwall,' Margaret observed.

'That would not have happened if Edward had followed me.' Amelia glared at her friend, her voice harsh with pain and indignation. 'Instead he chose to return to Cornwall with his daughter.'

'Amelia, you are making too much of this.' Margaret lost patience. 'The yard is in debt. This has been a difficult year for Edward. It is not as though he deliberately flaunted Tamasine's existence. He did not know of it himself until the summer. You cannot condemn him for a liaison which happened so long before he met you.'

Amelia stood up, her manner stiff with injured pride. 'I thought as my friend you would understand how I feel.'

'Edward is my brother. I admire and respect him. If he had known of Tamasine's existence before your marriage, he would have told you. He loves you. He will be hurt at the way you left Cornwall.' When Amelia remained tense and condemning, Margaret lost her temper. 'It is not as though he has been unfaithful to you. Few men are so considerate of their wives. Even my own dear Charles had a peccadillo while we were wed. I thought my heart would break when I learned of it. He gave her up when I told him I would not countenance such a betrayal. He proved that he loved me and not her, but the pain of his infidelity was unbearable for months. I do not think I ever quite got over it before he died. Then it became insignificant against the pain of losing him.'

'And you forgave him?' Amelia stared at her with shock. 'You never spoke of this before.'

'Apart from his one indiscretion, he was always the most adoring and supportive of husbands. I only speak of it now because you judge Edward so harshly. He has a duty to that girl. Tamasine is not some common by-blow; her mother was a noblewoman. And if you are about to condemn the Lady Eleanor for loose morals, you would be wrong. Sir Arthur was a gross womaniser who sorely neglected his wife.

133

Eleanor loved Edward. When she returned to London after their affair, all the joy of living had gone out of her.'

'Is that supposed to make me feel better?'

Her friend's pain was obvious but Margaret's sympathies were for Edward. Amelia should be in Cornwall, supporting him at this difficult time. This attitude of her friend puzzled her. Amelia had always been rather strait-laced but Margaret had never considered that her outlook could be so puritanical. 'Have you written to Edward explaining how you feel?'

'He would never understand. I suppose out of loyalty you must take his side.' Amelia began to pull on her gloves. 'I should not have come.'

'Sit down, Amelia. This is so unlike you.'

Amelia sank on to the sofa and burst into tears. 'I know I should not blame Edward, but I was not brought up to accept the lax morality that the Lovedays seem to live by. When Edward asked me to marry him and he spoke of his sons and Japhet being wild and unconventional, nothing in my imagination could conceive how easily they would disregard the proprieties of normal living.'

'You were no child bride, Amelia. But you had led a sheltered life.'

'I was blessed with a peaceful marriage to my first husband. And I do love Edward, but . . .' She took a moment to regain her composure. 'Did you know that St John has been involved with smugglers? And Adam, though he is supposedly working for the

British Government, will now be little better than a pirate if he seizes an enemy ship.'

Margaret tilted her head to one side. 'If you love Edward that should be all that matters. Smuggling has always been a part of Cornish life. And during a war many respectable sea-going families become privateers.'

'But this side of your family shocks me. Edward is not the man I thought I married. I should leave.' Amelia stood up. 'I have the melancholy and am poor company.'

'Write to Edward,' Margaret insisted. 'Do not let this rift deepen by misunderstandings.'

Amelia swayed slightly, too pale and thin not to be suffering from ill health. 'I am not as you, Margaret. I was taught to guard my emotions. To speak of this with Edward would be too painful – too distressing.'

'Not to speak of it could cause irreparable damage to your marriage. Edward will view your behaviour as disloyal, and loyalty means a great deal to him.'

Chapter Ten

Japhet sat on the edge of the vast four-poster bed with its red and gold hangings. The window curtains were drawn, and though it was mid-afternoon, the room was lit with the light of four candles. Japhet had learned that Celestine shunned bright daylight, preferring the candlelight that was more flattering to her face and figure. When she ventured into the streets during the day, a wide brimmed hat shadowed her face.

He struggled to pull on his boots and when the clock on the mantel shelf chimed the hour, he silently cursed the lateness of the day. He had an appointment with a horse buyer half an hour ago and Japhet disliked being late for business dealings.

'Are you running off again so soon?' Celestine threw back the silk sheets to clasp her arms around his shoulders. 'We have another hour before Sir Pettigrew Osgood will visit. You are more fun and enjoyable a lover.'

Japhet grinned and turned to kiss her naked shoulder. 'Unlike Osgood I have to work to earn my money.

If you do not wish to see him, send him away.'

Celestine pouted. Her carefully applied makeup was smudged from their lovemaking and her blonde hair tumbled in disarray over her fleshy shoulders. 'I have a mountain of bills from dressmakers, milliners and shoemakers I need him to settle. That is unless you will oblige . . .' She regarded Japhet through heavy-lidded eyes, her tone low and seductive.

Japhet grinned at her. 'No chance of that, my lovely seductress. I told you from the outset I am not a wealthy man.'

Japhet had no intention of paying Celestine's bills. From the money she had amassed from wealthy protectors over the years, she had bought a dozen houses in the shadow of St Paul's Cathedral. These she leased at high rents to costermongers, dockworkers, and clerks' families. Her avarice was her least attractive quality, but her ardour and uninhibited passion compensated for it. She was as innovative a lover as she was promiscuous. Her bawdiness appealed to Japhet's sensual nature.

They had been lovers for three weeks, meeting in secret, as Celestine had no wish to alienate her wealthy protector. She would send word to Japhet's lodgings when she was free for him to call upon her. This suited Japhet since he wanted an affair with no ties.

'Can't you stay longer?' She pressed her body against him and wriggled suggestively. 'I hate being alone.'

'You will not be alone for long. Sir Pettigrew is to

accompany you to the theatre and there you will be thronged by dozens of ardent admirers.' He glanced around the untidy room to check he had left none of his possessions; the rumpled bed would show Osgood that she had been entertaining a lover.

'You are heartless.' Celestine whisked a sheet around her body like a Roman toga and sank on to the stool by her dressing table. The top was piled high with trinket boxes, fans, discarded bracelets and feathered headdresses. She picked up a perfume bottle and sprayed her neck and shoulders.

The heat in the room was already overpowering and the heavy scent made Japhet nauseous. He pulled on his waistcoat and stared over her shoulder into the looking-glass as he fastened his stock.

'I do not know why I bother with you, Japhet. You are a selfish rogue. You do not love me. You never buy me pretty things.'

He laughed and kissed her neck, his eyes level with her in the mirror. 'I never said I loved you and you have a houseful of pretty things. You bother with me, as you put it, because we are alike. Two free souls who have made our own way in the world, and who would have the world dance to our tune whenever possible. And besides,' his grin broadened, 'you find me irresistible because I do not fawn over you and pander to your every whim. I am no ladies' lapdog.'

'You will break my heart and see me penniless,' she pouted.

'Your heart is unbreakable,' he teased, 'and it is

138

your lovers you strip to their last shilling. Your seductive spell is their undoing.'

'Get out, I hate you.' She turned on him and flung a large powder puff at his head.

The white powder daubed his face and Japhet picked up a handkerchief from the cluttered dressing table to wipe the powder away. The handkerchief briefly covered part of his lower face and he saw from the reflection in the mirror that Celestine was watching him closely, her head tilted to one side.

'You said when you came to the green room that first night that we had never met, yet I feel I knew you before then.'

Japhet, ever the gallant, raised her hand to his lips. 'Do you think I could ever forget if our paths had crossed before? The "Darling of London" is incomparable.'

'Flatterer,' she giggled, her pique dispelling. 'How can I bear Osgood's company when you make me laugh, my Sir Devil-May-Care? With you I can forget the strain my position as London's foremost actress puts upon me. I can be natural.'

Life was one long melodrama for Celestine; everyone must fit into the role she chose for them. That she had almost recognised his half-hidden face alerted Japhet to the danger of continuing as her lover. If she realised that it was he who had robbed her and Osgood that night, his life could be at stake.

He was at the door ready to leave when she called over her shoulder, 'I shall be free tomorrow afternoon at four. Arrive at the back door as usual. My maid will tell you when it is safe to come to my room. I am lunching with Lord Sefton, who is inclined to linger.'

Japhet resented the way she expected him to be at her beck and call. 'Your pardon, my dear. I have business tomorrow in Greenwich. Then there is the race meeting at Newmarket, which will take me away for the rest of the week.'

'Cancel them.'

'I never renege on a business meeting, madam, as I am sure you would never fail your public by cancelling a performance.'

'There is no comparison. No one refuses my favours.' She flung her arms around him and kissed him with such passion that Japhet lost control of his senses, and the lovers fell to the floor, locked in a heated embrace.

When she finally rolled away from him there was triumph in her eyes. 'Tomorrow then. After all, it would pain me deeply to tell Sir Pettigrew of our special secret.'

'What secret would that be?' Japhet strove to appear nonchalant through the onset of alarm. His clothing adjusted, he picked up his hat from the chair and regarded her.

'Oh, a little matter of a meeting on Hampstead Heath.'

'I do not understand you, madam.'

She smiled. 'I think that you understand all too well. But do not fear, your secret is safe with me. While you continue to please me, why should I wish to see you locked away in Newgate?'

Japhet held her stare and laughed. 'What new fancy is this? I make a small enough profit at horse dealing that no one could accuse me of dishonesty. As a gambler I may have put a hole in many men's purses but I have never cheated at hazard or cards.'

'I know you were on the heath that night,' she persisted.

He laughed. 'Celestine, you have mistaken me for another.'

As he left he cursed her scheming mind. By calling her bluff he may convince her that she had been mistaken in believing him the highwayman who had robbed Osgood. It was a dangerous ruse. But to run would only be to place suspicion upon him. He must brazen it out.

The marionette show took place in a red, blue and gold striped booth and did not hold Lisette's attention for long. She was more interested in studying the other people there. The shadows were deepening around the Serpentine in Hyde Park and the mist that had hung over the city all day thickened. The first of the leaves were falling from the trees and the air was damp with an autumn chill.

Lisette fidgeted, her gaze constantly alighting upon four cavalry officers who were in conversation close by.

'Men in uniform are always so handsome and dashing,' Lisette giggled. 'Do you not agree, Gwen?'

The officers were immaculate in red and gold-braided uniforms, close-fitting white breeches and tall black helmets decorated with black plumes. They had dismounted and held the reins of their horses, and were talking to two women in an open carriage parked on the edge of the spectators.

Gwen glanced briefly in their direction and shrugged. 'It would take more than a uniform to impress me.'

'Oh, you have no eyes for anyone but that wicked Japhet,' Lisette responded. 'What good does that do you? You should flirt with more men when you have the opportunity. Who knows, you may even make Japhet jealous.' There was a spiteful glitter in her eye. Lisette had purchased a posy of yellow rosebuds from a street-seller and held it to her nose. 'You cannot think those officers are not handsome. They look so strong and dashing.'

Gwen pulled her blue pelisse more tightly across her shoulders; she regretted her decision to accompany Lisette. She had come in the vain hope that she might catch a glimpse of Japhet. Thomas had told her when they dined yesterday that Lucien had seen him in a chophouse and at the play. The strain of waiting for him to call at the Strand had frayed her patience. Lisette was too self-centred to be enjoyable company.

Gwen had little in common with the younger woman but she had done her utmost to entertain her this afternoon. Lisette had complained about the weather, how she considered London fashion to be so 'bourgeois', and how the city was dreary and lacked excitement – unlike Paris.

Constantly Lisette's glance searched the populace

to settle upon young, unattached men. Gwendolyn was growing impatient with the Frenchwoman's frivolous view on life. To silence her, she spoke sharply. 'Our gallant cavalry look well enough in their gaudy uniforms, but so many are arrogant and conceited. Most are younger sons with little income. A wise heiress avoids their attentions.'

'If one had such a man as a lover who would care if they have designs upon your wealth?' Lisette had caught the notice of a blond captain with wide sidewhiskers and could not take her gaze off him. She smiled and fluttered her eyelashes over the top of her posy of flowers.

When the officer did not join them, Lisette stamped her foot. 'Oh, your Englishmen, they have no idea of romance. A Frenchman would be flirting with me by now. Must I make it more obvious? I will go to him.'

Shocked, Gwen grabbed her arm. 'You cannot throw yourself at a stranger. What will he think of you? He will think you are a . . . a . . .' Gwen struggled to say the words, 'a common doxy.'

Lisette laughed in her face. 'But that would make him take notice of me, no?'

'It is time we returned to Mrs Mercer's house. The mist is closing in and the roads will become congested. Mrs Mercer will worry if we are late.' Gwen tugged at Lisette's arm.

'But I wish to meet this handsome soldier.' Lisette snatched her arm away and there was a cruel line to her carmined lips.

'You are a married woman and should be ashamed

of your behaviour.' Gwen was shocked at the spectacle Lisette was making of herself. Several heads had turned to watch them. 'Think of your husband. William Loveday is risking his life at sea. How could you betray him by wishing to flirt with another man?'

'You are such a child, Gwen.' The porcelain-white face framed by a peaked bonnet was tight with anger. 'I will do as I please. The handsome captain is approaching. Go away if you do not wish to see me enjoy myself. You are a staid old maid.'

'I will not leave you. Amelia would never forgive me.'

Lisette turned her back on Gwen, her attention centred upon the officer, who bowed to her. The open carriage left the park but Gwen refused to be drawn into conversation when his three companions joined the captain.

'You must forgive us, gentlemen, but we are expected at home,' she cut across their introductions. 'Since we have not been formerly introduced it is improper for us to speak with you.'

'Fiddle-de-dee, how you fuss, Gwen,' Lisette countered. 'These officers have been so kind as to introduce themselves. It would be rude of us to leave.'

Gwendolyn made several attempts to draw Lisette away and was ignored by the Frenchwoman. Short of leaving Lisette to her own devices, which would be unthinkable, Gwen had no choice but to stay. She grew more uncomfortable by the moment. It was embarrassing to witness the brazen manner in which Lisette flirted with the officers.

The last puppet show of the afternoon had started and several torches had been lit around the booth. As the daylight faded it was difficult to see the edge of the park through the mist. Still Lisette paid no attention to Gwen's plea that they leave. The officers flirted so outrageously Gwendolyn was mortified. She had never been an accomplished coquette and even in Japhet's company she could become tongue-tied.

In desperation she searched the park, praying that she would recognise someone she knew who would help her get Lisette away. Then her attention was caught by a tall, dark-haired man riding along Rotten Row on a horse that looked like Japhet's Sheba. Her heart missed a beat that she had finally found Japhet.

She broke away from the others to run in his direction, her hand raised to hail him. On closer regard she saw that she was mistaken. The rider was not Japhet. Downcast with disappointment, she stared into space for some moments, heedless of the number of people around her leaving the park. How long would it be before she encountered Japhet? Each day dragged like a month. And what would she say when she saw him? Had she been a fool to come to London?

Abruptly, she pulled her thoughts back to the present – such speculation was pointless and frustrating. When she returned to where she had left Lisette, the Frenchwoman had vanished and so had the officer she had been flirting with.

The other three men were already mounted as she called out, 'Where is my friend?'

The shortest of the three officers laughed and

preened his dark moustache. 'She has gone, my pretty. Archie has whisked her off. You will not see her before morning.'

'You must stop him,' Gwen implored each of the men, who laughed as they turned their horses away. 'She is a married woman. She has just come to London from the country.'

'Just the way Archie likes them.' An imposing officer with a scar disfiguring his brow halted his horse and lecherously eyed Gwen. 'Do not play the coy maiden with us. Which one of us suits you? We've rooms next to Archie. We could always make it a cosy foursome.'

Gwen's cheeks stained to crimson. 'How dare you make such a monstrous suggestion?' She faltered. Their leers and innuendo alarmed her and she was sick with panic at what had become of Lisette. 'Lisette must be rescued from your friend. Please, you must help me.'

'The woman went with him of her own accord. And from her eagerness to go to his rooms, she is no innocent,' the shortest officer guffawed. 'I can see that you are a woman of more refinement. Forget these other two buffoons, I know how to make a pretty woman happy.' He slid from his horse and reached out to take Gwen into his arms. 'Come with me.'

Gwen slapped his face and ran through the thinning crowd. She called Lisette's name in the vain hope that the officer had lied and that the Frenchwoman might be searching for her. Gwen searched until it was almost dark and she feared for her own safety in the park. Sobbing with distress, she ran to Piccadilly where she hailed a sedan chair to take her back to the Strand.

Margaret was taking tea with Georganna when Gwen burst into the room. Thomas had gone back to the bank for an appointment with a customer. Gwen sobbed out her story, blaming herself for not paying more attention to Lisette and forcing her to return home earlier.

'That wilful minx will do exactly as she pleases. It is not your fault, Gwen,' Margaret consoled. 'This is worse than anything I feared. Poor William. And Amelia . . . We must try to keep this from her. But something must be done. Lisette cannot be allowed to shame William by her conduct.'

'But what if she is harmed?' Gwen wrung her hands. 'To go off in such a manner . . . the danger . . .'

Margaret put an arm around Gwen. 'Lisette has survived far worse. I pray she will be safe, but she has brought this upon herself . . . and the consequences.'

It was impossible to keep the truth from Amelia, for Lisette did not appear for two days and then she was completely without remorse.

Chapter Eleven

Two days of arguments followed Lisette's return to Amelia's house. Amelia had been unable to eat or sleep she had been so upset at the Frenchwoman's conduct. Margaret came at her friend's summons to try to reason with Lisette, for the young woman refused to answer any of Amelia's questions. When Margaret arrived Lisette was in her bedchamber surrounded by a delivery of four new outfits from a dressmaker and hatboxes from several different milliners.

'So many new clothes,' Margaret said with surprise. 'Can William afford so much?'

'I lost the paltry allowance my husband gives me at cards the other evening,' Lisette said with scorn. 'I sold a necklace I brought from France to buy these.'

'Is that not very foolish?' Margaret began, but Lisette turned away from her, preening in front of a mirror in one of the new bonnets.

'I like pretty things. In France I had a lavish allowance. First from Papa – and the Marquis de Gramont was extremely generous; he expected his wife to dress in the highest fashion. I gave up my lovely title of marquise to marry William. I cannot believe he would begrudge me a few necessities.'

'You have gowns and hats aplenty.' Margaret lost patience with Lisette's selfishness. 'And William is a kind and generous man within his means, unlike your marquis, who was evil and subjected you to many degradations, if your tales of your life in France are to be believed.'

Lisette threw the hat on the floor and stamped on it, working herself up into a fury. 'You ruin my pleasure. I need to forget how bad that monster was.' The expensive hat was destroyed as her voice rose in hysteria. 'I cannot forget how I suffered when you would shut me away like a prisoner, and force me to live like an old maid. I need pretty things around me. I am young and beautiful, I need excitement.'

'You are acting like a spoiled child, Lisette. That hat cost two months of your husband's naval pay, and you destroy it in a fit of temper. Have you no respect for our values?'

'What do I care for your prim and stupid values?' Lisette kicked the battered hat across the room. 'I am married now. I do not need to be chaperoned. I will live my life as I wish. I will no longer burden your family with my presence. I shall take rooms in London. I can sell another necklace to pay the rent.'

Margaret was horrified at Lisette's plans. 'Our family will not allow you to shame us. Have we not arranged entertainments and diversions to amuse you? If you want your own rooms so that you can entertain a lover, the family will not allow that to happen.'

'You cannot stop me.' Lisette stood with her hands on her hips, her petite figure shaking with rage.

'There are many ways the family can restrain you from your wilful behaviour. You shame not only us by your conduct, but the memory of your beloved father and mother.' In the past only the threat of besmirching her father's reputation had any effect on Lisette's wild tantrums. Margaret could think of no other way of reasoning with the Frenchwoman. 'Many of your family's acquaintances and friends now live in England. They will have no respect for the memory of an honourable man when they see that he did not bring his daughter up to know the difference between decent and unacceptable behaviour. You have acted no better than a common harlot these last days – William will be appalled at your conduct.'

'William promised me a lovely house. He broke his word. He is not as nice as I believed. I thought he was like my papa, who adored me, who could deny me nothing.'

'You are no longer a little girl to be appeased with sweetmeats or a toy. Stop acting like a spoiled, ill-mannered child.'

Lisette stopped ranting and waving her arms. She stood motionless, her eyes filling with tears. 'I miss Papa. Only he truly loved me.'

The rapid mood swings, which were part of her illness, were always disconcerting. She threw herself to the floor in a cloud of billowing pink silk, her arms locked tight across her chest as she rocked back and forth, chanting, 'Papa . . . Papa . . . Papa . . . Why did you die? Why did you have to leave me?'

Margaret overcame her anger, hoping that now Lisette was calmer, she could reason with her. 'Let us help you, Lisette. Despite what you think, we all love you.'

The young woman did not appear to hear and was locked in some inner torment as her body swayed backwards and forwards. She began to sing a lullaby in French, her eyes large and staring into a world only she could see.

For two weeks after that, Lisette's behaviour was exemplary until an afternoon visit to the daughter of one of Margaret's friends with Georganna and Gwendolyn. Other guests were also visiting and, amid the conversation, Lisette slipped unnoticed from the room. It was not until the maid brought in a tray of tea that Georganna noticed Lisette was missing.

'Where is my cousin?' Georganna looked round with a puzzled frown.

A footman carrying in a tiered cake stand replied, 'The young lady who accompanied you, ma'am, left the house some minutes ago. She did not take her cloak.'

'Did she say where she was going?' Gwendolyn put her hand over her thudding heart, fearing that Lisette had run off again.

'The young lady spoke to no one,' the footman replied.

Georganna came to Gwendolyn's side. 'It is time we also left. I had not realised the hour was so late. Mrs Mercer wished me to collect a physic from the apothecary's for her and it will soon be dark. Forgive us for rushing away.'

As soon as the two women were outside. Georganna said, 'Where do we look for her?'

'There is no point. Lisette could be anywhere,' Gwendolyn groaned. 'I promised Mrs Mercer I would keep an eye on her. But when you were asked about Japhet, I forgot Lisette as I listened to your conversation. I failed Mrs Mercer and she has been so good to me.'

'You cannot blame yourself. Lisette was probably waiting for a chance to escape from us. She must face the consequences, for Amelia is no longer prepared to be tolerant of her wayward conduct.'

'What if Lisette does not return?' Georganna paused before entering the Mercers' carriage and scanned the street in the forlorn hope of seeing Lisette. 'She spoke of getting rooms to be free to follow her own life. We may never see her again.'

'I doubt she will abandon her clothes and jewels. She will have to return to Amelia's house, but this time no one will be taken in by her duplicity.'

Thomas and his family were at Amelia's when Lisette finally reappeared late in the afternoon of the following day. Gwendolyn had stayed away, conscious that she was an outsider and that this was family business. The Mercers were in the upper salon on the second floor of the tall Georgian house, which had escaped any damage by the unruly tenants. A fire burned in the hearth as the weather was grey and cold.

Lisette's colour was high and her eyes overbright as she entered the room. 'So many of the worthy Lovedays are here – have I missed some exciting entertainment? I thought it was planned to visit the playhouse tomorrow.'

'Where have you been?' Amelia demanded.

'With a friend.' Lisette pulled off her gloves and removed her high-domed hat. Her dark hair, which had grown to her shoulders after it had been shorn in France, was dishevelled, and several pins fell out as her coiffure collapsed into a straggling mess.

'Look at the state of you!' Amelia groaned. 'You have no decency or shame. You look like a penny harlot.'

Lisette shrugged, completely unrepentant. 'There is no shame in enjoying oneself.'

Amelia groaned and hid her face in her hands. 'Listen to her. This cannot go on.'

'I wish to bathe: send a maid to fill my bath. I am going to my room.' Lisette ignored them and walked to the door.

Thomas barred her way. 'Amelia is right. Your conduct is a disgrace. You shame us all. It will not be allowed to continue.'

'You cannot stop me,' Lisette shrieked, her arms waving in her agitation. 'William was too mean to buy me my own house but my handsome captain will set me up in rooms. I do not need you. I do not need anyone.'

'Now listen here . . .' Thomas grabbed her arm.

'Let her go, Thomas,' his mother intervened. 'She will not listen.'

Lisette ran up the stairs, singing at the top of her voice. Her bedroom door banged shut and Margaret spread her arms in defeat. 'We have done all we can. Dr Claver must be summoned. While Lisette is bathing her room will be locked, and will remain so until Dr Claver has examined her. I told Amelia's manservant to send for him the moment Lisette returned.'

A scream of rage was accompanied by frantic banging on Lisette's locked door. 'Let me out. I will not be your prisoner. You are wicked. Wicked. I hate you. I will kill you. Let me out.'

A stream of invectives followed both in English and French at the same time that Dr Claver arrived. He was a short, bespectacled man, with austere features and dressed in sober grey, although, incongruously, he teetered precariously on shoes with high stacked heels, and his frizzed powdered wig was so immense that it wobbled when he walked.

'You were right to summon me immediately. The woman is demented. She could cause serious harm to herself, or another,' he said without preamble. 'Classic symptoms, I fear. Your letter explained the young woman's ordeal in France. It has agitated the humours of her mind, soured her spleen and caused a surfeit of bile. I will need to inspect her stools and urine. She will need extensive medication and care. Treatment can take many months.'

A crash of smashing pottery and furniture being tipped over was followed by a further tantrum of rage.

'I fear for her own protection. The young woman will need restraining,' Dr Claver continued. 'She will, of course, be taken to my hospital for treatment, where we have the facilities to effect a cure.'

Another thud of falling furniture made Amelia flinch and hug her arms across her chest. 'How are you to sedate her? No one can get near her when she is in this state.'

'She will soon grow tired.'

Amelia shook her head. 'It can take hours. We have suffered this so many times at Trevowan.'

'And she could hurt herself.' Georganna had become very pale.

'When you spoke of how bad she could be, I did not realise the violence behind her attacks,' Margaret added.

Amelia clenched her fists and paced the blue and yellow salon. 'We have done everything we could to make her life comfortable and secure. This is how the little vixen repays us. The child is mad, is she not, Dr Claver?'

'One always hopes that the condition is temporary. As with our own dear King George. The cold-water baths can be efficacious and trepanning will allow the demons to escape and will lessen the pressure of ill-humours upon the brain.'

'Trepanning is very drastic.' Thomas looked concerned. 'It involves drilling three holes into the skull, does it not? Lisette was tortured in France when her château was overrun by the mob. Will not such treatment further unhinge her wits?'

'You wish the young lady to be cured, do you not?' Dr Claver regarded each of them fiercely. 'But trepanning is a last resort to release the most pernicious humours which possess the mind. I have many patients and my time is not to be wasted.'

The family glanced at each other, all ill at ease.

'Things cannot go on as they are.' Amelia was firm.

Margaret nodded. 'Georganna is right. Lisette will harm herself. Let alone the danger she is to others.'

'That is true,' Amelia declared. 'There was that time in Truro when she attacked a woman with her parasol when we were buying lace. The customer had picked up a piece Lisette had first discarded then decided it was what she wanted. The woman was severely cut on the cheek and her hat ruined. I had trouble appeasing her and stopping her calling the constables and charging Lisette with assault. And Lisette frequently strikes the servants, which is inexcusable.'

'Then Lisette will be placed in your charge, Dr Claver,' Thomas announced. 'How long do these cures take?'

The doctor shrugged. 'One cannot put a time on such cases. At the least a few months, sometimes it could be years. I will send regular reports. It is not good that they receive visitors. It often results in a relapse.'

'But it is our duty to ensure that she is well cared for.' Amelia glanced guiltily at Thomas and Margaret.

'What if William returns and is angry that Lisette has been committed to an asylum? I think this is a decision Edward should make.'

The screams and obscenities from upstairs had risen in volume. The women shuddered and Dr Claver pursed his lips. 'The woman is quite mad and a danger to the community. If you do not commit her, I will inform the authorities and have her locked up for the good of public safety.'

The family exchanged horrified glances.

'I will write to Uncle Edward,' Thomas suggested. 'Clearly Lisette needs immediate treatment. She will not allow us to help her. Perhaps she should be put into Dr Claver's care until William returns with the English fleet. It is for him to decide her future.'

'But William could be away for months.' Georganna was aghast. 'Poor Lisette.'

Amelia was crying softly. 'I cannot be responsible for her.'

Margaret put her arm around her friend. 'It is not an easy decision, but in this Thomas is right. Dr Claver, there must be a way that we can visit Lisette once a month and see how she is progressing, without her seeing us, if need be.'

The doctor bowed graciously. 'Many people wish such relatives to be locked away and forgotten. Your concern is a credit to you. It shall be as you wish.'

'Very well, let it be done.' Amelia clung to Margaret for support. 'How will I face William? We have failed him.'

'William should not have married in such haste,'

Margaret said. 'He would not listen to Edward when he tried to tell him of Lisette's wild behaviour.'

'But William adores Lisette,' Amelia groaned. 'He waited so long to marry and now for this to happen . . .'

'Elspeth told William that he was a fool.' Margaret led Amelia to a chair and sat beside her. 'For all his middle years and that he can rule men with a rod of iron in the navy, he has little experience of women. Lisette connived to marry him. With all the months William is at sea, she thought the marriage would give her freedom to indulge her baser nature.'

Amelia sighed and dabbed at her eyes. 'Let it be done discreetly. There must be no further gossip.'

It was two days before Lisette's temper ran its course and she fell into an exhausted sleep. Dr Claver was sent for. When Amelia unlocked the door, the stench of urine and excrement hit them. Lisette had smeared the walls with her excrement, the bed had been stripped of its hangings, the vases and china ornaments were smashed, and clothes torn from drawers and the closet, to be strewn amongst the filth on the floor. Lisette was slumped in a pool of blood inside the door. She had slashed one wrist with a shard of pottery.

'She's killed herself,' Amelia screamed.

Dr Claver stooped over the figure. 'She is alive.' He opened his medicine case and bound her wrist tightly to stop the bleeding. Then taking out a phial, he forced open her mouth and inserted several drops of an opium tincture. 'She must be kept sedated until she is safe within the hospital.'

Thomas lifted the petite figure and carried Lisette out to the doctor's closed carriage. As he shut the door on her unconscious figure he murmured, 'May God have mercy on her.'

Gwendolyn was shaken by the consequences of Lisette's wayward behaviour. Her conduct, no better than that of a hoyden or common doxy, could not be condoned, but to incarcerate her in a mental asylum seemed such a drastic act.

She said as much to Georganna when they were alone together in the rose arbour of the garden at the Mercers' house. Autumn had stripped the leaves from the trees but the sun was shining upon this sheltered corner of the garden where a few roses still bloomed, filling the air with their scent. 'Lisette was spoiled and undisciplined but to declare her insane . . . Surely it cannot be so.'

Georganna clutched the book she had been reading to her slender breast. 'Great writers portray such personalities in plays and turn the events into comedy. There was no amusement in witnessing Lisette's pain. Yet what sane woman of birth and breeding would act as Lisette has done?'

'She has no morals or apparent sense of decency but the only other mad person I have seen was some years ago when my family first moved to the Traherne estate after Roslyn's marriage.' Gwendolyn stared disconsolately at a flock of chirping sparrows in a holly bush.

'I once made the mistake of joining a party visiting Bedlam to view the inmates.' Georganna shuddered. 'It was dreadful to see their suffering. Some were tied to their beds as they screamed abuse. Others tore their own or each other's clothes, rolled on the ground like wild animals, or would take any sharp object and disfigure their bodies. Some openly fornicated, egged on by the inmates and bystanders. But what was worse was the way people went to view them as an entertainment. It gave me nightmares for weeks.'

'At least Dr Claver assured us that Lisette would be cared for in a manner befitting her station.' Gwen shook her head. 'The man at Traherne was terrifying to behold. The gamekeeper found him poaching on the Traherne estate. The vagrant wore nothing but a ragged army greatcoat and one boot. The gamekeeper brought him into the yard as Roslyn, Sir Henry and myself had returned from a ride. At first I felt sorry for the poacher. He was emaciated and had been beaten about the head, and looked as though he could barely stand. Then without warning he howled like some ghastly spectre and with unexpected vigour broke away from his captor. He capered inanely around the stable yard, stripped off his coat and was naked but for his boot.'

'What did you do? Was the man dangerous?'

Gwen blushed at the memory. 'I did not know where to look. Roslyn was mortified and Sir Henry quite apoplectic with rage that we should be subjected to such a sight within the precincts of his home. The poacher was overpowered and Roslyn and I hurried back into the house.'

'What happened to the man?' Georganna asked.

'He was bound in ropes and taken to Launceston Gaol.'

Both women lapsed into a worried silence until Gwendolyn added with a groan, 'If Lisette is forced to mix with others who act in such an inhuman manner, how will that affect her?'

'Dr Claver is held in the highest regard. Thomas did visit his hospital and found the conditions there to be satisfactory. Lisette will be kept in a room on her own. We must pray for her. And it is not as though the family have not tried to avoid such drastic treatment. She has brought this upon herself.'

'Ladies,' Thomas strode towards them, looking very dashing in a peacock-blue silk jacket and navy and silver waistcoat. 'Mama is quite overset by all that has happened. I have booked a box at the play for this evening. It will divert us. Go and ready yourselves. We leave in an hour.'

Georganna leaped up, her face alight with pleasure. 'Will Lucien be joining us? And in the interval you must read from your book of poems you have just published.'

'My dear, you know it would be impossible to keep Lucien away.' Thomas smiled at his wife. 'As for the poetry, we shall see. I inflict it too often upon my family. Mama has agreed we need the diversion and has persuaded Amelia to attend.'

'Is Amelia taking all this badly?' Georganna bit her

lip in her anxiety. 'It cannot be easy for her.'

Thomas shrugged. 'She has written to Edward and I am certain that my uncle will approve our actions concerning Lisette. But Amelia is worried about the gossip if anyone recognised Lisette with the officer.'

'Why is it everyone relishes gossip unless it happens to be about their own family? Amelia has been quick to gossip about other families when scandal is attached to them,' Gwen pointed out. 'It is better to face it and show the world that it cannot hurt you.'

'As you have done.' Georganna linked her arm through Gwen's. 'You were so brave to reject that dastardly Beaumont and have your mother retract the announcement of the engagement. There are plenty of charming young men for you to meet instead, and I know you are a good friend of Thomas's cousin Japhet, who has many acquaintances among society to introduce you to.'

'Do you think that Japhet may be at the play tonight?' Gwen could not stop herself asking. 'Lucien saw him some weeks ago. Why has he not called upon you?'

'He has been conducting some horse-trading out of the city, so I heard,' Thomas replied. 'If Japhet is in London, he will be where any diversions are to be found. Now, away with you, ladies, to primp and preen. We must put this unfortunate incident behind us.'

'What play are we to see?' Georganna paused. 'Not one with Celestine Yorke, I pray. She did nothing but simper and play up to Lord Sefton in his box the last time I saw her act. Her performance ruined a good play. The Yorke woman is more interested in gaining a wealthy paramour than doing justice to the work of a great playwright.'

'The people love her antics,' Thomas laughed, 'and to her a great playwright is of no importance. She constantly corrupts even the works of Sheridan and Garrick to suit her own designs. That is sacrilege. Tonight we shall enjoy Sheridan's *The School for Scandal* and I assure you that the "Darling of London" will not offend your sensibilities by the massacre of the words of a maestro. The playhouse manager is too discerning to employ her.'

'They say Celestine is very beautiful and notorious,' Gwen observed. 'Mama does not approve of any actress, and Celestine Yorke most of all. It would be rather naughty and exciting to see so infamous a woman perform while I am in London.'

'Then we shall see her another time,' Thomas promised. 'But not tonight. Tonight is for those of us with more discerning taste. And the real joy will be if, as it is rumoured, Sheridan himself attends – his political duties permitting. It was a sad day for the theatre when Sheridan entered Parliament.'

Gwendolyn, who had only seen travelling players of indeterminate talent, was entranced by the spectacle awaiting her at Drury Lane. The theatre, with its tiers of gilded boxes and the excited chattering of the audience, was unlike anything she had witnessed before. She searched the rows of boxes, peering into their gloomy interiors to behold lords, ladies, gentry, and city dignitaries in all their finery. The noise of conversation was all but deafening, as acquaintances called to one another across the crowded theatre. Friendships were renewed, liaisons speculated upon, trysts unashamedly made between lovers, and business conducted between the men.

Her restless stare roamed over each new arrival, searching for Japhet's tall figure. Always she was disappointed but nevertheless remained hopeful that this night would see them reunited.

The musicians struck up a tune. The theatre was lit only by the oil lamps within the more expensive boxes and the footlights smoking at the edge of the stage. There was no abatement to the level of conversation, and cries and catcalls continued from the cheapest seats in the open area directly below the stage.

The first actors came upon the stage and it was several minutes before a hush descended enough for Gwen to hear their speeches. Even so, she was captivated. She sat forward in her seat and, watching the spectacle enacted before her, forgot to continue her search for Japhet. The play made her laugh so hard her sides ached. When a commotion broke out amongst the audience below them, she paid scant heed as heads craned back to stare at a box two along from where her party were seated. Gwen glanced towards the box, where a well-endowed blonde woman waved to the crowd. Since it was not a member of the royal family, she was annoyed that someone could be so ignorant as to arrive late and interrupt the play.

Seated beside Gwen, Georganna gave a disgusted snort. 'That's your infamous Celestine Yorke, Gwen. See how she cares nothing that her entrance has stolen the attention of the public from the actors upon the stage.'

With greater interest Gwen studied the box. Celestine Yorke was now seated with her profile to Gwen. The box was full of the actress's acolytes, and the woman kept leaning back in her chair to converse with a companion who was hidden from Gwen's vision by a curtain.

'You would think she was royalty,' Georganna complained. 'She will play up to her public all evening and the play will be ruined.'

Their discourse was interrupted by the late arrival of Lucien Greene. 'A thousand pardons, dear friends,' he cooed, and sat behind Thomas. He nodded to the ladies and his smile wavered as he greeted Gwendolyn. She did not notice, for the play had again caught her attention and the comedy antics brought tears of laughter to her eyes.

With an anxious glance in Gwendolyn's direction, Lucien leaned forward to whisper in Thomas's ear. His manner was so clandestine that it made Georganna tap him with her fan and mouth, 'What is amiss?'

Lucien shook his head, refusing to answer, and Georganna was startled when Thomas left the box without an explanation.

'Lucien, where has Thomas gone? He will miss the rest of the first act.'

The poet shrugged and appeared absorbed in the play. Georganna would have none of it. She slapped his arm with her fan, demanding, 'What did you say to Tom to make him take off like that? He hates to miss part of a play.'

'It is nothing to trouble yourself over, my dear. A client of the bank needed to speak with him urgently.' Lucien stared at the stage, presenting a frigid countenance to the women.

'That is too bad,' Margaret frowned. 'What can be so urgent that a customer cannot talk to Thomas when the bank opens in the morning?'

'There is something you are not telling us, Lucien,' Georganna whispered behind her fan.

'How cruelly you malign me, sweet lady. I am mortified to the core. Indeed, I am so cast down that the play is quite ruined for me.' He affected an air of wounded innocence.

Georganna restrained the urge to press the poet on the matter. Lucien was being deliberately evasive. Perhaps Thomas had arranged a surprise for them during the interval. She smiled to herself at the thoughtfulness of her husband. She loved Thomas dearly and knew that she had been singularly blessed by having him as a husband. Thomas had allowed her to enter the world of playwrights and poets, which had always been her dream. That Lucien Greene was his lover did not trouble her. It was part of the pact they had made before their betrothal. Georganna had seen her mother die after a drawn-out labour that had ended in a stillbirth. She was terrified of conceiving a child of her own. It was a relief that Thomas had no wish to share her bed. He lavished her with affection, and adored her like an older brother. She was content to remain a virgin if it meant she would not have to face the ordeal of childbirth.

When Thomas slipped back into his seat, he looked strained and uneasy. The first act ended, and in the interval Georganna spotted Richard Sheridan in a box opposite them. 'Will we be able to meet him, Tom? Sadly for us, his box already looks full of friends claiming his attention.'

'It may be necessary to leave as soon as the play is over.'

There was a joyful cry from Margaret as the curtains at the back of their box were pulled back. 'Japhet, this is a wonderful surprise. We had begun to think that you had decided against visiting London after all.'

Gwendolyn had been so engrossed in searching the theatre for sight of him that she jumped in surprise as his deep voice answered his aunt. 'I have been busy visiting some stud farms in the country.'

He bowed to his aunt, Amelia and Georganna. When he saw Gwendolyn, though he smiled, his expression was taut and he turned quickly back to his aunt. 'I regret I cannot join you. I am with a party of friends, and one is interested in buying a stallion. I will call upon you later in the week.'

'Gwendolyn is staying with us,' Margaret informed him.

He nodded, but there was a stiffness about his

manner that wounded Gwen. He did not seem pleased to see her.

'Is Uncle Edward not with you?' he asked Amelia.

'Sadly, he has too many affairs to attend in the yard,' Margaret explained to avoid Amelia any embarrassment. 'He is overburdened now both St John and Adam are away. Amelia is here because Lisette is receiving treatment from Dr Claver.'

'Not before time.' Japhet still did not look at Gwendolyn and seemed eager to be on his way. 'Thomas, did St John change his plans? I thought I saw Meriel riding in Lord Wycham's phaeton through the park last week.'

Amelia sucked in her breath and Georganna, who could be more impulsive than diplomatic, blurted out, 'St John sailed to America with Adam. Did you not know that Meriel had left him? She ran off with Lord Wycham.'

Amelia covered her face with her hands. 'How could she be so brazen as to flout her affair so publicly? There will be no avoiding a scandal.' She stood up. 'Please, Thomas, would you summon a sedan chair for me? I could not watch the rest of the play now.'

Margaret was about to tell Amelia to sit down and not be so foolish, when she saw how pale her friend had become. Amelia looked close to swooning.

'You cannot travel the streets alone,' Thomas insisted. 'Perhaps we should all leave.'

'That would be foolish; Gwen so looked forward to this evening,' Margaret protested. 'Could Gwen and

Georganna not join your party, Japhet? It would be such a shame for their pleasure to be curtailed.'

Japhet tensed and looked ill at ease. Gwendolyn's stomach churned with fear at his obvious reluctance. 'At any other time, aunt—' he began.

Too proud to hear his rejection, Gwendolyn interrupted, 'I would be happy to leave with Amelia. I have the headache and it is getting worse.'

Japhet turned his stare upon her and fleetingly she saw regret in his eyes. He bowed to her. 'I will visit you soon.'

'Then the least you can do is wait with us while Thomas summons the coach.' Margaret was not about to let Japhet escape so easily. She was determined to make a match between him and Gwendolyn.

Outside the boxes people milled in the corridor and called out to acquaintances. Japhet remained tense as he politely helped his aunt and Amelia with their shawls.

'So this is where you ran off to, you naughty man,' a stentorian feminine voice cut through their conversation. Celestine Yorke sashayed through a crowd that parted before her. 'Are you not going to introduce me to your friends, Japhet?'

Irritation tightened Japhet's jaw as the actress possessively linked both arms through his. 'Who are these people that they keep you so long from my company?'

'My family.' Japhet disengaged her arms. 'And I am sure that you need no introduction.' He bowed briefly to his aunt. 'Your pardon.' With that he took Celestine's arm and escorted her back to their box.

Gwendolyn was rigid with shock. If Japhet was with such a notorious woman as Celestine Yorke then she must be his mistress. She had never condemned his affairs in the past, but then she had never so blatantly had to endure the presence of his mistress.

'I am sorry that happened, Gwen.' Georganna linked her arm through her friend's as they walked through the foyer of the theatre.

'The actress is very beautiful, her life bold and exciting. What can I offer Japhet compared to such women? I was foolish to come to London.'

'You are beautiful, Gwen.'

'I am not beautiful. And she is dazzling and sought after – everyone adores her for her wit. I am dull and provincial. How can I compete with her?'

'Celestine Yorke is no wit,' Georganna derided. 'She is funny on stage because she recites lines written by others. Japhet will soon tire of her.'

'Everything seemed so different in Cornwall, but it was an illusion. This is the life Japhet prefers.' Gwendolyn would not be consoled. The pain she felt at seeing Japhet with a mistress was corrosive. She was angry with him for destroying the illusion she had fostered in Cornwall, but she was angrier with herself for believing that Japhet's reputation could not hurt her, and that loving him she could forgive him anything. Images of Japhet making love with Celestine Yorke tormented her, the pain lacerating her heart until she wanted to tear it out to stop the agony.

Chapter Twelve

A mile along the coast from Trevowan, the fishing village of Penruan lay at the base of a combe that opened out into the sea. The granite stone cottages were tiered on the steep slopes of the wooded hills surrounding the small harbour. Along one side of the quay were the cleaning sheds, which were never free of the reek of fish from where the women gutted and salted the catch. At the opposite end of the quay was the general store that had been owned by Thadeous Lanyon before his murder.

The new owner, who insisted on being known only as Goldie, was busy sorting through the stock. Marigold Lanyon wore a bright yellow wig, her black eyes hard and calculating as a pawnbroker as she worked. She was trying to assess what merchandise was required or was appropriate for the needs of the village. Her head ached from the task for she could neither read nor write, relying on her sharp memory to recall an inventory of the stock.

She picked up a jug with a hole chipped in its side

and put it with other uselessly damaged articles in a sack. The range of goods for sale included haberdashery, ironmongery, flour, wickerwork, pots, cutlery, candles and soap. Some of the stock was discoloured, tarnished or cracked with age and had been in the store for years. The place was cluttered and, to Goldie's mind, disorganised, and many of the items were overpriced. Lanyon had charged high prices for everyday necessities, knowing that many of the villagers had no choice but to buy from him, or else travel vast distances to the nearest market.

She shook her head. Goldie had suffered the hardships of poverty for too long not to be disgusted by Lanyon's greed. The profit on goods in a shop like this should be sufficient without robbing the customers blind. It offended her sense of fairness.

For years Goldie had built a barricade around her heart, refusing to allow herself to be governed by her emotions. She had been reviled and abused throughout her years as a whore, and forced to live as a social outcast. The shame of that life had always haunted her, for until she married Thadeous Lanyon she had lived a hard-working but honest and decent life, her parents respected by their community.

'Damn your worthless soul, Lanyon.' She shook her fist at the desk at the rear of the shop where Thadeous Lanyon had written in his ledgers. 'You brought me to ruin and shame. But I am worth more than that. Here I intend to hold my head high again. I will be accepted as part of this community.'

Her life had been one of stark survival since the

fateful day she had met Thadeous Lanyon, thirty years ago. Married, abandoned – or rather at the age of sixteen sold off to a brothel by Lanyon – she had refused to use her married name since. She was well rid of the evil monster who had wed her for the small farm she had inherited from her parents, who had died within a week of each other from smallpox.

Lanyon had sold the farm and once the money was gone, he had regularly beaten Goldie into submission to his will. To supply his need for ale, Lanyon had sold Goldie's body to any man for a couple of pennies. She had hated her life, too terrified of Lanyon's threats to kill her to try to escape. It had not taken long to learn to numb her feelings and block her emotions to guard herself from pain. The degradation Lanyon had inflicted on her had toughened her to life within the brothel. It had enabled her to survive when many other young women had died of disease or mistreatment.

She had endured the brothel for five years before managing to escape. During that time there had never been enough to eat and the woman who had been sold into virtual slavery received no money.

All Goldie knew was the life of a whore. In her youth she had been pretty, and when she escaped from the brothel she headed for Bristol and the anonymity provided by a large and busy port. A retired bosun became a regular customer and, after a couple of years, suggested that they set up a lodging house together. She agreed and he invested his meagre savings in a dilapidated three-storey building in the poorest district of the port. Though they continued to live in poverty, running the lodging house gave Goldie a new sense of achievement. Her lover gave her regular money and wanted her exclusively for his bed. When he died from a stab wound after being robbed one night on his way home from a tavern, Goldie found she had been left the lodging house in his will.

At last Goldie felt that she could make something of her life and she dreamed of one day moving to a better part of the town. To achieve this she needed a greater income than her lodgers could provide. She used the only talents she possessed, tripled the sailors' rent and provided them with the services of her bed.

Everything had changed the day a dwarf had entered the house. He was dressed in threadbare clothes and she assumed that he had come from a travelling circus or freak show.

'This bain't no bordello. I only take in regular lodgers.' Goldie was sweeping the step and raised the besom to shoo him away.

'I'm not after such services or lodgings. I believe you knew Thadeous Lanyon.'

The name still had the power to terrify Goldie. 'Don't know no man of that name. Get you gone.' She brandished the broom. When he did not move she made a jab at him but the small man deftly sidestepped. Fear gripped her. Had Lanyon found her and sent this man to kill her? She had heard some years ago that he had wed a wealthy woman in Penruan. The existence of a first wife could see him thrown in prison if anyone discovered his secret.

'Get you gone,' she screeched. 'Go or I will call for help. I've two burly sailors in their rooms upstairs to protect me.'

'Madam, I mean you no harm.' The soft cultured voice was at odds with the man's appearance and she lowered the broom. He put up his hands showing that he was unarmed. 'Do not fear me. And I assure you that you have no need to fear Thadeous Lanyon. He is dead. You are Marigold Lanyon, are you not?'

His manner was so authoritative that she nodded and self-consciously patted a stray tendril of hair back into place.

'Forgive my appearance,' he continued. 'It has taken me many days to find you and I did not wish to draw attention to myself in this part of the port. Permit me to introduce myself. I am known as Long Tom. Your husband was murdered and thrown into the river at Truro.'

'Why should that be of interest to me? I'm glad he be dead.' She remained wary and defensive. 'And what has it to do with you either, for that matter?'

'I am here on behalf of the family of the man who will shortly stand trial for the murder of Thadeous Lanyon. He is innocent and the evidence brought against him is circumstantial. I need someone to speak at the trial to tell the world the truth about Lanyon's disreputable life.'

'I bain't about to go in no court for no one.' Goldie shook her head. ''Sides, I got a business to run.' She turned to go inside the lodging house and shut the door on Long Tom.

'Thadeous Lanyon died a wealthy man,' Long Tom clipped out. 'A very wealthy man. His widow could live a life of luxury if she so chose. But the world believes that Thadeous Lanyon's widow is living in Penruan.'

'That bain't no marriage.' Goldie was overtaken by greed at the thought of what riches could be hers. 'I be his only true wife. His first wife. Any other marriage bain't legal, not while I still be alive.'

'That is correct.' Long Tom showed no expression as he studied her. 'To claim your inheritance you must attend the trial and inform the court of your status. Do you have any documents to prove that Lanyon wed you?'

'It will be written in the register of Altarnum church and I got a copy of my marriage lines somewhere. The Lord knows why I kept them. I hated the bastard, but I reckoned that someday I could pay him back for all the suffering he caused me. 'Cept I never had the courage. If I showed my face anywhere near Penruan he would have killed me for sure.'

'Now he is dead. His evil cannot touch you.'

'Aye, you be right,' Goldie nodded. 'I'll attend the trial. I don't reckon any man should swing for ridding the world of that evil bastard.'

It was not until the trial that she learned that Lanyon had bigamously married three other women for their money: two of whom had died within a few years of the marriage from his brutality. The fourth wife was expecting his child. At the time of the trial Goldie had given little thought to the woman who was to lose everything when her marriage to Lanyon was proved to be invalid.

When Goldie moved to Penruan, she realised that Lanyon's wife, a local woman, Hester, had been as much a victim of his cruelty as herself. Goldie pitied Hester, but she had lived too long fearing destitution to surrender anything of her inheritance. The people of Penruan had hated Lanyon, but they did not welcome the arrival of an unknown wife, who had ousted one of their own women from a comfortable widowhood.

Goldie had since learned that Hester's father, the local chandler, had disowned her when her marriage was proved invalid. It was also speculated within the village that the child Hester carried was not Lanyon's at all, but Harry Sawle's. Hester and Harry had been courting for years before Lanyon married Hester. It was also said that Sawle and Lanyon were archenemies, as Sawle was the leader of another gang of smugglers, and equally dangerous to cross.

When Goldie had taken residence in Lanyon's large house on the hill and reopened the shop, the Penruan villagers had shown their antagonism towards her by their stony glares of disapproval. Even though necessity forced them to use the store for provisions, they ignored any conversation she attempted with them. Goldie had faced public censure for too many years to allow it to affect her.

She gave little thought to the dispossessed Hester Moyle. Yet on the one occasion she had seen Hester from a distance, obviously close to her time, her belly large, she had felt a twinge of remorse. Hester dragged her body wearily through the street, her lovely face pinched with grief. Not for Lanyon, if rumour be true, but for Sawle. On discovering that Hester would get nothing of Lanyon's property Harry Sawle had abandoned her and was now said to be paying court to a woman in Launceston, the wealthy widow of a town dignitary.

Until now Hester had never known poverty. She would have been destitute and homeless when her father disowned her had it not been for the intervention of the Reverend Mr Snell, who had given her one of the alms cottages when the last occupant had died.

'Lanyon may have abused Hester as cruelly as he did me,' Goldie spoke aloud in the empty shop, 'but she bain't done too badly. She be kept by the parish and bain't had to sell her body like me to stay alive.'

Goldie shook off her thoughts. Hester Moyle was not her concern. Goldie reckoned that she was more than entitled to Lanyon's wealth after he had squandered her own inheritance and made her life so miserable.

In a rush of diligence Goldie sorted through the shelves and the storeroom of goods, wondering what she could do to increase trade. She had expected that the life of a shopkeeper would provide her with an easy and respectable income.

'Increase trade?' She gave a derisive laugh that echoed eerily in the deserted shop. 'No matter how friendly I be to the customers, they still distrust me as an outsider who has usurped the rights of one of their own. Is it my fault that Thadeous Lanyon was a bigamist and duped the village for years with his treachery? Anyone would think I be some kind of ogre.' Goldie glanced across at the red and blue macaw on his perch by the side of the cluttered counter. 'What do you think, Poppy, my old lover?'

'Poppy wants a good time. Give us a shilling, darling. I'll make you happy,' the bird squawked, and bobbed his head up and down as he strutted along his perch. The bird had been named Poppy as a short-ened term for popinjay, the old name for parrots, and also for a foppish, conceited and overtalkative man. Goldie had met too many such men in her time. 'Poppy wants a good time. Poppy be the best.'

'Poppy do be the best, and less trouble than any man, my darling,' Goldie laughed, and gave the parrot a walnut to crack open. 'I shall have to clean up your speech. No naughty talk here. We be respectable now and not in a bawdy house.'

'Goldie's best bawdy house in town,' Poppy craned back his neck to preen himself.

Goldie shook her head. 'Oh dear, I really will have to teach you some new phrases.' A sailor who went off one night never to return had left the bird at the lodging house in Bristol. He had either been mur-dered in a drunken fight, or more likely taken by the press-gang. Poppy had been popular with Goldie's lodgers, and in the ten years they had been together, she had become very fond of him.

It was late afternoon and the light in the shop was fading. Goldie shook her head as she frowned at the rows of drawers behind the counter, holding various goods. The shelves along each wall were also piled high, and iron pans, spades and various-shaped baskets were hung from the ceiling beams so that she often had to duck her head as she crossed the floor. 'Lord, Poppy, there be so much stock but how can I tell what we sell in a week, a month, or a year? As for these, Poppy, my lover . . .' She fingered the three thick leather-bound books laid on Lanyon's desk. Each contained pages crammed with columns of figures. Despite her lack of learning Goldie knew a money ledger when she saw one and they looked to record a great many transactions that could represent a huge fortune.

Last week a lawyer from Bodmin had come to the shop and introduced himself as having dealt with Lanyon's affairs for several years, and offered her his services. She had hesitated, not sure if she trusted lawyers and the like, never having dealt with them in the past.

Perhaps Lanyon's bankers should deal with the books? Goldie wrestled with the problem, knowing it was not wise to allow things to continue as they were. She guessed there could be a great deal of money at stake. But if her late husband was the smuggler he was purported to be, would she find herself in trouble with the law from any information about his illegal activities contained in the books?

It was a dilemma, for she did not know who to trust. She was used to dealing with money as it came into her hands and stowing it in a secret place in the chimney. Banks, lawyers, ledgers, and facts and figures in books alarmed her.

She wiped her dusty hands on her apron. 'I shall have to find someone I can trust to help me to understand these books. Someone who bain't about to steal all my money and me none the wiser. That lawyer in Bodmin do reckon I be a wealthy woman. What do you say to that, Poppy?'

'Give us a shilling. Give us a shilling.'

Goldie continued to talk to the parrot as though he was a person. Indeed, he was often a confidant to her deepest thoughts and emotions. She was cautious about anyone who would handle so much of her income. 'That will not be an easy post to fill, will it, Poppy? And I am going to need a maid and a woman to help in the shop. That will mean a day at the next hiring fair. No one from the village has applied for the work and the notice has been in the window all week.'

'Goldie's be best bawdy house in town,' Poppy cackled. The phrase had always annoyed Goldie for the bird had been taught it by one of her more disagreeable lodgers.

'Goldie's be best shop in town, Polly. That old life is behind us. Don't you go upsetting the customers.'

She stared out of the tiny panes of the bow-fronted shop and wondered if it would be possible to get the bird to change his less acceptable phrases. It would be better to keep him in the house instead of the shop, yet she spent long hours here rather than returning to an empty house.

Goldie frowned. Life had been so much simpler in

Bristol, but nothing came easy, and Lanyon's money would likely set her up in comfort. She could sell the shop and other businesses and properties that Lanyon also owned. There were the smoking sheds on the quay, the Gun Inn and three cottages rented to fishermen. Yet to sell up would seem like admitting defeat, and, used to hard work, Goldie did not relish the boredom of a life of inactivity.

The heavy downpour of rain hammering against the windowpanes was a depressing sight. It did not help her mood. The shop was not her only problem. The Gun Inn had not had a single customer since she had taken it over. Unwilling to continue paying the barman's wages, she had closed it last week. She was tempted to sell it, but remained undecided. The shop and the inn should be bringing her in a good income, or Lanyon would have sold them long ago.

From the corner of the window Goldie could see towards the centre of the village. A woman, hunched against the driving wind and rain, was seated under the lych-gate of the church. A man came out of the Dolphin Inn that was the rival tavern to the Gun. The woman in the churchyard ran across the space and as her cloak parted in the wind, Goldie saw from her swollen figure that it was Hester. The young woman clung to the man's arm and looked to be pleading with him. He roughly pushed her away and when she tried to grab his arm, he struck her and she fell back across the side of a stone horse trough. The man swaggered away as though he was some cock of the roost and he did not look back.

Goldie felt a rush of anger towards the man. Brutality sickened her, for she had suffered it too often. The woman had not moved from where she had fallen. The village was deserted of people, kept indoors by the bad weather. The poor wretch must be drenched. Goldie opened the shop door and reached for her shawl. No one else had seen the woman fall and even though Hester would no doubt regard her as an enemy, she could not stand by and see her suffer.

The rain chilled Goldie as she hurried across the quay. By the time she reached Hester, the woman was struggling to rise with one hand clamped over her stomach. She groaned and fell back. Hester was also sobbing uncontrollably, and seemed unaware of her predicament or surroundings. Her hair was loose and hung in wet tendrils across her face. Her eyes were hollowed and darkly circled and her cheekbones were too prominent. A bout of coughing momentarily halted the sobs.

'Let me help you,' Goldie offered, placing her shoulder under the woman's arm and heaving her upright. Hester was ashen and shivering in her sodden clothes, and Goldie could feel the bones of her ribcage through the soaking cloak and gown.

At the sound of a kindly voice, Hester clutched hold of Goldie's hand, her face screwed up in pain and misery. She was bent over and did not look at Goldie's face. 'Baby be coming.'

'How long have you been having pains?'

'They started in the night and I got little sleep. But

I had to see Harry. Harry will look after me. He promised.'

'If that were your Harry who hit you, he bain't gonna do nothing for you. Forget him be my advice. I'll take you back to the almshouse and send someone for the midwife.'

'I don't want Ginny Rundle.' She pulled herself upright and gasped at recognising Goldie. 'I don't want your help. Go away.' She tried to pull away but Goldie held her too firmly.

'There bain't no one else here to help you. Do you want to have your child in the gutter?'

Hester staggered towards the seat in the lych-gate. 'I need to rest. Let me be.'

Goldie helped her until she was seated. Hester groaned and clutched her stomach. No one else came to her aid, though several cottages overlooked the churchyard.

'You can't stay here, Miss Moyle. Why do you not wish Ginny Rundle to tend you?'

'Ginny always said that Harry be no good, and she's a friend of Sal Sawle. The Sawles don't want anyone to have anything to do with me. The villagers are scared of Harry. Too many depend on him.' Hester glared at Goldie. 'I don't want your help. If it hadn't been for you, Harry would have wed me. Everything would have been all right.'

'And right miserable he would have made you if all he wanted was Lanyon's money,' Goldie informed her. 'What about Mrs Snell, the reverend's wife, will she help you? You should have a woman with you for a day or so after the birth. Did I not hear that you had a sister who married the doctor? I shall send for him.'

Hester tried to rise but doubled over as she was struck by another contraction. 'Mrs Snell be visiting her sister in Polmasryn. I can manage. I don't need you.'

'Where does the doctor live?' Goldie ignored the woman's hostility, supporting her until the contraction ended. 'Your sister will comfort you.'

Hester pulled herself upright and stared into the distance, her tone bitter. 'Chegwidden won't come. He'd like to see the child and me dead. Since he wed my sister Annie last month, he be ashamed we be family. He sees me as a fallen woman, and won't let Annie have nothing to do with me. Pa also says I have shamed him. They don't want me in Penruan. I stayed 'cos of Harry. Once the baby comes, he'll do right by me.'

Hester struggled to her feet, sobs shaking her body. Goldie gave her a rough shake. 'Who can I send for to tend you? You need help.'

'Send for Senara Loveday over at Trevowan Hard.' Hester refused to look at Goldie. 'Senara will not charge. Mayhap Keziah Sawle will come. She's been a good friend, although her Clem be Harry's brother. Keziah is not scared of Harry. But she be no midwife.'

Goldie stared at the sodden, hostile woman and felt a moment's respect for Hester. Despite her helplessness, Hester showed a stubborn resilience against Goldie, whom she saw as her enemy. It proved Hester had once been a fighter and Goldie admired that.

'Happen I've seen a babe or two born in my time. I can do what be needed if there be no complication. You'd best come to my house.'

'I bain't going in there.' Hester wrenched herself free of Goldie's grip. 'Have I not enough to endure that you would humiliate me by giving me charity in what used to be my home?'

Goldie lost patience. 'Cut your whining. You'll die if you don't accept my help. It don't sound like no one else is gonna take you in. I'll get you settled, then send for the Loveday woman and Keziah Sawle. Keziah be the only woman who's spoken pleasantly to me when she came into the shop.'

Another pain stopped Hester's protests and when it passed the fight had gone out of her and she allowed Goldie to help her up the hill to Lanyon's old house. Goldie put Hester into her own bed and lit the fire already prepared in the grate. The pains were coming faster and Hester gripped the two sheets that Goldie tied on each of the bedposts behind the pillows.

'We've got to get you out of those wet clothes.' Goldie took out a rough linen chemise from a coffer. 'Reckon it don't matter if this be ruined; it be time I treated myself to something better.'

'With my money, damn you,' Hester wailed. 'I don't want to be here. Get Kezzie.' She pushed Goldie's hand away as she tried to unfasten the lacing of Hester's gown.

'I'll get Keziah once you are out of those wet clothes. Now you either let me help you, or I shall cut them off you.' Goldie had enough experience of dealing with drunken sailors who could be stubborn and belligerent, and she had no intention allowing Hester to dictate to her in her own home.

Hester regarded her sullenly as Goldie helped her out of her garments and into the chemise. Twice they had to stop whilst Hester arched her back in the grip of a contraction.

'Now get Kezzie,' Hester sobbed, but her words were cut off with a scream and she drew up her legs.

Goldie lifted the sheets. 'Baby's head just appeared. I bain't gonna leave you now. Come on, old girl, next pain you push hard and it will be all over.'

The baby was born with remarkable ease, much to Goldie's relief. Goldie wrapped it in a sheet and tended to the mother, who lay back exhausted.

'Give me my baby,' Hester demanded. When Goldie placed it in her arms she clutched it tight to her breast and broke down in tears.

Goldie left the room. 'You'll be needing some broth to get back your strength. I'll go get Keziah, if you want, but I bain't about to turn you out on the street until you are ready to leave here.'

She was at the door before a weak voice answered, 'Thank you. The hour be late. Don't trouble Kezzie now. I reckon you bain't as bad as I thought. That don't mean that I don't still hate you for what you took from me. Life with Lanyon was hell. I worked like a slave in that shop, and for what? You got everything.'

'Lanyon were a bastard. He ruined my life,' Goldie confided. 'He deserved to die the way he did.'

Once Hester and the baby, who had been laid into a
drawer for a crib, were asleep, Goldie sat in front of
the kitchen range in a wooden rocking chair. The
house with its three bedrooms, parlour, dining room
and separate kitchen was one of the grandest in
Penruan, but Goldie felt ill at ease here. It carried
Lanyon's presence as forcefully as if he haunted it.
The kitchen was the only place other than the smallest
of the bedrooms, which she had taken for herself, that
had not been tainted by him.

The birth of the child had affected her. She pitied
Hester. Sawle was no better than that bastard Lanyon.
It would be a fine thing to make him pay for his
cruelty. By getting at Sawle, Goldie would appease her
anger for all the indignities that Lanyon had heaped
upon her.

Chapter Thirteen

Lieutenant Francis Beaumont avoided patrolling the southern shores of Cornwall. He had taken his cutter, *Challenger*, to the northern coast, where he was not so well known. He had no great love for the sea and had entered the navy as a midshipman only because his grandfather had insisted. Life at sea involved too much deprivation of the luxuries Beaumont desired. But until he came into his inheritance, he was forced to pursue a career afloat.

The bad weather of the last weeks had added to his discontent. He was weary of chasing smugglers in seas that pitched and heaved, and threatened the lives of all on board. Tonight as they patrolled the waters off Land's End he was lying on his bunk in his cabin. Above him his second in command shouted orders and men pounded across the deck to obey. Beaumont took no interest; in another four hours it would be too light for smugglers to risk a landing, and he could return to port.

Not that on land he would find much solace. Since

Gwendolyn Druce had left for London rather than wed him, he risked ridicule in his old ports and haunts. His grandfather had been furious that a betrothal was announced and then retracted. Unless Francis found a suitable bride and married her within two months, before his cousin was due to give birth to her first child, his grandfather would disinherit him in favour of his cousin. Francis was not about to allow that to happen – his grandfather's estate was in excess of forty thousand pounds, even without the house and grounds in Hampshire.

Time was short and lack of availability of an heiress of marriageable age made a choice difficult. Many families whose daughters were pretty and would inherit a fortune considered an excise officer too lowly, even if he was the heir of Admiral Algernon Beaumont.

He had approached three families in Cornwall and all had refused him. In desperation he was contemplating sailing to the Somerset ports. But that could prove too costly in time. He needed a betrothal to be announced immediately. The only family with an eligible daughter fell far below his expectations. He had no choice but to visit the Thackwell family tomorrow at their estate three miles inland from St Ives.

After another night with no success at apprehending smugglers, Beaumont hired a horse and, with little enthusiasm, rode to pay court to Maria Thackwell. The Thackwells owned a hundred acres and three productive tin mines. The L-shaped house of a dozen rooms was built of local stone, unpretentious and plain in appearance – very much like its owners. John and Mary Thackwell greeted him heartily when he was ushered into a drawing room by their maid. Maria was squinting over her embroidery, the material turned grey from her sweating palms. She bundled it aside and giggled as he bowed over her hand.

He forced a smile. Maria's mousy hair was frizzed in tight unattractive curls at the front and the rest was hidden under a gauze mobcap. She was eight years older than he, with red apple cheeks, and close-set eyes. She was the image of her portly parents and together the family must weigh in excess of fifty stone.

'Lieutenant Beaumont, it is a pleasure to have you dine with us.' John Thackwell led him into the dining room. 'There is no time to waste, as you will want to return to your ship before dark. A special meal of nine courses has been prepared in your honour.'

Beaumont was bloated and uncomfortable before half the dishes were served. Throughout the meal, John Thackwell enquired into every aspect of his family and life. Mrs Thackwell and Maria were silent, except for the steady chomping of their food and clatter of cutlery as they piled more helpings on to their plates.

'It is good to see you have a hearty appetite, Lieutenant Beaumont.' Mr Thackwell pressed more fish pie on him. 'My little Maria has been brought up to know the value of good food. No one can say I keep my family short. Anything they want is theirs for the asking.' He eyed Beaumont's slender figure with derision, the only note of censure from the mine owner.

Maria giggled and blushed as she glanced across the table at Beaumont. He hid his distaste that he found her unattractive as he piled her and her mother with false compliments. Thackwell obviously assessed a man's success and wealth by his girth. The family's table manners were appalling as they slurped and chomped their food. As the meal progressed it was obvious that Mr Thackwell was an opinionated boor and his wife and daughter inane, poorly educated and frivolous.

Beaumont swallowed another mouthful of food with difficulty and smiled. 'Sir, you have indeed shown your love for your family by your generosity.' During his visit he assessed the value of the expensive items of china, paintings and silver on display, but only his desperation to comply with his grandfather's ultimatum kept him from running out of the house.

The ladies finally excused themselves after eating several pieces of sugared fruit and marchpane. The room smelled of the rich food that had been served, and was stuffy and overhot from the roaring fire in the hearth. Everything the Thackwells did they did in excess.

Beaumont took the port and cigar offered to him and was overcome with a sudden rush of panic. The family were ghastly and Maria Thackwell held no attraction for him other than her money. He finished the port and stood up, straightening his uniform jacket. 'I have been made most welcome in your house, sir. So welcome and, indeed so overwhelmed by the hospitality of your family, that I fear I may offend by presuming upon so short an acquaintance to ask for your daughter's hand in marriage.'

Thackwell laughed. 'You want her for her money. I'm not a fool, Lieutenant. Five thousand a year has attracted fortune-hunters in the past, but none Mrs Thackwell cared for. However, she finds you most presentable.'

Beaumont stiffened in affront but before he could protest, Thackwell added, 'Sir yourself down and let us talk, sir. My dear wife will not be happy until she has a grandchild to dangle on her knee. Maria is taken with you and has made it plain to me that she wants you for her husband. What my wife and daughter want, they shall have. When do you wish the wedding to take place? I insist upon a grand affair with the whole of St Ives celebrating my Maria's good fortune.'

'A grand wedding would take time to arrange. Unfortunately my grandfather, Admiral Beaumont, is in failing health.' Beaumont lied to make plausible the excuse of a hasty wedding, which would take place before his cousin produced her child. 'This, of course, is not common knowledge; the admiral's role in the war with France is too important and could affect morale. But my grandfather was pleased when I wrote to him of my intentions. He suggested a wedding early next month before he joins the fleet. He is presently at the Admiralty in Plymouth.'

'This I must discuss with my wife and daughter. They had plans for a large affair.'

'Many people consider it romantic that the couple wish to take their vows without too long a delay. I am not involved in the war directly, but one never knows what role the Admiralty may wish the revenue service to take, if the French sail too close to our shores. It could mean a delay of several months if the French Navy try to invade.'

'That is not likely, is it?' John Thackwell viewed him with suspicion.

Beaumont shrugged. 'There is always that danger – my grandfather intimated as much. He is party to records and information concerning the whereabouts and intent of the French fleet.'

Thackwell resisted Beaumont's arguments but the lieutenant was adamant the wedding would take place in the next month or after the war with France was over. It was a gamble and took some persuasion before Thackwell agreed. Once the arrangements were finally made, Beaumont felt more resentment than joy at the prospect of his marriage.

In a sour mood, he blamed his ill fortune entirely upon the Lovedays. He was convinced that St John had been implicated in some way in Lanyon's murder and he had escaped the law. The death of Thadeous Lanyon had ended a profitable partnership. Lanyon had paid him handsomely to keep the revenue ship away from the coves where the smuggler landed his cargoes. That loss of income was due to St John Loveday. Japhet Loveday was the cause of him losing a wealthy, attractive bride, and Adam Loveday had been a thorn in his side for years, since they had duelled and both been cashiered from the navy.

But the Lovedays had not escaped completely. Before Beaumont had left Fowey he had paid two local villains, who had been in Lanyon's pay, to cause havoc at the Loveday shipyard. They were to steal what they could and would be paid a bonus for any damage that resulted in a ship being delayed in its launch. The destruction in the carpentry shop had cost him five guineas but the cost to Edward Loveday would be a hundred times more in extra wages and the penalty clause imposed by late delivery.

However, Beaumont was not satisfied. He was not finished with the Lovedays. Adam, Japhet and St John were out of his reach for the moment, but he had already set in motion a plan to show them how vulnerable even men such as Edward Loveday could be.

Celestine Yorke was a demanding and a possessive mistress, although she did not keep herself exclusively for Japhet, who refused to meet her bills. This suited Japhet, who had never wanted their liaison to be more than a casual affair. Among her other lovers, Sir Pettigrew Osgood was Celestine's main protector, but she expected Japhet to be at her beck and call. She was an insatiable lover, often sending for Japhet to attend her within an hour of Osgood leaving her. Usually, Japhet had made other arrangements and would send his apologies, for no matter how exciting Celestine could be he was no woman's lackey to be summoned on a whim. It led to many quarrels and

Japhet was growing weary of her tantrums.

There was no matinée performance today and Celestine had insisted that they visit one of the dozens of freak shows set up in London. Her taste in entertainment was rarely to Japhet's liking, but today he was in the mood to humour her. The show she had chosen was in an alley off Soho. There was snow in the air but that did not daunt Celestine, who was wrapped in a sable-lined velvet cloak.

When they alighted from her carriage into the dingy street a dozen barefoot urchins surrounded them, begging for alms. Celestine held a nosegay to her face. 'Get those disgusting creatures away from me.'

Her manner made the beggars more persistent. The alleys between the rat-infested tenement buildings were narrow and dark. Poverty was rife and many of the children were horribly disfigured. In the rookeries, which were the most squalid and poverty-stricken areas of London, the children were condemned from birth to lives of beggary. Infants had their bones deliberately broken so that they grew twisted. Children had saltpetre rubbed into open sores so that the flesh became ulcerated and the wounds exhibited to obtain alms. Other beggars feigned hideous wounds by covering a patch of skin with a layer of soap and then applying strong vinegar, giving the appearance of large yellow suppurating wounds.

Aware of these tricks, Japhet nevertheless pitied the wretched lives of the children, and tossed a handful of coppers on to the cobblestones. Whilst the beggars grabbed and fought over them he escorted Celestine safely into the freak show. It was in a dark and poorly lit warehouse, which smelled of mildew and boiled cabbage water. Each exhibit was on a dais in a cell-like room, or in a cage lit by a single candle. A corpulent, bearded lady reclined on a day bed, and a man wearing only red woollen hose had his upper body pierced with porcupine quills. Another man was tattooed on his face and torso to resemble a tiger, with quills inserted into his cheeks as whiskers. In two stalls were a two-headed foal, whose second head flopped and looked in danger of falling off every time the animal shook its head. Obviously it was filled with straw and fixed by fine wires and the foal had been trying to rid himself of the irritation for hours. A six-legged calf had the two extra legs hanging beneath its belly, again attached by thin wire, which had started to cut into the animal's flesh.

Celestine gasped in amazement at the exhibits and Japhet hid a smile at their obvious fakery. Celestine was too vain to admit that she was short-sighted. A family of dwarfs with three children lived in a toadstool-shaped construction in the corner of the warehouse and they had been dressed up as gnomes. The star of the freak show was a satyr in a wooden byre draped in dead ivy. The creature, with long ginger matted hair and beard, had the legs of a goat and lay propped against the stump of a tree. Even in the poor light the satyr was clearly a man sitting inside the hollowed tree stump and who had strapped on the stuffed legs of a goat.

'Have you ever seen so much tomfoolery?' Japhet

could not contain his laughter.

'You are too much of a sceptic, Japhet,' Celestine chided. 'They are real. It is such a pity the merman is no longer here. He was a sight to behold and lay in a large tank, his scaly tail like a fish.'

'Have you seen enough?' Japhet guided her away. The smell in the warehouse was turning his stomach.

'But it is still early. We could go to Newgate and pay to see the men in the condemned hold. There's to be a hanging at Tyburn tomorrow and I want to see that also. We must leave early to be sure of a place near the gallows.'

'What pleasure is there in seeing a man turned off?' Japhet retorted.

'But he is a highwayman, my dear.' Celestine looked at him through lowered lashes. 'Surely you cannot have forgotten that I was robbed. The villain has not been caught. Such men deserve to hang, do they not?'

Celestine was deliberately taunting him and he refused to rise to her baiting. He made his voice sound indifferent. 'I see no pleasure in seeing a man choking out his life's breath from the end of the rope. And neither do I enjoy the dubious delights of Newgate Gaol. Osgood can take you if you wish to see such spectacles.'

'But I prefer your company.' A sly smile twisted her lips. 'Or do you fear that the fate of those men could one day be yours?'

'I tire of your silly insinuations, Celestine.' Japhet felt himself tangled deeper into the insidious web she had woven around him. 'Is your life not filled with drama enough, that you must invent some mystery surrounding me?'

They were again in the street and the urchins and beggars clamoured around them. 'Off with you.' Japhet directed his anger over Celestine's insinuations at the urchins. 'I've given you money already.'

The youths jeered and jostled. 'Giv us a penny, mister. A penny ain't nothing ter yer. You're a regular toff. Ain't that Celestine Yorke? She could afford a shilling.' One lad with open sores around his nose and mouth thrust his face closer to Celestine, who screamed.

Japhet moved swiftly to stand in front of Celestine and drew the dagger secreted inside his jacket. The blade flashed in front of the urchins. 'I said be gone, or shall I split a nose or two for your impertinence?'

The youths backed off. 'Didn't mean nothing by it, sir. You looked a regular toff. I need a shilling ter get me sick mother some physic.'

'You want it to spend on gin. I know your sort.' Japhet stood his ground, jabbing the dagger towards any who tried to get closer.

The youths began to melt away into the shadows, leaving only the two oldest, who had been the loudest in their demands.

'I jus' gotta whistle and me gang will be on yer,' one threatened. 'The wench has some pretty gewgaws in 'er ears. They'll do for starters.'

Japhet's hand darted out, the blade slicing the lobe from the youth's ear. He yelped and clutched his hand to his head as blood seeped through his fingers. 'You want the other ear nicked? Or what about your mate here?'

'I don't want no trouble, mister.' The second youth ran off. And without the support of his companions, the last beggar backed away.

Japhet glanced at Celestine, who was breathing heavily, her eyes gleaming with a feral light. 'They could have killed us over a few measly coppers.'

Japhet regarded her seriously. 'Only if they thought they could get the upper hand. They are bullies. Confront them and they will back down. Bullies are usually cowards. They rely on gang force to back them up. You only have to show them that you mean business and are capable of defending yourself and they will seek easier game.'

'But I could have been robbed or assaulted.'

'Not with me to protect you,' Japhet smiled.

He handed her into her carriage and when he sat opposite her, her head was tilted to one side in an assessing manner. 'You are very sure of yourself. I admire that in a man. But to know the behaviour of such men, you must have mixed with them.'

'You are making assumptions again.' His grin hid his disquiet. 'I know human nature and have fought my share of duels. A man can see alarm or fearlessness in another's eyes and will decide whether a challenge is worth the risk involved to himself.'

Celestine laughed. 'That's why I adore you, Japhet. You never bore me. Osgood would have handed over his money and anything of value I had with me. But then you know that. Have you still got that bracelet of mine from that night on the heath? I would like it back or one to replace it.'

'Keep your demands for your wealthy lovers. I have no time for your foolish games.' He banged on the roof of the coach to signal the driver to stop.

Celestine grabbed his arm as he made to step down into the road. 'They are no games, my handsome lover. I know you are the highwayman we named Gentleman James. An actress has an ear for voices and you disguised yours that night on the heath. When you threatened those youths your manner changed and there was a certain inflection in your tone – the same inflection you used when you threatened Osgood on the heath. Gentleman James, get back into the coach. No man walks out on me until I dismiss them. Come back to my rooms. I have a hunger to be alone with you, my bold highwayman.'

Japhet hesitated and Celestine patted the seat beside her. 'There is a hundred guineas on your head, but your freedom is precious to me. It would be a pity to inform Sir Pettigrew that I know the identity of the man who robbed him. He has vowed to see you hang.'

Japhet remained outside the coach, but his stare was wary as he studied her. 'I make my living as an honest horse dealer, nothing else.'

She leaned forward and ran a hand along his clean-shaven cheek. 'You are too exciting a lover to hang, and as a partnership we can both become very rich. You have very remarkable eyes, long-lashed and hazel in colour. They are the eyes of Gentleman James and they were clearly visible in the light from the coach lantern.'

'Celestine, my dear, it is time for this game to end. It is not amusing. I am not Gentleman James. You must seek such sport elsewhere.'

The feral glitter in her eyes intensified. 'You have such memorable eyes, Gentleman James – eyes a woman would not easily forget.' When Japhet stepped back with every sign of impatience, her expression hardened. 'Osgood will remember when I point these facts out to him. It is time for Gentleman James to be generous with his booty and I shall have the pick of the jewels you steal for myself. That is the price of your freedom.'

Again Japhet felt a noose tightening around his throat. The novelty and excitement of his affair with Celestine had turned sour. He knew he could not risk ending their relationship immediately, for Celestine had a vengeful streak. She would not hesitate to denounce him for the publicity his trial would bring her. Had the actress been a man, he would have fought her in a duel to defend his honour. There was no such retribution for a woman. For now he could see no other way but to play along with her schemes and extricate himself from her clutches when an opportunity arose.

He cursed his foolishness. He had always been reckless but never this foolhardy. To win such a notorious woman as Celestine for a mistress, when wealthy men could not always buy her favours, had been an irresistible lure, a seductive challenge that had paid no heed to reason. It had soothed his wounded pride over the treatment he had received from Gwendolyn's mother. Now he saw the full danger of allowing his emotions to control his head. He had misjudged the depth of the actress's greed and spite. He had seen what he had wanted to see, heard only what he wanted to hear, and risked everything in his quest to possess her. And he believed his wits would extricate him from any repercussions.

As he wavered the triumph was clear on Celestine's face. He had to dash it or be crushed. 'Celestine, I am your devoted servant in all things. The gift of your favours has been my greatest joy, but I cannot fulfil this role you would place upon me.' He bowed to her. 'I am mortified that as a humble horse dealer I cannot afford to lavish upon you the jewels you deserve. You are the Darling of London – the city is at your feet. How can I, poor country gentleman that I am, hope to be worthy of you? Farewell, dear lady.'

Celestine could not believe that Japhet would walk away from her ultimatum. Her face mottled with fury as he strode unmolested through the crowd of beggars in the alley. She yelled at the coachman to drive her home and refused to look at Japhet as they passed. She would not receive the knave again. Anger turned quickly to malice. No, she would not let him so easily off her hook. In the loneliness of her carriage she admitted the pain of her heartache. She loved the knave. 'What I want, I make sure I have,' she vowed. 'And I want you, Japhet Loveday. By fair means or foul. I shall have you.'

Japhet could not dismiss his unease as he walked away from Celestine. He could not risk her informing the authorities of her suspicions.

At the mess he had woven about his life, Japhet regretted his recklessness. By his pursuit of gratification he had put not only his life in danger, but would bring heartbreak and shame to his family. That he found unacceptable.

And what of Gwendolyn? When he had seen Gwen at the theatre and Celestine had brazenly demanded his attention, Gwen's misery had been obvious. Guilt at the pain he had seen in Gwen's eyes had made him stay away from visiting the Mercers' house in the last weeks.

His mind churned in turmoil. He had been reckless and irresponsible in the past but never like this. Celestine had lured him as powerfully as a Siren and, like the Sirens of ancient myth, she had used him for her own ends. Could he avoid destroying himself on the rocks that had awaited the shipwrecked sailors lured by those Sirens of old?

St John joined Adam and Long Tom on the quarterdeck as *Pegasus* sailed through the wide expanse and length of Chesapeake Bay. Adam was at the helm, and Long Tom leaned his back against the rail overlooking the half-deck as they chatted and laughed together. St John nodded to them both. Conversation between him and Adam had been sparse since their fight. St

John was still unconvinced that Rowena was his daughter and not his brother's.

'We should be at the Penhaligan plantation within the hour,' Adam addressed St John as he followed a ship ahead of them along the mid-channel.

The three men had changed out of the sea-stained jackets and breeches worn during the voyage. The day was overcast but there was no sea mist and Adam had studied the landscape as they sailed past.

Tidewater Virginia extending south-eastward towards the Chesapeake Bay was a rich lowland, which was intersected by several deep and navigable rivers: the Potomac, the Rappahannock and the James. Along these rivers ran a web of smaller rivers, many of which were large enough to carry ships out to the ocean. The seaway was busier than he had expected, although from the merchants and chart makers he had spoken to in England, he knew that slave ships from Africa and the West Indies were a frequent sight. Other ships carried clothing and household furnishings, as did *Pegasus*. And vessels left Virginia laden with hogsheads of tobacco from the vast plantations spread along the coast.

From his own cargo, Adam expected to reap a handsome profit. He intended to fill the hold with tobacco for the return voyage to England. Also the letters of marque given to him by the British Government gave him permission to attack and seize any French ship they encountered. Such a venture could make his fortune, enabling him to rebuild Boscabel, or result in him losing everything including his life.

Adam did not contemplate failure. He was a sea-soned sailor and, with his years in the navy, the thrill of battle was in his blood. If he were to rebuild Boscabel to its full glory, life as a buccaneer would provide him with the fortune he needed.

An hour later they pulled alongside the wooden dock of Greenbanks, the Penhaligan plantation. Adam hailed the shore, awaiting an invitation before he stepped on land.

'Ahoy, Greenbanks! We are *Pegasus* out of Fowey, England. I am Captain Adam Loveday and cousin to Mr Garfield Penhaligan. Do I have your permission to dock?'

It was some minutes before a man strode on to the dock. He wore buckskin trousers and a loose-fitting jacket, and carried a shotgun over his arm. Adam repeated his greeting.

'Loveday, you say?' the man queried. 'Adam Loveday, the cousin from England?'

'Yes,' Adam returned. 'And my brother St John.'

'Mr Penhaligan is expecting you. Tie up. I am Hamish McLean, the overseer. I shall send word to the house.'

By the time *Pegasus* was safely moored a tall, slender man in his sixties had arrived at the dock and greeted them as they walked down the gangplank.

'Welcome to Greenbanks, cousins. Garfield Penhaligan at your service. We had no idea when you would arrive. We received your father's letter only last month.' He eyed the twins with a fierce blue stare and spread his hands. His silvery hair was completely white at the temples and ears, and tied back with a black satin bow. 'You are not alike enough to be taken for twins but there is no mistaking that you are brothers. Which is which?'

Adam made the introductions and turned to Long Tom. 'May I present my friend Sir Gregory Kilmarthen.'

Garfield Penhaligan looked taken aback but quickly recovered. 'We don't get too many titled gentlemen down this way. You will be the toast of the county, Sir Gregory. Welcome to Virginia, gentlemen.' He looked at the ship and frowned. 'Were not your wife and daughter to journey with you, St John?'

'My wife is dead, sir,' St John clipped out, his expression set. 'We thought it best if Rowena stayed with her grandparents, whom she adores. She is young, and a long sea voyage would have been upsetting for her.'

At his blatant lies, Adam glanced at St John. What had made his brother make such a statement? He could hardly contradict him about a matter of such import in front of a cousin they had just met.

Garfield Penhaligan led the way across the dock to where a carriage had pulled up. 'It is a half-mile to the house,' he explained. 'I thought your wife and daughter may be tired. My condolences and sympathy on your sad loss. Did it happen suddenly? When your father wrote six months past—'

'It was sudden and I find it painful to discuss,' St John interrupted.

Garfield nodded. 'I understand. It will change some

of the arrangements we had planned. A young widower will wish to mourn—'

'I came to Virginia to put many aspects of the past behind me. It would be discourteous not to join in any diversions or entertainments you may have planned, sir.'

In response Garfield lifted a white brow but made no comment. 'As you wish.'

As Garfield stepped into the carriage followed by Long Tom, Adam pulled St John to one side. 'What the devil was that all about?'

'Meriel is dead to me. I never want her name mentioned.' He shrugged off Adam's hold and entered the carriage.

Adam gazed across at the plantation as they sped towards the house. They passed a cluster of wooden buildings, with black women and small children sitting outside some of them, and he assumed they were the slaves' houses. Acres of land had been cleared, many of the fields lying fallow, though maize grew in those closer to the house.

'I thought Greenbanks was a tobacco plantation, sir.' Adam was curious.

'We are indeed,' Garfield said. 'But tobacco needs vast acres of lands. Within three years the soil is ruined and we have to clear more land. It is why you will see few towns in Virginia. The plantations are spread out and we try to grow or import what we need. Your ship is filled with expensive pieces of English and French furniture and oriental carpets, I trust. There will be great demand from our neighbours. I did write to your father with details concerning what is most required.'

'And we were most grateful for that information, sir,' Adam replied. 'We contacted an agent to procure what was needed in readiness for when I sailed.'

The carriage swung round a circular drive and Adam gazed up at a three-storeyed house with a white pillared portico. An elderly woman dressed in black, and a younger blonde woman stood at the top of the dozen steps that led to the entrance.

'My sister, Susannah, and my late wife's niece, Desiree Richmond.' Garfield introduced his family. 'Desiree is a widow. Her plantation, Broadacres, is ten miles downriver. It is somewhat isolated, and to our great delight she spends most of her time with us. My overseer, McLean, whom you have met, manages both estates.'

Desiree curtsied to the men, glancing from Adam to St John with pleasure. She was in her late twenties, her complexion fresh and her fair hair curled high on her head to fall in ringlets to her shoulders. 'I did not dare to hope that our cousins would be such handsome men. Such a pity they are both married.'

'My dear, our cousins will think you immodest,' Susannah Penhaligan remonstrated. She smiled at the twins. 'Eligible bachelors, especially young and handsome ones, are in short supply.'

'Tragically, St John has recently been widowed,' Garfield explained.

Desiree studied St John, and Adam saw that his

brother was also appraising her with more interest than was seemly. She was pretty, with an hour-glass figure and a forthright stare.

She held out her hand to St John. 'You have my condolences on your sad loss, sir. I know the pain of losing a beloved partner. But time and pleasant company are great healers.'

Garfield introduced Long Tom, who had been observing the outbuildings and Negro slaves as they worked in the garden and fields. Long Tom bowed to the two women. 'I am honoured to make your acquaintance, ladies.'

'Sir Gregory, we are honoured to have you in our home.' Susannah, who had ignored Long Tom's presence, now turned a bright smile upon him.

'The pleasure is mine, dear lady.' He turned his attention back to Garfield Penhaligan. 'Your plantation is clearly run on very different lines from the estates in England. I look forward to many discussions with you, sir.'

Adam had also been studying the workings of the plantation, and at the sight of so many slaves he found it hard not to show his disapproval. Whilst in the navy they had come across a slave ship that had been demasted and damaged in a squall. The ship's captain, first mate and bosun had died of food poisoning some days earlier. The slave ship was in danger of sinking and Adam had been sent on board to arrange repairs so that the ship could be taken in salvage. The conditions, the smell of fear and inhuman suffering had sickened him. More than a quarter of the four hundred slaves on board had died, many of those still shackled to their companions. It disturbed him to see men and women stripped of their freedom and sold into bondage. At least the slaves at Greenbanks appeared well fed. In the distance he could hear some of them singing as they chopped wood for the winter fires.

He abruptly recalled himself to the present as the family filed into the house. St John walked at the side of Desiree Richmond and the young woman talked animatedly, her manner coquettish enough to alert Adam that St John had been unwise to declare Meriel dead. St John had been sent to Virginia to escape the scandal of his trial, not to create a new one by becoming embroiled in the affections of an attractive and wealthy widow.

Chapter Fourteen

'I don't want you mixed up with that Hester Moyle.' Clem faced his wife, Keziah, across the kitchen table, his mood sour and threatening. He had been out with the fishing fleet all night and the catch had been poor. On the return to Penruan the weather had changed and he had battled back to harbour in rain and gale-force winds. Clem was tired and cold and in no mood for his wife's stubborn disregard of his wishes.

Keziah was tall and strappingly built, her amber hair straggling in wiry curls that hung unrestrained to her waist. Before speaking, she placed a hot toddy of brandy and water on the table for Clem and ladled out the thick rabbit stew that had been simmering on the range since she had lit it at first light.

'Hester has asked for me. She is my friend.' Keziah had never submitted to Clem's menacing behaviour. He had the reputation of a bully that rivalled that of his brother Harry, but he had never hit her and he knew that Keziah would leave him if he ever raised a hand to her. 'Hester's child be your niece, and precious little help she be getting from your family or her own.'

'She got what was coming to her.' Clem flung himself down on the wooden chair by the range and peeled off his sodden jacket and shirt. His hands were swollen with chilblains, and the pain from them shortened his temper. 'Hester made a fool out of our Harry when she wed Lanyon. It's her lookout that her marriage to Lanyon were illegal and she got nothing on his death.'

'The child is Harry's – the whole village knows that.' Keziah folded her arms across her chest, her eyes flashing as she prepared for a verbal battle.

Clem scowled and broke off some bread to dip into the stew. He was shivering and his sharp features were pinched and white. Usually Keziah fussed around him when he returned in such foul weather. Penruan cemetery was strewn with the graves of fishermen who had drowned and for the last three hours she had been worried about his safety.

But now, with her fears allayed, his surly manner antagonised her. 'Your brother promised to wed Hester if Lanyon were out of the way. He should stand by her. Her father threw her out. How's she gonna live and support a child?' Keziah scooped up a mound of risen dough from a bowl and kneaded it on the table with angry thumps.

'That be Harry's concern, not mine.' Clem downed his hot toddy and hunched over the table to spoon the hot stew into his mouth. He was still in his wet

213

breeches, which steamed from the heat of the fire in the range.

'I will not abandon a woman in need.' Keziah continued to pummel the dough with such vigour a cloud of flour formed around her. 'Hester be one of the few women who accepted me when I came to the village. Even now, some of the village women distrust me as an outsider and we've been wed eighteen months.'

'Hester used you to get near to Harry. We stuck by her when Lanyon were killed and Harry could not be found. That were enough. Harry don't want to know her and I'll stand by my brother, not his scheming whore.'

Keziah slammed the dough on to the table so hard, Clem splashed some hot stew over his hand and let out a disgruntled snarl. Keziah realised it was no use trying to reason with him. 'So a Sawle's word don't stand for much then, is that what you be saying?'

'The Sawles stand by each other.' Clem waved a stubby finger at his wife. 'You remember that, woman.'

'Don't you give me none of that talk, Clem Sawle. I've got my principles and I stick by them.'

She cut the dough into two and placed it into two tins and put them on the top of the range to continue to rise. While Clem finished his meal she went upstairs, lifted young Zach from his bed and, with her shawl wrapped around them both, carried him downstairs. She was also carrying a bundle wrapped in oilcloth.

As she walked past her husband to the door, he roared, 'Where you going and what you got there? I won't have you going to Hester. Do you hear me, woman?'

'I hear you, you old windbag,' Keziah snapped. At the sound of her raised voice Baltasar, the billy goat who followed his mistress everywhere like a dog, looked up from where he had been munching on some turnips that had rolled out of the store box in the corner of the kitchen.

The goat trotted to Keziah's side, his head lowered as he studied Clem. It would not be the first time the goat had butted Clem when his mistress and master had quarrelled. Clem, who feared no man, eyed the goat warily. Baltasar could charge without warning. Keziah doted on the beast and if Clem raised a hand to harm him, he would find himself exiled from her bed for a month.

'I just want to see that Hester be all right,' Keziah reasoned. 'It were a rum do the way that Goldie took her in. There be a few baby clothes of Zach's in the bundle. I bain't likely to need them.' Keziah's voice cracked with pain. She found it hard to accept that she was barren. Zach had been Clem's child by Tilly Glasson, sired before he wed Keziah. Tilly had worked in the Dolphin Inn, owned by his parents, and, unable to care for him, Tilly had left her child on Clem's doorstep after his marriage, her body found on the moor some days later.

Clem heard the pain in his wife's voice. He loved Keziah, who was the only woman who stood up to him and was not afraid to put him in his place if he stepped out of line. Few men would risk telling Clem Sawle their opinion of him.

He scratched the stubble on his chin. 'Give her the clothes if you must, but I bain't having Hester living here. I bain't falling out with Harry over this.'

Keziah opened her mouth to protest and snapped it shut. After a moment she said, 'Hester has an alms cottage to live in, but I will do what else I can for her. Harry can talk to me if he doesn't like it.'

She left the house and her long bouncing stride soon covered the distance down the hill to Lanyon's old house. She knocked loudly on the door, but stood waiting with some trepidation for it to open. Goldie Lanyon had scarcely been welcomed with open arms by the fishermen's wives, and Keziah had done no more than exchange a few polite words with the woman, when she had needed something from the shop.

Goldie opened the door and stepped back for Keziah to enter. The face of Lanyon's first wife was expressionless but the lines around her eyes and tightness to her mouth showed the hardness of the life that she had previously endured.

'Hester be upstairs,' Goldie said. 'Second door on the left.'

Hester was dozing, the baby in a drawer by the side of the bed. She woke up as Keziah approached the bed. 'Kezzie, I be so glad you came. I got no one I could turn to.'

'Looks like you bain't done too bad. Goldie Lanyon

had no need to take you in.'

Hester eased herself further up on the pillows. 'She be the last person I thought would help me, but Goldie has been really kind. It makes it hard to hate her. But for her I would be rich, and Harry—'

'There bain't no point in talking that way.' Keziah cut her short and picked up the baby to hold in her arms. 'What you gonna call her?'

'I thought Harriet.'

Keziah regarded her sombrely. 'That would be foolish to have her named after Harry. Forget him, Hester. He bain't no good.'

Hester started to weep and Keziah sat on the bed to console her. 'You have a beautiful daughter. She be the important one. Think of a name that be more fitting. Something joyful. The little mite deserves that at least. You could call her Joy, or Merry.'

'Merry Moyle don't sound too good,' Hester sighed.

Keziah patted her arm in gentle encouragement. 'You must make a new life for yourself.'

'But how? I be a fallen woman. Who will employ me? I don't want to work as a servant or in a tavern. I was good at my schooling but no one will employ a governess who has a child.'

'You got reading and writing?' Goldie said as she entered, carrying a silver tea tray and three porcelain cups. She put it on the table by the bed. 'Lanyon bain't stinted himself with every luxury. When I were with him all we had was wooden bowls and beakers. He sold my parents' pewterware to spend on drink.'

'Yes, I can read and write.' Hester tipped back her head with a show of pride. 'My father taught me.'

'Do you know figures and the like?' Goldie's stare was shrewd as she watched Hester whilst she poured the tea.

'Of course.'

'Um.' Without further explanation Goldie left the room and Hester glanced apprehensively at Keziah.

'She be a strange one. I'm gonna have to get out of here. The house gives me the creeps – this were Phyllis's room. Lanyon used to visit her at nights; she was useless as a servant.'

'Poor lass be dead now. Murdered by Lanyon when she stole his money.' Keziah passed Hester a cup of tea. 'You've got yourself in a mess and no mistake. I can give you some money to start a new life somewheres. You could go where you bain't known and call yourself a widow.'

'It wouldn't be right to take your money, Kezzie. But that be right kind of you. I don't want charity from the Sawles. It be for Harry to do right by me and keep his word.'

They fell silent at the sound of Goldie coming back up the stairs. She came into the room and threw one of the leather-bound ledgers on to the bed. 'Do you know anything about what be written in these?'

'Why should I tell you?'

'That be right, why should you?' Goldie shrugged and made to pick up the ledger.

'Lanyon were a moneylender, a banker for the smugglers and he owned property. The ledgers list the details.' Hester eyed the woman she regarded as her enemy with a sullen pout. 'I'm telling you that so I bain't beholding to you for taking me in like you did. This were my house—'

'Thank you.' Goldie put the ledger on the window-sill. 'I reckon not all his deals were legal.'

'Lanyon never discussed his business with me. Smuggling bain't legal, is it though?'

'You should go to a lawyer, Mrs Lanyon,' Keziah suggested. 'They will settle any business matter for you.'

'It's Goldie. I don't use that bastard's name. And I don't trust lawyers.'

Hester gave a dry laugh. She had been studying the older woman. 'You can't read, can you?'

'Happen I can, or happen I can't.'

'You must get some advice, Goldie.' Keziah was worried. 'Do you want me to look at the books? There could be something in there that may incriminate you in some way. Lanyon was pretty underhand in all his dealings. I know he charged extortionate interest rates to any he loaned money to, or who was in financial debt to him in some other way.'

'You understand these things?' Goldie persisted.

'No, but Hester does. She used to help her father with his books.'

Hester did not look pleased that Keziah had been so outspoken but she was proud of her education and accomplishments. There was a flash of her old defiant spirit as she replied, 'My father be a chandler. I helped in the shop and would sometimes tot up the figures at

219

the end of the week, if his eyes were tired.'

Goldie studied Hester. 'Did you love Lanyon, or marry him for his money?'

'That be a cruel question.' Keziah was horrified that after all Hester had suffered Goldie could challenge her in such a manner.

'It be reasonable enough in the circumstances.' Goldie folded her arms across her chest. 'I knew Lanyon for the bastard he was. He were brutal and mean and far from handsome. So what was the attraction to you, Hester?'

'I was scared of him.' Her face crumpled in misery. 'He paid me attention when Harry was unfaithful to me and brought me pretty things. I took them to spite Harry – make him jealous. I was a fool. Lanyon don't allow himself to be used. He threatened to ruin my father if I did not wed him and I think he would have killed me. Life with him was hell. I never wanted Lanyon. I never wanted his money when he was alive. Though I reckoned after all I had gone through it was compensation after his death. Harry and I would have had a grand life together.' She began to sob.

'And now your lover has abandoned you. You don't have much luck with men, do you?'

The baby started to whimper and Goldie watched as Hester, still snivelling, placed her to her breast. 'That kid ain't Lanyon's, is it?'

'Really, Mrs Lanyon, I do not think Hester should be subjected to—' Keziah interceded but was abruptly cut short.

'I be Goldie, I told you. Just Goldie. And, if that kid bain't Lanyon's then this young woman gets my respect and admiration for daring to put a cuckold's horns on him.'

Hester gave a muffled cry and looked up at Goldie in astonishment. 'This child is not Lanyon's. Her father bain't be much better from the way he lied and cheated on me. You be right, Goldie. I don't have no luck with men.' She kissed the baby's brow. 'I wanted a boy, thinking that would bring Harry back to me. It wouldn't. He told me just afore you found me on the quay that he only took me back to get his revenge on Lanyon. He was the one who wanted Lanyon's money. Harry did not love me.' She swallowed against her misery, but a more determined light brightened her eyes. 'I be glad the baby be a girl. I don't want to spend my life looking into Harry's face.'

Goldie nodded and Keziah, overcome with emotion at all Hester had suffered, put her arms around her. 'There, my lovely, you cry all you need. You deserve better than Harry Sawle. But what are you going to do now? You need to support the child.'

'I shall start life afresh where no one knows me. If I apply for a post as a widow, mayhap I can get work as a housekeeper. I'd be good at that and maybe I'd even get a fine house to live in. Here all I've got is an almshouse and everyone will either pity me or revile me. I could not stand that.'

'No one is going to pity you,' Goldie announced. 'I got you wrong. I thought you'd wed Lanyon for his money. I mistook the misery you were suffering as weakness. But you bain't weak. You've just shown that. I reckon we've got a lot in common, Hester Moyle-cum-Lanyon. You shook off his name fast enough once you knew how he had duped you. Many would have clung to it for the sake of respectability or sympathy.'

'The very sound of Lanyon's name stuck in my throat and made me feel sick,' Hester grimaced.

Goldie gave a dry laugh. 'Aye, it does, doesn't it? I need you to answer one more question. If you had Lanyon's money and your Harry came back to you, would you take him back?'

Hester stared down at the baby for a long moment before replying, 'If I did that I would have no respect for myself. He would always lie and cheat on me. No, I would not take him back if I had money to support my child alone.'

'Then you shall have that money.' Goldie became serious as she regarded the two women, who were slack-jawed with astonishment. 'I bain't just handing it over. I suffered at that bastard's hands far more than you. But I don't have no learning like you. I could never understand these books, or know if I'd been swindled or cheated. I reckon if we were business partners, you would appreciate what I could do for you and not cheat me.'

'How could we possibly be business partners? I don't want your charity.'

'It won't be charity. You'll work hard, same as I intend to.' Goldie placed her hands on her hips, her chin jutted and her face resuming its harsh lines. 'I bain't never lived alone. A bawdy house and the lodgings I ran were always full of people. And this house gives me the creeps. I can feel the malevolence of his presence. I could take his money and set up home in a grand house and never need to work again, but I would not be happy with an idle life. The property and businesses remain mine, but I'll pay you half the profits to keep the books and help me with the running of the business.'

Hester burst into tears and Goldie stiffened with affront. 'Well, if that don't suit, that's fine by me.' She walked briskly to the door.

'Don't go.' Hester recovered enough to speak. 'Please. I be crying because it be all so unexpected. Why are you so generous?'

'It bain't generosity. It be common sense. I reckon we both want to show the people here, and the world in general, that women may become the prey of men, but they do not have to become victims.'

'I accept your offer, Goldie.' Hester continued to look stunned, then she stared into her new partner's eyes and laughed. 'It will be good to show Harry Sawle how well I can do without him.'

She held out the baby to Keziah. 'Say hello to Joy Marigold Keziah Moyle. I want you both to be her godmothers. Do you think Clem will allow you?'

'He'd better not try and stop me,' Keziah grinned.

Goldie wiped a tear from her eye. 'I lost two kids when they were babbies – not Lanyon's either. It will be grand to be godmother to this little one.' She took

Hester's hand. 'The little one will want for nothing. She will be a seal upon our partnership, Hester Moyle. There'll be some rum gossip in Penruan when this all gets out. It will be good for trade, you see if it won't.'

Admiral Algernon Beaumont received his nephew and new bride propped up in a huge four-poster bed in his house overlooking Plymouth Sound. He was bed-ridden with a broken hip that refused to mend, following a fall some weeks ago. His mood was irascible from the pain and frustration that his injury prevented him from attending war councils at the Admiralty.

Oak linen-fold panelling lined the room and over the black marble fireplace hung a painting of the first ship the admiral had commanded. On a tailor's wooden figure was the admiral's uniform heavily adorned with gold braid. The sight of it intimidated Francis. It was as though it was there as a reminder that he had been cashiered from the navy, the disgrace of which his grandfather had vowed he would never forgive him.

The room reeked of rum, which the admiral drank copiously to dull the pain of his injury. The spirit aggravated an inflammation in his gut that also added to his ill humour.

'So you finally towed the line and got yourself a bride,' Admiral Beaumont barked. At sixty-seven, even with his nightshirt and black-embroidered gold dressing robe covering his skeletal figure, his manner remained autocratic. A red turban covered his bald head and his hooded eyes regarded his visitors over a beaked nose.

Francis Beaumont stood to attention at the foot of the bed and glared at his wife, who was giggling in an inane fashion, whilst partially concealing herself behind a navy-blue bed hanging. 'May I present my wife, Maria, sir?'

'It is such an honour, sir.' Maria bobbed a curtsy and giggled nervously under the fierceness of his glare.

'Not an imbecile, is she?' the admiral barked. 'Come forward, woman, and let me see you. And enough of that foolish simpering. Can't abide women who gush and simper.'

Maria cringed at his tone and moved closer to Beaumont to cling to his arm. He angrily shook off her hand. Her touch and presence nauseated him.

'What settlement did Thackwell make on her?' the admiral demanded.

'Five thousand, sir.' A tic appeared in Beaumont's eye as he evaded the full truth. John Thackwell had waited until the betrothal was announced before informing Francis that his daughter's settlement would be put into the care of his lawyers. Money would be paid out for a suitable house for the couple and thereafter two hundred pounds a year would be paid to them. Once Maria produced their second son, the money would be released plus a further two thousand paid into the account.

Beaumont had been furious. John Thackwell was

aware that the couple's first son would one day inherit the admiral's estate, and was equally determined that a grandson of his would inherit in his own right the tin mines and the Thackwell estate. Beaumont had been tempted to call off the match, but that could mean that he was ostracised by society. It was only two months since his engagement announcement to Gwendolyn Druce had so disastrously backfired. For it to happen a second time would make him a laughing stock.

'Only five thousand. A paltry sum for Thackwell to cough up. Though I suppose that since your wife is the heir to Thackwell's tin mines and estate the interim sum is adequate.' His grandfather nodded. 'I'm not getting any younger. I want to see you produce a son before I die.'

'You said I need but marry to secure my inheritance,' Francis raged.

'Remember to whom you speak,' the admiral rapped out, making Beaumont flinch. 'I have not forgotten the shame you brought to our family when you were cashiered from the navy. Six generations of Beaumonts have served in high office and you lost your commission as a lowly lieutenant. A great-grandson is what I need – another Beaumont to carry on the honourable tradition of serving the Admiralty and our country.'

The interview with his grandfather fuelled Francis's hatred for the Lovedays. His grandfather would never forgive him for the duel with Adam Loveday, which had resulted in his lost commission. To produce a son, he was forced to live with a woman he neither liked nor desired. The Lovedays were responsible for all the ills that had befallen him. The time had come for them to pay for the indignities he had suffered.

Chapter Fifteen

'Thomas, you must seek out Japhet and talk some sense into him.' Margaret Mercer stood at the foot of the stairs to waylay her son as he was leaving for the bank. 'Japhet is avoiding us. He promised to call; that was a month ago.'

'Japhet probably feels guilty about Gwen.' Thomas was late for an appointment and had no wish to meddle in his cousin's life.

'And so he should.' Margaret Mercer ushered Thomas into the privacy of the empty dining room to continue the conversation. 'Gwen is miserable. If Japhet were not so besotted with that Yorke woman, he would be paying court to Gwen. From what Gwen had told me of their relationship, Japhet reveres her more than any other woman.'

'We cannot presume to know what Japhet feels for Gwen.' Thomas knew it was pointless trying to deter his mother from her matchmaking. For years she had been driven to find a wife for himself when he had had no inclination to marry. But Thomas liked

Gwendolyn Druce and it disturbed him to witness the way she was suffering at Japhet's neglect.

'Japhet is never easy to track down if he does not want to be found. I will leave messages at his lodgings and usual haunts for him to contact me. Mama, you may be making too much of this. Japhet is not a man to avoid our company just because Gwen is here, but he may prefer not to encounter her. He is loyal to his family, but I suspect he feels that his presence would upset Gwen.'

'Because he cares for her and is too stubborn to admit it.' Margaret would not be halted in her desire to see the couple united. She picked up a yellow hot-house rose that had fallen from its vase and twisted it in her fingers.

Thomas kissed his mother's cheek. 'Mama, you cannot meddle in this. You only succeed in driving Japhet away. If Japhet cares for Gwen he will come to that conclusion in his own time.'

Margaret threw up her hands in exasperation. 'When will that be? When Gwen is old and grey? I've tried to make Gwen take an interest in other men, but she will have none of them. Perhaps a dose of jealousy will stir Japhet from his complacency.'

'He may think it is for the best that Gwen has found herself another suitor. He is oddly protective of her welfare and has said many times that she would be happier with someone else.'

Margaret jabbed the rose into the vase with such force that its stem snapped. 'He is making excuses to cling to his freedom. I know you think I am interfering, but I have seen the way Japhet looks at Gwen. He cares deeply for her. And Gwen is also becoming stubborn; she will take only so many blows to her pride. She is an independent woman.'

Agitated, Margaret removed the broken flower from the vase and picked at its petals. 'Gwen was talking yesterday of taking rooms of her own. She believes that she is becoming a burden to us. Which is nonsense. I enjoy her company, but she will not listen.'

'I cannot approve of Gwen living on her own.' Thomas voiced his concern. 'But we are not her family and she has the means to support herself.'

'Then get Japhet to talk to her. Only he can resolve this matter one way or another.' Margaret pressed home her intent. 'The Christmas season is almost upon us. I will be offended if Japhet is in London and does not spend the festivities with us.'

Thomas left the house to walk the quarter-mile to Mercer and Lascalles Bank. It was a bleak and dreary morning, a sulphurous mist distorting the outline of buildings and turning the populace into ghostly spectres. Even the cries of the costers sounded mournful.

The gloomy weather added to Thomas's sense of foreboding about his cousin. He was troubled by Japhet's behaviour. He had not seen Japhet to speak to since they had met at the theatre a month ago, when his cousin had accompanied Celestine Yorke. Twice since then Japhet had been at the theatre at the same time as Thomas, but his cousin took pains to avoid his family.

It was obvious that Celestine Yorke was Japhet's mistress, and she was a self-centred and heartless woman who, Thomas feared, was dangerous to his cousin. Celestine demanded that everyone pander to her vanity and delighted in playing her lovers against one another. It was rumoured that Celestine was also Sir Pettigrew Osgood's mistress and that he paid her bills.

This worried Thomas, especially when he heard that Osgood had a vengeful streak. He would resent paying a mistress's bills if the woman did not keep herself solely for his pleasure. Japhet could be hot-headed and, an accomplished swordsman, he had duelled before now when his pride had been slighted. Although duels were illegal and frowned upon, they were still fought over matters of honour.

Thomas shook his head to rationalise his thoughts. Japhet may have a wild streak but Thomas had always known him to be inherently decent in his dealings with others.

The next three evenings Thomas visited all of Japhet's known haunts, leaving messages for his elusive cousin. The landlord of his lodgings informed him that Japhet spent infrequent nights in his rooms. Thomas knew that his cousin was still in London because Lucien had seen him escorting Celestine Yorke to a cockfight. The actress was not currently performing in a play or Thomas would also have left messages at the theatre.

Japhet was usually more discerning about the women he became embroiled with. The last two plays

Celestine Yorke had appeared in had played to dwindling audiences, and it was rumoured that many of the theatre managers were tired of her demands and tantrums. Thomas was amazed that an actress with dubious talent had kept her popularity with playgoers for so long. The public were fickle and demanded freshness and excitement, and now younger actresses were usurping Celestine's hold on audiences' affections. As her popularity waned so her meanness of spirit and manner became more apparent in her attitude on stage. She ignored the common people and pandered to the depleting number of wealthy gallants who aspired to win her favours.

At the end of the week Thomas was at his office at the bank when his clerk announced, 'Mr Japhet Loveday has called, Mr Mercer. He sends his compliments and asks if you are free to see him. Your next appointment is not for an hour, sir.'

Thomas set aside the papers he had been studying on a new mining investment. 'Show Mr Loveday in.'

The oak-panelled office was dominated by portraits of Thomas's father and grandfather; the Sheraton leather-topped desk piled high with ledgers and papers.

Japhet greeted Thomas with a grin and accepted the glass of claret Thomas offered to him, but he did not sit in the chair indicated and restlessly paced the office.

'How is Aunt Margaret?'

'Mama is well, though she is perplexed that you have not called.'

'And Amelia and Lisette? Are they well?' Japhet continued to pace.

'Amelia is troubled that Lisette has been admitted to Dr Claver's hospital.'

Japhet paused in mid-stride. 'Good God, I had no idea! Is Uncle Edward in London?'

'No.' Thomas briefly informed his cousin of the family news. 'If you had called on us you would know this. What the devil has got into you, Japhet? You have never neglected the family before. And you have not asked about Gwen.'

'What is there to say? I was surprised to see her in London with you.' He sat down and crossed his legs, leaning back in the chair in a nonchalant manner. Thomas was not fooled. Something was troubling Japhet.

'Did you lead Gwen on?' Thomas accused, his patience with his cousin wearing thin. His mother had not given him a moment's peace that he had not ensured that Japhet came to their house and spoke with Gwen. Even Georganna had taken Gwen's side. 'It's none of my affair, but I have to live with Mama and her romantic ideals. Gwen is a level-headed woman. I suspect she would not have come to London if you had not shown her some encouragement as to your feelings towards her.'

Japhet did not answer and his face was devoid of emotion as he stared down into his empty claret glass. 'I never told Gwen that I cared for her in any way other than as a friend. What made her take it into her head to come to London?'

'Her mother was trying to force her to wed Lieutenant Beaumont. Lady Anne was making Gwen's life miserable. The betrothal was even announced in the *Mercury* without Gwen's knowledge or agreement to the match.'

Japhet let out a harsh breath, but kept his opinion to himself. Finally he said, 'That must have been hard on her. She had pluck to defy her mother. Now I suppose Aunt Margaret would see her wed and has a list of worthy beaux for her to be introduced to.'

'Is that all you can say?' Thomas banged the table with his hand and stood up to glare across at Japhet. 'Gwen loves you. What the devil was in your mind when you kissed her, if you did not care for her? She is not the type for dalliance.'

'Of course she is not. I was wrong to give in to my impulse as I did.'

Thomas studied his cousin, surprised at the tension in Japhet's tall figure. 'Why will you not admit that you care for her? Do you want to see her wed to another man? Is a fling with the Yorke woman worth causing Gwen so much misery?'

Pain creased Japhet's brow and he rubbed his hand across his jaw. 'I never meant to hurt Gwen. You know how I am, Tom? I am not ready for marriage. Gwen deserves better than anything I could offer her.'

'Yes she does, but she will never see that,' Thomas snapped. He was aware that Japhet was heading for disaster. There was little money left in his account with the bank after his recent sale of three horses. He was regularly drawing out large sums, which, if he was not buying horses, must be being lost at the gaming tables.

Thomas tried a different approach, appealing to Japhet's gallantry. 'You at least owe it to Gwen to speak with her. Otherwise she will wait all her life for you to come to your senses – or until you marry someone else.'

'Why can she not hate me?' Japhet frowned and sadly shook his head. 'Gwen must realise that Celestine is my mistress.'

'But you do not love Celestine Yorke, do you? While your heart remains free, Gwen will always hope that one day you will turn to her.'

'I wish it was that easy.' Japhet looked haggard. 'I've made a mess of my life since I came to London. I have been losing heavily at cards and have run up debts. I came here today to ask for a loan of one thousand pounds.'

Thomas frowned. 'You have no collateral, cousin. The bank cannot give you such a loan. And I have not that much spare cash. I have been paying back Uncle Edward for the Loveday losses sustained when the bank all but failed.'

'I should not have asked. It is my problem.' Anguish momentarily darkened Japhet's hazel eyes, and then he shrugged. 'I shall raise it somehow.'

There was an edge to Japhet's tone that alarmed Thomas. After some deliberation, he said, 'I shall personally guarantee your loan, Japhet. You would not have asked if you were not in dire need. You helped save me from debtors' prison when the bank was in trouble. There is no way you could raise such an amount by legal means.'

'I appreciate what you are doing, Tom.' Japhet brightened. 'Lady Luck has abandoned me at cards.'

'Is it not time to put that side of your life behind you, Japhet? I'll not see *you* in a debtors' prison.' Thomas sat down and leaned forward in his chair. 'You've never got in that deep before, Japhet. What madness is driving you?'

Japhet shrugged. 'I earn my living gambling.'

Thomas knew a lecture would only antagonise Japhet, so he added, 'The only condition to the loan is that you call at our home tomorrow and speak with Gwen. You have not treated her as she deserves. God knows what you put into her mind when you were in Cornwall. She is a family friend and her affections cannot be trifled with.'

'I have always been honest with Gwen,' Japhet heatedly defended.

'But have you been honest with yourself about your friendship with her?'

Japhet's expression froze and he linked his long fingers and flexed his knuckles until they cracked.

'My marriage to Georganna saved the bank. You would do well to consider Gwen as your bride.'

'I've no taste for marriage,' Japhet retorted.

'Do you think I found it easy to accept the married state? My reasons for avoiding marriage were far more relevant than yours, cousin. I have no taste for women. But in Georganna I found the solution that suited both of us. We have a perfect friendship.'

'But is Georganna happy?' Japhet fired back with unusual virulence that surprised Thomas.

'Yes. She hated her old life and loves the theatre world.' He hesitated briefly before adding, 'She has no wish for children.'

'Then you were fortunate in your choice.'

'As you would be with Gwen. She truly cares for you, Japhet, and her fortune would solve all your problems. Do you intend to lead this shiftless life for the rest of your days? I thought your dream was to raise racehorses? Marry Gwen and all that will be possible.'

Japhet shook his head, his jaw set in a stubborn line.

'Then at least make your peace with her. She deserves that. To make it easier for you, I shall ensure that Georganna takes Mama shopping for the afternoon. Gwen will be at the house alone. Mama also expects you to join us for the Christmas festivities.'

'It will be a pleasure to spend Christmas with you. Thank you for the loan. I need a draft from your bank to meet a debt of honour of eight hundred pounds this evening. I'll have fifty in gold now and the rest I intend to put aside for the horse sales.'

'And the fifty? Gambling is no way to recoup your losses,' Thomas warned.

'It has not failed me in the past. I feel lucky tonight and I want to repay my debt to you as soon as I can.' Before Thomas could comment, he grinned, adding, 'I will attend on Gwen tomorrow. At the very least she deserves an apology from me. But matchmaking ill suits you, coz.'

Thomas rang the bell on his desk and, when the clerk appeared, asked for the bank draft and gold coin to be brought to his office immediately. While they waited for the money to be delivered, Japhet paced the office, subjecting Thomas to a volley of questions about the play he was penning.

'Georganna insists that I spend at least two hours every day on my play and protects me against Mama's demands to escort her about town. But it progresses slowly. The Haymarket have shown an interest in putting it on in the spring.'

The clerk returned with the money and bank draft. As Japhet walked to the door, Thomas was prompted to say, 'Japhet, you cannot continue with the uncertainty of the life you are now leading. We all worry that you will destroy yourself.'

There was a haunted look in Japhet's eyes, although he shrugged and laughed: 'I value my life and liberty. But sometimes a devil rides my shoulder. It would be worse if I were foolish enough to marry a woman I did not love just for her money. That would destroy us both.'

The weather seemed determined to sabotage the launch of the brigantine at the Loveday shipyard. December was a notorious month for dense sea mists, storms and persistent rain. Only the most violent storms stopped the men from working, but even a sea mist could make the scaffolding slippery, and construction progressed slowly.

Usually a patient man, Edward found his temper

sorely tested as the strain of the last months took its toll. He missed his sons and he missed his wife more. It still rankled that Amelia had deserted him. The letter she had written informing him of Lisette's admittance to Dr Claver's hospital had held little warmth. Her manner angered him, and his reply condoning her actions for Lisette's treatment had been polite rather than affectionate.

With the need to complete the brig on time to avoid compensation payments, Edward laboured alongside the shipwrights. Weariness seeped into his bones and calluses hardened on his palms from shaping and fixing the supporting beams amidships. Following the long hours in the yard Edward would return to Trevowan and be up until midnight dealing with the problems of the estate. Then he would sleep fitfully, waking in the hour before dawn without the warmth and comfort of his wife at his side.

Sleep would desert him as he lay listening to the wind pummelling the windowpanes and groaning down the chimney. The edge of the Persian carpet flapped against the floorboards from the draught under the door, and the ticking of a clock was as persistent as a heartbeat. Every sound drove sleep further from him, the problems of the day stripping away any chance of rest.

He could not comprehend Amelia's censure of his affair with Eleanor. It had taken place so long before he had met his wife that he could not see how it affected the love and regard in which he held Amelia. Edward accepted that Amelia's sensibilities were offended, but the past was over and done with, and he felt no regrets or guilt at his love for Eleanor, only the consequences that his beloved had suffered from her malicious husband. Amelia had deserted him, judging him without allowing him to tell her of his feelings at Tamasine's arrival. Such conduct he found reprehensible, especially when so many problems beset his family and their finances.

He was grateful that Elspeth did her best to support him by efficiently running the house, though his sister resented the time she must spend away from the hunt, and never ceased to remind him that Amelia had abandoned her duties. Elspeth would also absent herself from his company in the evenings, when Rowena would wake crying and calling out for her parents. Edward had never felt so alone, or his responsibilities so onerous.

Another day dawned bleak and forbidding, and heavy rain accompanied Edward on his ride to the yard. The men were already at work. Two horses pulling a large tree trunk from the woodpile stacked behind the cottages to the sawpit splashed through the puddles, their heads bent against the rain. Edward gave Ben Mumford his orders for the day and scanned the chink of light that was brightening the horizon.

'God willing, the rain will let up today,' he said to Ben. 'If we had two weeks without rain we could achieve so much.'

'Bain't much we can do about the weather, sir, but men want the brig finished on time. It be a matter of their pride.'

Edward spent an hour prioritising which bills could be paid that week and the wages met. Several creditors were becoming impatient and were threatening not to deliver the next order without payment. The dividend money from his investments that Thomas had brought to Cornwall when he attended the trial was all but spent.

He threw down his quill, the figures in front of him blurring, and he pushed the papers aside and dropped his head into his hands. Outside he heard the sound of Tamasine's laughter as she called Scamp to his food. His daughter's arrival into his life was another complication, but he did not regret having fathered a child with Eleanor. He regretted only that his daughter could not be openly acknowledged, and that she had been hidden away for so many years. With his family away from Trevowan, Edward was drawn to become better acquainted with Tamasine. He would often look up from his paperwork to see her gazing across at the office. It had become a habit to ask her to join him and they would regularly share the brew of tea Pru Jansen brought to him of an afternoon. Each renewal of their acquaintance brought him increasing pleasure, and in her company the pressure of his burdens eased.

The commencement of hammering in the yard told him that the shipwrights had returned from lunch. To complete the cutter on time the men were working from six in the morning until nine at night, starting and ending the day using lanterns hung inside the vessel and along the scaffolding to illuminate their work.

241

Edward rose, put on his greatcoat and wrapped a muffler around his neck. Outside his boots squelched in the churned-up mud in the yard. Ben Mumford was by the water's edge when Edward approached him.

Ben doffed his cap. 'The rope for the rigging arrived this afternoon and has been stacked in the storeroom, Mr Loveday. And Seth Wakeley says that the ship's rails will be completed in another two weeks. Also Moyle has sent the pulleys you ordered from his chandlery.'

Edward nodded. 'I saw the bills on my desk. To stand any chance of meeting the completion date to hand over to the owner by the end of February, the brigantine must be launched by mid-January and the masts fitted when she is afloat within a week of that date.'

'With the extra carpenters you brought in, that shouldn't be a problem, sir.'

'Good. The men have done well, despite the weather.' He glanced at the sky as he walked to the blacksmith's to check that the anchor chain would be completed by the weekend. The rain clouds were clearing and a watery sun was trying to break through. He hoped it was a good omen and that the weather would be drier for some days. It would help them to make up for lost time. The setback caused by the break-ins at the yard was disastrous in terms of both time and money he could ill-afford.

The sight of the empty dry dock was a continual frustration to Edward. Since Thadeous Lanyon had spread his rumours that the wreck of his ship was caused by poor design and workmanship, the dry dock had been empty. The malicious rumours had lost Edward all his customers, and the expense of the construction of the dry dock had been the cause of the last loan Edward had raised on the yard – a loan he was still struggling to repay.

As he crossed to the forge he heard the children in the schoolhouse singing a carol. It made his step falter. Christmas was but two weeks away and for the first time that he could remember his sons and close family, except for Elspeth, would not be around him. The wave of longing he felt for Amelia was angrily stamped down, her lack of loyalty cutting deeper. The situation between himself and his wife was intolerable but unless she came to her senses and returned to Trevowan, he feared the rift between them would only get worse.

Chapter Sixteen

Japhet awoke to his head pounding and his tongue feeling that he had a mouthful of fleece. He had fallen asleep fully dressed on his bed; even his boots had not been removed. He staggered upright and clutched his aching skull with his hands. With a groan, he plunged his head into the washing bowl of cold water and held it there to try to clear the pain. It did little to help.

'The devil mocks me for I drank little last night.' Japhet peered into his shaving mirror and grimaced at the sight of his bloodshot eyes. There was a bitter aftertaste in his mouth that had accompanied the last three mornings after drinking and gaming at Celestine's house.

When he examined his money pouch he was dismayed to discover that it was empty. Last night he had arrived at Celestine's with fifty guineas, hoping to recoup his losses at a gaming party. There was little left of the loan from Thomas after he had settled his gaming debts. With bitter reverie Japhet grimaced at his reflection in the mirror. Lady Luck had never turned so cruelly against him in the past. Celestine brought him nothing but ill fortune. He winced as he remembered that he had promised Thomas that he would visit Gwendolyn today. Never had he felt less proud of himself.

He shaved and changed his crumpled clothing. Taking care to appear at his best. He may have paved the path to his own damnation but with the Christmas festivities almost upon them, he would not allow his family to see how bleak his future had become. His usual optimism returned. Something might yet come up, for opportunities were often there to a man who kept his wits about him.

Stubbornly he refused to consider Thomas's suggestions that he wed Gwendolyn to solve his financial problems. Aunt Margaret's matchmaking had been the bane of his life for years and he had no intention of succumbing to her schemes now.

An hour later none of his misgivings showed in his manner as he bowed over Gwendolyn's hand when she received him in the drawing room at his aunt's house.

'Japhet, how good of you to call. Your aunt has gone to the Royal Exchange with Georganna.' There was coolness to her tone and her lashes veiled her eyes. She wore pale blue, a colour that always made the best of her creamy complexion and enhanced the richness of her chestnut hair.

'It is you I came to see, Gwen. Thomas said that your mother made your life difficult after I left Cornwall. That was my fault.'

'How could I blame you for leaving? Mama was wicked to say the things she did about you.'

Her loyalty touched him. He reached for her hand and again lifted it to his lips. 'Why do you tolerate me? I am unworthy of your esteem.'

'Should I not be the judge of that?' She removed her hand from his hold and sat on a padded settle in the centre of the room. 'Do sit, Japhet. I shall have a crick in my neck if I have to look up at you.'

He sat next to her and searched for the words to make amends. 'I do not know what to say to you, Gwen. I wish I did. I know only that there would be a barrenness in my life, if I thought I would never see you again.'

She hung her head, shielding her eyes from his gaze. Her quiet dignity tore at his conscience and he sighed. 'I am a knave to neglect you so. There is so much to see in London. Permit me to escort you to some diversion this afternoon. Where would you like to go? A freak show? The menagerie at the Tower of London?'

'I do not want you to be kind to me out of pity.'

'Pity is the last emotion with which I regard you, Gwen. Where do you get these notions? I am here because I enjoy your company. Will that suffice?'

She stood up and walked away from him, and her voice sounded strained when she spoke. 'I have the headache and must decline your kind offer.'

'Then I shall call tomorrow. If the weather conditions are appropriate, a hot-air balloon is taking to the skies in St James's Park. It is a marvellous spectacle to behold.'

'I am busy tomorrow, Japhet. I saw such a sight some weeks ago with Georganna and Thomas. Another time perhaps.'

Her refusal shocked him. 'As you wish.'

He stayed another half-hour but Gwendolyn remained distracted throughout. Even his wittiest jokes raised only a wan smile. That left him discomfited. His life was in chaos and he had expected his meeting with Gwen to bring him a sense of peace.

'You are cross with me,' he said as he took his leave. 'I ask your pardon for offending you at the theatre, Gwen. I never meant to hurt you.'

Anger flared in her eyes. 'You have not offended me, Japhet. I know well enough the way you conduct your life. If it gives you satisfaction there is no more to say. I thought you more worthy . . . but no mind.' She shook her head as though impatient with herself. 'You must live your life and spend it in the company you choose.'

'You *are* angry that I have so neglected you.'

'You presume too much, sir,' she responded with heat. 'I do not like to see a friend who is capable of achieving so much, wasting his life in the mindless pursuit of pleasure.'

'Is that how you regard me?' Now that she had finally voiced her censure of his conduct, he was shocked at how deeply it cut into his self-esteem.

They were interrupted by the arrival of Amelia, followed by his aunt and Georganna's return. After greeting them Japhet looked for Gwendolyn and found that she was no longer in the drawing room.

Disconcerted by her manner, he left, declining his aunt's invitation to dine with them. Gwendolyn's criticism still rankled and out of a perverse sense of rebellion against it he called upon Celestine. When he arrived at her house he found that the gaming tables were out in readiness for an evening of cards.

He viewed them with little enthusiasm. Painful as Gwendolyn's censure had been, he acknowledged that she was right. It was time to end his relationship with Celestine and regain his self-respect and integrity. He had enough money to invest on a couple of horses, which he could sell at a profit.

It was galling to admit that he had also been unnerved by the actress's threats to denounce him as a highwayman. Celestine was capable of such a vengeful act. It was time to extricate himself from her clutches but to do so, and ensure that he kept his freedom, he needed to handle the situation with care. A handsome piece of jewellery would buy her off, but for that he needed more cash. He decided to bide his time whilst gradually allowing his relationship with Celestine to cool. That would also take diplomacy, for each time they were apart she quizzed him with growing jealousy, and her demands on his time were becoming more frequent and onerous.

It was an hour and a half before Celestine's evening guests usually arrived. At such a time Celestine would be awaiting Japhet in her bedchamber and they would make love before she dressed for the evening. Tonight the maid showed him straight to the parlour where Celestine was attired in a low-cut scarlet evening gown. Her hair was elaborately coiffured and topped by a new headdress of white ostrich feathers held in place by a large diamond-studded clip. Two dandified men were lounging in chairs.

'Dear Japhet, Sir Marcus and his friend Barty Bannister are to dine with us,' Celestine said after their greeting. 'They so enjoyed their evening at cards last week that I have invited more of my friends to attend later.'

Japhet bowed to the men, who returned to their conversation, which was praising a recent performance by Celestine. Both men had been at Celestine's gaming party last week and it was to Sir Marcus that Japhet had lost so heavily. Sir Marcus was portly and indolent by nature, and Japhet had summed the baronet up as something of a buffoon, which was why he had been so surprised to have lost so much money to him. He would pay his gaming debt to Sir Marcus and take his leave. 'Celestine, I came to see you, not to gamble.'

She smiled ingenuously. 'Are you jealous, my darling? You did not come to me when I sent my maid with a message that I was free this afternoon and you left early last evening because Sir Pettigrew was here. I would rather it was you who had stayed.'

'I had a business appointment this afternoon,' Japhet replied, unaffected by her ploy to rouse his jealousy.

'You are cross that we cannot be alone now,' she simpered, and rubbed her hip against his thigh. 'How I wish it could be so. Sir Marcus called unexpectedly and brought me a lavish gift. He adored my performance in my last play. I felt obligated to invite him to dine.'

'You may see who you wish, dear lady. Since you have guests I will not keep you from them.' He stared at her headdress. 'That, I presume, is the present from Sir Marcus. How well it suits you.'

She patted the diamond clip. 'He is most generous. Of course, he wishes to become my lover.'

'Then I am reassured that you will not miss my company tonight. I regret I cannot stay.'

'You will not leave.'

Japhet raised a dark brow at her strident tone. 'Do not dictate to me, madam.'

Anger sparked in Celestine's eyes and her lowered voice was laced with conspiracy: 'I have been keeping Sir Marcus sweet for your benefit. He was concerned that you would not be able to honour your gaming debt to him. I reassured him, of course.'

'How very thoughtful of you.' Japhet did not conceal his sarcasm. 'But why would he assume that I would not pay him – unless you put the notion into his mind? I have a draft on my bank for him in my pocket.'

Celestine looked momentarily disconcerted. 'Eight hundred pounds is a great deal of money. Last week you lost all your money, or so you said. Or did you cry poverty to avoid buying that bracelet I so wanted as a token of your devotion.'

He curbed his irritation at her greed. The light in the room was subdued, flattering her features, but for

Japhet Celestine Yorke had lost her charm. It was not the lines of age around her eyes or mouth that made him no longer desire her, but the cruelty and malice in her expression. He concealed his annoyance behind a charming smile and raised her fingers to his lips, his voice husky and seductive. Although Celestine no longer held any allure for him, it was not his nature to part from a woman with harsh words.

'You would have seen how ardently I appreciate you had you not chosen other company this night. I will pay my debt to Sir Marcus; then I regret that I must leave.'

'But I insist that you stay.' She pouted, feigning hurt, but her eyes were brittle and scheming. 'They wanted me to tell them how I fared at the hands of Gentleman James, but that is not something I talk about . . .' She faltered when Japhet failed to respond to her baiting, her tone now peevish. 'And I thought you so enjoyed a night at the tables. My wish was to please you.'

'It is your company that pleases me.' Japhet felt it politic to appease her.

Fortunately, Barty Bannister coming over to whisper in her ear diverted Celestine's attention. Japhet used the opportunity to pay Sir Marcus the money he owed to him.

Sir Marcus Grundy was an amiable man, with a ruddy face and flaring blond side-whiskers. 'Tonight you will have your chance to win back some of your losses.'

'I regret I have an appointment elsewhere.' Japhet

refused to give in to Celestine's attempt to blackmail him into obeying her commands.

Sir Marcus shook his head. 'My dear fellow, that simply is not done. You must have your chance to win some of your money back.'

'Perhaps he thinks that you will win more money from him, Marcus, old boy,' Barty Bannister sniggered. He had been lecherously eyeing Celestine while she spoke with Japhet, and it was obvious that he was jealous that Japhet was her lover.

Sir Marcus's laugh grated like a nail drawn across a slate tablet. 'Is that it, Loveday? Do you fear losing? I thought you a redoubtable gambler.' He rose unsteadily to help himself from the brandy decanter.

'There, you must stay, Japhet,' Celestine taunted. 'It would not do for Sir Marcus to think that you had lost your nerve.'

'Indeed you must stay, Loveday,' Barty Bannister challenged, 'unless you fear old Marcus here is the better man.'

Japhet ignored the gibe. What money remained from the bank loan he needed to buy horses. At that moment the maid announced Sir Pettigrew Osgood.

The atmosphere in the room changed when Osgood entered – sexual tension sparked between the other men. Osgood started at seeing Japhet and his eyes flashed with annoyance. 'Good day, gentleman, I thought you would be alone, Celestine.'

'As you see, I am not.'

'Perhaps we should leave,' Barty Bannister suggested.

'We were invited for a gaming evening.' Sir Marcus was drunk enough to be belligerent.

'I was about to leave.' Japhet bowed to Celestine.

The actress stamped her foot. 'No, I will not have it. I have invited my friends for a night of gaming. Sir Pettigrew may join us. And, Japhet, I will not hear of you leaving.' Her stare was challenging.

Japhet reconsidered. Celestine had told him that Osgood had asked her to stop seeing him, and if he left it would make the baronet believe he was in some way intimidated by him. Also, he disliked Bannister and wanted to teach him a lesson. He also noticed that Sir Marcus's breath reeked of brandy and the baronet was weaving backwards and forwards on the balls of his feet. Japhet did not like being in debt to Thomas. If Sir Marcus was intoxicated and Bannister wanted to impress Celestine, they were likely to play recklessly for high stakes. The odds were in Japhet's favour that he would recoup his losses.

'It would be churlish of me to refuse in such circumstances.'

Osgood remained antagonistic, clearly annoyed not to have Celestine to himself. They dined first on an excellent meal, and Japhet was sparing in his intake of wine and brandy. Celestine flirted outrageously with all her guests but it was to Japhet she gave the most attention, until it made him uncomfortable. Osgood's mood became surlier with each glass of wine he partook. As the men left the dining room Sir Pettigrew deliberately blocked Japhet's passage until the others were out of the room.

'If you know what is good for you, Loveday, you'll stay away from Celestine.'

The threat raised Japhet's hackles. He may have decided to finish with the actress but he certainly had no intention of allowing Osgood to think that it was because of his threats. 'I go where I please and visit where I am made welcome, sir.'

'Not in this matter.'

'And how do you intend to stop me? Pistols at dawn would be too absurd, don't you consider?'

At the mention of a duel Osgood's bluster faded. He had heard that Loveday was an accomplished duellist, both with the sword and pistol. He had challenged men in the past, but only those he knew he had an edge over. Loveday was a wild card.

'I do not duel with the lower orders. Or over the reputation of an actress.'

The insult to himself roused Japhet's temper. If he struck Osgood and challenged him, the baronet would have no choice but to fight him. Then common sense reasserted itself. He had resolved to put his old ways behind him and, besides, he wanted to be rid of Celestine. A duel would only feed her ardour and vanity.

Japhet gave a mocking laugh. 'As it pleases you, Sir Pettigrew.'

Celestine returned, and her stare was speculative upon her two lovers. 'What are you two about? You look so fierce.' She clapped her hands. 'You are not going to fight over me, are you? That would be so exciting and once the news got out the public would be clamouring to see me in a play.'

'Duels are fought over a man's honour – not to pander to a woman's vanity,' Osgood retaliated. 'You forget that I am married, madam. Do you think I would shame my wife by fighting over the affections of an actress?'

'Then leave my house, sir,' Celestine demanded. 'I thought you cared for me. You do not.'

Sir Marcus ambled back into the dining room. 'I thought we were to play cards. Perhaps since Celestine challenges your affections, we should play for who wins her this night?'

Celestine rounded on Sir Marcus. 'I will not subject myself to be the prize of a wager.'

He shrugged. 'Are we to play cards, or not? If not, Barty and I are off to White's.'

Celestine was angry at Osgood both for refusing to fight a duel over her and also for ruining the plans she had made for this night. Japhet would also leave. If she did not have him in her bed tonight, she needed to ensure her hold over him in other ways.

'If any of you leave then I shall not forgive you.' She was desperate now for the gaming to begin. And later Osgood would pay dearly for not being willing to fight a duel over her. It was time he brought her another trinket to show his undying affection. She pouted. 'You are quite ruining the entertainment I had planned. It is too bad of you.'

Throughout her tirade Japhet had held Osgood's antagonistic stare. The baronet pulled Celestine to him and kissed her possessively. She did not resist and was smiling as she drew away.

As they moved to the gaming table, Sir Pettigrew fired a parting shot at Japhet. 'I neither trust nor like you. Take care you do not overstep the mark. Nothing would give me greater pleasure than to denounce you as a blackguard.'

When they were seated at the card table, Celestine brought Japhet a large glass of brandy, which he sipped sparingly. Even so, as the evening progressed, he found it hard to concentrate on the run of cards, and by the end of the evening he had lost another three hundred pounds. He was surprised at how drunk he felt when he rose from the card table. Osgood had a pile of coins in front of him and smirked at Japhet's losses. He resented the hold Japhet had on Celestine's affections, and his conceit was such that he did not like sharing his mistress with another. From the malicious glitter in Osgood's eyes, Japhet knew he had made an enemy.

Before leaving the yard on Christmas Eve, Edward called at Mariner's House. Senara and Tamasine were plucking a brace of pheasants in the kitchen when he walked in unannounced. Speckled russet feathers escaped from the sack Senara was collecting them in and floated in the air. They stuck to the women's curls and they laughed when one tickled their noses. Nathan was seated on the floor, his fist clutching a honey biscuit as he chewed it contentedly.

Flustered by Edward's appearance, Senara laid the pheasant on the table and smoothed the strands of hair that had escaped from her chignon.

'Please do not stop your work on my account. I am intruding.' Edward looked ill at ease.

'I must thank you for the pheasants, sir. Dick Nance brought them yesterday for us from the estate,' Senara replied.

He waved her gratitude aside. 'They are nothing. I thought I should explain that in the circumstances I do not feel that it is appropriate for Tamasine to attend at Trevowan tomorrow. Although as Adam's wife normally we would wish you to join us, Senara.'

'I did not expect such an invitation, sir,' Tamasine was quick to point out. 'Any form of celebration was frowned on at the academy. After we attended church in the morning the girls were locked in their dormitories and given a French essay to write.'

Senara was always horrified at the restrictions Tamasine had been forced to endure and wanted to do everything in her power to make life more enjoyable for the young woman. 'Sir, with Adam away I would prefer to spend the day here with my mother and sister.'

He nodded, looking relieved, and held out a carved wooden ship. 'This is for the boy. It used to be Adam's. I carved it for him for his first birthday. I am sure that he would wish Nathan to have it. The child is a year old now, is he not?'

'He was born at the winter solstice. The ship is beautiful, sir.' Senara ran her fingers over the smooth contours of the bow, feeling a pulse deep within the wood that carried an echo of her husband's presence from the hours he had played with the toy. She held it out to Nathan, who seized it with a cry of pleasure. Nathan's birthday also marked her first wedding anniversary to Adam and it would be hard to spend it apart from her husband.

'Is your brother's family to join you tomorrow?' Senara asked.

'Yes, together with Peter, but Hannah will not leave the farm as Oswald has again been taken ill. His chest is worse this winter than last. It will be a small gathering this year without the twins and Japhet. I trust you will both be at the service tomorrow morning at Trewenna church? It would not be out of place for Tamasine to be seen in church as your companion. You do not attend as often as I would wish, Senara.'

Senara did not wish to explain her absence to him. It was not an issue with Adam.

At her silence Edward frowned. 'Your absence adds fuel to the gossip surrounding Tamasine. I know you did not always attend the service with Adam, but I would not have it speculated that my son's family are less than godly. It will not reflect well upon Nathan in later life if you allow gossip to spread concerning such matters. Also, if Tamasine is to be accepted within our community, there must be no slur upon her reputation.

Senara was about to retort that if Adam accepted that she did not believe it necessary to enter a church to lead a good and honest life, then she would not be influenced by his father's orders, but Nathan chose that moment to crawl forward, pushing his ship along the floor. Senara saw that Edward was watching the child intently with a smile. Upon Adam's marriage to Senara, Edward had been so set against his grandson's gypsy blood that it had almost cost Adam his inheritance of the shipyard. Was the toy ship a sign that Edward's attitude was mellowing? In the circumstances Senara decided to refrain from replying, but as she had already made her own venerations at the solstice, she would attend church to celebrate the Nativity.

When Edward left, Senara was troubled that Tamasine would feel excluded from the family by Edward's decision. 'Your father does not wish to offend his wife's sensibilities, even though she is absent from Trevowan. That is why he cannot invite you to the house.'

Tamasine shrugged. 'What do I care what Mr Loveday's foolish wife feels? Or his dragon of a sister? I like living here with you and I can see Mr Loveday most days. I doubt I would have so much fun at the big house as I do here, or so much freedom.'

Senara could not help wondering if too much freedom was bad for such a headstrong woman as Tamasine.

Chapter Seventeen

It was two weeks after the finish of the Christmas festivities and Celestine had not seen Japhet for several days. She was bored and drummed her fingers on her dressing table as she watched the snoring figure sprawled across her bed. Sir Marcus had rolled on to his back after their lovemaking. He was still partially clothed, for in his haste he had only removed his jacket and breeches. She picked up his jacket from the floor and, with a glance to ensure that he remained asleep, took out his money pouch and removed fifty gold coins. Sir Marcus had been so drunk he would never remember the exact amount of his winnings that night. Celestine placed the coins in her own purse on the dressing table and patted the pouch with satisfaction.

Her gaze lifted to her reflection in the looking-glass. Her hair was a mess, and her thick white face powder and rouge were streaked across her face. Celestine grimaced; even in the flickering candlelight she looked old and haggard. Fear clutched at her stomach. She was losing her popularity on the stage and her looks would soon also fail her.

At a snore from Sir Marcus she turned to glare at him. He was an unsatisfactory lover, caring only for his own gratification. Celestine was a sensual woman who enjoyed sex, which was why she was so promiscuous. Yet it was rare that a lover lived up to her expectations – except Japhet.

She closed her eyes against a rush of jealousy. From the moment Japhet's family had returned to London and they had been seen at the playhouse together, he had become less attentive towards her. She found such neglect impossible to tolerate, and if this had been any other lover she would have dismissed him.

Celestine simmered with anger as she recalled the coolness she had received from the women of his family. They had regarded her as a whore and not the great actress who deserved acclaim. But what had roused her displeasure most was the pain in the eyes of the young, chestnut-haired woman with the party when Celestine had possessively taken Japhet's arm. Clearly the woman was in love with Japhet, though she was too plain to consider as a serious rival. But Celestine could not so easily dismiss that Japhet's ardour was cooling, and that alarmed her.

Her hand clenched, the jewels on her rings digging into her fingers until they drew blood. Always her affections and heart had been hardened, ruled by avarice. With Japhet she had broken her own rules for survival. Idiot that she was, she had fallen in love with him.

For the first time since her mother had abandoned her, Celestine felt the pain of rejection. Angered by the way she felt that her heart had tricked her, Celestine wanted to strike back at Japhet for not loving her with the same passion. To keep Japhet, Celestine needed to entrap him. But how? She was not entirely certain that he was the highwayman who had waylaid Sir Pettigrew's coach, but his growing indifference to her charms was making her desperate. Japhet needed to be taught the lesson that he could not dally with her affections with impunity. The money he had recently lost at her gaming parties was proof she could trick him when she chose. Why then did her triumph taste so bitter, or give her no sense of peace?

Even with her thoughts in turmoil, Celestine did not forget the role she needed to play when entertaining a lover. She picked up a powder puff and patted it over her cheeks and repinned her hair. The need always to look her best was now more important than ever.

She climbed back into the bed and was about to shake Sir Marcus awake when she saw his emerald stock pin on the sheet. The stone was the size of her thumbnail and worth a small fortune. She picked it up and studied it. Sir Marcus gave a loud snore, which started him awake and instinctively Celestine hid the stock pin in her hand behind her back. She blurted out, 'It is time for you to leave, my dear.'

It took a moment for his gaze to focus and for him to remember where he was. Then he smiled at her and stroked her dimpled elbow. 'My sweet Celestine, it cannot be time for me to leave already? Come, let me embrace you.'

She was in no mood for his fumblings. She kissed his temple, then moved behind a screen to dress and hid the stock pin beneath a pile of petticoats. 'The hour is late and I have some papers to sign at my lawyer's in an hour. He is attending an auction of a tenement building and needs my signed proxy to bid for it.'

With a groan Sir Marcus rolled from the bed to pull on his breeches.

'Have you not enough property?'

'Now I have decided to retire from the stage it is how I make a living.' She emerged from the screen and presented her back to him. 'Lace me, if you please. The maid has gone to Billingsgate. I had a mind for kippers for supper.'

He tugged at the laces of her gown. 'You're getting a bit stout, old girl.'

'Stout! You dare call me stout!' Her voice rose with hysteria. 'Get out of my boudoir. And don't show your face near me again. You are a poor excuse for a lover.'

'Then I will take back the topaz necklace I gave you.' His mood turned ugly at her disparagement of his prowess. 'There are plenty of younger and more popular actresses who will be grateful for my patronage. You've had your day.'

She hurled a vase at his head, but missed, and he picked up his jacket and scurried to the door, retying his cravat.

'You can whistle for your necklace. I earned it putting up with your complacent fumblings!' she screamed after him.

He spun round. 'Where is my stock pin?'

'What stock pin? You were not wearing one. Now get out.'

He ignored her and searched the bed, then kneeled on the floor to look under it. 'I was wearing my emerald pin. I'm not leaving without it.'

'And I say you wore no pin. You were so drunk when you arrived you either did not put it on or lost it on the way here. You had been to your club and walked here. Perhaps you were robbed.'

'I would have remembered that.' His stare became accusing.

Celestine blazed, 'You were in no state to remember anything. Ask that fool Barty. Now get out. You insult me and I am weary of you.'

The last time Sir Marcus had driven with her in the park she had noticed his gaze wandering to some of the young actresses in their carriages. If he was about to discard her, the stock pin would be her compensation. She could not get him out of her house fast enough.

When she heard the front door of her house slam shut the fight went out of her. His insult had rung uncomfortably true.

It made her even more desperate to reclaim Japhet's affection. On several occasions when Japhet had attended her card tables she had drugged his drink whilst he gambled. Only with his money gone would

Japhet again turn to highway robbery, and then she would demand a half share of his plunder as the price of her silence. And once she had the evidence that he was a highwayman, he would never dare to leave her.

With her popularity waning, Celestine was determined to hoard as much money as she could to protect herself from poverty in later years. The rent she earned from the dozen houses she owned she discounted as too little to sustain the life of luxury she desired. Even the fortune in jewels, which were locked away in a bank, could so easily be squandered if she had to resort to selling them.

Although she loved Japhet, she still resented the fact that her handsome lover had never brought her jewels or expensive gifts. She may enjoy the pleasure he gave to her as a lover, but Celestine never did anything without reward. Japhet would pay for his arrogance in assuming that her favours came free. He would pay the same as all her lovers, and they all had paid very dearly indeed.

When the sun broke through the clouds, Senara set aside the frayed hem of the petticoat she was sewing. The gypsy in her abhorred being constrained within a house for too long; the open air with the song of the birds and scent of woodlands and meadows was invigorating and uplifting.

Tamasine was slumped in a chair reading and had been complaining for the last two days at the thick mist that had prevented their usual ride. Senara glanced out of the window and saw that the mist was lifting and they could see the trees on the far side of the river inlet. 'There is still time to ride to Boscabel, if you wish?'

'That would be wonderful.' Tamasine jumped up and rushed up the stairs to change into her riding habit. She shouted from her bedroom. 'If there is time can we call upon Bridie? I have not seen her in days.'

Senara climbed the stairs at a more sedate pace. In two months her child would be born and her movements were slowing. 'We shall make time.' Senara had been worried about encouraging Tamasine to make friends with her sister unless Edward approved. He had seen the two young women together on several occasions and not indicated that he wished them kept apart. Both of the young women were outcasts in their own way: Tamasine by her birth and Bridie through her deformity.

Senara paused to give instructions about Nathan's needs to Carrie Jansen, who was tidying the nursery. 'Make sure he has the tincture I prepared rubbed into his gums when he awakes. He was restless again last night with his teething.'

Senara was only half changed into her riding habit when she heard Tamasine call out as she ran down the stairs, 'Hurry up, slow coach. I'll saddle the horses.'

'No running in the yard,' Senara reminded Tamasine. 'Mr Loveday would not approve.' She laughed at the young woman's enthusiasm for life. Having Tamasine for company had made living at Mariner's House without Adam easier.

Scamp joined them as they rode out of the yard, his

legs muddy from chasing seagulls along the edge of the inlet at low tide. When they rode past the crumbling pillars that stood each side of the track to mark the boundary of Boscabel, the roof and chimneys of the house were visible through the leafless branches of the surrounding wood. A herd of roe deer, startled from their grazing by the sound of the mares' approach, bounded in front of them for several yards before crashing through the dying brown leaves of the bracken.

The two women rode through the arched gateway, which was missing its rusted gates with broken hinges, as they had been taken to Trevowan Hard for the blacksmith to repair. Senara dismounted by the leaf-filled basin of the fountain and stared up at the roof of the house. New timbers and shingles covered the oldest section of the open hall and solar wing, and temporary repairs had been made to other holes in the roof, giving the shingles a mosaic effect of greens and browns. The work had stopped before Christmas, all the carpenters and shipwrights working extra hours at the yard in the urgency to launch the brigantine on time.

The iron-studded oak door creaked on its hinges and Tamasine hesitated to follow Senara inside. 'Don't you find this old house a bit scary? It's not been lived in for so long and it is such a ruin. And it is so isolated. What if some vagrants break in and are waiting to murder us?'

'You have too vivid an imagination,' Senara laughed. 'And did we not take on Rudge, after

Beaumont accosted Gwendolyn Druce on our land? There is nothing to fear.'

The house smelled of mildew, dust and long neglect. The splashes of weak sunlight dappling the floor brought no warmth to the draughty entrance. Temporary boards had been placed over the broken windowpanes, and Senara had removed the drapery of cobwebs from the walls, swept the floors free of debris and washed them, so that the red and black pattern of the tiles showed that life and a time of caring had returned to the dwelling.

'Rudge, are you there?' Senara called to the retainer, who had been provided with a room at the rear of the old kitchen for his accommodation.

'You have need of me, Mrs Loveday?' Senara started at the sound of the retainer's voice close by.

He appeared silently from the passageway leading to the back of the house. For a man of bearlike build, he walked with surprising stealth. Eli Rudge was employed to clear the debris from the house and grounds and keep a general eye on the property. He wore an old battered flat hat on his bald head. His face was permanently ruddy and a fox-coloured beard hung to his chest.

'I wanted to check that the repairs to the roof have not let in water.'

'They be fine, Mrs Loveday. I've been clearing out the well. There be old bits of plough, mattresses, barrels and the like, and some kind of broken platform in it. Couldn't be sure but I reckon it's been used at some time by smugglers to hide their goods.'

'That would not surprise me, as the place has been deserted for so long. But there can be no such allowances given to the smugglers in the future.' She was aware that the retainer was watching her with a wary expression. Too many people would take bribes from the smuggling gangs to turn a blind eye when they worked in the district. 'It will be part of your duties to ensure that the smugglers do not cross our land. You must take care, though, for they are dangerous men, Rudge.'

Rudge removed his cap and scratched his head. 'There were some man from Penruan here two days past. I caught him snooping round and he seemed up to no good. He were surprised to find someone here. Mean-looking cove he be, said he be related to the Lovedays.'

'That is likely to be Harry Sawle and he knows I will have no dealings with smugglers.'

'He don't look the type to take no for an answer.'

'If he is on the estate again I want to be told and I shall confront him.' Senara was not intimidated by Harry Sawle, for she had saved his life when a rival smuggling gang had shot him, but if she did not stand up to him, he would do exactly as he pleased. Any contraband found on this land would set the authorities against the Lovedays. There had been too much unhealthy speculation about St John's involvement with the Sawle gang at his trial.

Senara was unsettled by Harry Sawle's interest in their land. He was a wily devil, who would promise one thing and still believe himself above retribution and able to do exactly as he pleased. It would not trouble Sawle if he brought the Lovedays to greater disrepute.

She wondered if she should approach Edward about the matter, but he had so many problems she did not want to burden him with another. She could be making too much of the incident. She put the matter from her mind, inspected the rest of the house and gave Eli a list of jobs to be done in the following week.

Tamasine had been wandering around the grounds. When Senara joined her Tamasine wrinkled her nose at the house. 'It is so old. I would have thought Adam would tear it down and build a new mansion.'

Senara frowned. 'This house has a special atmosphere of its own that would be lacking in a new mansion. However, it will never be Trevowan and that will always be a cause of sadness for Adam. He loves his old home. But Boscabel will be his refuge and his pride. I could not ask for more.'

'Have you finished here? Can we ride now to visit Bridie?' Tamasine was impatient to leave. A cloud had passed over the sun and the house looked menacing in the deepening shadows.

'I will race you there.' Senara hurried to her mare, holding her side as the activity caused the child to kick against her ribs. It would be good to escape the responsibilities of her new life with an hour or two in the company of her mother and sister.

They arrived at the cottage in the wood to discover a horse tethered to the fence around the vegetable garden. A large black spotted sow grunted and rose up on her back legs to peer over the top of her sty, her snout dredging the air in anticipation of the arrival of her food. Outside the barn a dozen chickens pecked at the ground, foraging for the remnants of the corn scattered for them.

The presence of the horse made Senara uneasy. A dog lying outside the door with his nose on his paws, rose stiffly at their approach. Old age, and the goring from the horns of bulls, when he had been used in bull baiting before Senara had rescued him and nursed him back to life, had stripped him of his agility. Angel was no longer the guard dog that most men would fear to encounter.

The cottage was so isolated that Senara's family received few visitors. When she entered her old home, she was surprised to see Peter Loveday seated on a wooden chair by the fire, sipping a glass of Leah's elderberry wine.

Peter rose at her entrance and was forced to duck his head from tangling with the bunches of dried herbs that hung from the central rafter. 'Good day, cousin. You must find it strange to discover me here?'

'A little.' Senara was guarded. Pious Peter, as his family referred to him, had never hidden his dislike for Senara's heathenish ways, as he regarded them. He was a religious bigot and had none of the common touch or understanding and compassion for his fellow man that his father, the Reverend Mr Joshua Loveday, did. 'What brings you to call upon my family? I thought you had left the district to preach elsewhere.'

'It is true there is much work to be done in the Lord's name, but since Japhet shows no sign of relinquishing his wayward life, I have decided to help Papa in his work in the parish.'

His patronising manner annoyed Senara. 'You are an example to us all, Peter. But that does not mean that we should condemn those who do not live up to the expectation of others.'

Peter sucked in his lips. 'Cousin, I must protest. It is the duty of all God's children to heed—'

'Cousin Peter, with respect, I did not visit my mother and sister to hear a sermon.' Senara lost her patience.

Bridie limped forward. 'Senara, please do not be mean to Mr Loveday. You should be glad that a member of your husband's family has called upon us.'

'It is the reason that Mr Loveday has called which concerns me.' She faced Peter across the room. 'Did you come to pay your respects to my family, or to harangue them upon our heathenish ways?'

'It has always distressed my father that you and your family rarely attend Trewenna church.'

'We could go more often, couldn't we, Ma?' Bridie interrupted. 'Now I have my pony, I can travel further.'

'Trewenna church is still a long way for Ma to walk, Bridie.' Senara glanced at her mother. Leah held herself upright but her face was lined with pain, her knees and joints swollen from years of walking long distances in the worst of weathers.

'The Reverend Mr Loveday did say how pleased he

was that we attended the carol service,' Bridie went on. 'He also suggested that it would serve you better if you attend church more regularly, Senara.'

She could tell by Bridie's flushed face and over-bright eyes that Adam's handsome cousin had made an impression on her. Bridie was fifteen and growing more beautiful each day. Her crippled leg was no longer so apparent since Adam had insisted he buy her specially built-up shoes. Leah's expert sewing and padding in the bodice of Bridie's gown cleverly disguised the slight twisting of her spine, which deformed one shoulder.

'Now that Senara is married to Adam, it is her duty to set an example to our parishioners,' Peter admonished.

Before Senara could retaliate, Peter bowed to Bridie. 'It pleases me to learn that you are so well read after attending the school at the shipyard. I will leave this bible with you and will call again in a few days.'

'I cannot allow my daughter to accept a gift from you, Mr Loveday.' Leah was agitated at having to confront him. 'It be not right for a young woman to take gifts from a man.'

'A bible cannot be considered an improper gift, Mrs Polglase.'

Bridie clasped the bible tight in her hands. 'Please, Ma. I bain't never had a book of my own. I do love the stories of Jesus healing the sick and of Noah and the animals.'

Leah exchanged an anxious glance with Senara,

before saying, 'Mr Loveday, I'm sure you mean well, but it bain't right for a man to be giving my daughter gifts.'

'Think of it not as a gift from me but from the Lord himself. They are his words, his laws and commandments, and we are but his servants to obey his will.' He picked up the bible from where he had placed it on the table with his hat, and bowed to the women. 'Good day, ladies. I trust we will see you all in church for the service on Sunday.'

On his way to the door he stopped before Tamasine. 'I will send a bible to Mariner's House for your use. You have much to atone for. A child born in sin must cast out the devil which has tainted her blood.'

Tamasine's hand was a blur as she slapped the arrogance from his face. 'Take care when you cast the first stones, sir, that you are without sin. Pride and false vanity in one's own superiority is a sin, is it not? And did not your Lord and Master say, "Blessed are the meek for they shall inherit the earth"?'

Peter's face flushed with anger. 'I see no meekness in your brazen outburst. The bible also says, "Suffer not a woman to teach, nor usurp authority over the man, but to be in silence." It is time you knew your place both within the world and within our family.'

He marched from the room and Bridie rounded upon Tamasine. 'How could you be so mean, Tam? Mr Loveday came to us out of kindness.' She burst into tears.

'Bridie, I did not mean to upset you. But he was so rude and arrogant—' Tamasine began, but Bridie stumbled into the bedroom of the two-roomed cottage, slamming the door behind her.

Exasperated, Senara interrupted. 'Leave her, Tamasine.' She turned to her mother. 'Bridie is growing up faster than we thought. Peter is a handsome man. I had better speak with him. I would hate for Bridie to allow her affections to be taken by him and she become hurt.'

Chapter Eighteen

Nathan had been fretful and restless all day. He was teething and would not settle, and he would allow only Senara to comfort him. For the third time since she had retired for the night, Senara awoke to the sound of her son's cries. The cup of tisane that she had prepared to ease his suffering was empty and needed replenishing. She wrapped a woollen shawl over her night-rail and carried the distraught child downstairs. As she passed Tamasine's chamber, the light from the embers in the hearth showed the young woman's figure buried beneath the bedclothes. Tamasine always slept soundly, and even the most violent thunderstorm would not rouse her.

Loss of sleep made Senara's steps slow and she yawned constantly as she descended the stairs. A faint ruddy glow from the Cornish range took some of the bite out of the cold night, but even so, Senara drew her shawl tighter around her shoulders. The window shutters were closed and the large oak table and dresser showed as indistinct forms in the near total darkness.

With Nathan propped on her hip and refusing to be pacified, Senara lit a candle, then threw more wood on to the range and kept the iron door of the oven ajar to take the night chill from the air. She warmed some milk and added some drops of clove tincture and honey. Scamp scratched at the kitchen door and she let him out into the yard, shutting the door quickly to keep out the cold.

Senara calmed her son enough to spoon some of the milk into his mouth. Within minutes Nathan stopped crying but showed no sign of falling asleep. Outside, Scamp was barking. Senara sighed. 'The stupid dog will wake the shipwrights and that will not make him popular.'

When she opened the door the pungent smell of smoke chased the sleep from her brain. Dawn was two hours away and it was too early for the women to have stoked up their fires for the day. Then her sharp ears detected a distant sound of crackling wood and her heart jolted in alarm.

'Fire!' she shouted. 'Tamasine, wake up! There's a fire in the yard.' There was no time to check that the girl had heard her and, holding Nathan tight to her chest, Senara ran barefoot across the yard to Edward's office. Smoke was drifting from below the decks of the brigantine in its cradle. A bell hung from a bracket by the door of the office and she rang it to rouse the men.

She was appalled to see how quickly the fire was building in pace, the flames writhing like eels through the open decking to illuminate the yard with an eerie orange glow. Senara could feel the heat on her face and arms.

Doors banged open from the cottages and more shouts of 'Fire!' echoed around the yard. Everyone would be needed to fight the flames, and when she heard Ben Mumford yelling to the men to form a fire line to pass the water buckets, Senara ran to Seth Wakeley's cottage. His son, Timmy, ran out of the house as she approached and she grabbed his arm.

'Tim, saddle Hera and ride to Trevowan to inform Mr Loveday of the fire.'

Martha Wakeley and her daughter, Lottie, appeared in the doorway. 'Heaven save us all! It be a fire. If it spreads the whole yard and cottages could go up,' Martha wailed. 'Lottie help your pa strap on his wooden leg.'

'I need Lottie to take care of Nathan while I do what I can,' Senara interrupted. 'For safety the children should be taken to the schoolhouse, which lies further back. Lottie and the older girls can look after them. The women are needed on the bucket line.'

Lottie took Nathan, who had fallen silent at all the noise and bustle capturing his attention. Senara sped back to the brigantine where a line of men and women were passing buckets, filled from the river, to the scaffolding around the ship.

The fire was difficult to reach as it appeared to have started within the ship's hold, and the buckets had to be passed up the scaffolding ladders, then down into the hold. Fortunately, the recent rain had dampened the outer timbers and the flames were slow to take hold. Senara glanced at the sky. No stars or moon were visible and she could smell rain in the air. Why did it not come? A downpour now would put out the fire.

'Get 'em buckets up here faster,' Ben Mumford shouted from the scaffolding. 'We'll lose 'er if 'ee don't get a move on.'

There was a creaking of timbers and a deafening crash as the upper deck gave way. Flames lit the sky like fireworks, sparks shooting out in all directions. A woman screamed when some landed on her, setting her hair alight. The man next to her threw a bucket of water over her to douse the flames and Senara left her place in the line to run to the woman who had fallen to the ground and was groaning. The side of her face was painfully blistered; the injury was more superficial than deep, but her hair had been burned short as straw stubble.

'Keep a wet cloth on your face and come to me as soon as the fire is out,' Senara instructed the woman. 'It should not leave a scar and I will give you a salve and physic for the pain.'

She rejoined the line and saw Tamasine working at the foot of the scaffolding, her hair and coat she had put over her nightdress drenched from the water spilling over her as she raised her arms to lift the buckets. There was little wind but what breeze there was wafted the smoke across the fire fighters, making them cough, and their eyes sting and stream with tears. Puddles of icy water slopped from the buckets and formed around their feet; many of the workers had emerged without shoes in their haste to help. Sometimes in their panic and urgency a bucket would be dropped and angry words and curses rose above the hiss and crackle of flames.

A steady rhythm was set up as the full buckets were passed along the line and the empty ones passed back. Senara was sweating from her exertions, and her clothes sodden from the water splashing over her from the buckets. Desperation to put out the fire drove everyone beyond their normal endurance. Hands became chapped, blisters broke and rubbed raw, muscles strained, whilst pain knifed through backs that bent and heaved in constant motion. No one complained. No one faltered. Too much was at stake. The yard was their livelihood and without it they would all starve.

The spit and crack of the flames devouring timber was relentless, and the fire fighters were being driven back. Faces glistened with sweat and smoke, and clothing smouldered beneath the constant bombardment of sparks. The older children and women were losing their strength and several had been forced to rest, coughing and choking in the thickening smoke.

'Be strong, good people,' Senara urged. 'We are winning. The brig can be saved.'

Some of the women responded but the children were too exhausted and some were crying from where the flying sparks had burned them. The smoke hung too thickly around the brigantine for Senara to see how much damage had been done, but it did seem as the sky brightened with the rising sun that the flames were being beaten back, though the damage to the hold was bound to be extensive.

Gradually the flames dwindled and the smoke lessened. Senara, together with the other women, dropped back from the line, holding their sides as they struggled to regain their breath. Tamasine was amongst them, looking about to drop from exhaustion.

Senara nodded to Pru Jansen, who ran the kiddley. 'The workers deserve a quart of ale and a tot of rum after they have finished their work. Tamasine will help you. I've some raspberry cordial in the house for the children.'

'Fire's out!' A shout came from the depths of the ship. The workers gave a collected sigh of relief and most of them sank down into the mud and put their heads between their knees as they recovered their breath.

Edward Loveday rode into the yard and leaped to the ground to stare with horror at the blackened timbers of his ship. 'How the devil did a fire break out?' he raged. 'Who was careless in not dousing the lanterns?'

'The lanterns were all extinguished when the men finished work,' Ben Mumford informed him. 'I checked them all myself. I heard a couple of dogs barking and after what happened in the carpentry shed, I looked out of the window but could see nothing. My cottage faces away from the brig, sir.'

'First I knew of it was the fire bell ringing,' Seth Wakeley observed. 'That were Mrs Loveday's doing. Reckon if she had not roused the men the entire ship could've gone up.'

'I bain't done a full inspection,' Ben Mumford added, 'but I reckon the damage bain't too great that the hold can't be repaired.'

Edward struck his riding whip against his leg to release his fury. 'It will take months to put right, if it can be done at all.'

Toby Jansen came forward. 'Mrs Loveday asked the wife to serve the men with ale and a tot of rum, sir. Reckon they could do with it. It's taken over an hour to put out the fire.'

'Let the men drink their fill, but I want no sore heads. The repair work must be started by mid-morning. I shall have inspected the ship by then.'

As the morning light brightened the yard, Edward clambered over the charred timbers. The dampness of the timber from a week of rain had saved the bulk of the ship. The deck that had fallen in could be refitted and other damaged beams cut away and replaced without endangering the stability of the ship. The fire had been contained in a relatively small area thanks to Senara's fast intervention, but the repairs would still take up to two months and each day would incur penalty costs to the owner. Any profit from the ship would be swallowed up and Edward would need to raise another loan to continue to pay the shipwrights' wages.

This further catastrophe could bring them to the

brink of ruin. Mumford had been adamant that no lanterns had been left unattended. How the fire started was a mystery. Could it be arson? But who would do such a terrible thing? It was the same with the break-ins. It seemed somebody was deliberately out to destroy the yard.

Anger surged through Edward. Arson was a coward's way of extracting revenge. With the family's old adversary, Thadeous Lanyon, dead, he had no idea who would wish to see him ruined.

With the reputation of the yard already in jeopardy, the fire would undermine his customers' faith in his ability to honour a contract on time. Further orders were likely to be lost and everything that the family had worked for over four generations could be jeopardised.

It was mid-January before Adam was ready to sail to England. The hospitality lavished on him by Garfield Penhaligan had made it impossible to leave earlier. Garfield was a prominent leader in the local assembly and he had introduced Adam to many of his Virginian neighbours. Several had shown interest in shipping their tobacco to England on *Pegasus*. This had meant a delay of some weeks to finalise the contracts, for the American gentlemen took a leisurely approach to business that Adam found frustrating. His patience had been rewarded, however, and four plantation owners had agreed to shipments. The hold of *Pegasus* was filled with barrels of tobacco and Adam had a list of goods that the plantation owners wanted imported on his next voyage to Virginia.

Tonight was his last meal with the Penhaligan family. The dining room was lit by two crystal and gilt chandeliers, which each held a score of candles, and their light danced off the diamonds at the women's throats and wrists. The diners were dressed as formally as though they were attending a ball, for the Penhaligans had insisted on making this a special occasion. Adam had lost count of the number of dinners, balls, and musical evenings they had attended at various plantations along the river. Tonight was a small affair with Adam, St John, Long Tom, the Penhaligans, and Desiree Richmond, who had been in almost permanent residence at Greenbanks since their arrival.

When the meal was over Susannah Penhaligan rose and gestured for Desiree to join her and allow the men to enjoy their port and cigars. Desiree cast a lingering glance in St John's direction and declared, 'St John has prevailed upon me to play the harpsichord later. Gentlemen, do not linger over your port too long now, or I shall be too mortified to play.'

Garfield inhaled deeply on his cigar and turned to Adam. 'We shall miss you when you sail. You must prevail upon your good father and his lady wife to visit us sometime.'

'I will do that with pleasure, sir.'

'And your stay has not been without its rewards.' Garfield nodded with satisfaction. 'Now that you have the tobacco contracts we shall expect you regularly to grace our plantation with your company. And may we hope that your good wife and children will join you on your next voyage?'

'I am sure that Senara would find your country most fascinating, but while we are at war with France, I would prefer that my family remain safe in England. An English merchantman is a prime target for French privateers in wartime.'

'As will any French ship be for you,' Garfield chuckled, 'though with my tobacco on board I trust you will not engage in fire upon the enemy.'

'Certainly not, unless I am fired upon first and must defend myself and your cargo.' Adam had resolved that with a full hold it would be foolish to risk an encounter with a French corsair. 'Sir, be reassured that the cannon on board *Pegasus* will protect your cargo from any attack.'

'And I trust Sir Gregory has enjoyed his stay?' Garfield smiled at Long Tom.

'Indeed. Your friends have made me most welcome. Plantation life is very different from farming in England. And your form of democratic government interests me. I may well consider purchasing land here one day.'

'I find that strange that you support our democracy when you are part of the ruling class of England, Sir Gregory.'

'My family has always had strong Jacobite sympathies, though we managed to hold on to our estates after the 'forty-five rebellion.'

'Yet you risked your life for your country in France.' Garfield showed his surprise.

'The Jacobites were routed fifty years ago, and the Hanoverian line is firmly established on our throne. I have allegiance to my country and prefer a life of adventure to being tied to an estate, or the wrangling of the Whig and Tory parties to gain power in Parliament.'

The cigars were half smoked when the strains from the harpsichord were apparent.

St John stubbed out his cigar and drained his port glass. 'Desiree grows impatient. It would be discourteous to neglect her.' He excused himself and left the room.

Garfield was thoughtful as he watched St John depart. 'A pity your brother must spend a year in mourning. A match between my wife's niece and St John would be most beneficial to both our families.'

Adam was alarmed. St John had been a fool to declare that Meriel was dead. His twin's pride could be his undoing. He was troubled throughout the musical recital. St John stood over Desiree, turning the pages of her music score. Several times their arms touched as he leaned forward. Desiree did not hide her pleasure at his attention and smiled at St John in an intimate and provocative manner.

When the family retired for the night, St John and Desiree sat in deep conversation on a window seat. Adam approached his brother. 'Desiree, will you forgive me if I take my brother outside for a talk? There is a family matter I wish to discuss before I sail tomorrow.'

'I have been selfish. St John is such witty and

charming company.' She fluttered her fan and smiled at St John. 'There must be much you need to discuss. St John will have messages for his family.'

St John was frowning as he accompanied Adam outside. He took a thin cheroot from a gold case in his pocket and lit it. 'We've scarcely spoken while you have been here. I see no point in changing the situation now. You have been busy feathering your own nest with contracts to transport tobacco to England.'

'You need to be honest with Garfield about Meriel,' Adam challenged. 'He speaks as though he expects you to make an offer for Desiree once you are free of your mourning.'

'Did he now?' St John chuckled. 'Well, Desiree would make a wife that Father would be proud to acknowledge. Her plantation is ten times the size of Trevowan and her husband left her a fortune.'

'But you are not free, St John. Garfield must be told. It is not honourable to encourage Desiree's affections.'

St John rounded on Adam. 'You're a fine one to talk of honour. You wasted no time after your betrothal to Lisette to seduce Meriel and get her with child.'

'Let us not go into that.' Adam refused to be sidetracked. Rowena's parentage still troubled him, but it was best for St John to believe he was her father. 'Rowena is as likely to be your child as mine. And Meriel used us both to get what she wanted. Desiree is another matter. Garfield has received us with open arms. You cannot repay his trust and hospitality by playing Desiree false. Either you promise to tell Garfield the truth before I leave tomorrow, or I will speak to him.'

'What I do in America is my affair. I did not ask for this exile. Father wanted me out of the way until the scandal of Lanyon's murder died down — a murder I did not commit. I am banished because my presence in Cornwall could endanger the precious shipyard's reputation.'

'And you intend to repay Garfield's trust by dis-honouring his niece.'

'Of course not.' St John paced away from Adam. 'I intend to use my time in America to my advantage. As a single man I have a greater freedom to cultivate friendships than if I am married. I've already had a couple of business propositions put my way by men eager to win my favour, as they have daughters of marriageable age.'

'Such dishonesty is bound to have repercussions.' Adam strode after St John and grabbed his arm. 'Desiree is obviously setting her cap at you. You cannot deceive her. Garfield will not tolerate his niece being duped. You have to tell him the truth.'

St John shook off Adam's hold, his stare cold and mutinous. 'How would it look if I did tell him I am married? That does not reflect well on either of us that I have lied to him all these weeks and that you were party to the deception. He is not going to think you are so trustworthy, is he? He could even cancel his contract to ship his tobacco.'

'At least he would know that we did not intend to

deceive him. I would rather risk his anger now than bring shame to our family by being considered a liar.'

'And you would be gone from here and not have to face the ridicule,' St John flared. 'I will not tell him the truth. There will be no need. I shall keep more distance from Desiree. She is a complication I did not plan for and I could do without.'

'Do I have your word on that?' Adam insisted, not sure he could trust his brother.

'If I cause a scandal here, Father will cut me off in favour of Rafe or yourself. Do you think I will risk that?'

Adam conceded that St John would not risk so much, even so he left America on the morning tide with an uncomfortable feeling that St John was heading for trouble by not being honest about still being married.

Lisette lay exhausted on her bed in the tiny cell at the asylum. She was tied to the bed with ropes fastened around her body. Her wrists, knees and ankles were also bound. Her throat was raw from a night of continual screaming and every muscle in her body ached from where she had tried to thrash herself free of her bonds.

'I hate the Lovedays,' she snarled. 'I hate them. Hate them. They will pay for what they have made me suffer.'

She slumped exhausted on the narrow pallet. The mid-morning sun shone through the tiny window high on the wall, its bars throwing shadows across the ceiling. The only clothing she was allowed was a rough linen gown and this was ripped down the front where she had torn it in her rage. All her clothing had ended as no more than rags, rent asunder in her anger. Fresh gouges on her arms and legs crisscrossed old scars where she had mutilated herself with any sharp instrument or surface she could find. To stop the mutilations, they had cut her fingernails short, and she was not even allowed a spoon with which to eat her food. She was given a thick wooden bowl and had to use her fingers.

The spy hole in her cell door was snapped open. Lisette raised her head enough to see the upper part of Dr Claver's face. She screamed a torrent of abuse at him in French. Amelia Loveday's face replaced the doctor's in the aperture.

'Please, Lisette, you must calm yourself. Such conduct makes it more difficult for us to help you,' Amelia pleaded.

'Bitch! Get me out of here.' Lisette's face twisted in fury. 'You shut me away because you hate me. You never wanted me to be a part of your life. You are jealous that your husband was kind to me. He was kind because he loved me. That's why he made Adam promise to wed me. Edward Loveday wanted me in his bed.'

Amelia gasped with horror and stepped back. Dr Claver shook his head. 'I am sorry you had to hear that. The woman is sick. She says whatever will hurt someone most.'

'I can hear you,' Lisette screamed. 'What are you

plotting? You all hate me. Adam hated me. He did not come to France so we could marry. I was made to marry de Gramont. He made me sick and your family is to blame.'

'Adam rescued you from France,' Amelia tried to reason. 'You must calm yourself. This delusion—'

'I will not be shut away.' Lisette would not let Amelia finish. 'William will hear of this. I am his wife. He will protect me. You have no right to treat me like this.' Another torrent of obscenities followed, this time in English.

Amelia gasped, her face turning scarlet as she hid it behind her hands. 'She gets worse. The shame of such conduct . . . I had hoped that she would have improved and could leave here soon. This is so distressing.'

'A cure takes time. Her mind is damaged by her ordeal in France. Some poor souls never fully recover from such trauma.'

'She must get better. Do everything you can. But to bind her like a wild dog . . .' Amelia wiped a tear from her eye. 'She is gently reared. For a woman to be treated thus does not seem right.'

'You are free to take her away any time you choose,' Dr Claver snapped. 'My methods have been proven. If you do not agree with them—'

His manner alarmed Amelia. She turned to Margaret, who looked pale and equally shocked.

'Lisette needs help,' Margaret said. 'Dr Claver treated our sovereign. We have to do what is best for Lisette. But it is upsetting to see her like this.'

Amelia nodded. 'It has been several weeks. People are asking what has become of her. I had hoped that she could come home soon.'

'That would be most unwise,' Dr Claver insisted. 'Your niece is far from stable. She could do a violence to herself – perhaps even to another.'

'What caused the marks on her arms?' Margaret asked as Dr Claver gestured for them to follow him to his office.

The corridor contained several rooms, all with spy holes in the doors. From behind the doors could be heard bestial grunts, inane laughter or incoherent rambling voices. A small window was at the far end, affording little light. The place was as gloomy as a prison, the wooden floor scuffed and unpolished and the plaster on the walls cracked and dented in places as though it had been struck with a hard object. Both women held scented nosegays to their faces to counter the stench of urine, excrement and vomit.

Dr Claver walked rapidly, forcing Margaret and Amelia to hurry at an undignified pace to keep up. 'On one of her more rational days, or so we thought, your niece was left unsupervised for some minutes in the dining room. She hid a spoon about her person and later managed to sharpen the handle so that one side was rough. She sawed this across her skin until she was bleeding profusely from several lesions.'

'The child is quite deranged,' Amelia groaned. 'Is there hope of a cure, Dr Claver?'

'The last week has not been encouraging, but there have been periods of rational thought and reasonable conduct. It is an auspicious sign that her madness comes and goes. I have every confidence in a complete recovery.'

'I pray that will be so.' Amelia was unable to control a sob of anguish. The atmosphere of the asylum was oppressive without comfortable furnishings or adornments of any kind on the walls. Above them someone began to scream and they were joined by others in an inhuman cacophony.

'Will you partake of a dish of tea before you leave, ladies?' Dr Claver seemed unaware of the dreadful voices above them.

'We have another appointment, Dr Claver,' Margaret lied, unable to stand another moment in the asylum. She could see Amelia looked close to swooning and took her sister-in-law's arm as they hurried to the coach.

As it pulled away Margaret voiced her dismay. 'I cannot believe that Lisette can benefit from such treatment. I will instruct Thomas to look further into the matter.'

Amelia nodded, an attack of nausea leaving her incapable of a reply. She pressed her nosegay to her face to draw in its reviving scent, and her other hand was laid across her stomach. The child within kicked as though demanding acknowledgement of its presence. This was a secret she had not even disclosed to Margaret. Amelia blinked aside an onrush of tears and pushed away a feeling of guilt. She had not informed her husband that she was almost four months gone with child. Not long after St John's trial she had begun to suspect that she was again enceinte. Stubbornness had prevented her from telling Edward of her condition in her letters.

The intensity of her emotions swirled like a millrace through her mind and she pressed a hand to her mouth.

Margaret leaned forward, concerned. 'Are you unwell, Amelia? It was upsetting seeing Lisette in such a place. But I am sure that it is for the best.'

'I wish Edward was here to decide what is to be done for her.'

'Do you miss him?'

'Of course.'

'Then why do you not return to Cornwall and allow Thomas to deal with Lisette?'

'How can I return whilst that child remains in Cornwall?' Amelia closed her eyes against an onrush of misery. The letter she had received from her husband, informing her that Tamasine would not be attending school and that she was residing with Senara at Trevowan Hard, had been cold and informal in tone. There had been no words of love, no entreaty that she return, or an apology at the indignity that she had been subjected to by the arrival of Tamasine.

'I will not live in Cornwall whilst that child stays nearby. I have had to accept the presence of the daughters of a tavern-keeper and a gypsy at my table because both St John and Adam chose unsuitable wives. I accepted them out of duty to Edward. But I will not accept the humiliation of Tamasine living within our community. It is wrong of Edward to expect so much.'

'Edward has not openly acknowledged Tamasine as his daughter. If he intends that she remain Senara's companion until Edward can arrange a marriage, surely your paths need not cross.'

'But people will gossip. I have to bear the brunt of it.'

Margaret lost patience with her friend. 'People will always gossip, Amelia. It is for us to rise above it. I held my head high throughout the crisis our bank suffered last year. When Charles was found drowned there was unpleasant talk of suicide, which would have destroyed Charles's good name and brought the bank down with it. By staying away from Cornwall you but add to the speculation.'

'I am not strong like you. Too much has happened.'

'You are one of the strongest women I know, Amelia. You refused many suitors during your years of widowhood. And you raised Richard to be an exceptional young man. He will do well in the navy.'

'I worry about my son. The sea is dangerous and now we are at war. His ship could be attacked at any time. But I can cope with that. Such a fate is in God's hands. It is the gossip surrounding the Lovedays in Cornwall I find so undermining.'

'Are you not losing perspective of what is important, Amelia?' Margaret said. 'Is it not better to face the gossip and therefore negate malicious talk? Edward is striving to rebuild the reputation of the shipyard after Lanyon's ship was wrecked. That evil man tried to ruin Edward's reputation as a reputable shipbuilder.'

'You think I am weak and foolish.' Amelia stared disconsolately out of the window, the clamour and street noise of London unnoticed in her misery. 'But Edward has not asked once in his letters that I should return.'

'Nor will he, since you chose to leave without consulting him. Edward will see your absence as betrayal. He has a duty to provide for Tamasine and would not willing cause you pain. The longer you stay, the greater the rift that will form between you. Do you want that?'

Amelia shook her head, but she had made a stand and her pride would not allow her to back down. Throughout her life every whim had been granted; first by her parents, then her first husband, and until now by Edward. She had never had to exert her authority or accept a compromise.

Chapter Nineteen

A pale halo ringed the moon and the heath glowed with an eerie phosphorescent light from the thick dusting of frost covering the ground and gorse. Swathed in a thick greatcoat, muffler and gauntlets, Japhet was stiff from the cold. It had been madness to come here and try his luck again as a highwayman. He had been reluctant to use robbery as a means to extricate himself from his debts, but he could discern no other solution. Last night he had lost all his money at another gaming session at Celestine's house, and he needed money to settle a gaming debt of fifty guineas or his honour would be lost.

Thoughts of Celestine made him angry. He had resolved to keep away from the actress's gaming sessions and in recent weeks he had won several hundred pounds at various gaming parties over Christmas. But Celestine would not keep her claws out of his affairs. Japhet had been bombarded with missives from the actress, demanding his presence. When he had ignored them, their content had changed from jealous tirades accusing him of playing her false, to unpleasant demands threatening to expose him to Sir Pettigrew Osgood as Gentleman James.

The ache in his joints from the penetrating cold further soured Japhet's mood. He had thought he had convinced Celestine that she had been mistaken in believing he had held up her coach. Clearly the actress intended to use her suspicions as a weapon to keep him at her side. He could deny the notion as absurd, but Osgood would relish being seen as the man who had brought Gentleman James to justice after posting the reward for his capture.

Japhet had finally given in to Celestine's insistence that he call, and he had arrived to find some dozen men already seated at cards. He was known to most of them and it would have been considered bad form to refuse to join them. Although he drank little he found he had soon become light-headed and found it difficult to concentrate on the cards. As a consequence he had lost heavily.

How could he face his family when his life was in such a mess? He needed to be free of Celestine, and to do so without rousing her malice, she would need a very expensive gift to buy her silence. One more robbery could get him out of her clutches and give him enough money to buy the horses he needed to continue his business in a legitimate manner.

The choice should be simple but lately dishonesty sat uneasily on Japhet's conscience. In the past he had been a deft pickpocket and relieved many a drunken gentleman of his money pouch without a second thought when the need arose. The recent coolness he had received from Gwendolyn had left him unsettled. He had not realised how much Gwen's opinion was part of how he viewed his actions.

'This is not the time to get a conscience.' He stood up to pace the ground, thumping his arms across his chest to create some warmth in stiffening limbs. When his teeth began to rattle together from the cold, Japhet clenched his jaw. This was truly madness. He had been on the heath for two hours since the light began to fade, hoping to waylay a traveller returning late to the city. The frost had not cleared from the previous day and when darkness fell and the temperature plummeted he was reluctant to continue his vigil. Desperation made him linger. If he did not succeed in a robbery tonight he would have to sell Sheba to pay off his gaming debt.

Without Sheba he would not have the thoroughbred line to start a stud farm. During the time he had spent with his family over the festivities the conversation had often been about his plans to raise horses. He ran a gloved hand along the mare's neck. It would devastate him to part with Sheba. She was the only thing he possessed in life he had truly valued.

The heath remained silent, and he doubted anyone would travel so late in such weather. He had failed to use a robbery to solve his problems.

Despondent, Japhet pulled off the mask that hid his lower features and mounted Sheba to return to his lodgings. He had not travelled far, when in the distance, he heard the sound of a gunshot. Other robbers were abroad this night and they had found prey leaving London for the country. That settled it. He had missed his chance tonight.

A second shot warned him that the hold-up had not gone smoothly. Perhaps, after all, he had had a lucky escape.

He veered away from the direction of the gunshots and later heard a coach and four speeding along the road away from the city. His hand strayed to Sheba's mane, stroking it absently as he closed his mind to the prospect of losing her. The cold and his dejection made him lethargic and he lost interest in his surroundings. He wanted this madness over and to be back in his rooms with a warming tot of brandy to lift his spirits.

'Stop or I shoot!'

The shout startled Japhet out of his reverie and he automatically drew the pistol from his saddle to lay along his thigh. A man appeared from behind a gorse bush and grabbed Sheba's bridle. His pistol was pointed at Japhet's heart.

'Step down from yer 'orse.'

Fate was mocking him: now he found himself the one being robbed at gunpoint. Anger tightened Japhet's gut at this further indignity. He would give his life before he surrendered Sheba.

'You're out of luck. I've no money.' As Japhet spoke he freed his foot from the stirrup.

'Quit yer gabbing. I want yer 'orse.'

Japhet kicked out, his boot catching the horse-thief

on the jaw. The man fell back but still held on to Sheba's bridle, viciously jerking the bit in the mare's mouth.

Unused to such cruelty Sheba whinnied and shied. When her hoofs hit the ground she wheeled around, throwing the horse thief to one side. Japhet stayed in the saddle, gripping the mare's sides with his thighs. The mare reared a second time and Japhet used his knees to bring her down, but Sheba was frightened and backed into the gorse bush. Her hoofs tangled with the stirrups of a saddle that Japhet's assailant must have been carrying, and Japhet assumed that the thief's horse had been shot from under him.

Japhet's reactions were fast, sharpened by his instincts for survival. He glimpsed another object on the ground and as Sheba jostled against it, he heard the chink of coins. Still clutching his pistol, Japhet fought to bring the mare under control, his gaze now riveted upon his attacker. The moonlight glinted off the horse thief's pistol as he took aim. Years of swordplay had honed Japhet's reflexes. His own hand jerked up and he fired before his assailant had a chance to retaliate.

The reins were freed as the attacker fell to the ground. Japhet pulled his second pistol from his belt to train it on the figure, who now lay unmoving. He thought he had only winged him, but this was not a time to investigate if the man was dead or alive. Sheba was between the man and the saddle and bag and, as she kicked out, Japhet again heard the ring of coins.

There may yet be a chance to redeem something

from this night, Japhet surmised as he swung his upper body towards the ground and scooped up the bag Sheba had trodden on. It was heavy and gave another satisfying chink of coins as Japhet placed it across the pommel of his own saddle. Was his attacker the highwayman involved in the earlier shooting?

There was a groan from the assailant as he began to stir. Japhet dug his heels into Sheba's side, urging her to a gallop, his heart thundering as loudly as the mare's hoofs as she made their escape.

A shouted curse from the recovering horse thief was followed by a shot. Then a bullet blazed a trail of fire across Japhet's ribs, slamming his body forward over the pommel. A dark form of a horse lay on the ground in front of them and Sheba veered sharply to avoid the animal and almost unseated Japhet. He clung on, glimpsing the stain of blood shining in the moonlight along the highwayman's dead animal's neck as they rode past. Japhet grinned. Lady Luck, it seemed, was again with him.

But soon the pain in Japhet's side blotted everything from his mind except the need to reach his rooms and safety. An hour later he waved aside the groom, who ran out to lead Sheba into her stall at the inn where he stabled her. He always attended to Sheba himself and this time he was grateful that his actions would arouse no comment. The wound in his side continued to bleed and if the groom had detected any blood on the mare, it could rouse suspicion that he had been up to no good.

Japhet was weak from loss of blood when he finally

entered his rooms. He dropped the bag he had taken
from the highwayman on to the bed and in the dim
light of a single candle found it contained a bulging
pouch of money and a cache of diamond jewellery. A
low whistle escaped him at the size of his haul. It was
the answer to his prayers. Once sold it would solve all
his financial problems and enable him to buy some
land and start his stud farm. He was about to examine
the contents more closely when he staggered, weak
from loss of blood. On the point of fainting, he hid
the bag under his bed and as he straightened he
lurched alarmingly. The room swirled crazily around
him and he crashed unconscious on to the bed.

'Out of my way, woman! Do you not know who I am?'
Celestine attempted to push aside the stout figure of
Mrs Ruskin, who had stepped out of her parlour on
the ground floor of the four-storey house in Brook
Street where Japhet had taken rooms.

'Madam, I have no idea who you are, nor from your
appalling manners do I care to be acquainted.' Mrs
Ruskin folded her arms across her chest, her gimlet
eyes sweeping disparagingly over the actress's low-cut
gown. 'I keep a decent house here. No whores are
allowed in the rooms.'

'How dare you call me a whore! I am Celestine
Yorke, the actress, and I have business with Mr
Loveday.'

Mrs Ruskin continued to bar the way. A prim lace
collar edged the high neck of her navy woollen gown
and tight rosebud curls marched in double file across

303

her temple, the rest of her hair hidden by a plain mobcap. She gave a sniff of disapproval. 'Never did hear of any actress whose reputation as a whore did not take precedence over her abilities on the stage. No decent woman demands admittance to a gentleman's rooms. If you are who you say you are, why is Mr Loveday not calling on you?'

'Because I have to be on stage in an hour and I need to see him urgently. Now out of my way.' Celestine lost patience and elbowed the landlady aside.

At the commotion Charlie Ruskin came to his wife's side. An ex-army sergeant, he puffed out his chest and stood to rigid attention as he scrutinised the actress. He lifted a tufted brow and smacked his lips in a salacious manner. 'Yer are indeed Celestine Yorke. Welcome to our 'umble 'ome. This is indeed an honour.' He rounded on his haughty wife and snapped, 'Ain't yer got work ter do in the kitchen, woman? This place don't run itself.'

'This is a respectable house,' Mrs Ruskin persisted but the fire had gone from her voice. When her husband raised a fist to her, she flinched, fear stark in her eyes from a life of enduring his brutality. Without another word she withdrew, like a tortoise back in its shell, into the parlour.

Ruskin edged closer to Celestine. 'Pay no mind to the wife. I've seen every one of yer plays. Loved 'em all.'

'You are a man of discernment, sir.' Celestine accepted his adoration as her due. 'I have urgent business with Mr Loveday. Which is his room?'

'I've not heard 'im about yet. 'E came in late last night. May I offer yer good self the comfort of our parlour while I summon 'im?'

'That will not be necessary, my good man. His room, which is it?'

'Top of stairs, third on right. Lucky beggar,' he finished as he watched Celestine's swaying hips as she climbed the stairs.

Celestine did not bother to knock but barged into Japhet's room. She was furious with him for ignoring her notes demanding that he attend on her. He was asleep on the bed still in the clothes he had worn the previous evening. She was about to shake him awake and give him a piece of her mind when curiosity got the better of her. She had never been in his rooms before and Japhet was very close-mouthed about his family and life.

There were few possessions in the room. His shaving equipment was by the washstand in a corner. A dagger, two silver-handled pistols, and a powder cask lay on a table by the bed, and a sword belt hung from a wall hook. The door of a hanging closet was open and she examined the jackets on its hooks, not hesitating to put her hand in the pockets in search of some new information about him. She found nothing of interest. The clothes smelled of his scent and as she ran her fingers over the velvet, her body ached with desire for him.

'Come, slug-a-bed, and see what joy the morning has brought you,' she laughed, and began to pull the pins from her ostrich-feather-trimmed hat. Japhet did not stir. Something glittered in the sunlight that splashed across the floorboards at the foot of the bed, drawing her attention. Only a piece of jewellery would sparkle in that fashion.

Her heart beat faster and, careful now to move quietly so that she did not wake her lover, she lifted the bedcover to reveal a leather saddlebag. The catch had not been fastened properly and a diamond bracelet was draped over the edge of the bag. When she flipped back the top flap of the bag she gasped with pleasure. Several pieces of diamond jewellery winked at her in the sunlight. She clutched them to her breast. There were two necklaces, a tiara, three bracelets, two pairs of ear drops and two enormous rings. One of the necklaces was an unusual design and she frowned as she examined it. Hadn't Lady Sefton worn just such a piece when she last attended the theatre? Their box had been at the side of the stage and Celestine had paused in the performance to flirt with Lord Sefton, and her avaricious glance had settled on the exquisite necklace, which was wasted on Lady Sefton's scrawny neck.

The touch of the diamonds was warm against her fingers. The necklace drew her irresistibly and she replaced the rest of the jewellery in the bag and paraded in front of the small shaving mirror with the necklace held against her throat.

A movement and groan from the bed made her thrust the necklace down her bodice and she turned to face her lover. Japhet owed her such a piece of jewellery for all the times she had entertained him, and she did not intend to be fobbed off with a mere bracelet or ring from this substantial haul.

Japhet groaned again and flung an arm across his chest. It was then she noticed the blood on his jacket. Her first thoughts were that he could discover she had found the cache of jewels, and she quickly pushed the bag back under the bed with her foot. A hasty touch of her hand on her bodice reassured her that the necklace was safely hidden from sight.

'Japhet, my darling. How late you are abed.' She decided to pretend she knew nothing of the jewels. Once she had the necklace safely hidden in her home he could accuse her of the theft and she would deny it. 'Oh, and is that blood? Whatever has happened?'

The sound of Celestine's voice was the last thing Japhet wanted to hear. His side ached abominably and if she suspected that he had been involved in a robbery, she would have a dangerous weapon to hold over his head. He could not even remember if he had hidden the saddlebag on his return. And what the devil was Celestine doing in his rooms anyway?

He shook his head to clear his mind and swung his feet to the floor. He could feel the sweat forming on his brow, and the pain in his side felt as though an iron had branded him. A rapid survey of the room showed that the saddlebag was nowhere in sight and he remembered that he had stashed it under the bed.

'How were you hurt?' Celestine persisted.

'A duel. A man was cheating at cards and I called him out. He nicked me with his sword but I had already drawn first blood so honour is satisfied.'

'Have you seen a physician?'

'I do not need a physician. And duelling is illegal. It is but a scratch.' He reached out to pull her down on to the bed, but she evaded him. The sudden movement had caused a rush of dizziness and he needed a moment to collect his composure. He was displeased to find her in his rooms but the quickest way to get rid of her was to placate her. 'What brings you here?'

'You have been ignoring me,' she simpered as she paraded in front of him. 'I would not stand for any other lover to treat me as you do.'

The sweet musky perfume with which she liberally sprayed her body was overpoweringly nauseous when he was weak from lack of sleep and loss of blood. He rose unsteadily to his feet and was forced to bite the inside of his lip at the pain in his side as he held himself tall and erect. If Celestine detected any weakness in him she would be relentless in her demands. He had wanted to end their relationship and instead he found himself needing to placate her. 'I have commitments to my family while they are in London. I thought you understood that. And I've been looking for horses. That is how I make my living.'

'And does it not concern you that I miss you?'

He caught her to him with a smile that disguised his growing unease in her company. The wound in his side was aching and he wanted her out of the way so that he could attend to it. He kissed her with a thoroughness that silenced her and her body swayed against him, her voice breathless in his ear.

'Japhet, you must know that I love you.'

Over the rooftops a church tower struck one o'clock. The single note was as menacing as a death knell. He had thought her too mercenary to love anyone but herself. He did not want her love: such declarations had always been the end of any past relationship. Her declaration was alarming, for a woman as parsimonious in her affections as Celestine, once smitten, would be doubly vengeful if she were rejected. Her long nails dug in to his back and he pulled away. 'I thought you had a matinée today. Should you not be at the theatre?'

Her lips twisted into an angry line. 'Is that all you can say, when I tell you that I love you?'

'I am deeply honoured.'

Celestine struck his arm with her fist, pouted and stamped her foot. 'It is abominable the way you treat me. Not once have you given me a gift to show how much you care.'

'Then perhaps I am not the right man for you.' He was in too much pain to reason with her. 'If I cannot give you what you want then you are better served by other lovers.'

'You care nothing for me!' Her voice rose with a shrill hysteria. 'Some of the highest and most noble men in the land have begged me to grant them my favours. How dare you, a common highwayman, treat me in so dastardly a fashion? I could see you rot in prison – hang even.'

Prickles of fear skimmed his flesh. 'Celestine, my dear, what madness is this? I will not pander to your romantic illusion that I am a tobyman. You burst into

309

my room and my wits are barely with me after my ordeal last night. I think only of your own interest. If I weary you so, other men would clamour to claim your attention.'

Celestine drew a sharp breath to combat a rush of tears that threatened to betray her. Even dishevelled from sleep Japhet was so damnably handsome. 'You are cruel. You never weary me, damn you. But you desert me for nights upon end.'

'Nights where you have not wanted for company, my angel.' He smiled. 'Have I not called upon you and you have been surrounded by admirers, or you have arranged a card party. You are a beautiful and accomplished woman, but I will not stand in line to be granted your favours.'

'You needed to be taught a lesson.' Her anger at him was dissipating, and her body craved for him to take her into his arms and tell her how much he loved her. But they were words that he had never spoken, nor had he ever promised her his undying devotion. Japhet was infuriatingly elusive when it came to voicing his emotions. Her vanity would not allow her to believe that he was not totally infatuated with her, and she had convinced herself that his aloofness was because he was in awe of her charms and beauty.

When Japhet remained on the far side of the room, she pouted prettily in a manner that usually made men protest their devotion. 'I am Celestine Yorke and no common doxy. Do you not care for me enough to give me a token of your esteem? I find that both insulting and upsetting.'

'Then you do yourself a disservice, my dear.'

It was not the reassurance she was seeking and she could not suppress a moment's spite. 'Do not take me for a fool. I know what you were up to last night, my darling. I do not believe this tale of a duel. I saw the jewels hidden in the bag under your bed, Gentleman James. No card player would wager such jewels. But a highwayman would have in his possession such booty. I deserve a small trinket, do I not?'

He did not move and his expression was dark and forbidding. There was something in the fathomless glitter in his hazel eyes that frightened her. It also made him the most fascinating man she had ever met. She had no intention of losing him as a lover.

She laughed seductively. 'Do you fear that I will betray you? It is far more exciting having Gentleman James paying court to me than plain Japhet Loveday.' She held out her arm. 'A bracelet – is that too much to expect? A token of your love which would bind us in secrecy.'

He shrugged but the dangerous glitter in his eyes intensified. 'Do not threaten me, Celestine. I am not Gentleman James. I won those jewels in a card game from a French countess who had more money than sense.'

Was he trying to trick her? She recognised the necklace as belonging to Lady Sefton, but could not mention that now that she had taken it. Celestine juggled her greed and desire for Japhet. Desire won. She had begun to fear that he was tiring of her. She had been a fool to speak of her love. Now he would take her for granted and that would not suit her at all.

'You are a rogue by nature, used to living on your wits. You may have been born a gentleman – but no gentleman carries the scars of a whip on his back as you do.' Her hands rested on her hips, and she was antagonistic and accusing.

Japhet had never removed his shirt during their romps together but it was likely that Celestine would have felt the ridges of the scars and been intrigued by them.

'How did you come by them, Japhet? Were you flogged for stealing in the past?'

'A sea captain returned unexpectedly and found me in bed with his wife. A sword is no match against the cat-o'-nine-tails when a fellow is naked.'

Celestine's eyes widened in amusement. 'Is that the truth?'

'Unfortunately, yes.' Japhet saw no point in lying. 'And you are not whipped for stealing, you are arrested and hanged.'

Again, Celestine felt that Japhet had outwitted her. He had never responded to her threats to win him; she must resort to more devious means. She changed tactics.

'I must away to the playhouse. Unfortunately Pettigrew is being tiresome and demanding that I entertain him tonight. I shall ensure that I am free after the performance tomorrow. There will be no gaming or other guests, I promise. Do not disappoint me and I shall be expecting a token worthy of the esteem in which you value my favours. I shall treasure it above everything else I possess.'

Japhet closed the door on Celestine with relief. The woman was becoming impossible. He was uneasy that she had found his cache of jewels but hoped that a sizeable trinket would ensure her silence. Celestine loved gossip and drama, and that was making her dangerous. It was time to end with her. A bracelet would be a fitting parting gift.

The ache across his ribs was troublesome but when he stripped off his shirt he found that the bullet had sliced through his flesh the depth of his little finger. It looked clean and uninfected but was still oozing blood. He fashioned a pad and a bandage to stop the bleeding and, once dressed, pulled the saddlebag out and opened it to assess the contents. He frowned. He had thought there were more jewels, but in his confused state of mind last night he must have been mistaken. The haul was still impressive.

Once the jewels were sold he would then deposit the cash in Thomas's bank, vowing to himself that no matter how dire his circumstances he would never rob again. His thoughts turned to Gwen. The last few weeks in her company had showed him the two contrasts of his life. Celestine represented all that was irresponsible and bad whereas Gwen, with her goodness, held out a light that could reclaim him.

Chapter Twenty

Celestine arrived at the playhouse in a buoyant mood; it soon dissipated when she walked on stage to discover the theatre was no more than half full. The same happened at the evening performance and in the second act she was even booed, and insults shouted when she forgot her lines. In one of the boxes she had glimpsed Sir Marcus Grundy arrive with the young actress Maggie Flynn languishing on his arm. The couple laughed uproariously throughout the catcalls. To cover her humiliation Celestine engaged the audience in some lewd asides, which usually won them over, but even those received a frosty reception.

Her anger sparked and she played every line of innuendo to the wealthier patrons in the boxes. Yet on several occasions she found the young dandies did not even halt in their conversation or show signs of acknowledging the tribute she was playing to them. Playhouses were always noisy throughout a performance, with the orange and lemonade sellers touting their wares, and people calling out greetings to friends. The gentry and merchants came to make secret assignations, pursue business deals, exchange gossip, or simply to be reacquainted with old friends. The common populace of London crowded into the pit: it was an opportunity to pick pockets, and for prostitutes to solicit customers. It was a rare customer who came solely to see the play. But Celestine was used to receiving the adoration of the men in the audience. Tonight, as with too many recent performances, she found that adoration missing. She was losing her popularity and it terrified her.

Only three men came to her dressing room after the show. Even Sir Pettigrew arrived late, and he had a smear of lipstick on his cravat and was drunk. Normally Celestine would have thrown him out, but none of the other men had anything close to a quarter of his fortune, and not one of them had brought her a gift. Her mood soured. A drunken Sir Pettigrew was a poor substitute for Japhet's prowess in bed.

As she pulled on her cloak and pushed her hands into her muff she felt the diamond necklace that she had stolen from Japhet's room, which was secreted in the lining. The diamond necklace was extremely valuable, but unfortunately the piece was easily recognisable, as Lady Sefton wore it often and it irked Celestine that it would be dangerous for her to wear it in public. She would have to sell it and the unscrupulous fence she used would not give her a fifth of its true value.

The brandy fumes from Sir Pettigrew's breath hit her full in the face and he stumbled against her as they walked through the dimly lit corridor to the stage door. The baronet could be an arrogant bore and she was growing weary of him. The manager of the theatre appeared at the door of his office. His powdered wig was askew, and red wine and snuff stained the front of his shirt.

'I'll have a word with you, Mrs Yorke, before you leave, if you please.'

Celestine did not like his tone. She stepped back to avoid the rank smell of mildew that always permeated his clothing. 'The hour is late and I have company, Mr Samuels. Tomorrow before the performance will be more convenient.'

'There will be no performance for you tomorrow.' Samuels snapped. 'And a relief it will be not to have to put up with your uppity ways. You ain't filled the house with an audience in months. Maggie Flynn is taking your part and she'll have the lead in the next play as well. You'll be playing her mother in that play.'

'Her mother! I'll play the lead or not at all.' Celestine could not believe that they would relegate her to a minor role and one that portrayed an older woman. It was mortifying.

The manager shrugged. 'Then we'll find someone else to play the mother and you can find another playhouse for your fading talents. Good day, Mrs Yorke.' He shut the door of his office before she could respond.

'Did you hear that, Sir Pettigrew? The indignity of it.'

'Hear what, my sweet?' He had fallen back against

the wall and his eyes were bleary as he struggled to keep them open.

Her mouth clamped shut. At least Sir Pettigrew had been too drunk to witness her shame. She grabbed his arm and propelled him to the door and his waiting coach. This was the third theatre to dispense of her services in a year. The ruse to regain her popularity by publicising the robbery by Gentleman James had failed.

She had seen too many actresses fade into obscurity and poverty, and was determined that would not happen to her. Without the notoriety of her popularity on the stage, it would not take long before invitations to entertainments would stop. It was a life she adored and was not prepared to give up. As age caught up with her and her looks began to fade, she could not expect to be kept as a courtesan. She needed a husband – a man of standing and good family. Sir Pettigrew was married, as were all the lovers she had recently taken. All except Japhet. Japhet was not rich, but he was a wily rogue and could earn a fortune from his gambling. She had been drugging his wine so that he lost at cards and would return to highway robbery. And Japhet was the only man whom she had loved, in her own fashion.

She could feel panic rising in her breast. Obscurity was looming threateningly close. To create a new life she needed to be respectably married to a man of status. Why should she not wed Japhet? Marriage to him would not only be exciting, it would ensure that she maintained the standard of life that she adored.

Their wedding would be a grand affair; the public loved a spectacle and she would reclaim favour in their eyes and restore her place as 'the Darling of London'.

The plan excited her. Was not Japhet's cousin Thomas Mercer, who was not only a banker but also a playwright of no little repute? Celestine knew it would be hard to live without the adoration of the public that she had enjoyed for so long. Once married to Japhet she could always return to the stage and, with a famous playwright now part of her family, she had no doubts that Thomas Mercer would be honoured to write a play with her as the central character.

As she sat in the coach listening to Sir Pettigrew snore as he slumped in the seat across from her, she touched the stolen necklace in the lining of her muff. Celestine knew that Japhet would not surrender his bachelor status easily, but she had never yet failed to get any man to do her bidding. The necklace was an added insurance that she would bring Japhet to heel.

Tonight Japhet intended to end his relationship with Celestine and to ease their parting he had brought her an amethyst and diamond bracelet. When he gave it to her he told her he was returning to Cornwall.

'I will not hear of it, my love,' she informed him. She admired the bracelet on her wrist. 'This tells me that you love me. You are angry that I still see Sir Pettigrew but that will all end when we marry. I love you, Japhet. We are right for each other.'

Her impassioned speech blinded her to the horror on his face. 'There will be no marriage, Celestine. The bracelet is a parting gift. My life is in Cornwall. London is where you belong. You would be bored in the country.'

'As will you, my darling. You make your living by gambling. The highest stakes are always in London. Where else will you find the excitement you crave?'

Japhet's expression hardened. 'You know me not at all, madam. It had always been my intent to own a stud farm and raise racehorses. Gambling is a pastime – London a place for brief diversion. Cornwall is my home. No true Cornishman can stray from its shores for long. It is a land that has a majesty of its own.'

'You talk like some country dolt!' she sneered. 'London is refined and civilised. It is where society blossoms.'

'We clearly view such matters differently. That is why it is time to part.'

'You cannot cast me aside like an unwanted glove. You should be honoured that I have given you my love. I have been wooed by nobles and prominent men at His Majesty's court.' Her face twisted with wrath, she whirled round and, with a sweep of her arms, dashed to the floor the vases, candlesticks and ornaments on the mantel shelf.

'I am honoured that you have shown me such affection and I am not worthy,' Japhet placated. The scene disturbed him and he wanted to escape as soon as possible.

Celestine's body shook from the rage that consumed her. 'You *will* marry me. I have decided upon it. If you do not I will inform the authorities that you are Gentleman James. Sir Pettigrew will declare the same. He wants to see the man who robbed him hanged.'

Though his blood ran cold at her threats, Japhet threw back his head and laughed aside her accusations. 'No one else has been robbed by this imaginary Gentleman James.'

'I heard Lord Sefton had been robbed on the heath last week,' she added slyly. 'It was the same night as you came by those jewels you claim you won in a card game.'

'As indeed I did, madam.'

'Which French countess was it you won them from?' She eyed him with a smug expression. 'I shall ask Sir Pettigrew to check your story.'

Japhet had sold the jewels and felt safe against her accusations. 'If you doubt my word it is for you to find out those facts, madam. Take care you do not make of yourself a laughing stock. Since your fall from favour on the stage there would be many to snigger that you are bent upon taking revenge upon a lover who has spurned you.'

Celestine gasped and burst into tears. 'Why must you be so cruel? Of course I do not doubt your word. Tell me there is no one else. Tell me that you do not leave London to pursue another woman. Tell me that you have no intention of wedding another.'

Japhet took her into his arms. 'There will never be another woman like you in my life,' he declared with bitter irony. 'I value my freedom too much to squander it. It will be years before my stud farm is successful enough to support a wife and family.'

She lifted her tear-lined face. 'This is the truth? You do not lie?'

'I give you my word. At this moment I have no intention of losing my freedom.'

To his relief Celestine stopped crying. 'When do you leave London?'

'Soon. I have plans to make and the roads will as yet be difficult.'

She wound her arms around him and rubbed her hips against his loins. 'Then we must make the most of what time we have.' She pulled him down on to the rug before the roaring fire, brushing aside the scattered ornaments with her foot.

Celestine gave herself to Japhet with abandon. She used every trick she knew to enslave a sensual man and refused to believe that Japhet would forsake her.

Japhet dined with his family after leaving Celestine. The actress's mood had unsettled him. He did not trust her. Celestine had come to represent all that was bad and wrong in his life. Her malevolence clung to him, insidious and choking as bindweed. In contrast, Gwendolyn's friendship became a refuge. If only his aunt was not so set upon matchmaking them as a couple, he would be completely at peace in Gwendolyn's company.

Japhet was restless to leave London. It was no longer safe for him. He had enough money to buy half a dozen brood mares and pay for them to be covered by a prize-winning racing stallion. Perhaps it was time to consider his future. He had spent over a decade evading the scrapes his wildness had created.

When he arrived at the house in the Strand it was to find Amelia being consoled by Georganna, and Aunt Margaret pacing between the marble fireplace and her walnut writing desk in the far corner. Gwendolyn sat on the window seat, tense and pale. You could cut the atmosphere with a knife.

Aunt Margaret clutched a letter in her hand and had her back to the door as Japhet entered. 'You must return to Cornwall at once, Amelia. Edward needs you.'

'If Edward had wanted me at his side, he would have written to me and not to you.' Amelia dabbed at her eyes.

'Edward is too proud to demand your return, but he would expect you to know your duty.' Margaret was angrier than Japhet had ever seen her. 'This is the opportunity for the two of you to make your peace.'

Georganna gripped Amelia's hand. 'I agree with Mama. You cannot mean for this coolness to continue in your marriage. Uncle Edward adores you.'

Amelia lay back on the padded settle and put a hand to her temple.

'What has happened?' Japhet asked, uncomfortable at finding himself in the middle of so personal a family quarrel.

Margaret thrust the letter into his hands. 'There's been a fire at the shipyard and the launch of the brigantine has been delayed by up to three months. Edwards makes light of it, but then he would not want us to worry unduly. Yet I am sure the repercussions of the fire are serious. He also speaks of lost orders.' She glanced impatiently towards Amelia, who kept her eyes covered with her hand. 'Edward stood by us last year in our time of need, and now he is facing this crisis alone. It is so unjust.'

Japhet scanned the letter and absently rubbed his ribs to ease the ache from his wound. 'I think the situation is more serious than Uncle Edward is saying, otherwise he would not have mentioned the incidents.'

Margaret sighed and nodded in agreement. 'Thomas intends to advance him the money he needs to complete the ship. It is the least we can do.'

'It cannot help that Adam and St John are away.' Japhet frowned into the distance for a long moment, then announced, 'I should return and offer to run Trevowan for him. That way Uncle Edward can devote all his time to the yard.'

'Japhet, with respect, when did you ever manage a large estate?' Margaret remarked.

'Japhet spent several weeks last summer helping his sister, Hannah, on their farm,' Gwen defended.

Amelia stood up, her manner strained. 'It is I who should return. I know you condemn me for deserting Edward. And I have tried to come to terms with the existence of that child – but it pains me deeply.' She inhaled sharply before announcing, 'Clearly, the issue of Edward's daughter will not be resolved while I am in London. Yet for me to travel at this time—' she broke off.

'The journey will be uncomfortable, but in the

circumstances . . .' Margaret remained scathing.

With a sob, Amelia announced, 'I am with child.'

For several moments everyone was too stunned by her news to speak.

'Then you cannot consider travelling.' Margaret recovered from her shock and her manner changed to compassion. 'The roads will be hazardous. Coach wheels frequently become stuck in the deep mud-filled ruts in winter. Even if the frost holds, you will be shaken and buffeted every mile of the way. It cannot be considered in your condition. Does Edward know of the child?'

Amelia shook her head. 'I was not certain myself when I left Cornwall. I was weak when Edward most needed me to be strong. I came to London to avoid the gossip and scandal plaguing our family in Cornwall. My lack of support must have contributed to the loss of orders. It will have added to the scandal and gossip.'

'You concern yourself too much with gossip, Amelia,' Gwendolyn observed. 'It is wonderful news that you are to have a child.'

'It is just what is needed to heal this silly rift between you and my brother,' Margaret encouraged. 'He will be the first to insist that in the circumstances you must remain in London until the roads are less injurious to your health.'

Georganna impetuously hugged Amelia. 'You are so brave to even consider travelling in your condition. There is no point in blaming yourself for what is done and past.'

Amelia rose with a new determination in her

manner. 'I will leave for Cornwall as soon as I am packed. I will hire a private coach and driver and take the journey in slow stages. Will you be returning with me, Gwendolyn?'

The younger woman started and looked flustered. 'I had intended to remain in London at least until late spring.'

'You too have allowed a rift with your family to continue for too long,' Margaret suggested. 'Perhaps it is time—'

'No. I will not return yet.' Gwendolyn tilted her chin in defiance. 'I have prevailed upon your generosity for too long. It is time I rented a house.'

Georganna intervened. 'You cannot live on your own. Of course you are welcome to stay here. Is she not, Mama?'

'I have no intention of turning you out, Gwendolyn,' Margaret replied. 'It would be unseemly for a single woman to live on her own.'

She followed Amelia from the room, having closed the subject to her satisfaction. Georganna also stood up. 'The sun is shining. How pleasant it would be to drive to the park. Gwen was saying earlier that it has been days since the weather allowed us to go out. Japhet, will you not join us, if you have no other appointment?'

Gwen made an excuse for him. 'I am sure that Japhet is busy.' He glanced at her but she did not meet his eye and continued in a rush, 'I have much with which to occupy myself this afternoon. I shall write a letter for Amelia to take to Mama. I do not want

Amelia to face any unpleasantness from my family because I choose to remain in London.'

Japhet was startled by Gwendolyn's excuse. She had always been so eager to accompany him that he had taken her acceptance for granted. 'Surely, there is time to write your letter this evening, Gwen. I have no arrangements and would be delighted to escort you.' His aunt returned to the salon and he added, 'Will you join us, Aunt Margaret?'

She shook her head. 'Not on this occasion. Mrs Bailey, my seamstress, is to call in an hour to deliver a dress and I have another for her to alter. I shall keep Japhet entertained until Georganna and Gwen have readied themselves. Wrap up warm, young ladies. Despite the sun there will still be a chill in the air.'

When Margaret was alone with Japhet she stared fixedly at her nephew. 'You have sadly neglected Gwendolyn. I am glad you will be escorting her this afternoon. I fear that she is lonely in London.' Her eyes were assessing and thoughtful. 'You do not look well, Japhet. You are pale. You do not look after yourself properly.'

Japhet felt his cheeks redden. His wound ached and the lovemaking that Celestine had instigated had been energetic, causing the wound to bleed profusely. He had needed to place a dressing on it before visiting his family.

Margaret had seated herself by the window and drawn a sewing frame towards her. As she lifted her basket of silks on her lap, she frowned at her nephew. 'From the look of you, you have been up to no good, nephew. Last time four of my friends called, they would talk of nothing but that your name has been linked with that of a common actress. Celestine Yorke has ruined the lives of several gentlemen, bleeding them dry of every penny that they possessed. One such gentleman shot himself when she discarded him when he had no money left to lavish upon her. It is time that you settled down, Japhet.'

Japhet crossed his long legs and clasped his hands in his lap. He had learned years ago not to contradict Aunt Margaret when she was in a mood to lecture. She was less of a virago than Elspeth but even so, when crossed, she could be formidable.

'I shall be leaving London soon. In the next weeks I shall be travelling to buy some brood mares. I thought I might rent a field from Hannah and stable them on the farm this year until they foal.'

'I would feel happier if Amelia did not travel alone in her condition.'

'Then I shall accompany her.' Japhet warmed to the idea. It was a legitimate excuse to leave London and it would allow his relationship with Celestine to cool. The actress could not take it amiss, if he escorted Amelia. In Cornwall he would offer his services to Edward. En route there were some stud farms he would visit while Amelia rested.

Gwendolyn and Georganna appeared in fur-lined cloaks, the hoods trimmed with miniver, and each woman carried a matching muff. Margaret sighed with pleasure. 'Do they not look charming, Japhet? Gwendolyn has become a real beauty, has she not?'

Japhet rose to bow over both women's hands. 'Gwen is more lovely each time I see her. As is Georganna.'

'Keep your flattery,' Georganna laughed. 'It is wasted upon me. I am plain and thin as a pikestaff. What my handsome Thomas ever saw in me still never ceases to amaze me.'

'You have the most brilliant wit and Thomas clearly adores you,' Japhet responded. Like many of the family when he had first met Georganna he had thought her plain. He had assumed that his cousin had married her for her half-share in Lascalles Bank when Mercer's Bank was in danger of failing. After several meetings with Georganna, Japhet had found her to be an exceptional woman. He had never heard her make a derogatory remark about another person. She encouraged Thomas to continue his play writing, which his mother saw as detrimental to the interests of the bank. It had made Japhet realise that beauty was not everything, especially within a marriage. The woman a man planned to spend the rest of his years with needed to be compassionate and understanding of her husband's nature.

Margaret walked to her desk. 'I must write to Edward before Mrs Bailey arrives. And also a letter to Lady Anne Druce to reassure her that all is well with Gwendolyn.' As Japhet escorted the younger women to the door, she called out, 'I will send word to Amelia that you will accompany her, Japhet.'

'You are to leave London?' Gwendolyn fidgeted with her muff and would not look at him.

'Yes. I will offer my services to Uncle Edward.' He handed Gwendolyn into the carriage but as he turned to Georganna she gasped in dismay. 'I have just remembered I need to consult with Mrs Bailey about a new dress for the ball we are to attend at the end of the month. Forgive me, but I must decline to join you for the drive.' She ran back into the house before they could protest.

Gwendolyn became flustered. 'Perhaps we should abandon the drive. I am sure you have many things you need to attend to, Japhet. Especially if you are to leave . . .' Her voice broke and she leaped to her feet. 'I will not detain you.'

He put his arm about her waist and drew her back on to the seat beside him as the coach moved off. 'Would you also desert me when my aunt and Georganna have clearly contrived this ruse to throw us together?'

'How can you jest? Your aunt embarrasses me with her matchmaking. She is almost as bad as mama.'

He kept his arm around her and could feel the tension in her figure. 'Perhaps you feel that your reputation would be in danger if we are seen together. There is the coachman, who passes as a chaperon.'

'When did I need a chaperon with you, Japhet?' Her voice was sharp and she shifted so that their bodies were not touching. She struggled to come to terms with the news that he would return to Cornwall. She had been a fool to come to London. Since the evening that she had seen him with Celestine Yorke, she had realised that she had allowed her romantic ideals to cloud her judgement. She had been deluded in believing that Japhet cared for her. Foolishly, she had read more into their parting in Bodmin than there had been. Japhet saw her as a friend and she would never be more than that to him.

In recent weeks she had steeled herself against the sway he held over her emotions. It had made her analyse her life and how she could find fulfilment and meaning within it. She still balked at marriage to a man she did not love. The strength she had found to defy her mother and come to London had shown her that she could break away from her mother's stifling influence. Yet an unmarried woman of her class could never live alone without being ostracised by society. A spinster was often an object of pity that she had been unable to catch a husband. However much she may resent it, she remained a prisoner to convention. If she lived alone she would be regarded as no better than a fallen woman.

The casual way that Japhet had decided to return to Cornwall had thrown her into confusion. Pride would keep her in London, for she could not bear to return to Cornwall and again be subject to her mother's dominance. Seated so close to Japhet in the coach was torture. All her dreams had been cast to the winds and her heart felt that it was breaking.

To shield her pain from him, her manner became unnaturally stiff, her voice cool and polite. 'You talk of buying mares. Does that mean you finally intend to start a stud farm?'

'I'll rent a field from Hannah and Oswald and

convert one of their barns into stables. Oswald has been ill again this winter. If I rented from them, not only would it help them financially, but also I could assist on the farm without Oswald feeling that he was beholden to me. I enjoyed working on the farm with them last summer.'

There was a deeper passion to his voice when he now spoke of his plans for his future. She hoped that it meant he was prepared to give up his wild life, which she always feared would be his undoing. 'Your sister will delight in having you, but somehow I cannot see you content for so long surrounded by her children. They are a noisy boisterous brood. Will you not soon miss your old life?'

The statement was without recrimination but it tweaked at Japhet's conscience. 'Undoubtedly, I will find it hard at first and I have reservations that a life of respectability may eventually suffocate me. I feel that I have failed Uncle Edward by leaving Cornwall, knowing that Adam and St John would be out of the country for months.'

'You were not to know that Mr Loveday would face so many problems at the yard this winter.'

'Uncle Edward was always generous to my parents and paid for my own and Pious Peter's education. On several occasions he has saved me from the consequences of a misspent youth.' Guilt continued to attack Japhet. 'If I had stayed in Cornwall I could have taken over some of St John's responsibilities on the estate. Now that there has been this fire, Uncle Edward must feel his family have deserted him when he was most in need of them.'

'Something deeper than your uncle's problems is troubling you, Japhet. What is it?'

Gwen's insight unnerved him. He forced a laugh to allay her fears. There were times when she seemed to know him better than he knew himself. 'It is nothing more than a touch of the megrims, as my dear mama would say. Winter always makes me restless.'

The coach lurched in a pothole in the road. Japhet's injured torso was thrown against the side of the vehicle and he put his hand to his mouth and coughed to disguise his grimace of pain.

Gwendolyn smoothed down her skirts in an agitated manner as the coach jolted. Her thigh brushed against Japhet's leg and she lowered her eyes. The close proximity of Japhet was making her heart race uncomfortably fast.

'I feel guilty that the dreadful things my mother said to you caused you to leave Cornwall.'

'Nothing the Lady Anne could say would drive me away if I had not thought it best for your reputation.'

'My mother is the one who did her best to destroy my reputation.'

'Beaumont should have been called to account for the way he treated you. He wasted no time in marrying another heiress. Maria Thackwell is damnably plain, if I remember aright.' Japhet laughed. 'There'll be no joy in that marriage bed for Beaumont.'

His words sparked a pain that clamped Gwendolyn's heart in a vice and she retaliated acerbically, 'Can a plain woman not make a man happy? Celestine Yorke is very beautiful. Are you happy with her?'

Japhet raised a dark brow. 'If Celestine did not have beauty, she would have nothing. Her looks brought her fame but she is a selfish, manipulative woman, who cares only for her own interests and not the welfare of others. But why do you mention her?'

'Because your name is linked with hers.' She became flustered and a blush heated her cheeks. Angry at allowing her jealousy to run roughshod over her composure, Gwendolyn clenched her fists and held them in her lap. 'Of late you have not been your carefree self and you look drawn and haggard, Japhet. Or does she play you false? She has many admirers.'

Japhet lifted her chin with his forefinger and his hazel eyes were dark with concern. 'Celestine cannot hold a candle to you. You are all that is sweet and innocent.'

Those words 'sweet and innocent' summed up all the reasons why Gwendolyn believed that Japhet would never love her. Her eyes flashed with a resurgence of her misery. 'Odious fortune-hunters like Beaumont woo me for my money, and to you I am too innocent to be of consequence.'

'You do yourself a disservice, my dear.' He looked bewildered, his hazel eyes teasing as he held her gaze.

Japhet stroked the side of her cheek with a forefinger, its warmth sent a frisson of pleasure through her and she caught her breath. Then she armoured herself against her emotions. She was in no mood for platitudes. 'I am being realistic.'

'Sweet, Gwen, what you have is rare and precious.'

He kissed her mouth, the touch of his lips tender but without passion.

Pain and rage exploded within her and she lashed out to strike Japhet's chest with both fists. 'Stop treating me like a child to be humoured.'

The colour drained from his face as she struck his wound. He caught her hands and attempted to jest when she struggled to be free. 'I had not realised you were such a termagant.' His voice and expression were strained and his grip was tight on her hands when she continued to fight him.

When she saw the white grooves of pain around his mouth, she stopped struggling to stare at him. 'You are in pain. What ails you?'

'Nothing.' He straightened his spine and his lips parted in a smile. It ended in a grimace and despite the chill in the air, there was a sheen of perspiration on his brow.

Gwendolyn pulled back from his hold and saw the smudge of blood on his waistcoat where she had struck him with her fists. 'You have been hurt. What new scrape caused this?'

'A disagreement at the card table. It is nothing. You must not concern yourself.'

Her lips still tingled from his kiss but her body now burned with a different emotion, that of exasperation and sadness. 'Japhet, what devil drives you? You'll end up dead over some stupid, irresponsible incident. You are worthy of so much more.' Tears glistened in her eyes. 'Take me home and get that wound seen to before you travel with Amelia. I despair of you, truly I do.'

She lapsed into silence and stared out of the window. Japhet was stung by her censure. She had never judged him before. He grinned and tried to make light of the matter. Gwen ignored him, her silence glacial as she refused to meet his gaze. He touched a silken tendril of her coppery hair and when she pulled away, he frowned. Her attitude discomfited him. There was a sadness around her, which roused his gallantry and, knowing that he was partly to blame, he felt an overriding desire to protect her and return the smile to her face.

'Are you returning to Cornwall with us?' he asked.

'There is nothing in Cornwall for me.' The ice remained in her voice. 'Mama will be more overbearing than ever. I doubt I will be made welcome by her acquaintances. I will be ridiculed as the woman who jilted Admiral Beaumont's grandson.'

'Cornwall will not be the same without you.' Japhet realised how much that would be true.

The stare she turned upon him was haunted by anguish. He had never seen her so dispirited and his arm tightened around her. 'What can I do to put things right between us, Gwen? I was wrong to neglect you while you were in London. I wish you'd come back to Cornwall.'

She shook her head. 'You take me too much for granted, Japhet. And I was a fool to let you do so. I have seen in these last months how you wish to conduct your life. You choose to consort with women like Celestine Yorke, who have no thought but their own self-gratification.'

'But I do not choose such a life – not if I am honest. It has become a habit.' He defended with unusual heat for he never made excuses about the way he lived his life.

'Yet you continue it with relish. Can you not see the pain it causes those who care for you?'

Now it was his gaze that could not hold hers. 'My life has become a shambles these last months. You do not know the half of it, Gwen. The fire at Trevowan Hard is a tragedy, but it has given me the excuse I need to get out of London. The capital is a dangerous place for me at the moment.'

'You frighten me when you speak like that.' Tears spilled from her eyes and he was immediately contrite. He brushed the tears aside and cupped her lovely face in his hands.

'Are you in debt through gambling, Japhet? Let me give you a loan as one friend to another.' Her voice was soft and ragged with pain. 'It will be my parting gift, for I will no longer be part of the life of someone who is so set upon destroying himself.'

The difference between all that was good and wonderful in Gwendolyn and all that was evil in Celestine struck him anew. He had taken Gwen's affection and friendship for granted. Now he feared that he could lose her.

Chapter Twenty-One

A week of torrential rain prevented Japhet and Amelia leaving London. Amelia was fretful at the delay but she feared too much for her unborn child to risk travelling. The roads would be dangerously rutted, and made more hazardous by soft mud in which a coach could sink up to its axle. The journey was postponed until a heavy frost made the highways more stable.

Japhet also fretted at the delay. Now that he had decided to leave London, he was eager to put behind him the disastrous events since his arrival in the capital. Each day he remained brought more demands from Celestine Yorke. She refused to accept that their relationship was over. If he did not obey her summons to visit her, she would come uninvited to his rooms. Her moods were erratic and she was often irrational and upset, declaring that her career on the stage was finished and that he was cruel to abandon her.

She had visited every theatre manager in the city

and all had refused to give her work as the leading actress. Some had refused outright to employ her, saying that she had a reputation for causing dissent within a company, or that she was no longer a favourite of the audiences. Their rejection terrified her.

After each rejection she came to Japhet's rooms demanding comfort and reassurance. Japhet felt sorry for her and inevitably whenever she visited him they made love. Each time before she left she pleaded with him to stay in London. He was uncomfortably aware that since he had not left London immediately Celestine believed she still had power over his affections and that he was wavering in his resolve.

To escape her unwelcome visits he had decided to spend the last nights in London staying with his cousin. He was packing his travelling trunk when Celestine called unexpectedly at his rooms. When she saw the half-filled trunk she burst into tears.

'How can you desert me when I need you more than ever? Everyone is forsaking me,' she wailed.

'I have explained that my family is facing ruin. I have no choice but to return to Cornwall.'

'You would have left without saying farewell.'

'I intended to call upon you later. I have several appointments to attend before I leave.'

'My life will be unbearable without you. You are heartless to use me and abandon me so,' Celestine sobbed into a handkerchief.

'You have admirers enough who will keep you

amused.' Japhet controlled his impatience for her to leave.

'Is it that you are jealous of my other lovers? I will give them up for you.' She threw herself into his arms and pressed fervent kisses upon his neck. 'I have made no man that promise before.'

'My duty to my family must come before my pleasure.' Japhet had never taken her protestations of love seriously and this desperate show of possessiveness was disturbing.

She pouted and pressed her body against his to rouse his ardour. 'Cornwall is at the other end of the earth. I will not see you for months.'

'I cannot help that.' He moved away, unwilling to be coerced by her seductive tricks. When he turned his back on her to continue folding his shirts to put in the trunk, she flung herself dramatically at his feet and clung to his legs.

'I will not lose you, Japhet. I love you.'

Appalled at her conduct, he gently removed her arms from around him. 'This is undignified, Celestine. Osgood adores you.'

She lay sobbing on the floor but when he ignored her, her lips twisted into a vengeful line. 'Don't you dare abandon me! I'll make you regret deserting me. You forget I know your secret, Gentleman James.'

Her threat brought him back to her side. She smirked. 'I knew that would make you change your tune. I have your life in my hands . . .'

The vitriolic words dried in her throat as he unceremoniously hauled her to her feet and pinned her against the wall, her arms trapped against her sides so that she was powerless to retaliate. The fear in her eyes made him control his fury. He had never struck a woman but she had goaded him so that he was close to shaking her until her teeth rattled.

'Madam, your spite astounds me. Had a man made those threats I would have called him out to defend my honour. I have heard enough of your foolish accusations. Our time together will always hold special memories for me and you would taint them with vile slander. Forget your foolish notion that I am Gentleman James. Clearly the robbery on the heath has coddled your wits.'

He could feel her trembling but it was not his way to end a relationship with bad feeling. He raised her hand to his lips. 'I count myself honoured to have won the affection of the Darling of London, the most exciting actress of our age. Think well of this poor horse dealer, who is, as ever, your most devoted servant.'

The violence of his temper had alarmed her but his words soothed her wounded pride. She had forgotten her ploy not to threaten him. Again she had misjudged her lover.

'Forgive my tears, my love. I could not bear to lose you. No lover has given me such pleasure.' She kissed him with lingering passion and when she felt his body respond, she pulled at his clothing. To her consternation, he put her from him.

'Tempting as you are, I must resist. I have much to attend to this evening. I leave London tomorrow.' The lie was to stop her pursuing him while he stayed with Thomas. He picked up a small jewel box, which contained a heart-shaped garnet brooch that he had bought for Gwen to apologise for neglecting her. He would have time to buy his friend another before he left, though it would seriously deplete his savings. He hoped the trinket would appease Celestine. 'Farewell, dear lady.'

She sighed with pleasure as she gazed at the brooch. 'Promise me there is no one else. That would be too much to bear.'

'There is no one else.' He kissed her again and adeptly guided her to her waiting coach.

Celestine held the brooch against her breast. 'You are too stubborn to admit it, but the brooch is a token of your love. Why else would it be in the shape of a heart? Return soon, my love.'

Japhet ran his hand through his hair and let out a relieved sigh as she left him. He did not trust the actress but he hoped that he had placated her. Her affections were fickle and she would soon forget him once she found a wealthy admirer. Even so, he was troubled. If Celestine's days on the stage were numbered, she would use everything in her power to keep her name in the mind of the public. Japhet was certain that Celestine had no proof against him as a highwayman. The jewels she had discovered in his lodgings were sold and, as for the robbery on the heath, that was now months ago and it would be her word against his. Who would believe her after she had been his mistress for so long?

It was a relief to spend his last days in London with Thomas. He was welcomed by his family, but was also unprepared for the effect of Gwendolyn's presence in the house. She seemed to be putting a distance between them and became elusive when he sought her company.

On his third evening after the family had dined Japhet found he could not settle and paced the music room. He had lost his appetite for gaming and had not sought out any of his friends in the last days. Georganna and Thomas were visiting Lucien Greene. Aunt Margaret had insisted that Gwendolyn play the harpsichord to entertain them, but had soon made an excuse to leave them alone.

Gwendolyn halted in mid-tune but Japhet did not seem to notice as he stood by the window and pulled back the hangings to peer up at the sky.

'Your mind is elsewhere this night, Japhet. I will leave you to your contemplations.' Gwendolyn picked up her shawl from where she had draped it across a chair.

'Please stay. I have seen little of you of late.' He again looked up at the sky, saying, 'At last the stars shine brightly. There will be a second night of frost tonight and the roads will be passable.'

There was a cosy intimacy about the room with its burgundy curtains and padded chairs. The fire in the marble fireplace and the single candelabra on the harpsichord bathed the room in an amber glow. Japhet was dressed in black breeches and jacket, the white ruffles of his cuffs and cravat accentuating his swarthy skin. His handsome looks always affected her, and Gwendolyn had to swallow against a throat dry with desire before speaking. 'Then you will be leaving with Amelia tomorrow.'

He nodded. 'If we make the journey in easy stages it could take us anything up to three weeks. I hope she can cope with it.'

'When Amelia first came to Cornwall I thought she was a strong and resourceful woman. She has had a lot to contend with in the last two years. The strain on her was noticeable during St John's trial. She has regained her vigour with this break away from the problems at home.'

She picked at the fringe of her shawl and kept her head bowed. Even so, the image of Japhet's tall, rakish figure was indelibly burned into her mind. Now that his departure was imminent Gwendolyn found herself perilously close to tears. She breathed deeply to keep them at bay. It had been both a joy and a torture for her with Japhet living in the same house. She could not stop loving him, although she acknowledged that to have that love returned was an impossible dream. He would never feel anything more than friendship for her. It had taken a toll on her composure to treat him as a friend when her heart ached so wretchedly.

When Japhet again paced the music room, the scent of the sandalwood that he favoured wafted tantalising around Gwendolyn and her heart fluttered erratically. She cursed herself for being so foolish, and said impulsively, 'You have been agitated these last few days. What is wrong, Japhet?'

'Why must something be wrong?' He shot her a sideways glance, his face thrown into shadow. 'Once I have set my mind to do something I find any delay irksome.'

'There is more to it than that.' She sensed he was not being entirely truthful. 'Is it to do with the wound you received?'

He glared fiercely at her. 'Why do women always believe there must be drama behind every action a man performs?'

'I am not such a woman, and well you know it.' She crossed to a settle, her silk skirts rustling from the briskness of her step. 'You forget how well I know you, Japhet.'

Japhet smoothed his hand over his ebony hair. 'Does nothing escape you? It's a damnable business, that is for certain.'

Gwendolyn sat down and folded her hands in her lap. 'Tell me about it. I may be able to help.'

'It is nothing.' He shrugged and she sensed he was keeping something important from her. 'It is the waiting. If it were not for Amelia I would have left London days ago.'

'Why do I have the feeling that you are in trouble?'

His expression darkened, alerting her that she had touched on the truth. She continued despite his glower. 'Will you tell me what trouble you are in?'

He shook his head. 'It is nothing with which to concern yourself.'

The cavalier way he dismissed her fears roused her indignation. 'Stop treating me like a child, or an idiot.'

She leaped to her feet and ran towards the door.

He was there before her, barring her way. 'Gwen, what has upset you?' He took her arms, his touch burning through the silk of her gown.

'When you will not tell me what is wrong, then I can only fear the worst. If you do not want to confide in me, then what more is there for us to say?'

'Perhaps I fear your censure. You have always kept your faith in me when others would condemn me. That is important.'

Her body was rigid with tension. 'Not important enough for you to trust me.' Her gaze lifted to search his hooded eyes. She pulled back. 'Since you are to leave tomorrow, I will bid you farewell now. Safe journey, Japhet.'

'You would go just like that?' He sounded shocked.

'It is for the best.' She walked away.

'Someone may accuse me of highway robbery on the heath.' Japhet surprised himself by blurting out the confidence.

Gwendolyn put a hand to the wall for support and turned slowly to face him. 'If you are innocent, surely you have nothing to fear.'

'I have done many things that I regret. It was some months ago and I was not thinking rationally at the time.' He spread his hands. 'Now you know the worst of me. Do you hate me?'

'Highway robbery is a hanging offence.' Her eyes were round with fear. 'If this is some jest, Japhet, it is a poor one.'

'It is no jest.'

'Then who seeks to accuse you if it happened so long ago? Have they proof?'

'I doubt it, but they say hell hath no fury like a woman scorned. When I finished with Celestine Yorke, she threatened to inform on me. I continued to see her in the last few weeks to placate her. I do not trust her.'

A lacerating pain tore at Gwendolyn's heart at his casual mention of his mistress. 'Did you confide in her?'

He gave a derisive laugh. 'It was Osgood's coach that I held up. Celestine was with him. I was masked and the light was too poor for her to be absolutely sure that she recognised me. It was before I knew her. Osgood wants revenge on the man who held up his coach and Celestine may decide to denounce me.'

'But has she proof?'

Japhet shrugged, unwilling to mention the jewels he had stolen from the highwayman that Celestine had seen.

Gwendolyn backed away from him. 'Was she worth risking so much for?' Her voice broke and the tears spilled unheeded down her cheeks.

Witnessing her misery, Japhet felt guilty. He had never meant to cause her such pain by his confession. 'She is not worth a single one of your tears. What have I done to you, Gwen? Your mother was right. I am a worthless rogue, but as God is my witness I never meant to hurt you. How can I make amends?'

She shook her head. 'By being true to yourself.

Now, forgive me, but this has all been too much for me.' She fled the room.

Japhet threw himself into a chair by the fire and sank his head into his hands. Gwen's outburst had shaken him. It was only now that he realised how badly he had let her down. She had suffered her mother's spite because of him. She had jilted Beaumont and was condemned to face an uncertain future. Yet even now, knowing how low he had sunk, she had not judged him.

For an hour he stared into the dying flames of the fire. He was in torment and only Gwendolyn could give him peace. How could he fare without her?

When he rose from the chair he strode purposely to Gwen's room. He tapped gently on the door but there was no answer. It was not locked and he opened it and went inside. A single candle burned beside the bed. Gwen lay on the bedcovers fully clothed, her hands over her face, which was still wet with her tears.

'I've been such a fool,' he said, sitting on the edge of the bed and gathering her close. 'You are a remarkable woman. I shall miss you in Cornwall. Will you not reconsider returning with us?'

She shook her head. 'My life would be intolerable. The only way I can redeem myself in Mama's eyes is to return married.'

'Then marry me. Though I am the most unworthy wretch alive to be blessed with you as my bride.'

'I am too tired for your jesting, Japhet.' She pushed him away.

He kneeled at her side and took her hands in his.

'And if I did not mock but spoke in earnest, what would you say?'

She stared at him for several moments in disbelief, her gaze searching his. He grinned roguishly. 'For years I have been so bent upon travelling widely to seek pleasure that I have not seen that my greatest joy was within a few miles of my home.'

'But you do not love me. And how many times have I heard you say that you value your freedom too much to be shackled to a wife?'

'Now you would mock me. I know of no one who could make me happier. I adore you, Gwen, but I have always felt you were not for me. I did not want your family labelling me another fortune-hunter. And I do not want you facing censure from them and feel that you cannot return home. Unless you choose to live in London.'

'I prefer Cornwall and the hunting.' Gwendolyn rose up on to her knees and put her hands on his shoulders. 'Is this truly what you feel?'

He had buried his complex feelings for Gwen for so long, now that they had surfaced with such magnitude, he felt humbled in her presence. 'A devil has been riding my shoulder since I left Cornwall because I believed you could be happier with some-one else.' Anguish darkened his features. 'It is madness to talk of our future together now. The timing is wrong. I could lose everything if Celestine accuses me of robbery. I could lose my life – at the least bring disgrace to any who are associated with me.'

'If Celestine Yorke cares for you, she will not want to see you harmed.'

'She has none of your sweetness, my darling. If it served her own ends to bring her back into the public eye, she would not hesitate.' He held Gwen close and breathed in the scent of her hair and skin and sighed. 'I should not have spoken. I will not risk bringing shame upon you. Perhaps by the end of summer, if Celestine keeps silent, you will view my proposal more favourably.'

'I have not refused you. Neither would I wish to wait.'

Japhet clasped her hands together and kissed them. 'I do not deserve your affection. My darling Gwendolyn, would you do me the honour of becoming my bride? We will marry at Trewenna. Father would not forgive me if someone else officiated at my wedding. Can you be ready to leave in the morning?'

She flung her arms around his neck. 'Oh yes, Japhet. I will. I will.'

Then she scrambled from the bed. 'I have to pack. Oh, I want to tell someone. I am so excited. Aunt Margaret will be delighted.' She giggled. 'Mama will be furious.'

Chapter Twenty-Two

'Nathan was never as active as this.' Senara rubbed her side where the baby's foot banged against her ribcage. 'This one is not still for a minute. It will be an adventurer like his father.'

Tamasine walked at her side as they picked their way through the dead bracken to the riverbank at Boscabel. 'I thought you said you believed the child would be a girl,' Tamasine remarked.

'Aye, so I did.' Senara paused to watch a lizard basking on a rock in the afternoon sunlight. 'I knew Nathan would be a boy from the first month. I believed that this would be a girl until last month, when I have become so large and heavy. And girls are usually more placid in the womb than boys. This one wriggles like an eel.'

'Should you be walking so far, if your time is growing near?' Tamasine had been inquisitive about every aspect of Senara's pregnancy as it was a topic that had never been discussed at the academy. She had been innocent of the act of procreation, there being no animals at her school for her to have seen mating. Her own monthly flux had been explained as God's punishment on Eve for tricking Adam into eating the apple, and was the stigma all women must bear. When Senara had explained its true function in the cycle of life, and also how babies were conceived, Tamasine had stared at her in abject horror, stating, 'But that makes us no different from the cows in the field, or the wild beasts.'

Senara had laughed and replied, 'That is exactly so. Is not every living thing part of God's great creation? Must not the plants be pollinated by insects before they can produce their seeds or fruit? It is why we should respect all life, yet the tragedy is that man cannot even get on with man.'

'The revolution in France is an example of that,' said Tamasine. 'Mr Loveday explained something of the cause of the war with France to me last week. So many people have been murdered upon the guillotine. The peasants rose up against their masters.'

'Or were fighting to right the injustice of poverty and discrimination against the poor,' Senara had corrected. 'But how can there be any justification in taking another's life? The gaols of England are crowded with men and women who have committed no greater crime than stealing a loaf of bread to feed their families, or taking a rabbit from the land of a wealthy landowner. They have been condemned to be hanged, and the judge will think himself lenient if they are spared death to face transportation to Botany Bay on the other side of the world. They will never see their families or loved ones again. There has always been one law for the rich and another for the poor.'

Senara had been unable to contain her sense of injustice and added, 'I should not voice those opinions to you – Mr Loveday would not approve – but I had to live with such injustice at first-hand when I lived with my father's family as a child.'

'You mean with the gypsies.' Tamasine was all curiosity again. 'What was such a life like?'

'I promised Mr Loveday that I would not talk of such matters with you. Suffice that it could be a hard life at times.'

Another painful kick from the child brought Senara back to the present. She was breathing heavily from her walk. In the distance she could hear the waterfall splashing over the rocks into the river below. The child would be born in a week or two and she wanted to give an offering to the old gods of nature for her safe delivery. The brown leaves of the dead bracken crackled and disintegrated as they were swept aside by the women's long skirts or were crushed underfoot.

The trees thinned at the bend in the river and the waterfall was clearly visible. It tumbled downwards between granite rocks; the white cascade, full from the winter rains, was divided by a huge boulder at the top. This gave the appearance of an opalescent angel, its wings outspread and rising towards the heavens. Senara could feel its vibrant energy and potency. To witness the glory of nature, and to feel its power as a harbinger of life, filled Senara with a sense of wonder and reverence. How could anyone believe God resided within the sterile columns of a church constructed by man? To her, the evidence of the Creator's magnificence was in the rustle of wind in the trees, or pulsated in the waters that were the arteries of the earth that sustained all life.

Senara sank down on to a boulder by the water's edge. She needed a moment alone to perform her secret ritual and make her offering to the ancient goddess to bless her forthcoming confinement. She was about to send Tamasine on an errand to collect some herbs when a movement by the waterfall caught her eye. A man had materialised in the shadows at the side of the falling water with the suddenness of a spectre.

She blinked, convinced that her eyes were playing tricks on her. But the man was no water sprite but solid in substance as he climbed the rocks. When he moved into the sunlight, Senara recognised Harry Sawle. If he was on Boscabel land, he was up to no good. Rudge had reported to her that he had not seen the smuggler to give him her instructions that no contraband was to be hidden on the estate. The morbid sore throat had broken out among the children at Trevowan Hard and Senara had been busy attending them. It had delayed her confronting Harry in Penruan. The winter storms were not over and few landings, if any, were made in these months, and she had believed the matter was not urgent. It looked as though she had been wrong.

'Harry Sawle, what is your purpose on our land?' She stood up and walked towards him. Near the waterfall the grass and boulders were slippery from the spray. If he heard her, he ignored her summons and continued climbing the steep bank. 'Sawle, do not walk away from me.'

She raised her voice above the roaring water and in her haste to apprehend him lost her footing. She landed with a painful jolt on the base of her spine. Behind her Tamasine screamed, 'Senara, are you hurt?'

Senara pushed herself to her feet. 'I am unharmed.' Then she saw that Harry Sawle had been alerted by the scream and had turned in their direction. She beckoned him towards her. For a moment he looked as though he would disobey, then with reluctance he retraced his steps. There was another insolent hesitation before he touched the brim of his slouch hat. She was discomfited to see that he was carrying a shotgun in the crook of his arm, the breech broken open to prevent it accidentally being fired whilst he walked.

'Good day to you, Mrs Loveday.'

'What is your purpose on our land, Harry?'

'I did not think Adam would begrudge me a rabbit or two. The old warren here is overrun with them. The fishing fleet has not brought in a catch in two weeks.'

'The warren is on the far side of the hill as you approach from Penruan. There are no rabbits in the wood or river. Rudge said you told him to look the other way when the moon is full and there could be a cask of brandy left at his door. There will be no cache of contraband stored at Boscabel, or transported across its land. Adam will not stand for it.'

He took a menacing step forward. 'Adam bain't here.'

'But I am, and as Mistress of Boscabel I could have you arrested for poaching. I will turn a blind eye to that for I would see no family go hungry, but I will not condone smuggling.' She was aware that Tamasine had drawn close to her, and from the corner of her eyes saw that the young woman had her fist clenched and her face was tight with fury.

Harry gave Tamasine a swift, assessing glance but dismissed her as unimportant, his attention centred upon Senara. 'I bain't about to be crossed, woman.'

'You cannot threaten Senara in that manner,' Tamasine bristled. 'I shall tell Mr Loveday. He will have you clapped in irons.'

Senara put a restraining hand on Tamasine's arm, though she admired her courage. 'I will deal with this.'

Harry scowled, snapping shut the breech of the shotgun with an ominous click. 'I need the use of the cave behind the waterfall to store some casks until the roads are passable. The riding officers have been sniffing round too close to where it be hidden. We couldn't get it away from the coast before the storms made the roads bad. It will be worth your while. It's gonna cost Adam a fortune to repair that ruin of a place.'

'The money will come from legal means or not at all.'

Anger flickered across Harry's rugged features. 'You bain't in a position to tell me what I can or can't do. I need to use the cave. If you be wise you'll forget we had this conversation. I bain't forgot you saved my life, but there be too much at stake here.' He brought the shotgun to his waist, his eyes dark and malignant as he waited for Senara to back down.

The threat chilled Senara's blood. Harry was a man without compassion. His treatment of Hester after Lanyon's death had proved how ruthless he could be when his plans were thwarted. 'Do not threaten me, Harry Sawle.' She was relieved her voice did not quiver, for her legs were turning to aspic.

The barrel of the gun was pointed at her heart and sweat trickled down between her shoulder blades and breasts. She strove to keep her expression impassive and drew a steadying breath. If Harry guessed the terror that was making her heart thunder in her throat, he would be without mercy and bully her into submission to his wishes. 'Put the gun away, Harry. Or do you fear that I will harm you?'

Harry was unused to being challenged, and uncertainty flickered behind his eyes. Then the hardness returned to his features. 'No one crosses Harry Sawle. There be men more powerful than Adam Loveday who lived to regret it. Some didn't live long at all.'

As she looked in to Harry Sawle's cold and pitiless eyes Senara knew he was capable of murder. During her life with the gypsies, she had faced persecution many times. It had taught her resilience and the ability not to show fear even though her insides were quaking. Harry was a bully. Senara had vowed that Adam would never regret his marriage to her. If she backed down at Harry's threats, she would dishonour the Loveday name.

Senara squared her shoulders. 'You may regard me as a feeble woman with no power to stay your commands, Harry Sawle, but Boscabel will not be used to hide your contraband. I would prefer not to go to Sir Henry Traherne with this matter, but I will if you force me. He is both Adam's friend and a magistrate. Find somewhere else to hide your goods, and I will have no quarrel with you, Sawle.'

He raised his fist and for a moment Senara thought he would strike her. Her chin shot up and she stared at him without flinching. Subtly, she felt a change in the atmosphere of the land and water around her. The birds stopped singing and there was stillness, as stark as any presence, which made her catch her breath. Something brushed against her hair, the touch light as gossamer, warm and reassuring. She took it as a sign that the old gods would protect her and was no longer fearful. 'You may strike a common gypsy wench without fear of retribution, Harry Sawle, but to strike the wife of a Loveday would earn you a long spell in prison.'

'No one threatens me!' Menace dripped from every syllable. His fist dropped to his side and he thrust his face into hers. His breath reeked of stale ale and a spray of spittle dashed her cheek. 'I take orders from no man, let alone a woman.'

The touch upon her hair came again and there was the sound of a twig snapping in the trees along the riverbank. Harry spun round, the shotgun raised to challenge an unknown foe.

A voice inside Senara's head made her speak the words she heard aloud. 'You do well to fear the unknown, Harry Sawle. I will not allow you to desecrate Boscabel with your contraband. *Boscabel* will not allow you to desecrate her land.'

As the words faded another twig snapped and from out of the trees appeared a mature stag, his antlers majestically spread like the branches of a young tree. Senara did not see a stag but an ancient guardian, a revered one – a horned stag the symbol of the ancient god Herne. Senara held out her arms to the apparition. Looking past Harry Sawle, her voice was low as she chanted in the Romany language, 'Oh Great Herne, Great Cerrunos: Lord of the Beasts, Protector of the fields and meadows, we honour you.'

The stag raised his head and seemed to look straight into Harry's eyes. The smuggler raised the shotgun and Senara saw that his hand was shaking. 'That be fine meat for our table tonight.'

'Do not shoot!' she screamed. 'He is the leader of the herd.'

The shotgun bucked and a flash of orange flame and black smoke erupted from its barrel. Harry yelled, and twisted metal was thrown from his blackened hands into the water. The side of his face was also stained with gunpowder, and scorched. He clutched his hands to his head and staggered backwards.

Senara's gaze had been riveted upon the stag while she prayed that it would be spared. When the smoke cleared, there was no sign of the deer. Harry was groaning and Senara pulled his hands from his face. A shotgun misfiring in such a manner could blow half a man's face away. The injury was not as bad as she feared. His face was bleeding, the flesh blackened and raw. But it would heal in a week or so, leaving the skin puckered and he would carry the black stains of the gunpowder all his life. Harry Sawle had lost his good looks.

'I will tend your wound for you,' she offered.

Harry continued to back away. 'Witch! Stay away from me. What devil was it that you summoned?'

'It was no devil and well you know it, Harry. Your shotgun misfired. You must have got dirt in the barrel.'

Harry stared at the shotgun, the white of his eyes bulging. 'Bain't nothing wrong with that gun. It were the devil's work. I heard you summon him.'

She had never seen Harry frightened of anything and was surprised that he was so superstitious. Senara had regarded the appearance of the stag as a sign of the success of the secret rituals she had performed on the land during a full, or new moon, to preserve her future home from danger. Clearly, threats would not deter Harry Sawle, but superstition might prove her ally.

'It was no demon, Harry,' she emphasised, 'but Boscabel will not be desecrated. You would do well to remember the curse placed on those who would plunder this land by Lady Guinevere Polfennick when the roundheads hanged her from her own gatehouse. No family has prospered here since her day, but her spirit has accepted us because she knows that we will

honour Boscabel, and never abuse the riches the
estate will yield to us. Get off my land, Harry Sawle,
and do not return unless you are invited.'

Harry pulled the kerchief from his neck and held it
to his injured face. 'I bain't afeared of you, or your
witchery. Because you saved my life, I will repay the
debt and not use Boscabel *this* time.'

He climbed the rocks of the bank without a backward glance and Senara raised her voice. 'You will not
use Boscabel at all. I shall inform the authorities if
contraband is found on our land.'

Harry gave no sign that he had heard her. When he
disappeared from sight, Senara found that she was
shaking. Tamasine appeared at her shoulder.

'What an objectionable beast,' the young woman
observed. 'You were so brave to stand up to him. But
that was the strangest thing that happened with the
deer. It seemed to vanish in the smoke like a phantom.'

Senara shook her head and rubbed the ache low in
her back. 'Deer are plentiful around here and they are
very fleet of foot.'

Tamasine continued to study Senara with an appre-
hensive frown. 'What was that he said about you being
a witch?'

Senara was about to dismiss her words with a laugh,
but then she was moved to explain. 'My grandmother
was known as a wise woman. She taught me to respect
Mother Nature and the elements that sustain us.
There is the air that we breathe and the water we
drink, without which we could not survive. The earth
provides the food we eat and the herbs to cure our ills,

and fire warms and lights our homes. I tell you this only because I do not want you to be afraid of the old ways. It is against our law to harm anyone.' Senara picked up the mangled gun from the river and carefully picked her way along the slippery bank to the waterfall where Harry had appeared.

'But I thought witches cast spells, ill-wished others and had sold their souls to the devil.' Tamasine was breathing heavily as she concentrated on keeping her footing and not falling into the water.

'So your Church tells us. But the word "witch" means "wise one".'

'Your words were strange. Was it some ancient god that you called upon?' She looked worried. 'Are you a heathen, Senara?'

'The gods of yesterday are the devils of today. What of today's gods? Will in future centuries they become the devils of tomorrow?'

'That is blasphemy, Senara.' Tamasine was horrified.

Still shaken by the incident with Harry Sawle, Senara had spoken without her usual caution concerning her beliefs. It was not surprising that Tamasine was shocked. She was quick to reassure her. 'I do not consider myself a heathen. Jesus preached of love and peace and turning the other cheek. He spoke of love and compassion for all our fellow men and the creatures around us. That is what is important.'

'But people are rarely like that. Prejudice and injustice thrives.'

'That is the tragedy of mankind,' Senara replied. 'If

as the Bible says Adam was the first man and Eve the
first woman, then are we not all brothers and sisters?'

'That sounds like heresy.'

Senara laughed. 'Very likely, but then I am but a
simple gypsy woman with little education. What
would I know when great minds have decreed otherwise?' Her mood became serious. 'I have seen how
power and fear corrupt. My race is feared because our
way of life is different. That fear resulted in my father
being hanged. A horse was stolen from a farm and
because my father was seen in the area it was assumed
that he had taken it. One less gypsy was seen as one
less problem for the Parish. He was innocent. The
horse was found after his death in the possession of
the farmer's nephew, who had stolen it when he
learned he had been cut from his uncle's will.'

'Did such injustice not make you angry? Or want
his death avenged?'

'I was angry when I was young. I loved my father.
But his death taught me how easily fear can rule
people. Fear is our greatest enemy, not another person, race or religion. Allowing fear to rule your life is
to listen to the demon that can destroy us all.'

'But Harry Sawle is feared by many because he is a
brutal and violent man,' Tamasine said. 'No one at the
shipyard has a good word to say about him. Do you
not fear what he could do to you if you cross him?'

Senara did not answer immediately, needing a
moment to find the right words to express her feelings. 'Fear gives him power. But he is no more than an
unscrupulous bully. I do not say that he does not

frighten me with his threats: he does. But I will not allow my fear for my personal safety to make me his pawn.'

'So did you cast a spell on him for his gun to blow up? Was that not a form of using Harry's fear of superstition to warn him from using your land?'

Tamasine exasperated Senara by bringing the conversation back to the original subject. 'That was not my intent. My concern was for the stag. It is also a hanging offence to kill the King's deer.'

They had reached the waterfall and Senara examined the rock face. 'Harry spoke of a cave. To have such knowledge he must have used it before. I know of no such cave, but he appeared by the side of the waterfall as though he had materialised out of the air.'

A delicate spray of cool mist from the cascading water fanned across her face and arms. There was thick overgrowth of ivy where Harry had appeared. Senara touched it and found that it moved beneath her hand. She raised it and discovered a crevice the width of a stout man.

Senara squeezed inside, the sides of the entrance brushing against her back and swollen stomach. Little light penetrated from the aperture but the roof was as high as a man standing on another's shoulders. She advanced slowly, allowing her eyes to become accustomed to the gloom. The cave was narrow: no more than three yards wide and twice that deep. The air was stale and musty but the floor was dry. She could see why Harry wanted to hide his contraband here. It would be perfect. Although Sawle was a dangerous man to cross, she had no intention of allowing him to use their land to stow his goods. She would tell Eli Rudge to check the cave every day.

As she turned to leave a fierce pain arrowed through her back. She bent over and gasped, sweat breaking out on her brow and between her breasts. It was several moments before the pain receded enough for her to straighten.

Tamasine had been watching a kingfisher diving from a branch of a tree into the river and was shocked to see how ashen Senara had become. 'Are you all right?'

'Yes, but I must return to Mariner's House. The baby is coming. Do not look so alarmed. It will be some hours yet, even if it is eager to be born earlier than expected. There is time aplenty to return to the shipyard and have everything in readiness for its arrival.'

Several times during the walk back along the river-bank and through the wood, Senara was forced to stop as pain tore through her body. 'Tamasine, run ahead and get Rudge to summon my mother to the shipyard. This baby is more impatient than others to be born.'

'Are you able to ride?' Tamasine hesitated.

Senara nodded. 'Go to Rudge. I will meet you at the stables.'

Four hours later, with Senara warm and safe at Mariner's House, her daughter Rhianne was born.

'She is tiny, but a perfect little angel.' Leah wrapped her in a linen towel and her heart swelled with love as she stared into the depths of her granddaughter's eyes. The tiny brow wrinkled and the cupid bow's mouth curved into what Leah would swear was a smile. A soft contented sigh came from the child as her thumb found its way into her mouth.

Leah was about to lay her on Senara's breast when her daughter's eyes screwed tight with another pain and her body arched. Leah handed the baby to Bridie, fearful that something was seriously amiss. She examined Senara and relaxed. 'Well now, is this not a surprise! Your labours are not done yet, my girl.'

Fifteen minutes later Joel Loveday gave an indignant yell at being foist into a cold and chilly world from the warmth of his mother's womb. When the linen cloth was wrapped around his body, his face reddened with rage and his arms and legs kicked against the constraint to his freedom. Leah chuckled. 'This be a feisty one, Senara. Just like your brother, Caleph, when he were born. He be a Romany and no mistake. Don't know what Mr Loveday will make of that.'

Chapter Twenty-Three

Harry Sawle was in a malignant mood when he called at Chegwidden's house. The pain in his face was tortuous. The doctor had sent their maid to inform Harry that he was indisposed and could not treat him. Chegwidden was known for his reluctance to treat the fishermen of the village and most could not afford his high fees.

'My money be as good as any mewling gentleman,' Harry shouted, and he pushed the maid aside and strode through the house. He discovered Simon Chegwidden taking tea with his young daughter, Clarice, and his new wife, Annie, who was Hester's sister. The girl screamed at the sight of Harry's injury, and hid her face in her hands. Her pale hair hung in ringlets and was tied up with two red ribbons, her face pasty and her manner as haughty as her father's. 'That man is so ugly. Make him go away, Papa.'

Chegwidden jumped to his feet, knocking over the cup of tea he was stirring with a spoon. His thin, arrogant features were pinched with outrage. 'How dare you force yourself into my home? I will not treat a man of your scurrilous reputation. Get out!' He was white and shaking, and clutched the teaspoon to his chest as though it would somehow protect him from an attack by the intruder.

Harry grabbed the doctor by his jacket, and Annie and his scrawny daughter screamed in terror. 'I bain't here to pass pleasantries with you. My face needs tending. And stop those stupid women's caterwauling.' He opened his jacket to show a pistol thrust into the waistband of his trousers. 'I got money to pay for your services. I bain't no charity case.' Still holding Chegwidden's lapels he spun round to Annie, whom he had never liked. 'I bain't gonna hurt you, and silence the girl.'

'Take Clarice to her room, Annie, my dear,' Chegwidden ordered, attempting to regain his dignity.

'Stay where you are. Girl, get your pa's medical bag.'

Clarice ran sobbing from the room and returned carrying a leather bag. Her face was red and puffy from her tears and she refused to go anywhere near to Harry. She banged the bag on to the table and hid behind Annie.

Annie Chegwidden stared at Harry's disfigured cheek and shuddered. 'Lost your pretty-boy looks from the sight of it. Did you get your comeuppance from the excisemen?'

Harry released the doctor, who nodded to his wife. 'Ask the maid to bring me hot water and bandages.'

Annie did not instantly obey and glared at Harry.

Her eyes were close-set and she had a masculine square cleft chin. Her figure was too skinny for Harry's taste and she was wearing an unflattering, high-necked, grey velvet gown trimmed with red braid and her hair was pulled back in a tight coil. 'You've got a nerve coming here after the way you treated my sister.' As the daughter of a ship's chandler she had thought herself above the other women in the village, much as Harry's own sister, Meriel, had done.

Harry laughed menacingly. 'You were the first to turn your back on Hester after the trial. And your father be no better.'

'My sister shamed us. She is rearing your bastard child. What happened to your promises to wed her?' Annie whisked back her long skirts to avoid them touching him and left the room.

Chegwidden was far from gentle when he bathed the wound, forcing Harry to bite the inside of his other cheek to stifle a groan of pain.

'This is a nasty wound. You've lost the lobe of your ear. How did you come by such an injury?'

'That be none of your concern,' Harry snapped. His face throbbed with pain and his ear was ringing, the doctor's words muffled and sounding far away. 'I bain't gonna be deaf in that ear, am I?'

'Probably. I've seen injuries like this in the navy when a marine has not cleaned his rifle properly and it has misfired,' Chegwidden observed. 'If you were poaching, then you received your just punishment. You were lucky it did not shatter your jaw.'

'You got the wrong Sawle brother. I bain't no

pauper who needs to steal a rabbit to stop me family from starving.'

Chegwidden puffed out his chest in sanctimonious censure. 'You live by ill-gotten gains.' Throughout his tending the wound, Dr Chegwidden had lectured Harry. 'Come to see me again in three days. The wound will take some weeks to heal and will leave a disfiguring scar. That will be a guinea for my services, Mr Sawle.'

'And you say I live by ill-gotten gains. Your fees rob a man blind.'

'Then take yourself to the Loveday woman; she tends the peasants who cannot afford a proper physician's fees.'

Harry slammed the money on the table. His mood was sour as he strode through the village and across the cobbled square in front of the church.

Harry bowed his head to enter the low door of the Dolphin Inn. The interior was dim and the smell of stale ale, and the rabbit stew bubbling in the iron pot on the kitchen range, filled the air.

When he straightened, his mother, Sal, cried out in alarm. 'What you done to yourself, son?'

There were no customers in the tavern. Most of the fishermen now avoided the Dolphin and Reuban Sawle's drunken moods. They would send children along with jugs to be filled with ale and drink them in their own homes. Sal ambled from behind the tap-room bar, her body a shapeless mound under a brown dress and huge white apron. The last of the gilding had gone from her once blonde hair, and the white and grey streaks were hidden under a bonnet that fastened under her chin.

'My shotgun misfired. Damn near blew my ear off.' When Sal started to fuss he waved her aside. A thick padded bandage covered the side of his face. 'Chegwidden saw to the wound. It looks worse than it is,' he reassured his mother to stop her fussing around him. 'Get me a large brandy. Several of them.' Sal waddled away; she had long ago hardened her heart to both Harry's surliness and his dangerous pursuits.

Reuban sat behind the bar on a high stool that had been fitted with wheels, the stumps of his legs covered by a blanket. He had lost his legs when Thadeous Lanyon's coach had run him down.

'Bain't like you to be careless.' Reuban's words were slurred and he gave a caustic laugh. His cadaverous face was yellow and sunken with pain, and his long stringy beard resting on his chest was matted. As usual his breath smelled of brandy, for he started drinking as soon as he rose in the morning. He swayed unsteadily on the stool and his red-rimmed eyes slowly focused on his son. He tapped the side of his nose, aware that most of Harry's dealings were illegal. 'Hope you showed 'em who be boss, son. Sawles don't take no nonsense from no one.'

'I know how to look after my interests, Pa.'

Reuban wheezed and waved a dirt-ingrained finger at his son. 'You had better remember it. I never took no nonsense from no one. If I still had me legs—'

'We've heard it all afore, Reuban,' Sal cut in. 'Don't

you go getting Harry all riled. He should be more like Clem – keeping his nose clean.'

Harry tossed back his brandy and signalled to his mother to pour him another. Sal got little conversation out of Reuban and was eager to gossip.

'Have you heard the news, Harry? Senara Loveday has been brought to bed with twins. A boy and a girl. They do say Mr Loveday be right proud.' She sighed. 'Perhaps the twins will heal the rift in his family caused by Adam's marriage. Grandchildren are our future. Bain't nothing like them to make a soul feel they have served some purpose with their life.'

Harry scowled, his mood malignant. The Loveday woman needed to learn that he was not a man to cross. She had been the cause of his disfigurement and she would pay. She'd be too involved with the twins to get to Boscabel for a few weeks. He would use the time well.

Sal was continuing to gossip and Harry paid little heed to his mother's words. 'Who'd've thought I'd have a pretty thing like Rowena for a grandchild?' Sal gave a rare smile. 'She'll marry well and be a real gentlewoman. Clem's Zacky be into everything now. Got a sharp mind, that one.' Then her eyes clouded and her face set into grim lines. 'I'll get no pleasure out of Hester's child. She were carrying the little one back to the big house yesterday and crossed the street to avoid me.'

'Stay away from Hester and her brat.' Harry glowered at his mother.

Sal rested her knuckles on her wide hips,

undaunted by his churlishness. 'You and Hester were good together. She bain't a bad sort. You could do a lot worse than by doing the right thing by her. Do you want to see your kid brought up without a father?'

'The kid be Lanyon's. He were her husband.'

'Lanyon didn't have it in him to sire a child. He had three other wives who were barren. That kid be yours. You'd have enjoyed putting the cuckold horns on Lanyon.'

'Keep your nose out of my business, Ma.' Harry took his brandy to a dark corner of the tavern. His face hurt abominably and the brandy was having no effect at numbing the pain. He cursed Hester and then he cursed Senara for his suffering. No woman was going to get the better of him. He needed to use that cave within the next day or so.

He left the inn to walk down to the quay. An evening fog was coming inland from the sea and already obscured the headland. A sloop from Guernsey had been trying to land a cargo for three nights, but the excise ship had been vigilant in the area. He had been unable to get his usual bribe to the officer so that the cutter would stay away. The sloop had been unable to make the landing. The fog was a smuggler's ally. The sloop could slip into coastal waters undetected. The weeks of rain had made the roads and tracks difficult for the laden pack ponies to negotiate. The goods needed to be hidden until they could be safely distributed. As had been proved, Beaumont could not be relied upon to keep out of these waters more than three weeks of every month – despite the bribe Harry paid him. Harry was now the most ruthless smuggler on this coast. He was impatient to acquire wealth – no longer content with small infrequent hauls.

On the quay, Gabe Rundle was unloading the last of his catch. The Rundle family of seven men owned four fishing smacks. From the number of vessels bobbing in the water, half the fleet had already unloaded and the rest were still at sea. Harry hailed Gabe. 'Get word to the men in Penruan, there'll be a landing tonight.'

Rheumy eyes stared up at him from out of a craggy, line-scored face. Although not yet forty Gabe had lost most of his teeth and he lisped through the gaps. 'How we gonna get the cargo away? Beaumont's cutter were moored at St Mawes when we sailed past. He could be in our waters again tonight.'

'The fog will shield the cargo boat. The goods will be stashed on land.'

'And what happened to your face?'

'That bain't none of your affair,' Harry warned.

Gabe Rundle put aside his nets, his beetle legs scurrying away to the nearest cottage to deliver Harry's message.

Another fishing smack sailed into the harbour and Harry recognised Clem at the tiller. Clem lowered the single triangular sail as the ship drifted to its mooring and, once close to the quay, Clem threw Harry the rope to attach to an iron ring set into the wall.

A woman, who had approached unnoticed by Harry earlier, had caught the gist of Harry's conversation with Gabe Rundle and had drawn back behind a fisherman's shed to avoid being seen by the men. She was curious to discover what Sawle was up to and pulled her shawl over her head, holding the edges together to conceal her lower face.

'What the devil has happened to you?' Clem stared at his brother's face.

'Me shotgun misfired. These things happen.'

His intone indicated he did not intend to discuss the matter and Clem knew it would be pointless to pursue it. He worried about Harry these days and knew he was up to no good.

'Bain't seen you around much of late, brother,' Clem said as he stepped on to the quay. 'It's been some weeks since you fished with the fleet.'

'I've got bigger fish to catch than mackerel or pilchards. Though Beaumont bain't making it easy. His damned excise cutter has been in the area all week.'

'Thought you'd have Beaumont in your pay by now,' Clem said as he hauled a meagre catch of mackerel in a wicker basket on to the quay. Two of the fish fell on to the flagstones and several seagulls swooped around Clem's head as he flipped the fish back into the basket before the birds could steal them.

'Beaumont's got a yellow streak. His superiors are suspicious as to why so few cargos have been confiscated in this region. Especially after all Lanyon's dealings came up at St John Loveday's trial, people wondered how come the revenue men were never on to Lanyon as a smuggler. That be just a step before they question whether Beaumont took bribes.'

The sound of voices made the brothers turn their heads towards the far side of the quay. Under the slope of the hill were the row of drying sheds for the fish and the sprawling building of the general store. The door to this had opened and two customers laughed as they headed towards their homes. A light in the shop showed Harry the silhouettes of two other figures inside.

'Lanyon's so-called widow is coining it from that place.' Harry shook his fist at the shop. 'That money should be mine, not that upstart whore's. That Goldie reckon she be someone, don't she? Well, she bain't. She thought she were clever, taking Hester in. It got the villagers on her side. They're taken to using the Gun Inn again and the Dolphin be empty most nights.'

'And Pa's moods have driven the customers away,' Clem stated. 'Many think you should've done right by Hester. Most guess her child be your daughter.'

'No one has got the guts to say that to my face.' Harry hooked his thumbs over the waistband of his breeches. His thick brows drew down as he scanned the rows of fishermen's cottages clinging like barnacles to the side of the hill around the harbour. 'I warned Hester to get herself out of Penruan.'

'Leave her in peace, Harry.' Clem threw a pebble at a gull that was hovering over his catch.

'That Goldie's got a lot to answer for.' Harry swung away, then turned back to stare derisively at his brother's catch. 'Bain't much there to keep the wolf from the door. I be needing tub men tonight.'

'I be done with all that.' Clem sounded half-hearted.

'Kezzie wearing the trousers in your house then?' Harry jeered. 'The catch has been poor all winter. You could make more tonight than you've done in months.'

Clem hesitated; money had been tight this winter. A gale had taken half the slates off the roof of Blackthorn Cottage, smashing them on the ground, and they had been expensive to replace. He rubbed his unshaven jaw as he stared at the pitiful catch, the result of twelve hours at sea, shivering in the cold.

'It bain't just Beaumont you got to look out for. There be riding officers over St Austell way. They be as bad a curse on land as Beaumont is at sea. They found a cache of brandy stored in a disused tin mine last month.'

'I've found a place where they will never think of looking. The cave at Boscabel.'

Clem's head shot up. 'The one behind the waterfall? But that land be Adam Loveday's now. Pa used it in the old days when the house were derelict.'

'But the place bain't lived on. There be just a manservant doing odd jobs. Sides, the cargo will only be there a week at most. It's quality stuff – silk, lace, tea. Goods that be light and easy to shift. Are you with me, brother?'

Again Clem hesitated and the woman, who had ducked behind a wall on seeing the brothers, held her breath. She had no score to settle with Clem Sawle. His brother was another matter.

'I gave my word to Kezzie. I won't break it.'

'She got you under her thumb,' Harry scoffed as he swaggered away. 'A woman be only good for two things. Fornicating and a hefty dowry. But neither do give them the right to think they can rule a man's life.'

Clem shook his head at his brother's back, and jumped back on his boat to finish stowing the tackle. While his back was turned Goldie emerged from her hiding place. While Hester served in the store, Goldie had been delivering a box of cabbages and turnips to Mrs Snell for the poor of the parish. It was a weekly task she took upon herself to be more accepted by the villagers.

'That young man thinks he's cock o' the roost,' she muttered under her breath. 'He's a mean bastard, thinking he can get away with all the lies he told Hester – not to mention his threats to run her out of the village.' Goldie lengthened her stride. She had suffered at the hands of men like Harry Sawle when Lanyon had sold her to the brothel. She hated the way they had used her, often brutally, with no regard to her feelings. 'It be time that one got some of his own medicine. A word sent to Lieutenant Beaumont where the cargo is hidden will hit Harry Sawle where it will hurt most – his pocket.'

It did not cross Goldie's mind that others would be implicated if contraband was found on their land.

The arrival of Japhet and Gwendolyn with Amelia at Trevowan caused a stir of excitement. Edward was at the yard and Elspeth, bored from being unable to hunt in the bad weather, had spent the morning following the maids around the house, giving them extra duties. Her hip ached in the cold and damp, and the house had become as gloomy as a mausoleum since Amelia and the twins had left. She was even denied Rowena's company, for the girl was in the nursery with Hannah's two eldest children, Davey and Abigail, taking their daily lessons with the governess Edward had engaged.

Elspeth had gone to the stables with an apple for each of her mares when Jasper Fraddon shouted out for a groom to attend the coach that had arrived. Elspeth entered the house to discover a pile of travelling chests in the hallway. Rafe's nursemaid was carrying the sleeping child up the stairs and she heard Japhet's voice coming from the winter parlour.

'Why did you not send word you were coming?' Elspeth said by way of greeting, though she smiled to see that Amelia had also returned. Edward's wife was stretched out on the chaise longue by the fire, looking pale and tired. Japhet stood with his back to the fire and Gwendolyn was rubbing her reddened hands to bring some warmth into them. 'At last common sense has prevailed and you have returned to the fold. Amelia, you look dreadful.'

'It has been a gruelling journey,' Amelia replied. 'Seventeen days, all told. We needed to break the journey, staying an extra day at inns on four occasions. I am about ready to take to my bed now.'

Elspeth saw Gwendolyn watching Japhet, her face glowing. 'Your mama will be pleased that you also have come to your senses, young lady.' Elspeth raised a brow at her nephew. 'And what brings you back? Margaret's last letter said you were in London. Time you stopped your vagabond roaming and settled down.'

'How perceptive you are, dear aunt.' He kissed her hand in an exaggerated fashion. 'I may yet surprise you. There is much news to tell Uncle Edward.'

Amelia gestured to Gwendolyn to pour the tea a maid had brought in, then asked, 'What news is there since I have been away?'

'You would have missed the messenger with the news that Senara was brought to bed with twins. Bonny babies both of them. A girl, Rhianne, and a boy, Joel.'

'Twins!' Amelia did not sound pleased. 'More gypsy blood to taint our family. What did Edward say?'

'He was delighted for Adam.' Elspeth regarded her sister-in-law with impatience. 'It is unlikely that St John will give him more children. I thought you would be pleased. Rafe will inherit Trevowan.'

'How are the baby twins?' Gwendolyn interrupted. 'Are they healthy? And how is Senara? The birth must have been an ordeal for her.'

'Senara is already up and about and suffering no ill effects,' replied Elspeth. 'The twins are hale and so lusty that Senara has had to engage a wet nurse to help to satisfy their hunger. It's as well that Tamasine is on hand to help her, for Nathan is not much more than an infant himself.'

'So the girl is still here?' Amelia whitened with anger.

'She lives at the yard and everyone believes she is a distant cousin that Edward has given a home to. She does not visit Trevowan.' Elspeth regarded Amelia with fierceness. 'I had hoped your return meant that you had come to your senses over that matter. And whatever you may feel about Tamasine, her mother was a noblewoman.'

Amelia sucked in her breath sharply. 'And what about when spring comes and we entertain more? People will expect her to be present at any gathering that includes Senara.'

'Sometimes, for the good of all, you have to accept what may otherwise be unacceptable, Amelia,' Elspeth responded.

Amelia rose wearily from the chaise longue. 'I will bathe and take supper in my rooms tonight.'

Before she could leave the winter parlour Edward strode in. He greeted them all warmly and kissed his wife's cheek. Amelia reseated herself on the chaise longue but did not meet her husband's gaze.

The initial greetings over, Edward accepted a glass of mulled wine and stood behind Amelia. 'We did not expect you to return until later in the year, Japhet.'

'Sir, I thought you might have need of my services in some way. The fire at the yard sounded serious, and spring is always a busy time on the estate, with the lambing and ploughing. If not, I know Hannah can do with extra help on the farm. I understood that Oswald has been ill again this winter.'

'Your offer is appreciated, Japhet.' Edward, who had looked strained and tense, relaxed. 'We have the rebuilding on the brigantine in hand at the yard. But it has made us late in delivering and, of course, laying down another keel.'

'This may be of help to you, sir.' Japhet handed over a letter and large money pouch from Thomas.

Edward read the letter and more of the strain eased from his face. 'It is more than welcome. And what of you, Japhet? Joshua and Cecily will be delighted you are to remain in Cornwall. It sounds that you plan to stay for some while.'

Japhet grinned and walked to Gwendolyn's side. She had been quiet throughout the meeting and now she blushed. 'I have many plans and they include remaining in Cornwall. Gwendolyn has agreed to marry me. I have obtained a special licence and will ask Father to marry us straight away.'

'That is wonderful news. Congratulations.' He nodded approval to the couple. 'But what of the Lady Anne, Gwendolyn? She has always been against you and Japhet marrying.'

'That is why I asked Japhet to obtain a special licence. I would have preferred to be married in London so that Mama could not interfere, but Japhet wanted his father to marry us, which is understandable.'

'Joshua would naturally be upset if someone else had performed the service,' Edward replied. 'Do you think that your mother will cause difficulties?'

'I fear so. Japhet and I will visit them next to discuss the wedding. I know Japhet's parents will have no objection.' Her chin jutted with defiance. 'I am of age, and Mama cannot stop me marrying whom I choose.'

'Bah!' Elspeth retorted. 'I should think Lady Anne will be relieved that you will be married after the damage she did to your reputation. When your forthcoming marriage to that Beaumont fellow was announced in the newssheet, then retracted, he lost no time in selecting another wealthy bride. You were well shot of the knave.'

Some of the brightness dimmed in Gwendolyn's eyes. 'If Mama proves unreasonable, would you permit me to stay at Trevowan until the wedding, Mr Loveday?'

'Of course, but I would prefer that the matter is settled amiably with Lady Anne.'

Gwendolyn rose. 'We will speak with Mama now and get it over with.'

After the couple left, Elspeth excused herself, leaving Edward and Amelia alone.

Edward stooped to kiss his wife's cheek. 'I have missed you, my dear. I trust the journey was not too onerous.'

She shrugged. 'Duty dictated that I should return. Lisette will be in the asylum for some months, according to Dr Claver. Thomas will keep us informed of her progress.'

The lack of warmth in her tone pained Edward. 'You are still angry with me. I thought you more benevolent, my dear. I have no regrets about my liaison with the Lady Eleanor. It was too many years before I met you for it to affect the esteem in which I hold you. Tamasine is living with Senara.'

'So Elspeth informed me.'

'I cannot turn my back on her. Once she is sixteen a suitable marriage will be arranged and her presence will no longer be a burden to you.'

Amelia swung her legs to the floor and stood up. 'I am weary. I shall bathe and rest in my room. In three months I shall bear our second child.'

Though he was sad that she had not informed him before this, he made to take her into his arms, his eyes smiling. 'That is the most marvellous news. I am delighted, my love.'

When he would have kissed her, she turned her mouth away so that his lips brushed her cheek. 'I hope it is a girl – a legitimate daughter for you.'

The words showed Edward that the rift between himself and his wife had not been healed.

Chapter Twenty-Four

'How dare you presume to march in here and inform us that you are to be married?' Lady Anne Druce spat the words at her daughter. 'I told you I would never countenance a match with this knave.'

Gwendolyn turned away from her mother, her eyes bright with anger. She had been dreading this confrontation and it reflected her worst fears. The afternoon light was fading and the chandeliers in the yellow drawing room had yet to be lit. The gilded cherubs on the plasterwork around the fireplace grinned encouragement to Gwen.

Japhet stepped forward to address Sir Henry Traherne, who had been his friend for many years. Sir Henry stood with his back to the window and his expression was in shadow.

'I will make Gwen happy,' Japhet declared. 'I have done with my wild ways. Do we have your blessing to marry, Sir Henry?'

'I too would see Gwendolyn happy. How do you propose to support her?'

'With her own money,' snapped Lady Anne. 'How else can they live?'

Gwendolyn stiffened, her heart aching at the insults Japhet was being subjected to.

Though his jaw was clenched with anger, he ignored the barb. 'I have enough money to buy several mares and start a stud farm. But if Gwendolyn is to live as befits her station, then her dowry will buy us a house and land. I do not hide that from you.'

'That is if you do not gamble her inheritance away first.' Roslyn sided with her mother in her accusations. Her fingers drummed on the gold brocade of the chair.

'I would never risk my wife's home at a card table,' Japhet clipped out. He stood tall, his shoulders squared.

Gwendolyn slid her arm possessively through his and her eyes flashed with a dangerous light. 'You do Japhet a grave disservice. Mama had no qualms when Beaumont would wed me purely for my money. His conduct at St John's trial showed him to be a black-guard, yet it did not change your opinion of him. Beaumont had no care for me at all. Japhet loves me. And he would honour and protect me with his life.'

'Japhet loves all women,' mocked Roslyn. Her sneer made her protruding teeth even more prominent. There had never been much flesh on her bones, and since the birth of her third child Roslyn had become as wiry as a man. There was little softness about her nature either, and each year she became more critical of others and was always ready to find fault.

Sir Henry rubbed his angular chin and regarded Japhet in concerned silence for several moments. A ginger lock of hair flopped over his brow and he pushed it back with an impatient gesture. 'Have you changed your ways, Japhet? I never thought to see you settle down.'

'A leopard cannot change its spots,' Lady Anne retorted with contempt, a rash of angry colour flecking her neck and face.

'My father drastically changed his way of life when he was my age. I will not go so far as to take the cloth, but there is no shame in breeding racehorses. Gwendolyn loves horses as much as I do. It will be a good life and I will revere her above all women.'

Sir Henry continued to remain thoughtful. 'Japhet's intentions seem honourable enough. And with Gwendolyn's reputation in ruins—'

'Her reputation was destroyed through nothing Gwen had done,' Japhet defended with heat.

'Is she with child?' Lady Anne glared at her daughter. 'Are we to bear the shame of a baby arriving six months after the wedding?'

'Lady Anne, you besmirch the honour and integrity of a woman of unimpeachable character.' Japhet clenched and unclenched his hands, his stare harsh and challenging upon Sir Henry. 'I'd call out any man who so vilified my fiancée's honour.'

'Japhet has always been a perfect gentlemen towards me,' Gwendolyn pronounced. 'I have heard enough. If you do not give your permission I will wed Japhet anyway. Reverend Joshua Loveday will marry us by special licence next week.'

'Is this arranged?' Lady Anne flicked open her white lace fan and waved it imperiously. 'I find that outrageous, and our family not even consulted.'

Roslyn's thin face was pinched with condemnation. 'Mama, what else should we expect from a man who for years has thought only of his own pleasure? And Gwendolyn is an ungrateful wretch after all you have done for her.'

'Stop it, both of you.' Gwendolyn's face was aglow with passion, all her former timidity banished as she faced her mother and sister. 'Nothing as yet is arranged. Japhet insisted that we ask for your blessing before setting a date with his father.'

'Sir Henry, why do you not put an end to this nonsense?' Lady Anne turned her ire upon the baronet.

'Do you want this marriage, Gwendolyn?' Sir Henry asked softly.

'For years it is all I have ever wanted.' She ran forward to throw her arms about Sir Henry. 'You will not stop my only chance of happiness, will you?'

He smiled down at her. 'I give you both my blessing.'

Lady Anne sank against the back of the armchair, an arm flung across her face. 'My smelling salts. Gwendolyn, fetch my smelling salts. I cannot breathe.'

Gwendolyn ignored her mother's histrionics. It was an old ploy her mother used to get her own way when her will was thwarted.

Japhet smiled and held out his hand to Sir Henry. 'Thank you. Your blessing means a great deal to us.'

Sir Henry remained serious. 'There is one thing. If you are to marry, then it is best done with proper ceremony. Gwendolyn deserves that. It will also stop any malicious gossip. I ask that you delay until you can offer Gwendolyn a proper home.'

'I do not wish to wait.' Gwen looked fearful, and turned a fierce glare upon her mother. 'I will not be dissuaded. We can live with Hannah and Oswald Rabson until we have a property of our own.'

Sir Henry shook his head. 'Two months! Is that too much to ask? There is a manor for sale that may be of interest to you, Japhet. It is three miles from Trewenna. Lord Fetherington's cousin is selling it to pay off his debts. He has three other properties.'

'I know the place. He rarely stayed there and it has been neglected.'

'Which should make the price reasonable. It has a good stable block, as I recall,' Sir Henry said with enthusiasm.

Japhet held out his hand to his friend. 'Two months will bring us to Easter.' Japhet was prepared to compromise for the sake of an amicable agreement. 'What do you say to being an Easter bride, my dear? Sir Henry is right. I would wed you in the manner you deserve.'

A shiver of apprehension sped along Gwendolyn's spine. Two months seemed a lifetime away. So much could happen in that time. Every moment with Japhet was precious and she still felt that her happiness could be threatened.

★ ★ ★

Adverse winds had blown *Pegasus* off course. The crew had been away from England for several months and were restless. They had thought to engage enemy French ships as a privateer, earning a share of the ship's money for any prize taken. Yet no French ships had been sighted. And that may have been for the best. With the hold of *Pegasus* filled with tobacco, Adam had been reluctant to risk his own cargo.

Long Tom joined Adam as he took the midday sextant reading. After Adam had lowered the brass instrument from his eye and made a note of the reading to be put into the ship's log, Long Tom asked, 'How many days do you reckon before we reach Bristol?'

'Eight or nine, if this wind holds.' They were under full sail and Adam scanned the taut canvas and watched the men at work scrubbing the decks. He believed in keeping a restless crew busy, so that they fell into their hammocks too tired to stir up dissension. The delay irked Adam. He had hoped to dock at Trevowan with his cargo unloaded a month ago. Now he doubted that he would be home before the birth of his child. It could take up to another week to unload and sail from Bristol to Trevowan Hard.

'Do you regret missing out on the adventure you had planned?' Long Tom screwed his eyes against the sun's rays and tipped back his head to look up at Adam. 'The prize money from a French ship would have paid for most of the renovations needed at Boscabel.'

'Any encounter with the French is not without risk. Our guns may be the match against a merchantman, but a naval corsair would be another matter. I am content with the profit from the tobacco. What will you do when we get back, Long Tom? Will you return to your country seat?'

'For as short a time as possible. Will you be returning to America for another cargo?'

Adam scratched his clean-shaven jaw. 'For the next year or so I will need to captain *Pegasus* to fund the work at Boscabel. But life at sea has lost its joy for me. I have missed my wife and family more than I thought possible. Once Boscabel is refurbished I will be content to settle down as a shipwright.'

'The same cannot be said for St John.' Long Tom rubbed the lobe of his ear. 'He was enjoying the attention he received at Greenbanks.'

'Liking it too much.' Adam shook his head. 'He has little care for his family responsibilities in England. But then Meriel stirred up a cauldron of trouble by her behaviour. I wonder what I will find on my return. I hope Lisette has caused no trouble for Senara.'

'Your wife is a spirited woman. She can take care of herself, as I am sure you are aware.'

Adam grinned and was about to reply when a shout from the crow's nest made him look up at the mast. 'Ship to starboard. She's flying the French flag.'

A cheer rose from the sailors, eager to fight. Adam felt his gut tighten in apprehension. As a privateer here was his chance to take on a French ship and end the financial straits facing his family. He felt his pulse quicken, and his hand clutched the hilt of his sword at his waist in anticipation of a fight.

'Two ships to starboard,' the man in the crow's nest corrected. 'Bearing down on us fast.'

Adam raised his spyglass and studied the horizon. Two ships would be dangerous to take on. His heart clenched in dread.

'They be corsairs, cap'n. And there be three of 'em.' The cry was hoarse with the sailor's alarm. 'Three French ships to starboard. May God have mercy on us.' The announcement cut through the hubbub that had broken out on deck. The men's faces had changed from excitement to fear.

'Clear the decks for action. Hard to port and full sail,' Adam ordered. His glance was strained as it settled upon Long Tom. 'The hunter has just become the hunted. Only *Pegasus*' speed can save us. Her guns never will.'

Celestine Yorke sat in an open carriage in Hyde Park, surrounded by half a dozen admirers. Two were foppish lads, two ageing roués, and seated in the carriage with her were Sir Pettigrew Osgood and Sir Marcus Grundy. They all bored her to distraction. Although the afternoon was pleasantly sunny Celestine remained wrapped in her furs. It was warm enough for an open carriage, where Celestine could parade through the park and see and be seen, for she thirsted for recognition from the public. These days few people cheered her outings in the capital. It made her mood sour and dangerous.

Japhet had left London six weeks ago and she still could not get him out of her mind. He had said he would return before too long, but Cornwall was the other end of England. To Celestine, who had been born in London, it was a remote desolate place. It took days to reach even in good weather and may as well be at the other end of the world. Japhet seemed so far out of reach and she missed him terribly.

A weak jest from Sir Marcus, which lacked the finesse or cutting edge of Japhet's wit, grated on her nerves, but Celestine painted on a smile for her admirers. Inwardly her heart ached and she felt wretched. She clung to the belief that her dashing lover would return to her. It was inconceivable to believe otherwise. No lover had ever discarded her; it was she who always dismissed them when their usefulness to her had come to an end.

The men's conversation had turned to politics, which she abhorred. 'Fiddle-de-dee, gentlemen, have you no amusing anecdotes or gossip with which to amuse me? Talk of Whigs and Tories is so dull.'

Sir Marcus apologised. 'And rightly so – what woman wants to trouble her pretty head with such mundane matters? I meant to tell you that I ran into Phillimore Gilchrist. He is a friend of Thomas Mercer, the banker fellow who dabbles in play writing – a cousin to that Japhet Loveday chap who was so often at your gaming tables, my dear.'

'Yes, I know who Gilchrist is.' Celestine was impatient; her breathing had quickened at the mention of Japhet's name. 'The knave wrote a damning lampoon on my performance recently. The man does not interest me.'

'But he had news of Loveday,' Sir Marcus grinned. 'I always reckoned Loveday was a confirmed bachelor. Seems he's got himself betrothed to a country heiress. She was staying with the Mercers while Japhet was in London. Apparently they are neighbours in Cornwall. Can't say I can place the woman.'

'You cannot have your facts right, Sir Marcus. Loveday is not the marrying kind.' But despite her defiant words, Celestine held her breath in growing fear.

'Gilchrist heard it from Lucien Greene, and you know how close Greene is to Mercer. That fellow Loveday always was a dark horse.' He chuckled. 'Or should I say black sheep of the family.' His feeble wit earned him a scowl from Celestine, whose stomach churned with nausea and fear.

Unaware of her discomfort, Sir Marcus declared, 'The wedding is to be at Easter. A grand affair by all accounts.'

'The sun has gone in,' Celestine announced sharply. 'I will catch a chill if we stay out too long.' She was fighting back tears but by the time the carriage arrived at her house, her pain had turned to a searing, vengeful anger.

She invited Sir Pettigrew and Sir Marcus to take tea with her. Once they were settled comfortably before the fire and the tea had been poured she said in an offhand manner, 'Sir Pettigrew, did you ever wonder what happened about Gentleman James, who robbed us on the heath? There have been few reported robberies of late.'

'Likely the knave has taken his ill-gotten gains and gone to ground,' Sir Pettigrew snarled. 'I'd still like to get my hands on the thief.'

Celestine put her head thoughtfully on one side. 'Did you ever notice a similarity in height and build between Gentleman James and Japhet Loveday?'

'I can't say I did.' Sir Pettigrew frowned. 'Then I could never see what you saw in the fellow, my dear. The man had the touch of a rogue about him.'

'That is what I mean,' Celestine prompted. 'There were times when I saw a ruthless streak in him. He was never short of money to pay his gaming debts.' She turned to Sir Marcus to confirm her statement. 'Yet he conducted little business to bring himself an income. His father is a parson, so Loveday had no inheritance.'

'That still does not make him a highwayman.' Sir Marcus shook his head. 'I like the fellow.'

Celestine put down her teacup and left the room. She returned holding out the stock pin that she had stolen from the baronet while he slept. 'Sir Marcus, this is yours, I believe.'

He looked taken aback. 'It is indeed. Did your maid find it?'

'I wish I could say that she had.' Celestine gave an anguished sob. 'The last time I saw Japhet Loveday he was wearing it. I recognised it at once and demanded that it be returned to you. It was only when I threatened to call the watch that he handed it to me.'

She clenched a fist and struck it against her temple. 'I should have returned it to you at once, but I had hoped to find a way to give it to you without you knowing how I came by it. That would have been wrong.'

Sir Marcus was so relieved at the return of the valuable stock pin that his wife had given him, he did not question Celestine further.

'Why was none of this mentioned before?' Sir Pettigrew was agitated. 'I never trusted Loveday. If the man stole Sir Marcus's pin the authorities should be informed.'

'He said he found it in the street outside the house,' Celestine slyly fed his antagonism. 'The night we were robbed on the heath haunts me still. There were times when Loveday moved or spoke that he resembled the highwayman, but I thought I was being fanciful.'

Sir Pettigrew jumped to his feet. He had resented the way that Japhet had stolen Celestine's affections from him. 'Now that you mention it, there was some similarities between Loveday and the man who robbed us. I never trusted him: he was a wily rogue, too slick-tongued by far.'

Sir Marcus did not like to think that Japhet had duped him. If he had stolen his stock pin then he deserved to face the consequences. 'The matter should be investigated. I shall speak with the authorities. Though they will need more than our word to arrest him. He would have needed to have robbed others who will bear witness against him.'

It would pain Celestine to part with the necklace

that she had stolen from Japhet's saddlebag. But she would return it to Lady Sefton with a carefully worded note to ensure that another complaint was placed before the authorities suspecting Japhet Loveday of highway robbery. He would be dragged back to the city and gaoled in Newgate to stand trial. There would be no wedding. And if called to bear witness Celestine would deny her statements so that Japhet went free – providing that he promised to marry her. And, of course, any notoriety surrounding the arrest of her lover would have the playhouse managers begging her to return to the stage.

The announcement of the wedding in Cornwall roused another to a vengeful anger. Lieutenant Beaumont was in his house on the cliffs overlooking Falmouth, which had been a wedding gift from Maria's father. It was a substantial residence with large sash windows and an imposing portico. Though sparsely furnished, the furniture was of the best quality and latest fashion that Thackwell could purchase for his daughter. Francis Beaumont saw none of its beauty or luxury. However gilded his home may be, it was still a cage – a cheerless prison where he was tied to a woman he despised.

He resented his wife and was repulsed by her childish whining complaints, and her bovine features and gluttony. The wedding night had been a disaster. He had drunk a flagon of claret to brace himself to consummate the marriage. Maria had screamed her disgust at what was expected of her. She was, however, desperate for a child, and on other occasions she lay as wooden as a plank beneath him, her flesh quivering with revulsion. Three months after their marriage she had announced that she was with child and banned him from her bedchamber. Francis departed with relief that the baby would appease his grandfather and secure his inheritance. He rented a cottage at Port Isaac and installed a pretty young mistress there.

This evening Beaumont was dining with Maria, who was attacking her food with her usual vigour. She slurped her soup in her haste to refill her bowl, and made smacking noises with her lips when the wine and herb sauce ran down her chin from the chicken she was eating. Throughout she chattered incessantly, constantly repeating any gossip she had learned. Beaumont ignored her, or answered in monosyllables, yawning, making no attempt to hide his boredom.

'They say the wedding will be a grand affair. Then Miss Druce is one of the wealthiest heiresses in the country. Anyone who is anyone is invited. I do think it is most discourteous that we have not received an invitation – your grandfather is, after all, a lord and an admiral. You knew the family, did you not?'

The mention of Gwendolyn Druce's name penetrated Beaumont's ennui and made the overspiced meal lurch queasily in his stomach.

'Miss Druce . . .' Maria continued with a smirk. 'Wasn't she the one who jilted you? You thought I was too stupid to know about that, didn't you? I was tired of being mocked by acquaintances for my spinsterhood. Marrying the grandson of an admiral soon silenced their spite.' She giggled inanely. 'The Druce woman is to marry a Loveday – the one who is the black sheep of the family. That shows how desperate she is. They say the family is putting on a brave face – but the man has no income and has a reputation as a womaniser . . .'

Maria continued to bombard her husband with the gossip she had gleaned about the wedding.

Beaumont was frozen in his seat. It could only be Japhet Loveday that Gwendolyn Druce was marrying. Yet again that family had humiliated him. First Adam by the duel that had resulted in Beaumont being cashiered from the navy; then St John by stealing Lanyon's contraband from the customs house that Beaumont's men were guarding. It also irked that Beaumont was convinced that St John was Harry Sawle's partner in smuggling, but he had never been able to prove it as the pair had an uncanny knack of outwitting him. Now Japhet had won the wealthy bride Beaumont had wanted for himself. He did not love Gwendolyn Druce but her dowry was twice that of Maria Thackwell. And at least she was intelligent and presentable in public, whereas Maria was a constant embarrassment to his vanity and pride.

Francis Beaumont withdrew to his study and reread the poorly penned missive that had been waiting for him on his return to Falmouth. It had been written anonymously, stating a certain unscrupulous smuggler from Penruan had a hoard of contraband stored in a cave behind a waterfall on the old Boscabel estate. Beaumont knew that land now belonged to Adam Loveday. This was his chance to get back at his old enemy. He could be incarcerated for allowing contraband to be stored on his land.

Then he remembered that Adam had sailed to America. It would be harder to implicate him in any involvement with the smugglers. Also his twin, St John, had accompanied him on the voyage. Beaumont guessed that the anonymous missive referred to Harry Sawle. Yet Sawle paid him to stay out of local waters when he was landing a cargo. That bribe money had been enough for Beaumont to rent the cottage in Port Isaac for the next year and support his mistress in some style.

The paper was returned to his pocket. It was lucky that he had not destroyed it, seeking to protect Harry Sawle. If the smuggler was hiding his cargo at Boscabel, then the Lovedays could not be entirely ignorant of the fact. His vow of vengeance upon the family had so far had little impact. The break-in that he had arranged at the yard, which had destroyed the work in the carpentry shop, had caused Edward Loveday little more than inconvenience. Even the fire he had hired men to start had been discovered before it could do too much damage to the nearly completed ship.

He patted the paper in his pocket with malicious pleasure. He would post men along the river at Boscabel and discover this waterfall. Sawle paid him to keep clear of his landings; there was nothing in his agreement about contraband stored on land. Beaumont rubbed his hands in anticipation. This could bring the ruin and shame upon the Lovedays that he had awaited for so long.

Chapter Twenty-Five

Until the birth of the twins Senara had always been blessed with abundant energy and vitality. Now she was exhausted with her nights broken with one or the other of them crying. Every time a twin cried, Senara would go to comfort the baby, and be unable to fall asleep again. Often the twins' cries would also disturb Nathan, who had become more demanding of his mother's time since their birth.

The days became a haze of tending to the children's needs and those of the patients who still sought her remedies. Despite the hard work Senara was fulfilled as a mother and she was fortunate in her helpers. Leah and Bridie called every day to assist with the work. Nan Walker, who had been engaged as a wet nurse, came from Trewenna twice a day to help Senara feed the twins, and had a two-month baby of her own. Bridie was proficient in collecting the herbs and brewing the potions Senara needed for her patients. Her sister took Tamasine on her foraging for herbs, and several times the two young women had returned giggling after they had encountered Pious Peter, who would preach to them.

'There are times when I cannot believe that Peter is Japhet's brother. They are so different.' Tamasine shook her head and laughed as she recounted Peter's latest sermon to Senara, who was seated by the parlour fire feeding Joel. 'Peter said that my soul was in danger of corruption if I denied the Lord. He also said that it was scandalous that you had not been churched since the birth of the twins. He worked himself into quite a taking, saying—'

'I can imagine what he said.' Senara did not want to hear Peter's sermon, even at second-hand. 'Though I can see that he would regard me as a poor guardian of your morals. It has been some weeks since you attended church. I am surprised that Adam's father has not mentioned it.'

Pain shadowed Tamasine's expressive eyes and her chin came up in a moment of rebellion. 'I can hardly attend Trewenna church now that Amelia is back at Trevowan. And I told Pious Peter as much in no uncertain terms. Neither do I care for the pontificating of the Reverend Mr Snell at Penruan.'

Senara chewed her lip. She had not realised how complicated life could be trying to keep the peace amongst the diverse personalities of the Loveday family. She did not reply at once, taking time to concentrate on the needs of her son. When she laid him in his crib, his hands clenched and his face reddened as he continued to cry, demanding his mother's attention. Senara picked him up and put

402

him against her shoulder, knowing from experience that nothing else would pacify him. 'I am too tired to worry about what Peter thinks. I have better things with which to occupy myself than his sanctimonious belief in what is right.'

'I told him as much.' Tamasine toyed with a silver rattle, shaking it to make Joel smile. 'Poor Bridie tried to placate him. She became very upset when he stormed away.'

This struck Senara as the more serious issue. 'Leah is concerned that Bridie is going to Trewenna church twice on a Sunday. She is always quoting what Peter says.'

'I think she is a little in love with him,' Tamasine said with a laugh. 'She gets very defensive whenever he is criticised.'

Senara was worried about her sister's infatuation with Adam's cousin. 'Bridie is young and impressionable. Strangely, she never mentions Peter to me.'

'She knows you do not approve.'

'And does Peter show an undue interest in her?'

'I think he sees her as another convert to the faith and through her he will win you and your mother back into the fold.'

Senara walked through to the kitchen, where Leah and Bridie were helping Carrie Jensen with the weekly washing. Bridie was stirring a wooden paddle through the soiled baby linen in an iron pot on the range. She was red-faced from the heat and singing a popular love ballad. Bridie, with her elfin looks and thick tumble of rich brown hair, was fast becoming a beautiful woman. There was a fullness to her breasts and hips and in another year she would be ready for marriage.

Joel quietened at the sound of Bridie's singing and Senara paused to listen. Her sister's voice held the poignant note of a woman yearning to experience the joy of romance, to be wooed by the man of her dreams. Senara hoped that her sister's infatuation with Peter was temporary. At least Peter showed no sign of returning the young woman's feelings. Bridie needed to be introduced to other young men of her age.

Scamp came running into the kitchen from the yard with muddy paws and, after a yell from Leah, Tamasine ran through from the parlour and shooed the dog back into the garden. When she returned her shoulders were squared in defiance. 'Peter exasperates me. He has such a narrow view of everything. He makes me feel guilty that I do not attend church when I would spare Amelia's feelings. But I suppose I was wrong to impose on my guardian as I did. I should have stayed at the academy, even though I was miserable.'

'These things happen in the way that they do for a reason,' Senara replied. 'It is good that you can get to know some of your family.'

Leah paused in twisting the wooden dolly in the barrel used to wash the household linen. 'It must be awful to have no one at all to call your own.'

'Amelia considers only herself and what society will think.' Bridie joined in the conversation. 'I never knew my father, neither do I want to. He were a nasty piece of work, forcing himself on my mother the way he did. But I have been brought up surrounded by love from Senara and my mother. It gives me the strength to ignore the taunts that a bastard always faces. I have been fortunate in that my half-brother, Caleph, and the gypsies treat me no different from how they treat Senara, though I'm not their kin.'

Leah had dropped the wooden dolly and tears filled her eyes. 'You weren't to blame for what happened to me. I always loved you.'

'I know, Ma.' Bridie shifted her weight from her leg with the built-up shoe to the other, to ease the pain she suffered constantly. 'But sometimes I felt that my twisted back were punishment for the sin my father committed upon you. Peter says for me to enter into heaven I do need to repent daily because of the sins of my father.'

'That Peter Loveday do have more hair than wit at times.' Leah flushed with anger. 'What would he know of the wickedness and ways of the world? What do he know of the injustices suffered by the poor, or the prejudice and discrimination against my late husband's people? Or the fear people show against any poor soul who be different, like my Bridie? If I hear he be upsetting you again, child, he shall feel the weight of my broom on his shoulders. I won't have a sweet child like you reviled by no jack-a-dandy hedge-priest.'

'But, Ma, Peter Loveday be a man of God. He do but have the welfare of my soul in his care.' Bridie became visibly distressed. 'His father, Parson Loveday, is very kind to me. And despite what you say, Peter

Loveday be kind too. There bain't many folk trouble themselves to give me the time of day.' Bridie continued to tackle the baby cloths as though they were a hidden enemy.

Senara sighed. To say anything about Peter would only increase her sister's attraction to him. That was the way of young love.

Tamasine followed Senara back into the parlour. 'Everyone is so busy – so absorbed in their own problems. You let me do little to help in the house.'

'You are here as my companion, not a servant,' Senara reminded her.

'Mr Loveday is too busy for my afternoon visits. Besides, his wife does not approve of our meetings,' Tamasine answered with a sigh. She was always careful never to refer to Edward as her father and always used the formal manner of address. She pulled at a ringlet of dark hair in her agitation. 'You have the twins and Nathan to care for. Bridie is engrossed in making the remedies and you will not let me help.'

Senara understood Tamasine's plight and sympathised with the young woman. 'Mr Loveday may be content to allow myself and my sister to help those who are sick, but some of the knowledge of ancient lore that I gained from my grandmother is not something he would care for his ward to learn.'

Senara rocked her son in her arms and her gaze misted as she stared along the inlet of the Fowey river towards the sea. Whenever she looked at the river she always thought of Adam. He should have returned by now from his voyage. With each passing day Senara became more uneasy, her longing for her husband making her fear for his safety. She offered up a prayer that he was safe and well. She longed to see the surprise and joy on his face when he saw the twins.

'It has been so long since we visited Boscabel.' Tamasine broke through Senara's thoughts. 'It has been almost a month.' She laughed. 'You gave that man we met by the waterfall such a scare.'

A hollow feeling of panic gripped Senara. How could she have forgotten such a potentially dangerous situation? With the birth of the babies she had never got round to warning Eli Rudge to ensure that smugglers did not use the cave. Tamasine announced that she would wash Scamp's feet before he ran back into the house and left Senara staring out of the window, concerned at her oversight, as she rocked Joel to sleep.

Above the noise of the hammering and sawing in the yard, Senara heard Edward's voice raised in command. As so often of late it sounded tense and strained. The family from Trevowan had visited the twins. Edward was openly delighted, Elspeth fussing and proud, and constantly reminiscing upon the birth of St John and Adam. She took particular concern over the health of Rhianne, recalling that Edward's own twin sister, Rowena, had died at birth. Amelia, heavy with her own pregnancy, had sent excuses not to attend. Senara had hoped that the close proximity of the birth of their children would have formed a bond between the two women. Clearly not. From the little that Elspeth had said, it was obvious that Amelia would never come to Mariner's House while Tamasine remained in residence.

Worried about Harry Sawle's interest in the cave, Senara decided to visit Boscabel that afternoon. The weather was dry but overcast and she could return before the twins needed their feed. She asked Bridie to join her for the ride. Her sister declined, happy to spend the afternoon keeping Nathan amused. Senara found Tamasine in the flag-stoned yard of the garden, the young woman's skirt splashed from the bucket of water that she had been using to wash Scamp's feet.

Tamasine laughed at her offer to ride with her. 'You waited until I got this mutt clean before you asked that. Now he will get dirty again. I'd love a ride.'

At Boscabel Tamasine took Scamp off to explore the gardens while Senara did her rounds of the house. Rudge had worked hard in her absence. Any broken windowpanes in the house had been replaced and the yard was cleared of debris, the barn door and broken struts in the animal stalls repaired. It was with trepidation that Senara searched for Rudge and found him in the nearest field, rebuilding a dry-stone wall.

'You have done so much,' she said with pleasure before broaching the subject of the cave. 'Has it been used by Sawle?'

'I bain't seen nothing amiss. Though I had me work cut out up here.' He refused to meet her stare and shuffled away. 'I got work to be finished afore nightfall. The old barn be overrun with rats, and they be getting into the house. I got traps laid that need checking. Caught thirty of the varmints yesterday.'

'Rudge, have you checked down by the river that no cargo has been landed? I told Sawle I'd report him to the authorities if he dared to use our land.'

Rudge stopped in his tracks, his stare constantly shifting. 'You don't want to be interferin' in that business . . . There were a problem with Sawle . . .' He seemed to be dragging the words up from his boots and sweat broke out on his brow and upper lip. 'It were when you were abed with the twins . . . Mr Loveday dealt with it. It weren't nothing to do with me. I don't want to lose me job . . .'

'Is there contraband in the cave?' Senara demanded.

'Couldn't say. I bain't been near the place.'

'Then come with me and if there is anything in that cave, the authorities will be told.' Senara flicked the skirts of her riding habit with her riding whip and strode towards the horses, tethered by the fountain in the courtyard. 'I warned Harry Sawle I would not have contraband on our land.'

Rudge ran ahead of her, halting her progress. 'It bain't safe to go there. Sawle bain't a man to allow no one to interfere with his goods. Best you talk with Mr Loveday.'

Icy fingers of dread ran down Senara's spine but her growing anger that Harry had disregarded her orders overrode her fear. Something untoward was happening here. 'Is Japhet involved with Sawle? I can't believe he would put the family at risk. He is soon to wed Miss Druce.' She put a hand to her head, her thoughts chaotic.

'It be Mr Edward Loveday you should talk with.'

At the pronouncement Senara stepped back with shock. 'Adam's father! he would never permit anything underhand. What has been going on here, Rudge?'

He looked surly. 'I were told to stay away from the river. That's all I know. And it be best if you do the same. If there be goods hidden and you be seen in the area you could be implicated.' He shambled off.

Despite his warning Senara's first instinct was to go to the cave. She was halfway to the river when her temper had cooled enough to be more rational. What had Rudge meant by being implicated? If the excisemen found the cargo, she could plead innocence of its existence. Yet it seemed Harry Sawle had blatantly flouted her wishes. Surely, if Edward Loveday had become involved he would never allow anything illegal to jeopardise their family. She would talk to Edward first.

She was silent for most of the journey home and then was stopped from confronting Edward by Joel's demand for a feed. Her nerves were taut, fearing that she would miss talking to Edward before he left the yard at the end of the day. Once Joel was replete, she hurried to the office, only to find it empty.

'Mr Loveday be with the blacksmith,' Ben Mumford called to her.

Senara waited outside the forge in the shipyard until Edward had finished his conversation. She was so fraught with worry that when he appeared, she blurted out her fears without preamble. 'Rudge says you've had words with Harry Sawle. He threatened to use a cave at Boscabel to store smuggled goods. I refused him.'

Edward glanced anxiously around the yard. 'Keep your voice down. You'd better come into the office. This is not the place to talk.'

'Then Rudge was right?' Senara felt her chest tighten with alarm as she followed Edward across the yard. The fire had been raked out of the hearth and the office was cold. The crimson rays of the setting sun lighted the interior. Edward offered her a seat, which she refused, her stare challenging as she held his gaze.

'I had not realised Sawle had approached you.' Edward was abrasive.

Senara informed him of their meeting by the waterfall, ending fiercely, 'I told him that I would inform the authorities if he used the cave.'

'You have not?' Edward paled and clasped his hands behind his back.

'You condone what Sawle intends?' Senara put a shaking hand to her mouth. Everything she believed about the integrity of this man and his family was brutally crushed. Her eyes flashed with fury. 'I thought you disapproved of St John's involvement with the smugglers. Have you allowed Sawle on to Adam's land? The laws are harsh about smuggling. Could not Adam face imprisonment? How could you allow this to happen?'

'I do not approve. But in this instance I had no choice.'

Senara reeled back from him, her eyes wide with horror. 'You do not risk Trevowan or yourself,' she accused. 'There is a cave in Trevowan Cove.'

'That cave is well known. Sawle said he found the one at Boscabel by chance. I doubt even Adam knew of it, and as lads he and St John often broke into the grounds of Boscabel to play when the place was derelict and deserted.' He put up his hand to stop a further outburst from Senara.

'I can understand that you are shocked,' he went on. 'Please hear me out. I think you should also sit down.'

He waited until she complied, there was a sinister ring to his voice that kept her silent.

'I have been trying to find the right time to break this news to you. I should have done so three weeks ago, but it was so soon after the birth of the twins . . . I wanted to wait until you were stronger. Then with each day it became harder to speak. Squire Penwithick has sent me word . . .'

At the mention of the squire's name, Senara closed her eyes against a sickening premonition that something had happened to Adam. 'It is Adam! But if he is dead why would you allow . . .?' Her voice broke, choked by her misery. She battled to still a scream rising in her throat.

'Adam is not dead,' Edward hastily assured. '*Pegasus* was captured by the French. Adam and his crew are prisoners in La Rochelle. The French are demanding a ransom for his release, money that I cannot hope to raise unless I sell large portions of land

– and though I would do so without hesitation, that takes time. When I learned from Eli Rudge that Harry Sawle had hidden contraband in the cave, I told him to get it off the land that night or I would inform the authorities. He offered to pay me a substantial sum if it could remain there a week. He also offered me a low-interest loan on any money I needed to keep the yard out of debt.

'I should have known better and kept out of his clutches, but I wanted Adam freed as soon as possible. Sawle loaned me the ransom money. I could not go to a local banker for they would ask too many questions.'

Senara was stunned by the news. At least Adam was safe but conditions in such a prison would be dire, and gaol fever could strip even the healthiest man of his life.

'Your nephew is a partner in a bank. You did not need Sawle's loan.'

'It could take a month to get the money from Thomas. I did not want to wait that long. Squire Penwithick is arranging for the French to be contacted and Adam released. It could still take some weeks.'

Senara covered her face with her hands, tears spilling through her fingers. Edward put a hand on her shoulder. 'We are doing everything we can. But if Sawle is still using the cave to hide his cargo then that was not our agreement. I will investigate. You must not worry about Sawle. Keep faith that everything is being done to rescue Adam as soon as possible. Now that you know, I will tell the rest of the family. We will be there to help you in any way we can.'

Senara lifted her tear-streaked face and gripped his hand. 'Dealing with Sawle cannot have rested easily with you. I pray that not only will Adam be returned to us soon, but that all else will be well.'

Edward patted her hand. Sawle must be dealt with. Edward had been naive to believe that the smuggler would keep his word. But he had been desperate, and desperation had a way of making a man careless.

Chapter Twenty-Six

Following his conversation with Senara, Edward rode straight to Boscabel. As a precaution he was armed with a pistol pushed into his waistband. A bonfire was burning to the rear of the house and he found Eli Rudge burning a mass of cut brambles. The bodies of a score of rats were waiting in a pile to be incinerated. He summoned the man to accompany him to the waterfall. Edward had paid the servant to keep his silence about the contraband, which had been stored there.

'Is the cave empty, Rudge?'

The older man shrugged. He wore a threadbare jacket with a frayed muffler of indeterminate colour around his neck. His large hands were cut and bleeding from the brambles and he had picked up a sharp short-handled scythe when summoned by Edward. 'I've kept away from there. I bain't gonna risk a bullet in me back for putting me nose where me nose bain't wanted. Sawle made that clear.'

'He was given permission to store the goods there

for a week. The pack ponies should have taken it away long before now.'

'Someone has been down that way,' Rudge offered as they walked through the wood to the riverbank. 'There be fresh footprints by the river a few days ago. I'd set some eel traps and were checking on them. But they were some way from the cave. I reckoned they be poachers. There be a lot of pheasants in them woods.'

'Part of your job is to keep poachers out,' Edward snapped, 'especially with illicit goods on the land.'

'I be but one man. I can't be everywhere at once. Got me work cut out putting some order into the house and grounds. I bain't been told I were to be no gamekeeper.' He remained truculent and he had kept the scythe held in front of him as though expecting a sudden attack from out of the undergrowth.

'Neither Mrs Loveday nor I have any complaints about your work, but it is part of your duties to ensure than no trespassers are on the land, Rudge.' Edward had allowed his anger at Sawle to turn against Rudge and, sensing the man's resentment, he amended, 'From what I have seen you have worked well to clear so much of the land. My son will be delighted.' The mention of Adam brought a resurgence of fear for his son's safety. There had been no further news from France concerning Adam's release, and the squire had warned him that it could take months for the negotiations to be completed.

On top of all the other worries, Edward had to deal with, Sawle's blatant disregard of their agreement incensed him. He was weary of so many tribulations.

Amelia remained cold towards him and was adamant that she would have nothing to do with Tamasine. His wife was in poor health, with her pregnancy causing pains in her legs and back, and most days she was so tired that she could not rouse herself from her bed. Chegwidden had attended upon Amelia and stated that it was more debilitating for a woman to have a child towards the end of her childbearing years than for a younger woman. Edward tried to be patient and understanding. He loved Amelia and missed the vibrant personality of the woman he had married.

When Amelia did rise from her bed she spent most of the day reclining on a chaise longue, and retired each evening directly after the family had eaten. It did not make reconciliation between them easy to achieve. He prayed that once she had been safely delivered of her child, the love they had shared would return in its full intensity.

They were close to the bank of the river inlet when Rudge halted abruptly, stepped behind a tree and gestured to Edward to do the same. He whispered, 'I heard voices, sir.'

Edward pressed his back against the wide girth of an ancient elm and peered around its trunk, drawing his pistol as he did so. The trees were closely packed but without their canopy of leaves, the winter sunshine made it easy to see some distance through the wood. Edward could hear the tumbling of the waterfall, and closer to, indistinct voices that appeared to come from at least three men. He edged forward.

Rudge hesitated to follow. 'There could be a parcel

of them rogues. They be dangerous men to cross. Shouldn't I get some help?' His voice was thin with fear.

'Who from? It is a mile to the nearest farm. They could be gone by the time you return. How close is the cave from here?'

'Aways yet, sir.' Rudge frowned. 'Mayhap it just be poachers.'

'Then they will be dealt with accordingly.' Edward advanced and signalled to Rudge to keep at his side.

Ahead he saw a man urinating against a tree and there was a ribald comment from one of his companions. Poachers did not usually work in groups. When the man fastened his breeches and returned to his companions, Edward's skin prickled with alarm. He was uncomfortably aware that they could be vastly outnumbered.

'Who is there?' he demanded. 'This is private land.'

There was a shout and twigs snapped underfoot as the men scattered. With his pistol raised in readiness to fire, Edward advanced. He glimpsed half a dozen roughly dressed, bearded men running through the trees.

'That has scared them off,' he said to Rudge. 'Now we will investigate the cave.'

Edward was impatient to discover if the cave was still being used. He had made a mistake in allowing Sawle access to this land, but Sawle had under-estimated him if he thought that Edward would meekly allow the smuggler to continue now that their agreement was at an end.

He was grimly silent as he and Rudge made their way to the waterfall and was surprised at how well the cave was hidden. If Senara had not explained that overhanging greenery hid the entrance, he would never have suspected its existence. There were footprints all over the mud close to the entrance of the cave. That increased Edward's anger. The smugglers had been careless, making no attempt to erase any sign of their presence.

The curtain of ivy moved easily and allowed enough light to penetrate the cave to reveal several dozen kegs stored there. Angrily, Edward dropped the ivy branches. 'Rudge, if the lot is not moved tonight, set fire to everything in the cave tomorrow morning. I'm tempted to do it now.'

'They'll kill us,' Rudge yelped. 'Cross Sawle and I'll be food for the fishes in a week. And he'll make you pay. He rules by terror. He bain't gonna allow no man – even one of position in the county – to get away with besting him. He'd lose control over his men if he did.'

'I do not give in to threats or intimidation,' Edward seethed. 'You sound as if you're in his pay, Rudge. I paid you for your loyalty to our family.'

The retainer was ashen and shaking. 'He gave me a keg of brandy to keep me nose out of his business. I reckoned there weren't no harm in that.'

Edward strode away. 'Sawle has got above himself this time.'

'Arrest those men!'

The shouted order made Edward swing round, and

he saw nine men with muskets trained on him and Rudge.

'I arrest you both in the King's name. Give yourselves up peacefully or my men will fire.'

The leader was too far away for Edward to see his features. Edward did not recognise any of the armed men. The smugglers and tubmen would all have been locals and he guessed that these were excisemen. He raised his hands. 'This is my son's land. I have just discovered a hoard of contraband here. I have no idea who put it there and will appreciate you impounding it.'

Lieutenant Beaumont stood behind the armed men. He had spent a cold and uncomfortable three days and nights with his crew watching this cave. Normally he would have sent his second-in-command to stay with the guard until the smugglers came to retrieve their goods. But as this was Loveday land, he hoped that Japhet was involved with the smugglers as St John had once been. This was his chance to get his revenge on the Loveday family, and he was determined to make it as unpleasant for them as possible.

Two men grabbed Edward's arms and, outraged, he attempted to shake them off. From the corner of his eye he saw Rudge being beaten. A blow to his head felled the servant and they hauled his slumped body away, his dragging feet leaving grooves in the muddy riverbank.

When Edward continued to resist the leader shouted, 'Desist your struggles or I will fire.'

'I am no party to any smuggling band. This land

has been used without our permission.' Edward continued to fight as the two men twisted his arms behind his back. 'I am Edward Loveday of Trevowan. I am a shipwright, not a smuggler.'

'I know who you are, Mr Loveday, and that you also have a great many debts,' Beaumont sneered. 'You are not the first landed gentleman to clear his financial embarrassment by having an understanding with the smugglers. Why should I believe that you are innocent? Your son was a member of the gang who hid these goods.'

'My sons are both in America.'

'One fled the country to live down his trial for murder of another smuggler. I doubt you are as innocent as you would have the world believe, Mr Loveday.'

'This is ludicrous!' Edward raged, refusing to be taken like a common criminal.

'You are resisting arrest, Mr Loveday.' Beaumont raised his pistol and when Edward kicked out at his captors, he fired.

Pain slammed into Edward's shoulder, the impact of the bullet knocking him backwards. Then a cudgel blow to his head brought him to his knees before a second blow rendered him unconscious.

Edward and Rudge were taken to the lockup in Fowey. The small cell was fetid and the straw on its floor mildewed with age. Edward was still groggy from the blow to his skull and he cradled his arm to ease the pain from his injured shoulder.

'I demand that either Sir Henry Traherne or Squire Penwithick be sent for and this matter will be cleared up at once.'

'Concealing illicit goods on your land is a serious crime,' Lieutenant Beaumont informed him. 'Traherne and Penwithick are friends of yours. They will hardly deal with the matter in an unbiased fashion.'

'Then send for any justice of the peace,' Edward demanded. 'I am no common felon.' His head ached and he could not move his arm. 'I need a physician. The bullet needs to be removed from my shoulder.'

'All in good time.' Beaumont left the cell and the door was banged shut and locked.

No one came near them for an hour. Two drunken sailors had also been put in the cell with them and one had vomited on the floor before they both fell into a stupor and passed out. Edward rapped on the door, shouting for the turnkey.

A bearded face appeared at the grating in the door. 'I been told you're to get no special privileges, Mr Loveday.'

That the turnkey's tone was respectful heartened Edward. He studied the man. 'You're Joseph Ellman. You've done work at harvest time at Trevowan.' Edward held out a gold coin. 'This is yours if you send word to Sir Henry Traherne at Traherne Hall. Where is the physician I asked for?'

'Dr Tredinnick is attending a birth, sir. He sent word he'd be here as soon as he be able.'

'Then send to Penruan for Dr Chegwidden.'

'Chegwidden refuses to attend at the gaol.'

'He will if he is told who has summoned him, or he will find he is no longer our family physician. Will you send for Sir Henry Traherne?'

The turnkey reached for the money and Edward's fingers closed over the coin. 'You get this when Sir Henry arrives.'

Ellman hesitated. 'Beaumont will have me guts for garters. You be up afore the justice of the peace day after tomorrow, same as the other prisoners. If you be wanting something from the inn to eat and drink that will cost you.'

Edward took two silver coins from his money pouch. 'Get some wine and decent food for Rudge and myself. The gold is for you when Sir Henry Traherne arrives. Beaumont has overstepped his duty in arresting me.'

The money spoke louder than any threats Beaumont had made to the turnkey. A jug of cider and a cooked chicken and two pasties were delivered from an inn and Sir Henry arrived an hour later.

Sir Henry was splashed with mud from the speed of his ride. He pressed a handkerchief to his face to stifle the smell of vomit. 'Good Lord, Edward, I thought the man was raving when he said you had been arrested.' It took the baronet some moments to adjust his sight to the gloom. 'I say, there's blood on your shirt and jacket. Are you hurt?'

'I was shot for resisting arrest by that fool Beaumont. He found contraband hidden at Boscabel. I was checking that all was well on the estate and saw some suspicious footprints along the riverbank. I discovered

423

a cave behind the waterfall and it was full of brandy casks. Beaumont must have been lying in wait for the smugglers to return to catch them red-handed.'

'Beaumont is an arrogant fool, and he has no love for your family.' Sir Henry clasped his hands behind his back. 'Unfortunately, justice has to be seen to be done, Edward. No need for you to moulder here. Give me your word that you knew nothing of these goods on Adam's land and you can go free.'

Edward could not give his word of honour with a lie. 'I had a suspicion there could be goods hidden. Senara had encountered Harry Sawle trespassing on the riverbank at Boscabel just before she was brought to bed of the twins. The incident went out of her mind and she had only just recalled it. She was worried that her husband's property was being used for illegal means and it would rebound upon Adam.'

'So you think Sawle is involved?'

'Who else runs a smuggling gang in the area?' Loss of blood from the wound in his shoulder was making Edward light-headed, and he leaned against the wall of the cell, his breathing becoming laboured.

Sir Henry rubbed his jaw. 'Tricky business. I'm all for turning a blind eye when a bit of brandy is being brought ashore, but this is audacious. How large was the haul?'

'I would say the cave contained kegs from two or three landings. Sawle will be waiting until the roads are better before moving them. Rudge here was engaged by Senara to clear the debris from the house and land. He thought he saw some men in the area but they ran off when he challenged them and he reckoned that they were poachers.'

'Come forward into the light where I can see you, Rudge,' Sir Henry ordered. 'If you saw these men why did you not investigate the cave?'

'Did'na know there be a cave, sir. I jus' keeps a general eye on the property. I be employed like Mr Loveday says to clear out the rubbish and bring some order to the outbuildings and such. The place be in a rare state of neglect after so many years with no one living there.'

Sir Henry nodded. 'Rum do, all this, Edward. There were rumours that St John was involved with Sawle. Meriel was his sister, and St John could be pretty flush at the gaming tables when it was known the yard was struggling financially. Adam also needs a great deal of money to rebuild Boscabel.'

'Neither St John nor Adam is here to answer for himself. You are Adam's friend; you know he would never put his reputation, or property, at risk by allowing contraband to be stored on his land.'

'Indeed not!' Sir Henry stoutly declared. 'These questions needed to be asked and you have answered them to my satisfaction. You are free to go. Beaumont has been too eager in his work. Do you wish to press charges that you were shot, Edward?'

Edward shook his head. 'Enough harm has been done. Beaumont has a grudge against our family.'

'So it would appear, especially now that Japhet is to wed Gwendolyn at Easter.'

There was a commotion outside the cell and Dr

Simon Chegwidden entered with a nosegay pressed to his mouth. 'Mr Loveday, I was shocked to be summoned here. My fee will be double for the inconvenience,' he announced with cutting arrogance, and then he noticed Sir Henry and his manner mellowed. 'Sir Henry, you must be as outraged as myself to hear that a man of Mr Loveday's standing has been arrested and shot in the process.'

'Mr Loveday was shot by that idiot Lieutenant Beaumont,' Sir Henry informed the doctor. 'Contraband was found on his son's land. Since Adam is at sea, there can be no implication that the family was involved. I shall inform Beaumont's superiors of this. The fool could have killed Mr Loveday.'

Dr Chegwidden examined the wound. 'The bullet is in deep and inflamed. You are starting a fever. The bullet must be removed at once.' He took a flask of brandy from his bag and splashed some on the wound.

Edward shuddered and clenched his teeth to stop crying out from the pain.

'I advise you to drink the rest of the brandy.' Chegwidden pressed the flask into his hands. 'The experience will not be a pleasant one.' He turned to Joseph Ellman, who was hovering by the door. 'Fetch a chair for Mr Loveday, though a table would be better if I am to remove the bullet.'

'Bain't no table.'

'You cannot possibly remove the bullet in this cell.' Sir Henry was appalled.

'It would be dangerous to move the patient. The

bullet will work its way deeper into the body.'

'There will be a table at the inn,' Sir Henry suggested. 'That is but a few yards hence.'

Edward was led out of the cell to a back room off the inn. Sir Henry stayed in attendance. The bullet was lodged perilously close to Edward's left lung and he passed out as the knife probed deep into the cavity.

For half an hour Chegwidden sweated with nervous anxiety at his inability to remove the bullet. Blood smeared Edward's torso, covered Chegwidden's hands and dripped on to the floor. Sir Henry and Rudge held down Edward's body on the rough table and Sir Henry was close to fainting at the butchery he witnessed. Two or three times he thought to speak out, but knew his protest would not improve the physician's skill. There was now a hole the size of a man's fist in Edward's shoulder. Finally the bullet clattered on to the floor and Chegwidden wiped his brow with a handkerchief.

'This is a bad business. Mr Loveday really should not be moved but neither is it satisfactory for him to remain here. He needs the attentions of a skilled nurse. I suggest a boat is hired to take him to Trevowan on a stretcher. It is by far the less taxing journey.'

'How is Mr Loveday?' Sir Henry demanded.

Chegwidden shook his head. 'The prognosis is not good. He has lost a great deal of blood and the wound is infected. I have cleaned it as best that I could but the light here is poor. I shall engage a nurse to attend at Trevowan.'

'Senara Loveday is skilled in such matters. Is she not best suited to tend him?'

'I do not recognise her procedures; some are most irregular. For peasants with no money to pay for proper skills, Mrs Loveday's remedies give them some relief. Mr Loveday should have only the best.' Chegwidden nodded tersely and left.

Sir Henry instructed Eli Rudge, 'Ride to Trevowan and inform the family that Mr Loveday has been wounded. Then get Fraddon to take the coach to Trevowan Hard for Mrs Senara Loveday and her family to attend at the house. She successfully nursed Adam through a gunshot wound before they were married. Waste no time. Chegwidden has near-butchered Mr Loveday. The man is not fit to practise surgery.'

He glanced at Edward, who was sleeping after Chegwidden had administered a sedative. The injury to his friend angered him and he intended to seek out Beaumont before he left Fowey.

It was dark when Beaumont returned to the lockup. The turnkey did not bother to rise from his seat. Joseph Ellman had no regrets about releasing Beaumont's prisoners. He had enjoyed the benefits of illicit brandy too often to have any regard for the excisemen. The turnkey's two brothers were tubmen with Sawle's gang, and after Edward Loveday and Sir Henry went to the inn, Ellman sent word to Sawle at Penruan that his contraband had been found. Ellman reckoned such information would earn him another keg of brandy for his pains.

The revenue officer had enjoyed a fine meal and flagon of claret and spent an hour with a whore. He was replete and self-satisfied. Finally he had exacted his revenge upon the Lovedays. This would be another disgrace to blacken the family name and, as Edward himself was involved, the integrity of the shipyard would be jeopardised. Beaumont rubbed his hands in delight.

'Stand up, man, when an officer of the King approaches,' he barked at Ellman.

The turnkey rose with slow insolence. 'Dr Chegwidden and Sir Henry Traherne have taken your prisoners to the inn for Mr Loveday to have the bullet removed. Sir Henry Traherne do reckon that Mr Loveday be innocent of any knowledge that contraband were stored on his son's land.'

Ellman was grabbed by the scruff of his neck and thrown up against the wall by Beaumont. 'Who sent for him? I expressly gave orders—'

'Release that man!' An order was rapped out and Sir Henry stood behind Beaumont. 'An innocent man has been shot and lies close to death. You have exceeded your duty, Mr Beaumont.'

'He was shot for resisting arrest. He was seen with contraband on property owned by his family.' Beaumont released Ellman.

'You know as well as I that the smugglers use caves and old mine shafts without the landowner's permission,' Sir Henry raged. 'I will report this incident to your superiors. And where is this contraband you discovered? It has not been taken to the customs house, so I have been informed.'

'Our concern was to bring two men to justice. My men are guarding the goods, and arrangements have been made to transport it to the customs house. A considerable number of pack ponies were needed—'

Sir Henry cut him short. 'If Edward Loveday dies I'll see you tried for manslaughter. You're an arrogant, incompetent idiot.' He marched out of the lockup.

Beaumont was shaken. Traherne could get him dismissed from his post. Then the admiral, his grandfather, would likely disinherit him. He must act fast and redeem himself. The haul of contraband was vast from at least three runs. Sawle had become too confident. But the officer who captured such an illicit haul could counter any accusations Sir Henry Traherne may make against him.

By dawn the next day the cave was empty and the contraband locked in the customs house.

It was not until the following morning that Harry Sawle found a note from Ellman waiting for him on his return to the Dolphin, saying Beaumont had found the cave at Boscabel. Harry had been away arranging the distribution of the contraband. The customs haul was the talk of Penruan, as was the news of Edward Loveday's shooting.

Harry was furious. Much of his money had been tied up in those goods. He had thought the cave a secure hiding place. How had Beaumont learned of it? Someone must have betrayed him. That was a matter he would deal with later. But Beaumont had taken

Harry's money to stay away from his smuggling business. To impound the goods, which Beaumont must have guessed belonged to Harry, who ran all the smuggling in this area, was another act of betrayal.

Harry had thought Beaumont was in his pocket, but he had overlooked the revenue officer's hatred for the Loveday family. Too many of the Lovedays had made a fool of Beaumont. This was the lieutenant's revenge upon them. Now Beaumont would learn what it meant to feel the revenge of Harry Sawle.

Chapter Twenty-Seven

'Japhet, finally you have decided to marry and half the family are unable to attend.' Cecily Loveday voiced her only displeasure for the forthcoming events. She was seated at the long oak table in the panelled dining room, sorting through a pile of bed linen that was in need of sewing. Either the edges had frayed, or the sheets had worn so thin in the centres that they had ripped and needed to be cut and the sides restitched into a central seam. 'I have waited for this day for so long, and so few of the family will be celebrating with us. But I am happy for you.'

'I could put off the date for another year if you prefer,' Japhet teased. 'Though I doubt that Gwendolyn would approve. The Lady Anne is making life as difficult as possible for her.'

His mother shuddered and subjected him to a withering glare. 'Do not even jest about postponing the wedding. Gwendolyn has been more than patient waiting for you to come to your senses. And you'll never meet a more suitable bride.'

'I am aware of that.' Japhet had returned to Trewenna Rectory to change into evening dress before he dined at Traherne Hall. He had spent the day reinspecting the farm that Sir Henry had informed him was for sale. Gwendolyn was satisfied with the house, and the outbuildings could be extended to expand the stables. The only drawback was that the purchase would not be complete until after the wedding, and the couple would spend the first month of their marriage living with Hannah. Gwendolyn was happy to comply and had no intention of starting her marriage at Traherne Hall, as had been insisted upon by her mother.

With the wedding only ten days away, Japhet experienced moments of doubt that he could provide for Gwen the life that she deserved. And the thought of losing his freedom could still make him uneasy. Marriage meant rules and constraint, neither of which sat easily with him.

'Japhet, your thoughts are away with the fairy-folk – have you heard anything I have said?' Cecily put down the sheet she was examining.

'You regretted that so many of the Lovedays would be unable to attend the wedding, Mama.'

She sighed and repeated the rest of her news. 'While you were out a letter arrived from Margaret saying that she would arrive in four days, but not Thomas or Georganna. Thomas is needed at the bank.'

'I had not expected Aunt Margaret to travel so far at this time of year.'

'She is worried about Edward. His recovery is so slow and he remains too weak to leave his bed. And Amelia will be brought to bed soon with her child, so I doubt she will be at the wedding. She refuses to leave Edward's bedside.'

'I thought Uncle Edward was improving; he looked less feverish when I called yesterday morning and was working in his study. He spoke of visiting the yard today.'

'Which is exactly why the fever has returned. Your father is there now.' Cecily wiped a tear from her eye with a corner of a sheet. 'Edward will not rest despite Ben Mumford and Isaac Nance coping admirably with the work at the yard and on the estate. Elspeth found him collapsed over his desk in his study in the early hours of the morning.'

'He will not let me help.' Japhet was also anxious about his uncle's health. It had been a month since he had been shot and Edward should have recovered long before this. The wound had become infected and would not heal, and the fever kept returning. None of Dr Chegwidden or Senara's physics seemed to work.

'When will our troubles end?' Cecily shook her head. 'There has been no word of Adam. Edward paid the ransom the French had demanded and still they will not release him. Neither has St John bothered to write to inform his father that all is well with him. Edward frets St John may revert to his old wastrel ways.'

'I would have thought that St John had learned his lesson after his trial,' Japhet pronounced, more to reassure his mother than out of any conviction that this was true.

Cecily appeared not to have heard. She continued to dab at her eyes. 'We all worry about William, who is fighting the French. I dread hearing news of a battle at sea and that William's ship has been lost. Though what that dear man will find when he comes home . . . How will he take the news that his wife is locked up in an asylum?'

'Uncle William might be at sea for months to come. Lisette could be cured by then.' Japhet put his arms around his mother's shoulders. 'I thought my marriage would make you happy. It has made you worry more than ever.'

She dried her tears and smiled up at him. 'I am a foolish old woman. I am not usually so morbid. Edward will recover. He is strong. Adam will be home soon now that the ransom is paid. Squire Penwithick assured me it should not be long. And St John . . . I trust that the Lord will bless him as he has blessed you, and he will change his ways.'

Cecily drew her sewing basket towards her and searched for a needle and thread. She squinted in irritation at being unable to thread the needle. Japhet took it from her, threaded it and handed it back to her. 'We must fix you up with some spectacles, Mama.'

'There is nothing wrong with my eyesight,' she reprimanded. 'I am economising by not lighting a candle and the panelling makes this room so dark in the daytime.' She moved to sit by the window and continued her reservations about problems besetting the family. 'St John should be in England. Edward will not even write to him to return.'

'It would take many weeks for St John to receive a letter and find a passage home. Edward will be well long before then.'

Cecily shook her head as she sewed the hem of the sheet. 'St John's pride must be wounded at the way that strumpet Meriel deserted him. Margaret wrote that she had seen the baggage in London.' The strong use of language by his mother emphasised Cecily's distress. 'Meriel was no longer with Lord Wycham but on the arm of a prominent politician. At least she spares us the shame of dragging our name into the mire. She calls herself Meriel Merriweather now.'

'St John is still shackled to her while Meriel lives,' Japhet observed. 'He cannot find happiness with another wife, and he wants a son to inherit Trevowan after him. He will take no satisfaction to work all his life for the estate to pass to Rafe.'

'Now that you have come to your senses and chosen Gwendolyn as your bride, you will have no such problems. You have chosen more appropriately than either St John or Adam. Your father and I are very proud of you, and, more importantly, Gwendolyn will make you happy. You are dining at Traherne Hall tonight, are you not? This more respectable way of life you have led since your return pleases me. I give thanks to the good Lord that I no longer have to worry about you.'

When Margaret left London to travel to Cornwall for Japhet's wedding she charged Thomas to ensure that the treatment Lisette was undergoing with Dr Claver was proving beneficial. His fees were extortionate and Margaret feared that Lisette was showing little sign of improvement.

Thomas was concerned that his Uncle William would return with the fleet at any time and discover his wife incarcerated in a lunatic asylum.

He steeled himself for the visit to the asylum. Each month the fees were rising and this was beginning to disturb Thomas although he did expect the best treatment for his cousin. Because of his duties at the bank it was the first time he had attended for his mother had insisted that she was capable of dealing with the situation. Dr Claver also sent them monthly reports on Lisette's progress together with his bill for her treatment.

From the moment Thomas entered the courtyard of the asylum, he was struck by a feeling of oppression. On entering the premises he raised the nosegay to his face to obliterate the acid stench of urine and excrement. His ears were assaulted by the muffled shouts and low keening moans from the inmates. He shuddered, the narrow gloomy corridors adding to the melancholy atmosphere of the interior.

An Amazonian attendant rose from her chair in the dimly lit entrance, her angular face scored with harsh discordant lines. Her eyes were black and pitiless as a rearing viper. She was as tall as a man and held herself like a wrestler. A wart on her chin sprouted several dark hairs.

'Dr Claver has no appointments listed for this afternoon. Visitors are by appointment only.' She planted herself in the narrow entrance and folded her arms across her chest barring Thomas from proceeding.

Thomas suppressed his feelings of distaste at her appearance and her rudeness angered him. 'I am here to see my cousin, Lisette Loveday. I need no appointment.'

'Everyone needs an appointment, that's the rules.' Her jaw jutted with hostility. 'This ain't no freak show for the gentry like they 'as at Bedlam. This is a respectable hospital.'

'Which is why I pay handsomely for the expertise Dr Claver provides, and those fees provide your wages, madam. If Dr Claver is unavailable I expect your goodself or Dr Claver's assistant to take me to my cousin. I wish to ascertain that she is well provided for. She has been a patient here for some months. It distresses our family that there appears to be little improvement in her condition.'

A door opened and Dr Claver appeared. He was dressed in sober brown, his spectacles perched on the end of his hooked nose and his powdered bagwig frizzed in a halo around his aesthetic features.

'Mr Mercer, this is an unexpected pleasure. I heard your voice and altercation with Mrs Dibden. Of course, you need no appointment to visit with your cousin.' He turned to his servant with a flash of annoyance. 'In this matter you exceed your responsibilities, Mrs Dibden. I will escort Mr Mercer to his cousin's room.'

He walked ahead of Thomas, his short frame teetering on absurdly high red heeled shoes. 'Mrs Loveday's condition is most unfortunate. She is beset with ill-humours of the brain which cause her moods to fluctuate without reason. At those times she is a danger both to herself and others. I have high expectations that within three months she will be fully restored to health.'

'It will take so long? We had hoped that she would be cured by now.'

Dr Claver puffed out his chest and his small eyes regarded Thomas with hauteur. 'These matters cannot be rushed. Once a mind has become deranged it may never recover . . .'

'Lisette's behaviour in the past has been wilful and irrational. Are you telling us that she is mad?'

'That is not a term I use lightly.'

'Then how would you describe my cousin's condition?' Thomas lost his temper and shouted.

Dr Claver thrust his head forward in a belligerent manner. 'I am physician to the King and many members of the royal family and court. Do you presume to question my competence?'

The arrogance of the doctor's tone set Thomas's hackles rising. The doctor's manner and the forbidding atmosphere of the asylum made him increasingly uncomfortable. 'My cousin has been a patient here for many months. We had expected a greater improvement.' He pressed the nosegay to his face. The pervading stench of stale urine was everywhere.

Dr Claver looked through the spy hole in the door before entering Lisette's chamber. 'You will see your cousin is calm today. But she refuses to dress herself or be dressed by another.'

Lisette was in a larger room than his mother had described that was furnished with a pallet bed, a wooden chair and a washstand. She was lying on the bed with her eyes open and did not move as they entered. She wore a high-necked, long sleeved, night shift. A woollen grey dress and petticoat lay over the chair with a pair of stockings and stout shoes. Her feet were bare and her hair hung straight to her shoulders.

'Mrs Loveday, your cousin is here. Will you not greet him?'

Lisette turned dark eyes, which were deeply circled, upon him. Thomas was shocked at the dullness to her expression. He bent over her and raised her hand to his lips. There was a sweetish sharp smell on her breath that he recognised as some kind of opiate.

'How are you, Lisette?'

She continued to lie prone and each word was pronounced with a slow deliberation. 'Lisette wants to go home. Lisette does not like it here. Lisette will be good.'

Appalled at her strange manner, Thomas forced a strained smile. 'You will come home as soon as you are well, my dear. Dr Claver assures me you are much better.'

'Lisette wants to go home. Lisette does not like it here. Lisette will be good.'

He glanced at the doctor who shrugged his shoulders. He spoke reassuringly but his words did not seem to register and she repeated the same phrases again and again.

'Why is she so heavily sedated?' Thomas demanded.

'To prevent her doing harm to herself. It is only in the last week or so that we have no longer had to physically restrain her with ropes tied to her bed. As you see she refuses to dress herself and becomes violent if a nurse tries to assist her. When she dresses of her own accord she will be allowed to spend time in the common room with other patients – under supervision of course.' The doctor gestured that they leave the room.

'Lisette will be good. Lisette wants to go home.' Lisette cried out with greater passion as Thomas and Dr Claver made to leave.

Thomas tried once more to pierce her stupor. 'Look at me, Lisette. It is Thomas. You must do as Dr Claver says if you are to get well and come home.'

'Lisette wants to go home.' She stared unblinking into his face and with the abruptness of someone unlocking a door, her eyes cleared. 'Thomas. You have come to take me home.' Tears flooded down her cheeks.

He stepped to the bed and reached for her hand. 'Soon you will come home. You must do as Dr Claver says. I will visit you again in a few weeks.'

Her eyes rounded and bulged in panic and she scrambled from the bed to tear open the front of her gown to stand naked before them. 'Take me home, Thomas. Look what they do to me.'

Her flesh was blistered and raw from burn marks and her ribs were bruised. Tears ran down her face and her voice was high pitched with fear. 'I tell them I will be good. They do not listen. They only want to hurt me. Take me home Thomas. Please . . .' She fell to the floor and hugged her arms around her body as she rocked back and forth.

'What have you done to her?' Thomas rounded on the doctor.

'Blistering and cold baths are part of her treatment. The bruises she brings upon herself when she is hysterical and has to be restrained.'

Thomas was appalled. 'No woman should be treated in such a manner.' He knelt to hold out a hand to help Lisette to her feet and she flinched and threw her arms over her head as though he had meant to hit her. She was shaking uncontrollably.

'Lisette will be good,' she sobbed and held her head. 'No. No. I will be good. It is the other Lisette they hurt. The other Lisette who does bad things. I can make her go away, but still they hurt me. Then the other Lisette says I must do bad things.'

Dr Claver had gone to the door and yelled. 'Bertha, see to Mrs Loveday.'

'My cousin looks to me as though she has often been beaten,' Thomas grabbed the doctor and pushed him up against the wall.

'You are mistaken,' Dr Claver gabbled with fear. 'She can be violent and has to be forcibly restrained. You can hear how deranged she becomes by her speech. They are not the words of a sane woman.'

'Lisette is also clearly heavily drugged. She was not put under your care to be so abused. She is a gentlewoman and deserves respect.'

A monstrously large woman lumbered towards them and Thomas sidestepped to avoid contact with her heavy bulk. Bertha grinned showing blackened teeth as she passed him. She was foul of breath, noxious with incontinence and her flesh was pervaded with the rank sour smell of ulcerated legs. Around her bull-neck was a choker of pus-encrusted boils.

At her approach Lisette screamed and scuttled backwards across the floor on her buttocks, her eyes wide with terror.

'I've seen enough,' Thomas raged. 'I am taking my cousin out of here now.'

'You'll regret it,' Dr Claver shouted at him. 'The woman is mad, quite mad.'

Thomas held out a hand to Lisette, who yelped and tried to hit out at him. She no longer seemed to recognise him so deep was her terror.

'I am not going to hurt you, Lisette. Look at me. It is Thomas. Cousin Thomas. I have come to take you home. Calm yourself, you have nothing to fear.'

It was some moments before she quietened and the fear faded from her eyes. 'Thomas. Help me. I will be good. Lisette is a good girl.

Thomas realised that Lisette was far from cured,

but the treatment here was making no difference. He would consult other doctors and employ a full-time nurse to look after her. Even if it meant Lisette would have to be sedated while she lived with them, he owed it to his Uncle William to ensure that she received kindness and understanding.

He lifted Lisette into his arms. Her petite figure was as light as a child. 'My cousin suffered abominably at the hands of the rabble in France. She needs kindness to regain her wits not further cruelty. I am taking her home.'

Harry Sawle had been caught by Sal to bring up a barrel of ale from the cellar of the Dolphin Inn. His father was in a drunken sleep on a settle by the taproom fire, his head resting on an old barrel that served as a table. To save money the fire had been allowed to burn low and no candles had been lit to relieve the dingy interior of the taproom.

'Get another barman in to do the cellar work,' Harry snarled. 'I've more important work. Or get young Mark back here to run the place.'

'Mark is doing well as a groom working for the squire. He never had a liking for tavern work and is gifted with the horses. He's hoping that Japhet Loveday will take him on once his stables are established. Mark wants to work with racehorses. It's honest work.' Sal could not resist the dig at her son. 'And while you live here you can earn your keep.'

Sal slumped down on a stool, which creaked under her vast bulk. Her face was ravaged by time and her eyes had lost their fire since Meriel had run off with Lord Wycham. 'And don't you forget who you be talking to. I be your mother and deserve a bit of respect from my children. I can't afford to pay a barman to do your work. If you think you be some grand fellow that such work is beneath you, then you get yourself out of here. Clem bain't forgotten how I slaved to bring my children up right, and at least him and Mark allow me to keep my head held high. Meriel were no better than her sister, Rose, who run off with a lover, and few smugglers live to make old bones, Harry. One day the law will catch up with you.'

Her gaze alighted upon her husband and she sighed in frustration. 'This place barely makes a living for us. Reuben picks fault with everyone and has driven our regular customers away. The pain in his leg stumps is terrible.' She wiped a tear from her eye. 'He were such a fine, vigorous man. Bain't right he came to this.'

'You've changed your tune. Pa ran a smuggling band long before Lanyon came to Penruan. They'd been rivals for years. Lanyon got his comeuppance for running Pa down in his coach. Lanyon got his comeuppance for all his crimes.' Harry gave a bitter laugh.

The door opened, bringing a gust of fish-tainted air from the quay. The broad figure of Guy Mabbley filled the doorway. He was Harry's most trusted henchman. He was also brutal and ruthless and ensured that the name of the Sawle gang was the most feared in the district.

'Leave us, Ma. I got business to attend.'

Sal sniffed in disapproval and said under her breath,

'It be such business which ended in your pa losing his legs. And look at the state of your face. That weren't no accident. The trade does for a man . . .'

Harry pushed past her. The gunpowder-blackened skin on his cheek had healed into a puckered scar, and the wealthy widow from Bodmin to whom he had been paying court had stopped seeing him, repulsed by his disfigurement. It had made him more resentful and meaner than ever. 'Quit muttering, woman, and get us both a brandy. It be a cold night and I won't be back till morning.'

He handed the tot of brandy to Mabbley, who tossed it back, then grunted, 'We kidnapped Beaumont when he docked in Fowey. He's at the appointed place, awaiting your justice. It took a beating to keep him silent. He were squealing like a pig at being tied up.'

'He shall be made an example of to ensure that in the future no man crosses me.' Harry showed no emotion as he pronounced Beaumont's death.

The Lady Anne Druce criticised everything about the wedding plans. What Japhet had hoped would be a simple affair had turned into a hundred guests being invited, with the reception at Traherne Hall. Japhet needed to keep a tight rein on his temper as he dined with Gwendolyn's family and their guest, the Honourable Percy Fetherington. Japhet was relieved when the women adjourned from the table and the men were left to their port and cigars.

The dining room of Traherne Hall was overwarm, with the fire banked high in a marble fireplace decorated with carved vine leaves. The walls were covered with a fashionable striped wallpaper, and thirty candles in the gilded and crystal chandelier lit the room. The seven-course meal, with its richly spiced sauces and spun sugar desserts, sat uncomfortably in Japhet's stomach. Sir Henry had a fine wine cellar and they had consumed several bottles throughout the meal. Sir Henry and the Honourable Percy Fetherington were old friends, and Japhet relaxed in their company as he savoured his cigar and port. The respite was short-lived. Before they had finished their cigars, Lady Traherne was demanding that the men attend upon them. She was as peevish and as scathing as her mother, and Japhet wondered how Sir Henry could tolerate living with such shrewish women. But then Sir Henry had a mistress in Fowey and another in St Austell where he escaped from his wife's demands and complaints.

The reminder that marriage brought with it shackles and responsibilities unsettled Japhet. He made his excuses to leave and Gwendolyn slipped away to meet him in the entrance hall while he awaited Sheba being brought from the stables.

'Mama was mortifying this night. And you were so patient with her. I cannot understand why she is never content with her life.' Gwendolyn's eyes sparkled and her face was flushed with pleasure as she stared up at her betrothed. 'In another ten days I shall be free of her orders and recriminations. And we shall soon have our own house.'

He looked deeply into her eyes, needing to be sure

that this was what she wanted. 'As my wife you will not be able to live in the grand style that Roslyn demands. It will take years to establish the stud farm.'

'I do not care for grandeur. We shall be together. What must I do to convince you of that?' Her smile broadened. 'Like Hannah, I shall be with the man I love, and I shall be happy if that involves working with the horses.'

Japhet cupped her face in his hands, overwhelmed at the depth of his feelings for her. 'I have been such a fool this last year. I should never have waited so long to make you my own.'

In Gwendolyn's company he was so certain of what he wanted, but as he rode Sheba to the rectory, the old feelings that marriage was an entrapment returned to haunt him. With the wedding so close he knew he would not sleep while his mind was so unsettled. Once he would have ridden to Fowey to seek out a game of hazard or cards, or a nubile barmaid. Since his betrothal to Gwen he had resolved to put his gambling and wenching days behind him.

'You're a foolish fellow,' he chided himself. 'Gwen is not like her sister or mother. She understands me as no other woman could.'

The moon was bright and he decided he would ride across the moor and down to the coast before he returned to the rectory. He rode for an hour, keeping at a steady trot, and when the track was clear and well lit by the moon, urged Sheba to a canter. The power of Sheba's muscles beneath his legs was exhilarating, and the sound of her hoofs echoed the pounding of his heart. The wind whipped back Japhet's hair and fanned the heat of exertion that flushed his cheeks. His chest rose and fell, his breath harsh in his throat, matching the rhythmic rush of air from his mare's nostrils. The ride brought a glow to his muscles and dulled the turmoil within his mind.

Eventually he slowed Sheba to a walk as they approached a remote cove with steep-sided cliffs. The moon was reflected in the sea, and Japhet could make out the inky black line of cliffs for several miles to the next headland. Muffled sounds broke the silence of the night. He ignored the rustle of badgers in the undergrowth and distant bark of a fox or hoot of an owl. The sounds that had caught his attention were human in origin: the hushed drone of voices and crunch of heavy boots on the washed-up seaweed and flotsam in the cove. Were smugglers afoot this night? They would not take kindly to be spied upon. A man could be shot or beaten senseless if smugglers discovered that he had stumbled upon their work.

Japhet scanned the cove and saw a cluster of half a dozen men near the water's edge. There was an hour before high tide and the men were thigh-deep in the water with a man on horseback observing the party from the shore. There was no boat that Japhet could see. Had a revenue ship disturbed the smugglers when they had earlier tried to land a cargo? In such instances they would weigh the kegs with stones and sink them below the waves to be picked up later. But there were no pack ponies on the sand to transport a cargo.

Aware that Sheba needed to rest and recover her wind, Japhet was intrigued by the scene on the beach. He was hidden from the men in the cove by the tall gorse bushes spread along the cliff top. The cliff face was also steep enough to give him several minutes' lead if the men raised an alarm that he had been seen. He could see no lookouts in position.

Below him the men waded out of the water, which was rising fast. One alone stayed within the waves, which now reached his chest. The others on the beach stood waiting . . . or were they watching?

The blood chilled in Japhet's veins. The moonlight revealed a grisly spectacle. The men on the beach were witnessing an execution. The man in the sea had been tied to a stout post near an outcrop of rocks. The incoming tide would drown him. It was already crashing over the rocks and sending plumes of white spray into the air. The man must have betrayed the smugglers in some way. Japhet had heard tales of such executions but had believed them to be part of the folklore of the retribution given by smugglers to any who crossed them.

A command from the man on horseback summoned his men to follow him from the beach. Japhet was surprised that they did not wait to witness their victim's end. The temperature had dropped drastically and Japhet could feel the cold seeping through the thickness of his greatcoat. There was a kiddleywink about a mile inland from the cove. No doubt the smugglers intended to drink away the hours while the tide took the life of their victim. They would be back once the tide turned to remove the stake and allow the body to be washed up on the beach. The murder would appear as an ordinary drowning.

As the last of the smugglers left the beach, Japhet saw that the water had reached the man's shoulders. He could just make out the victim's frantic head movements as he tried to free himself and keep the waves from splashing into his mouth. It was a terrifying and gruesome way to die. Death had nudged closer to Japhet's shoulder this year, with his dreams often showing the hangman's noose that awaited a convicted highwayman. Japhet thanked Madame Fortune for allowing him to escape the fate that could so easily have overtaken him if he had been arrested in London.

It made him sympathetic with the victim in the water. Such a death was meted out to those who informed on the free-traders, or who they felt had betrayed them. If the man had killed one of his accomplices he would have been shot.

Now the smugglers had left, there was a chance that Japhet could save the man. He tethered Sheba to the gorse and slithered down the muddy cliff. The water was up to the man's neck and too deep for Japhet to wade out. He stripped off his greatcoat, jacket and embroidered waistcoat, pulled off his riding boots, and ran into the water. The dagger he had worn concealed beneath his coat was in his hand to cut the victim free.

Japhet was a strong swimmer. Along with his brother and cousins, he had learned to swim as a child. His grandfather, who respected the sea, knew the folly of a family being unable to swim yet earning their livelihood from the navy or the sea. The man tied to the post was frantically twisting his head from side to side to avoid the swell of the waves. Several had splashed over his head as Japhet approached. He was gagged, which had probably stopped the water filling his lungs. The whites of the man's eyes were bulging in his terror.

'I'll cut you free,' Japhet yelled before he dived. He felt for the rope around the man's body and sawed through it with his dagger. The thick rope was coiled around the man from his feet to his chest, and even the sharp blade had difficulty slicing through it. Japhet's lungs were bursting and he was twice forced to come to the surface for air. As he dived for a third time the man's body had gone limp. The rope finally parted and Japhet tore the bonds away. The man was unconscious, and Japhet hooked the fingers of one hand around the neckband of his jacket. He swam to the shore until the water was shallow enough to gain a firm footing and then he dragged the man on to the beach.

Japhet was breathing heavily as the rolled him on to his side. The man had stopped breathing. Japhet thumped him several times on the back and then rocked his body from side to side to get the water out of his lungs. Suddenly the man coughed and a gush of seawater spurted out his mouth, and Japhet left him to cough up the rest. He retrieved his clothes and boots and pulled a hipflask from the pocket of his jacket. He was shivering in his wet clothes and took a long swig before nudging the shoulder of the man who lay groaning on the sand.

'This will bring the life back to you.' He pushed the flask into the man's hands.

Japhet pulled off his sodden hose and pushed his feet into his boots.

'I owe you my life,' the man croaked, and levered himself on to his elbow.

Japhet stood up and held out his hand to assist the other to rise. His movement froze and his hand dropped to his side as he recognised Lieutenant Beaumont.

'If I had known who you were I would have left you to your fate.' Anger heated his chilled body. 'You would have dishonoured Gwendolyn Druce to get your hands on her inheritance.'

His temper got the better of him and he smashed his fist twice into Beaumont's face. The lieutenant curled into a ball to protect his head and body from further blows and began to whimper. 'Have mercy, I beg you.'

'As you would have shown mercy to Gwen.' Japhet punched him again and Beaumont sobbed like a frightened child.

'Spare me. I will give you anything. Name your price.'

Japhet grabbed Beaumont's collar and hauled him half upright. The terror on his bloodied face disgusted Japhet. He threw him back on the ground. Japhet had fought many duels and an uneven fight held no sense of justice for him. 'I could kill you for what you did to Gwen. What craven knave needs to compromise a woman to get her to marry him?'

'Spare me!' Beaumont wailed. 'I can pay you well.'

'I don't want your money. Or rather your wife's money. For all you wanted from Gwen was her money. You never cared for her.' Japhet was breathing heavily, his handsome features dark with hatred. 'But I will spare you. But only because death now would be too easy a punishment for you. In the morning the smugglers will discover that the rope was cut and you escaped their retribution. Who did you cross? Sawle?'

Beaumont continued to lie on the beach sobbing, a weak and pathetic sight. Japhet stepped back, still fighting against the urge to beat him senseless. 'Sawle will not rest until he achieves his revenge,' he taunted. 'Even if you leave the country and make a new life, Sawle will have his spies searching for you. It may take a few months, a year, or maybe several, but he *will* find you and kill you. You will spend the rest of your life looking over your shoulder in fear of an assassin's blade, or being shot in the back.'

Japhet strode away.

'You cannot leave me here,' Beaumont begged between sobs. 'I need help.'

'I would get yourself well away from this place, and as far away as possible if you want to live,' he replied. 'I have given you more help than your craven hide deserves.'

Chapter Twenty-Eight

Elspeth paced outside Edward's bedchamber, the sound of her walking cane echoing along the panelled corridor. Dust motes swirled in a beam of sunlight and the midday sun cast diamond patterns from the lattice window at the end of the passageway on to the wooden floorboards. For two nights Edward had been delirious with fever and Chegwidden had suggested that Joshua be called to administer the last rites. Her brother had clung tenaciously to life.

Dr Chegwidden was again closeted with Edward and the physician had turned the family out of the room while he administered a purge, bled his patient and applied heated glass cups to his skin to alleviate the fluid that had built on Edward's lung.

Amelia had been at her husband's side throughout his delirium. The fever had broken this morning and, exhausted, she had gone to her room to lie down. Within an hour she had declared that her labour pains had started. Aware that Dr Chegwidden would disapprove of her actions, she had summoned Senara.

Upon her arrival Senara had gone to talk with Amelia. Elspeth, who could spend all night coaxing a mare to give birth, found it difficult to cope with Amelia's pain and distress. Animals were more stoic and they did not engage in emotional outbursts of recrimination and guilt.

The anxiety Elspeth experienced grew with each passing minute. Impatience had governed her for years. Now the wait for Chegwidden's diagnosis flayed bare Elspeth's grazed nerves. For weeks Edward's life had hung on a precarious balance. Just as he appeared to be recovering, the fever would return.

A door opened and Senara came from Amelia's room. 'Amelia is sleeping. Her labour had started, though the baby is not due for a few weeks, but I doubt the child will be born before tomorrow morning. She needs to rest and conserve her strength. You should have told me how ill Mr Loveday had become and I would have tended him during the night.'

'You have enough to do with the twins. And have done so much already.' Elspeth rarely gave praise, and until Edward had been shot she had still harboured resentment that Adam had chosen Senara as his wife. It had been Senara's calmness and experience with maladies that had reassured the family, and her herbs had done much to aid Edward's recovery. She had also been insistent that he remained in bed until his full strength was restored. Edward had been too worried about the financial circumstances at the yard to heed her advice, which on this occasion echoed that of Dr Chegwidden.

Elspeth was grateful for all that Senara had done for Edward but, embarrassed by her own inadequacy in dealing with illness, her tongue remained sharp. 'Besides, you can hardly leave Tamasine alone at Mariner's House.' Elspeth thumped her cane on the floorboards as she continued to pace. Her slender body was tight with tension.

'My mother and Bridie would be with her,' Senara answered.

Elspeth sniffed and pursed her lips. 'They would not be the guardians Edward would wish for his daughter. It is a complicated and difficult situation. The girl has caused nothing but trouble since she arrived.'

'The only difficulty is from those who have created a problem from Tamasine's existence.' Senara held Elspeth's glare in a disconcerting manner. 'Tamasine is a lovely, good-natured young woman. She has inherited the Loveday wildness, but that has never been criticised in other members of the family.'

Elspeth was about to interrupt but Senara was incensed and cut across Elspeth's protest. 'Please give me the courtesy of hearing me out. I know Tamasine better than you, who did not meet her in the best of circumstances. The girl has never known more than a few hours of kindness a year from her mother, and feels acutely the censure of your family. She did not want to usurp anyone's place, or force Mr Loveday to openly acknowledge her. It took courage for her to run away from that dreadful school. Would you have acted any differently in the same circumstances?'

'You are presumptuous.' Elspeth chose to forget the reckless acts of her own youth. She eyed Senara over the top of her pince-nez with a judicial sternness. 'By running away from that school, Tamasine has shown herself to be wilful, with a callous disregard for the proprieties. It was scandalous the way she announced to our guests that she was a Loveday.'

'She was exhausted and never intended for it to happen that way. Why can you not forgive her? Tamasine is happy at Mariner's House, but she finds it hard to accept that she has no right to visit her father when he has been close to death.'

'She is a selfish and ungrateful wretch.' Elspeth turned her fears for Edward into anger against his daughter. 'Edward should have sent her to another school until a marriage, or a post as a governess, was found for her.'

Senara walked away, refusing to continue the conversation. The pain, visible on Elspeth's face, was making her irascible. Senara was also worried about Amelia, who was worn out from the weeks of worry and nursing Edward.

Both women were silent and the tension in the corridor thickened. When Dr Simon Chegwidden came out of Edward's room, he looked grave. Senara's heart constricted with alarm.

'Where is Mrs Loveday?' the doctor demanded in an arrogant voice. He ignored Senara's presence and addressed his comments to Elspeth. 'That Mr Loveday survived the night is heartening but he is not out of danger. How can I be expected to treat a man who will not obey my instructions to keep to his bed?'

'Mrs Loveday is resting,' Senara replied, angered by his rudeness. 'She is in the early stages of labour, but the child is coming early.'

'How is Edward?' Elspeth demanded.

'Still critical. The man seems bent upon killing himself. I cannot be responsible if he will not rest as I instructed.' Dr Chegwidden glared at Senara. 'I will not have you interfering with my patient. Tend upon Mrs Loveday, your skills are adequate enough as a midwife.'

The doctor turned his back on Senara and spoke to Elspeth. 'Mr Loveday is to be given five drops of the tincture I have left beside his bed every four hours. I shall attend upon him again in the morning. The fever has broken but he is very weak.'

He walked towards the stairs and Senara hurried to his side to speak in a low whisper so that Elspeth would not hear and be further worried. 'Will you be at home this evening? We may need to call you to attend Mrs Loveday or the child. It is coming before its time and it may not be strong.'

'The Reverend Mr Snell and his good wife are dining with us this evening. If your skills are not adequate to deal with the birth, send for me if you must. If you fear for the soul of the baby then send for a parson to baptise it as soon as possible. It is in God's hands.'

Senara bit back a retort at his heartlessness. She had spoken out of politeness, for she had no faith in Chegwidden's ability to deal with a complicated birth.

She checked on Amelia and found her asleep. That was heartening, as she would need all her strength in the hours ahead. She hoped the labour pains were a false alarm.

The corridor was empty, and seeing Edward's bed-chamber door open, Senara entered. Elspeth was on her knees praying by the bedside. Edward was asleep, his face sunken and flushed with fever. Senara picked up the bottle of tincture left by Dr Chegwidden and sniffed it. It was a strong opiate that would keep him too lethargic to get out of bed. She could detect nothing within it that would assist the healing Edward needed.

She put a hand on Elspeth's shoulder, indicating that she wanted to speak with her outside the room.

'If Amelia is in labour I will need my mother to help me with the birth. And your brother will recover faster if some herbs are prepared and put in some broth. He should be spoon-fed every few hours to give him the strength to stop the lung fever returning. Chegwidden has left nothing more than a sleeping draught. And he did not even change the dressing on his wound. I will do that now.'

'He is not going to die, is he? He is so weak. But how can you tend him and Amelia? The twins will need to be fed.'

'The wet nurse will bring them and Nathan to Trevowan and stay here until Amelia's child is born. I will feed the twins between Amelia needing my attention.'

During the next forty-eight hours at Trevowan only

the children were able to sleep. Amelia's pains had not stopped and the birth was protracted. Edward's health began to improve and Elspeth insisted on staying in his room to ensure that he took his medication and did not attempt to leave his bed. On the second morning an angry outburst of raised voices drew Senara to Edward's room, while she left Leah to tend to Amelia.

Edward was deathly pale, which was accentuated by the dark stubble on his sunken cheeks, and his eyes were darkly ringed. He had swung his legs over the side of the bed and had swayed to his feet.

'Are you trying to kill yourself, you fool?' Elspeth harangued.

'Get out of my way. I have to get to the yard.'

'Stop this,' ordered Senara. 'You are upsetting Amelia. Please, sir, you must get back into bed, or the fever will return.'

His expression was haggard. 'I cannot lie here listening to my wife's screams in childbirth. Will the child never be born?'

Edward had lost Adam and St John's mother at their birth and Senara could see his pain and fear at Amelia's travail.

'I am sure the baby will be born in a few hours. The labour is slow but Amelia is strong. I cannot tend two patients at once. Get back into bed so that I can return to your wife.'

'I am needed at the yard. There is a problem with a delivery from the chandler. And a customer needs reassurance from me that his vessel will be delivered on time or he will cancel his order.'

'Japhet will speak with the customer and the chandler,' Senara answered.

'Japhet gets married tomorrow. He has his own responsibilities.' Edward was forced to clutch hold of the carved post of the tester bed to stop himself from falling.

Elspeth waved her stick menacingly at her brother. 'If you do not get back into bed, Japhet and the rest of the family will be attending your funeral in a few days.'

He glared at the two women. 'I cannot afford to rest. You know our financial situation.'

'You are being a stubborn fool, Edward,' Elspeth rapped out. 'A week or ten days will see you fit and able to carry out your duties. Even a lost order is not worth putting your life at risk for. If you do not die you could end up an invalid. Is that what you want?'

'I need to ensure that the future of my family is secure.'

Another scream from Amelia stopped Edward's tirade. He sank down on to the bed and held his head in his hands. Senara put a hand on his shoulder.

'Amelia needs me,' she said firmly. 'For the greater good of your family I must ask you to rest, sir. Allow Japhet to repay you for all you have done for him in the past by giving him permission to speak with the customer and chandler. He has called at the house every day to enquire if you have need of his services. If you rest you will be well enough to speak with them both in a week.'

Edward pushed her away but as he stood up a wave of dizziness buckled his knees and he sank back on to the bed. 'Please, go to Amelia. She needs you. Elspeth will send word to Japhet.'

'At last you are showing some sense,' Elspeth remarked as Senara left the room.

Senara paused in the doorway to look back and saw Elspeth clutch her brother's hand and there were tears in the older woman's eyes as she said, 'You cannot do everything. You have given us so much and never failed us in the past, Edward.'

The baby was born an hour later. Both mother and child were weak and exhausted from the birth ordeal. The baby was tiny compared to the twins at birth and its chest heaved frantically as it battled to draw each breath. Leah took the infant while Senara finished tending to Amelia. The baby was not making a sound.

'My baby! Where is my baby?' Amelia implored. 'Give me my baby!'

'I must tend to you first,' Senara said.

'Show me my baby. Why is it not crying?' Amelia pushed at Senara and tried to raise her body from the mattress in her distress.

Leah appeared at Senara's shoulder. 'You have a lovely daughter, Mrs Loveday. She is very small but alive.'

'I have a daughter.' She sank back on to the pillows and took the baby into her arms. Amelia sighed and closed her eyes, her voice drowsy. 'I have a daughter, Elspeth. Edward always wanted a daughter. We had decided that she will be called Joan after his mother. A pretty, unfussy name. I do not care for fanciful names. Joan is good and honest.'

Senara was alerted by Amelia's possessive tone. The slur upon Tamasine's name was deliberate. Senara hoped the outburst was caused by Amelia's emotions after the trauma of the birth, and would not have sinister implications to Tamasine in the future.

The baby was slow to suckle and, since Amelia was so tired, Leah took the infant away to be fed by the wet nurse. The signs were not good that the baby would thrive.

Adam awoke with a start. He could see nothing in the pitch darkness of the prison cell. He had no idea what time of day or night it was, for there were no windows in the dungeon. The air was rank and foul from the press of bodies of the crew of *Pegasus*. Neither himself as captain, any of the ship's officers, or Sir Gregory Kilmarthen had been shown any privileges due their rank. Sir Gregory had given his name simply as Greg Marten when the French Provost Marshall had demanded each of their names. With aristocrats still being guillotined, Sir Gregory wisely preferred anonymity.

Adam was chilled to the bone as he lay on the mildewed straw, the leather jerkin that he had been wearing at the time of his capture gave him little protection against the cold. Several sailors were snoring, one man constantly coughed and spat out gobbets of phlegm. The inadequate bucket in the corner, which served as a privy, was overflowing and had not been emptied for two days.

His sensibilities were now numbed to the depriva-
tions they were forced to endure. His stomach
growled with hunger, their daily portion of thin gruel
and stale bread left him constantly hungry, and his
clothing hung loose on his frame. Adam scratched
absently at the fleas and lice that infested his body. At
the sound of squeaks and scuffing by his feet, he
kicked out at the rats which tormented the prisoners
with their bites.

'Do you think they will ever release us?' Long Tom
who lay beside Adam drew his short legs to his chest.
'If the ransom moneys they said they were demanding
had been paid, surely we should have been freed by
now. We've been here months.'

'They could have kept the money. Though I doubt
the government would have paid. War is too costly a
business to ransom prisoners. They would have
applied to our estates. Squire Penwithick knew you
sailed with me and would have recognised your alias.
Our family coffers are empty.' He shrugged fatalisti-
cally and ran a hand over his thick growth of beard.
All the prisoners were unshaven and unkempt. 'I
would not want my father risking the security of
Trevowan, or the yard, for my life. I chose to go to sea
while we were at war against his wishes.'

'I doubt my family will suffer any twinge of conscience if I rot here.' Long Tom observed without
rancour. 'My cousin George, will be rubbing his
hands with glee that he will inherit the estate sooner
than he expected. My father put it in trust to him,

having no faith that I would marry and produce an heir. And in that my father was right. But I am determined to make ancient bones merely to spite George and my mother and sister.' He gave a dry mirthless laugh. 'Confound them! I never intended to rot away in a French prison. It is ironic after evading capture during my years as a spy for Penwithick.'

Adam stared into the darkness. 'Hours seem like weeks in this place. Every time the bolts of the door are drawn back hope rises that we are to be freed, then dread follows that the authorities have discovered your identity as Long Tom and my own as Black Jack when I rescued you from a French prison last year. They would shoot us as English spies without a trial.'

'There will be no link between Black Jack and Adam Loveday merchant adventurer. We did not fire on the French. They overran us. With the hold filled with tobacco they have no reason to suspect that *Pegasus* is other than a British merchant ship for you burned the letters of marque before we were taken prisoner.'

Cramp attacked the muscles in Adam's leg and he grimaced as he rubbed it to ease the pain. He stood up but there was no room to walk and exercise in the confined space; bodies were sprawled with only inches between them across the floor. He drew a ragged breath, the fetid stench clawing at his throat. There were hours upon end when the torture of inactivity was almost unbearable. He would close his mind to the press of bodies and conjure up images of Senara and his family. Visions of Trevowan and Boscabel, the bustling activity of the shipyard, or imagining the rise and fall of the deck of *Pegasus* beneath his feet and an expanse of ocean as far as the eye could see, temporarily brought him peace from the torment of his incarceration.

There was a hollow ache in his chest as he yearned for news of his family and home. They had been given no news from England since their capture, though their gaolers taunted them that the English fleet was defeated and the English aristos and gentry had better look to their heads when the French marched gloriously into London.

Adam did not believe their taunts, the English fleet were supreme masters of the sea, but his fears for his family were not so easy to disregard.

How did the yard fare? And Senara? Did he have a son or a daughter? He thrust the questions aside for they added to his misery. All must be well. Senara and the child were hale and hearty. To think otherwise was to court insanity.

The clang of the bolt being drawn back echoed around the cell and Adam squared his shoulders and smoothed the creases in his shirt-sleeves.

A gaoler holding a lantern shuffled into the room. Behind him were four soldiers in uniform, the French tricolour tied around their waists and each armed with a musket.

'Loveday. Marten.'

Adam exchanged a stoic glance with Long Tom as the soldiers circled them and they were marched from the cell. They climbed a spiral staircase lit by flambeaux to a room high in the circular tower, which served as their prison. The brightness of the daylit room dazzled his eyes and it was some moments before he made out a figure standing by the window. The man's back was to them. He was in uniform with gold epaulettes and a tricolour plume adorned the bicorne he was still wearing.

'I will be alone with the prisoners.' A familiar voice made the hackles of Adam's neck rise.

'What if they try to overpower you?' a soldier queried.

The officer raised his arm to point a pistol at Adam's heart. 'I am armed and in no danger. Two of the escort may remain outside the door.'

As the soldiers filed out Adam held the glare of the French officer – a man who knew his and Long Tom's identity and who had long been his sworn enemy. A man who had vowed to see him dead.

'Loveday. Not so proud now are you? I have but to snap my fingers and you will be hauled before the firing squad as a spy. You and your friend.'

Adam did not answer and allowed his disparaging gaze to travel over the French uniform. The last time he had seen him was when they crossed swords during the fight when Adam had rescued Long Tom. 'Etienne Rivière. I see your charm has not changed. You are still a traitor to your class.'

The officer stiffened with affront. 'I know how to rise with the tide. And I am not the one mouldering in a foreign gaol.'

Again Adam ignored his baiting, their hostile glares

remained locked and the silence that stretched between them was charged with hatred.

The officer stepped forward and cocked the pistol. 'There are many reasons why I should kill you, are there not, cousin? Not least that your family locked my sister in a mental institution. I have my spies in England.'

'I have had no news from my family for some months since I left America. You will know that Lisette is married to William Loveday who is with the English Fleet. Her mind has been unstable ever since you sold her into marriage to a brutal and debauched husband.'

The pistol was uncocked and slammed into the side of Adam's temple. He reeled from the blow and recovered his balance to stare into Etienne Rivière's dark, malevolent eyes.

'You always were a reckless fool, Adam. A hopeless idealist.'

'I see no shame in loyalty to one's family and country.'

Etienne scowled and backed away to lean against an oak table by the window. 'How deep is that loyalty when your life is at stake?'

'I would die before I betray my honour.'

The officer's head tilted to one side and he nodded to the window that overlooked the harbour of La Rochelle. '*Pegasus* is a fine ship. She will be a splendid fighting vessel for my country. They have installed several more cannon and will use her against your countrymen. You built her well. How many Englishmen will die when she is used in battle against them?'

Adam inwardly flinched at the taunt and his jaw clenched to control his emotions.

Etienne laughed. 'That struck your pride, did it not? What will your children think of you and your ship design that was turned against their countrymen, or your father? That is if he lives to hear of it. Did you know he was dying?'

'You lie!' Adam challenged.

Etienne shrugged. 'Why should I lie? So you know nothing of your father's fate. He was shot on Boscabel land and implicated with local smugglers. Not so proud now are you cousin? Your father is a common felon.'

When Adam started forward his arm was grabbed by Long Tom. 'It could all be lies, Adam.'

'But they are not.' Etienne Rivière sneered. 'Why should I lie when the truth is so damning?'

Adam digested the news with mixed emotions. He had never felt so helpless or impotent. 'La Rochelle is a long way from your usual territory, Etienne. Even you would not travel so far merely to gloat at my misfortune. Is there a price on my head?'

'You flatter yourself, cousin.' Etienne turned to regard Long Tom for the first time. 'It is your friend whom the authorities would be interested in.'

'Our countries are at war,' Long Tom responded. 'We are not afraid to die for our country. But ransoms have been demanded. Does the French government renege of their diplomatic policies?'

'We do not ransom spies. Spies are executed.'

Etienne retaliated with venom. 'Your little friend, Adam, is the notorious English spy Long Tom.' Etienne chuckled. 'I have your lives in my hands, it would appear.'

Adam held his cousin's glare in silence. Etienne pushed his figure from the desk and went to the window beckoning Adam to join him. 'Why should I wish you dead, cousin? Your ship is a fine vessel. The swiftest in her class they say. She is set to sail at the end of the week. What if I were to offer you your freedom? We both know your father is in no position to raise the ransom. There are reasons that make it expedient I leave France. For that I need your ship and you to captain her.'

Suspicion furrowed Adam's brow. 'Is this a trick?'

'We are cousins. Where is your family loyalty now? I am offering you your life and the life of your men. I can arrange for it that the guards are drugged and we sail out of here.'

'Why should I trust you?' Adam countered.

Etienne grinned. 'Have you a choice if you want to see your family and home again? Your father could be dead? What will happen to the yard and your children?'

The need to escape pulsed through Adam's veins, but could he trust Etienne?

'Why do you need to leave France?'

'That is my affair but suffice to say, my own life could be in danger if I do not leave these shores soon. We can help each other to gain our freedom.'

Still Adam hesitated and Etienne goaded, 'Much

has happened to your family in the months you have been away. You are needed at home.'

'What news do you have of my family?' Adam could not stop himself asking. 'Is my father truly so close to death?'

'I need to start a new life in England. If you intend to rot away here then I shall find another means of leaving France.'

'Of course I want to escape. But tell me first of my family.'

'Edward is indeed gravely ill. You also have a new baby sister and the gypsy woman you married . . .' Etienne chuckled maliciously, 'I will have your word that you agree to my proposal before I say more.'

'I will do what ever it takes to recover my ship and return to England,' Adam ground out. 'What of my wife? Was she safely delivered of a child?'

'You are now the father of twins – a boy and a girl if my information is correct. I will need some days to finalise my plans. You have not only the prison to escape from; we must ensure that the chains across the harbour are also lowered to gain our freedom.'

Etienne listened to the guard's footsteps escorting his cousin fade away. His expression was cold and calculating. He had learned from a chance encounter with a fellow officer in a Bordeaux brothel that an English ship had been captured and her crew taken to La Rochelle. It was hailed as a triumph by the French and he soon heard that the captured ship was *Pegasus* and immediately he suspected that it was his cousin's ship. It was also rumoured that the captain and first mate were gentlemen and that ransoms had been demanded. A contact within a band of French smugglers delivering goods to Cornwall had kept him informed of the events happening to the Loveday family and also his sister Lisette.

It had taken several weeks for Etienne to use his influence to have a legitimate reason to visit La Rochelle on army business. He had been used before as an interpreter for the army as he spoke fluent English. Over the last two years he had amassed a fortune in stolen jewels from the aristocrats he had arrested in the name of the New Regime. But more than one superior officer was becoming suspicious and insurrection within the new government had seen the heads of several ministers meet the same fate from Madame Guillotine as the aristocrats those ministers had previously ordered to their deaths. Etienne knew his days in office were numbered. He needed to leave France and he intended to do so a rich man.

A bemused Adam was escorted back to his cell. He did not trust Etienne Rivière. And if his cousin needed to escape France, it was to save his own hide in some way. Yet Adam knew he had no choice but to trust Etienne in this. In wartime there was never any guarantee, even if ransoms were paid, that the captives were freed immediately. Negotiations could drag on for months.

The blood flowed hotly in Adam's veins. His ransom money would never free *Pegasus* from being a prize of war. Etienne's plan meant that not only would he return home but also that *Pegasus* would not be lost to him.

That night he slept soundly in the cell for the first time. His dreams were filled with his reunion with Senara and the joy of holding his twins in his arms.

Chapter Twenty-Nine

Dozens of carriages filled the single street of Trewenna village and were amassed around the green with its duck pond. The voices singing the final hymn faded away. Outside the church the villagers, dressed in their Sunday best, angled for a better view between the wide girths of the yew trees surrounding the churchyard. The early afternoon sun glistened on the drunkenly tilted headstones, the grass between the graves recently scythed and the gravel path cleared of weeds for the grandest wedding the church had witnessed in centuries. The bells began to peal, sending to flight a score of rooks from the trees, and several pigeons flapped noisily from the belfry window.

Inside the church Margaret and Cecily dabbed at their eyes as, after taking their vows, the smiling couple processed back down the aisle past the glittering array of nobles and gentry, their gaudy plumage bright against the plain stone walls.

Gwen dressed in oyster silk embroidered with gold thread, wore a garland of lilies of the valley in her hair.

She was radiant with happiness. Japhet grinned, smiling down at his wife with cool composure.

'Pinch me, Japhet,' Gwendolyn whispered. 'This is not all a dream, is it?'

'If it was a dream these new buckled shoes of mine would not be cramping my toes,' he teased, and closed his hand over her arm that was linked through his. He stroked the sensitive skin on the inside of her forearm with his finger and stooped to whisper against her ear, 'At last I can make you mine.'

Gwendolyn blushed crimson and the Honourable Percy Fetherington laughed aloud. 'Wait till you get your bride outside the church before you make love to her.'

'This is the house of God,' Pious Peter was quick to denounce the young nobleman. 'Have you no sense of what is seemly?'

'Your turn next Peter.' Fetherington was unabashed. 'Or will you become a monk?'

'Not much chance of that. Did you see the way the young Polglase girl was making eyes at him outside in the churchyard. He's made a conquest there,' another man chortled.

'You malign the honour of a sweet young girl, with your vile insinuations. I am a man of God, while you . . .' Peter started forward but Cecily put a restraining hand on him. 'Ignore them, Peter. I want no sermons from you today. Your father is in charge of his flock. We are celebrating your brother's wedding and ribaldry must be tolerated.'

Peter bristled and drew back.

Senara stood in a pew with Japhet's sister, Hannah, and her husband Oswald and their four children. Hannah was expecting her fifth child and was looking pale and drawn. Oswald had coughed throughout the ceremony and Senara had seen flecks of blood on his handkerchief. He was frailer than ever after this last winter and when she looked into his eyes, she knew that another winter could likely kill him. Senara had heard the comments from Fetherington and his company and they unsettled her. Bridie and her mother were amongst the locals who had turned out to watch the wedding. She had hoped that Bridie would have got over her infatuation for Peter by now.

As the bridal couple left the church, Lady Anne Druce and Lady Traherne walked stiffly and were unsmiling. Margaret Mercer joined Hannah, her eyes sparkling with mischief. 'The Lady Anne is taking this with bad grace. You would think the woman would be happy for her daughter. And I am sure that Japhet intends to change.'

Hannah was jubilant. 'Japhet speaks of nothing but the horses he will raise. He has already purchased three mares, which are in our stables. It will be another month before the papers are signed on the farm he will buy.'

'And in the meantime they will live with you,' Margaret said.

'Gwen refuses to stay at Traherne Hall,' Hannah sighed. 'It is such a pity there is this constraint between her and her mother. Roslyn has been equally unpleasant. For appearances' sake Gwen allowed the wedding breakfast to take place at Traherne Hall but they will not even spend their wedding night there. Squire Penwithick has offered them the use of his hunting lodge at Polmasyn and the couple will be travelling together to several stables to buy more horses. Gwendolyn is as excited as Japhet at the prospect.'

'I always said they were well suited,' Margaret said with satisfaction. 'I wish them well.'

'How are Uncle Edward and Amelia?' Hannah asked.

'Edward has finally come to his senses and has promised to stay in bed for another week. His health is improving. A customer hearing of Japhet's wedding has replaced the order at the yard for a brigantine that he had previously cancelled. That has eased his worries. Amelia is recovering quickly from her travail.'

'And how is baby Joan? When I saw her yesterday she was still slow to take her feed. She is very small.'

'Joan is a fighter,' Margaret answered. 'She is taking some milk and that is heartening. Amelia will not let her daughter out of her sight and I can see Joan will be in danger of being thoroughly spoiled.'

Hannah turned to Senara. 'As usual you have been in the thick of tending our family. How are the twins?'

'Joel is forever making his presence felt and demands his food in the most strident manner,' Senara laughed. 'Rhianne is no trouble at all and smiles at everyone.'

Hannah chuckled. 'There is no mistaking which one takes after which parent. Adam was a little terror when he was a child, always into trouble. Joel sounds just like him.' She nudged Senara to look over her shoulder where Peter was again talking to Bridie. 'Peter often mentions your sister.'

The carriages set off from Trewenna church to Traherne amidst great cheering from the villagers.

Peter stayed behind after the wedding guests departed. He knelt before the altar and lowered his head in prayer. His mind was tormented by the earthly passions that continually beset him. Aware that the wild, passionate nature of his brother ran as hotly in his blood, he prayed for the strength to overcome his lustful desires. Beautiful women were a constant temptation and difficult to resist, but he always despised their lack of morals after they succumbed to him. Even today, during the service in this holy place, he had seen the bold invitations sent to him in the eyes of three married women. Such women who were bored with their husbands were brazen in their means to seduce him. His piety seemed to spur them on to beguile a lay preacher into their bed.

He prayed harder to find the strength to resist the sins of the flesh, knowing that today, during the celebrations at Traherne Hall, temptation would be at his shoulder to fall from grace.

At the sound of a soft footstep behind him he suppressed his irritation at the intrusion and rose to his feet.

'I am sorry I thought everyone had left. I came to ensure that the church was tidy in readiness for tomorrow's service.' Bridie Polglase hovered uncertainly inside the door. Since summer she had taken on the duties of cleaning the church.

'I will not keep you from your work.' Peter answered.

'But I disturbed your prayers.'

Bridie was standing in a shaft of sunlight from the stained glass window depicting the slaying of the dragon by St George. Her elfin face was troubled, ethereal and beautiful. She blushed under his scrutiny and lowered her eyes. Her long straight brown hair was tied back with a blue ribbon and Peter could see a pulse fluttering at the side of her neck.

The impulse to kiss that throbbing flesh was so strong that he was appalled at his reaction.

'I must join my family at Traherne Hall,' he said abruptly. As he made to walk past her, her eyes lifted to hold his stare and he was caught by the adoration of her gaze. He halted at her side, the faint smell of lavender that she rubbed into her hair and clothing wafting around him.

Bridie became flustered and picked up a lily of the valley from the floor that had fallen from Gwendolyn's bouquet. She smelt the flower and sighed. 'Miss Druce looked so lovely and happy. She loves Japhet so very much. They will be happy together. Just like Senara and Adam.'

With a shy smile, she walked out of the church and Peter followed her, unable to take his gaze from her slender figure and the soft curve of her hips. Her innocence had always attracted him and it had moved him to bring her back into the fold of the church away from the heathenish ways of her sister.

She bent to recover a white satin ribbon from the wooden seat in the porch. 'One of the good luck favours has fallen from Miss Druce's dress. You must return it to her.' She held it out for Peter to take.

His fingers closed over her slender palm and the heat of flesh scorched him. His senses swirled and he pulled her into his arms and kissed her.

To his astonishment she wriggled like an eel, and then his face stung from her slap.

'How dare you!' She stared at him with dismay and backed away. 'You are a man of God. A woman should only kiss her husband in that way.'

When she turned to run away, Peter grabbed her arm. His heart was beating uncomfortably fast. 'Your pardon. My actions are inexcusable.'

She wrenched her arm free and hobbled from the church. Peter stared after her in a stupefied fashion. From her blushes in his company Peter knew Bridie was attracted to him. He had expected her to respond to his kiss and more. Instead she had reprimanded him. Her virtue was refreshing and tantalising. Peter put a hand to his temple to still his wayward thoughts. How easily he had nearly fallen from grace. His prayers had gone unheeded.

He returned to the church to pray now in penitence and it was an hour before he left to rejoin his family at Traherne Hall. He had frowned upon Adam for marrying beneath him to a woman who was little better than a gypsy. Peter was angry with himself that his own emotions had so betrayed him. Had Bridie Polglase bewitched him as he had believed that Senara had bewitched Adam? He saw clearly that to prove his love of the Lord he must save Bridie's soul from the devil.

Traherne Hall was decorated with masses of fresh-cut spring flowers and a sumptuous table was laid for the guests. Throughout, Gwendolyn had never been more vivacious, and Japhet seemed unable to take his eyes from his bride whenever they parted and mingled with their guests.

By mid-afternoon Japhet whisked Gwendolyn away from the revellers to be alone in her room. Her trunks were packed and a jade-green travelling gown laid on the bed for her to change into before they left for the hunting lodge.

Immediately the bedchamber door was closed behind them Japhet drew Gwendolyn into his arms. 'At last I have you alone and I can show you how irresistible you are as a woman. I have waited for this moment for such a long, long time.'

'As have I, my love. And now I fear that my inexperience will not please you. You are used to—'

He silenced her with a kiss and when he broke away, his voice was rough with anger. 'You are all I want, my darling Gwen. The past is over and done with. Your innocence is your most precious gift to me. The most precious gift any man could have. I never want to fail you or willingly cause you hurt as I hurt you in the past.'

Gwendolyn put a finger to his lips. The love and tenderness in his eyes set her heart racing. 'No promises, Japhet. This is a time for loving, not for recriminations. I have your love. That is what is important to me and I hope I will never disappoint you as a wife.'

'That would be impossible. Enough of words. Time for me to prove how much I do love you, my beloved.'

They could hear the laughter and music from downstairs and where the guests had spilled out into the garden, and became oblivious to the shouts for their reappearance when it was discovered that the couple were missing. They had time only for each other. Finally, as they lay replete in each other's arms, Japhet felt a deep contentment that he had never experienced before.

'Our future holds such promise, my darling.' He leaned over her and tenderly stroked her face. 'I do love you. Never doubt it.'

Gwendolyn glowed with happiness and it was some time before she became aware that the revellers had fallen silent. There was a heavy tread upon the stairs and along the landing to halt outside Gwendolyn's room. A loud banging on the door made her start and Japhet curse.

'Go away. We have no wish to be disturbed,' Japhet called out.

'You must dress and come downstairs at once, Japhet,' Sir Henry said in a grave and ominous manner.

Japhet laughed. 'Away with you, Henry. This is no time for japes.'

'I wish it was a jest, Japhet. This is serious and your presence is required.'

Japhet felt his euphoria drain away to be replaced by a sickening dread. He rolled from the bed and wrapped the bedcover around his naked figure and opened the door.

'Get dressed, Japhet.' Sir Henry looked shaken. 'There is an official downstairs demanding you attend upon him immediately. He has six armed men with him. I threatened to throw him off the estate but he would not be moved. I had him taken to my study. I did not want to cause a scene with so many guests. But they are suspicious that something is wrong.'

'I will be down directly.' Japhet closed the door and sank back against it, his face wet with sweat. He rubbed a shaking hand across his cheeks.

'My God, Gwen. I think they've come to arrest me!'

She ran to his side. 'That cannot be. It is a jape played by your friends.'

He shook his head and pulled on his breeches and shirt. In the fading sunlight the scars on his back were a chilling reminder of his wild past.

'If you truly fear the worst – then go. Get away from here as fast as you can.'

'I will not desert you on our wedding day.'

'Better that than they arrest you for the robbery on the heath. That is what you fear, is it not?'

Japhet shrugged his arms into his jacket and smoothed back his hair. His haggard expression spoke more poignantly than words. 'You deserve better than me abandoning you. I have to face this, Gwen. By running away I will only bring further shame upon you. I am so sorry. How can you ever forgive me?'

She gathered up her garments. 'Help me to dress. We will face this together. I am sure it is some wicked jest to disrupt our lovemaking. We will face it with dignity.'

Japhet prayed that Gwendolyn was right as he laced her into her travelling gown. She straightened his stock and adjusted the diamond pin before standing on tiptoe to kiss him, and he could feel that despite her brave words she was trembling.

Arm in arm and each with a bold smile they descended the stairs. Their families and friends had gathered at the foot of the staircase. The Honourable Percy Fetherington swayed tipsily as he raised his goblet to them. 'It is too bad of you, old boy, to hide away and desert us. Can't say that I blame you, though.'

There was a nervous laugh from several others and Gwendolyn was optimistic that Japhet's fear was in vain.

It was then she saw the seven men in military uniform all carrying muskets. One stepped forward.

'Japhet Loveday, otherwise known as Gentleman James, we arrest you in the King's name on suspicion of two counts of highway robbery.'

'This is outrageous,' Sir Henry declared. 'I have never heard anything so ridiculous. Mr Loveday is no thief and this is his wedding day. You can't arrest him.'

'I but do my duty.'

'I am a magistrate,' Sir Henry proclaimed. 'Japhet

will answer to me in the morning and this whole matter will be cleared up.'

'With respect, Sir Henry,' the official stood his ground and the soldiers raised their muskets in warning, 'Mr Loveday is to stand trial at the Old Bailey. He will be conveyed to Newgate Gaol. Several parties have given evidence as to his guilt.'

'There is no point in making this matter worse than it is.' Japhet disengaged his arm from Gwen's. 'I will come peaceably, gentlemen.'

The soldiers closed ranks around him and he was marched from the house to stunned silence from the guests.

Gwen ran after them and pushed aside a guard to fling herself into Japhet's arms. When a soldier would pull her away, Japhet said, 'One moment, if you please. This is difficult for my wife.'

The officer in charge clipped out without looking at Japhet, 'You have one minute to say what needs to be said. No tricks, sir.'

'Be brave, my darling. There can be no proof against me.'

'I believe in you, Japhet.' She clung to him in a final embrace. 'Whatever happens I will never abandon you. I will stand by you. We have come through so much. It cannot all be taken from us now.'

Japhet kissed her and then gently put her from him. His head was high and defiant as he was marched away between the soldiers to confront his fate.

Headline hopes that you have enjoyed reading THE LOVEDAY SCANDALS. We now invite you to sample the beginning of LOVEDAY HONOUR, the fifth book in this captivating series.

Chapter One

June 1794

'If a man does not have honour, he has nothing,' Edward Loveday declared to his wife. 'I will never sacrifice my honour simply to make life more comfortable, Amelia.'

Amelia ignored him and stared out of the window of the orangery at Trevowan, where they had taken their afternoon tea. Her auburn hair was coiled at the nape of her neck and partly hidden under a lace cap. The tilt of her chin was stubborn and the set of her shoulders uncompromising. There had been too many strained silences in recent months.

Edward had hoped that the birth of their daughter three months ago would heal their differences. He tried again to ease the tension between them. 'It is time to put the past behind us, my dear. Are you not allowing your recriminations to mar all that has been good in our lives?'

'Scandal is eroding the good name of the Loveday

family. How can you make it seem that I am the one in the wrong?' She kept her face averted and her chest rose and fell in growing agitation. 'Since our marriage your family has been linked to one scandal after another. Even *you* have not spared me. Where is the honour in that?'

'You twist my words. Have I not asked your forgiveness for the pain I have caused you? Are these times not difficult enough without your censure?'

'I cannot condone—' She broke off abruptly and took several deep breaths before resuming in a martyred tone. 'I pray daily that all members of this family will bring no further shame to our door.'

Edward suppressed a sigh and picked up his newssheet. Where Amelia saw shame in the actions of his family members, Edward was worried that fate and fortune had conspired against them and that their lives were in jeopardy. These were ruthless and uncertain times.

The strident tapping of a teaspoon against the bone china saucer soon made it impossible for him to read. He folded the newssheet and put it aside and studied the tense figure of his wife. Amelia was staring across the grounds of the estate, her eyes focused upon the spire of Trewenna church. Even in her late thirties, she was still lovely; her hair, though streaked with grey at the temples, was thick and luxuriant and her complexion creamy without the necessity of powder.

The tinkling peal of the spoon against the cup tested Edward's patience to its limit. He was relieved when a maid entered to clear the tea tray and Amelia relinquished her spoon with a terse sigh.

The afternoon sun dappled the leaves on the hawthorn, oak and elm trees on the hill behind the house and its rays slanted through the panes of glass of the orangery. The sunlight turned the white marble floor golden, and the leaves of the orange bushes in their stone urns cast shadows across the carved wood of the chairs and low tables. Edward squinted his blue eyes against the brightness of the glare. His heart was heavy, weighted by worries. He feared for the life of his son, Adam, a prisoner of the French; and also his nephew, Japhet, accused of highway robbery and now awaiting trial in London's most notorious prison – Newgate.

He reached out to touch a lock of Amelia's hair but she pulled back from him. This coldness between them was hard to bear. He was a passionate man and he did not want a loveless marriage. But if he had not yet won Amelia's understanding, how could he hope for her forgiveness? Honour bound him to the obligations of his past as well as the present, but he loved his wife, and was determined that his marriage would not be sacrificed on the altar of family duty.

Edward had lost patience with his wife's manner. The gentle, loving woman of their first four years of marriage had changed into a bitter, judgemental woman in the last year. This Amelia was a stranger to him. Edward did not condone Japhet's conduct or the circumstances that had led to the trial of his eldest son, St John. But Edward accepted the frailties of others. He was fiercely loyal to his family and expected no less loyalty from his wife.

A fit of coughing made him turn away from Amelia. Pain lanced through his chest and sweat stippled his upper lip and brow. He led a far from conventional life himself. His health had suffered from a recent run-in with Excise officers on Loveday land when they had found contraband hidden by a local smuggler. In the confrontation Edward had been shot and the wound was slow to heal.

'I have duties on the estate that must be attended to,' Edward announced.

He stood up too quickly, and, again, pain shot through his chest. Momentarily, the room spun around him. He dragged in a deep breath and caught sight of his reflection in the window. His tall, slender figure was slightly stooped and he straightened his spine. The movement sharpened the pain in his chest and he clenched his jaw to overcome it.

'You do too much, Edward,' she scolded. 'You must put your health first.'

He stared at her lovely face taut with unhappiness and fears and his love overrode his anger. Amelia had endured much in the last two years, and her sensibilities had often been offended. Even indiscretions from his own past had returned to put a further trial upon his marriage. But those indiscretions had been many years before he had met Amelia and he refused to be judged by her because of them. There was no reasoning with Amelia at the moment and he prayed that in time she would be more charitably disposed towards the tribulations they had faced during their marriage. He loved her deeply and wanted the rift between them to end.

'You should be resting, Edward. You were coughing through the night again. Dr Chegwidden says you do too much. There is a cold wind off the sea. You will get a fever if you go out.'

He disregarded her advice. He could not afford to pander to the pain in his chest and the bouts of weakness that struck him without warning. Too much depended on him rebuilding the reputation of the shipyard. 'I am well enough. You worry too much. And my dear, you must try not to dwell upon the misfortunes and trials that have beset us. It is the future that is important.' He bowed over her hand and lifted it to his lips. 'I will never abandon my duty to any member of my family, but your happiness is of great import to me. You were my rock in the first years of our marriage and have blessed me with two wonderful children. My feelings for you have not changed, my love. I esteem you above all women. It has been nearly a year since we have truly lived as man and wife. A family is only strong when it is united. Is it not time to put aside our differences?'

Her hand was cold and she redrew it to clasp both hands firmly in her lap. Her eyes were filled with tears and pain as she held his stare. 'Whilst your illegitimate daughter continues to live at the shipyard I feel humiliated and shamed. Send her away and I will be a true wife to you, Edward.'

Her conditions were unacceptable. The weight of

his burdens pressed down on him. A sharp pain shot through his chest each time he drew a deep breath. Amelia's stubbornness was a bitter betrayal. He knew he was pushing himself past the limits of his endurance, but he had never turned his back on his family or duty and whatever the cost he would not fail them now.

The sea mist rolled across the gently swelling waves and rose to obscure all but the tops of the stone chain towers built opposite each other at the mouth of the River Fowey. Behind the towers on each side of the river, the hills sloped down to the water's edge, sheltering the harbour from the storms and strong winds that could sweep this coast. Each side of the harbour rolling hills embraced the horizon, the grass and tree-lined slopes ink black against a milky sky.

Impatience rippled through the emaciated figure of Adam Loveday as he stood on the quarterdeck of his ship. The chain guarding Fowey harbour creaked as the winches within the towers lowered the chain to the riverbed. After nine months away from his home it was frustrating to be delayed further by this final barrier. But the chain across the harbour mouth was necessary to allow the citizens of the port to sleep safe in their beds from a surprise attack by a French warship.

Adam had dropped anchor whilst the harbour master was rowed out to inspect *Pegasus* and ensure that she was indeed under the command of her English captain. Several months ago word had reached Fowey that the French had captured *Pegasus* and her crew and that a ransom had been demanded for the release of the men. The harbour master was right to be suspicious. As a prize of war *Pegasus* could be used by the French to enter her homeport and then turn her guns on the people.

The ragged and emaciated condition of the crew bore testament to the months that they had lain fearing for their lives in a French prison at La Rochelle. As the sun broke through the morning mist, Adam lifted his head and breathed deeply to calm the thundering beat of his heart. He brushed aside a long tendril of black hair that had escaped from the leather strip that restrained it. He had been away for so many months, first visiting a cousin's plantation in Virginia, trading the cargo of furniture he had invested in to other plantation owners – English furniture was still prized in the old colony. It had been a prosperous venture and he had acquired many contracts from the tobacco plantations to ship their cargo to England. But on the return voyage *Pegasus* had been attacked by three French ships and overpowered.

Pegasus sailed past the quay at Fowey where several tall masted ships were docked; two more were anchored in the river channel waiting to be unloaded when a mooring on the quay was available. The fishing luggers bobbed and swayed in the shallow water and a ferryman rowed three passengers from the landing stage across the water at Polruan to Fowey. Now that the chains were lowered the fishermen would be preparing to set out to sea. From the shore at Polruan, the familiar hammering from a boatyard was audible, causing a dull ache of homesickness to rise in Adam's breast. How had his family shipyard at Trevowan Hard fared? Before Adam had sailed the yard had been struggling to survive. Several orders for new ships had been cancelled following the trial of his elder twin, St John, for the murder of the smuggler Thadeous Lanyon.

St John had been innocent but Thadeous Lanyon had long been a sworn enemy of the Loveday family and the reputation of the family had suffered as a result of the trial. To allow the gossip to die down, their father, Edward, had insisted that St John join Adam on his voyage to Virginia and remain for a year or so on the estate of Garfield Penhaligan, a cousin from his grandmother's side of the family. Adam had anticipated returning with a substantial profit that would ease the financial burdens of the yard. Instead he had been lucky to return with his ship and his life. The French had taken the cargo of tobacco he was transporting for the Virginian planters and his honour demanded that they be repaid.

He had failed his father and his family but at least *Pegasus* had been retaken from the French. When Adam and his crew escaped from the prison at La Rochelle, *Pegasus* had still been moored at the port. The French had repaired her main mast, which had been shattered by cannon fire in the fight before her capture. Unfortunately there had been no provisions other than ship's biscuits on board. The journey from La Rochelle had taken eight days as the winds had been against them, but they had managed to evade any French ships. With *Pegasus* again in his possession, he still had the chance to restore the family fortunes, even if that meant becoming a privateer and capturing any lone French ships he encountered while England remained at war with France.

A man climbed the steps to the quarterdeck, his swarthy features smug with satisfaction and his black eyes coldly arrogant. 'Cousin Adam, you have brought us safe to England's shore.' His French accent was obvious. 'You dealt with the harbour master well. It was inspired of you to suggest that I was a French Royalist who had information for your Squire Penwithick to pass on to your Prime Minister.'

Adam regarded his cousin with little liking. His dark hair was short and foppishly curled and wide side-whiskers emphasised the sallowness of his complexion. Etienne Rivière was immaculately dressed in black close-fitting breeches and a cut-away coat. The ruffles on his shirtfront and at his wrist were starched and pristine white. Standing beside him Adam felt like a vagabond in the crumpled and stained clothes he had been wearing in prison. Though Adam had shaved that morning and done his best to get the worst of the stench and grime washed from his shirt and breeches, lack of soap had made cleaning them difficult. He was ashamed to return home in such a bedraggled state.

There was a harshness to Etienne's angular face that showed him to be both ruthless and untrustworthy. The Frenchman's glance was mocking as it flickered over Adam's dishevelled clothing. In response Adam stiffened his spine. The ragged state of his clothing would never make him feel inferior to his cousin. They had been enemies for several years, but for reasons of his own, Etienne Rivière, had aided Adam's escape from the French prison on the condition that Adam allowed him to sail to England with them.

'I spoke the truth to the harbour master,' Adam curtly informed him. 'Squire Penwithick will be interested in any information you can give him. Shortly after the fall of the Bastille in Paris you joined the revolution to further your own interests and have served the French army for the last couple of years. I advise you to co-operate with our government. There will be those among your exiled countrymen who know you for a traitor and will suspect you of being a spy for the new regime. They will shoot you, given the chance.'

Etienne raised a brow in disbelief, then shrugged. 'I will talk to your squire. I have no intention of returning to France.'

'Because there is a price on your head?' Adam challenged. 'Your aristocratic wife and your daughter lost their lives on the guillotine. To save your own hide you abandoned them when you joined the army of the revolution. And before that you sacrificed your sister, Lisette, into a marriage with a debauched lecher.'

Etienne Rivière's thin lips lifted into a sneer. 'I arranged for Lisette to marry a Marquis when my father wanted her wed to you. I told you when the betrothal was announced that you would never have Lisette as your bride.'

Adam bristled at the insult but in truth it had no power to hurt him. He had never loved Lisette and would have wed her out of duty. Her marriage to the Marquis had left him free to marry the woman he loved. But Lisette had been young and innocent, and the debauched demands of her husband, coupled with her experiences during the early days of the revolution, had left her emotionally unstable. Her mood swings were volatile and perilously close to madness at times.

Adam resisted the urge to strike the arrogant sneer from his cousin's face. 'You callously bartered with Lisette's life. And your mother died because of your neglect. You are not welcome at our home. When you land give your report to Squire Penwithick and then leave Cornwall.'

'I will leave Cornwall when I am ready. You cannot stop me seeing my sister. The last news I heard of her was that your family had shut her away in an asylum. Edward Loveday has much to answer for.'

'Lisette despises you for the way you treated her,' Adam flared. 'And you forget she is now married to my Uncle William.'

'William Loveday is a naval captain with no land or property. He is unworthy of her. How can a naval captain support Lisette in the manner that she has been reared to accept?'

Adam stepped forward with his fist clenched. It was rare that he and Etienne met without the threat of physical violence. A short, stocky figure stepped between the two enraged cousins. The man's wavy cinnamon hair was worn loose and cut short above his shoulders. 'Gentlemen! Would you brawl in front of the men?'

Sir Gregory Kilmarthen stood four feet high in his socks. Despite the shortness of his figure, the voice carried the authority of his ancient family, which followed in an unbroken line of baronets since the days of William the Conqueror.

Adam controlled his temper and nodded to his friend. 'You are right, Long Tom.' Adam used the name by which Sir Gregory had been known to him when they first met. Long Tom had been an English spy in France and when he was captured Adam had been sent by Squire Penwithick to rescue the nobleman. Long Tom's dwarf stature had startled him at first, but it had provided Long Tom with an easy disguise to travel with strolling players providing entertainments in the cities and send information back to England. Sir Gregory Kilmarthen had the sharpest mind Adam had ever encountered. They had become close friends and Long Tom had joined Adam on this fateful voyage.

Adam turned to Etienne, delivering an ultimatum. 'Trevowan Hard is less than a mile downriver. My cousin will be leaving the ship and we will not meet socially again.'

A sarcastic laugh burst from Etienne Rivière. 'Indeed not! Your gypsy wife does not mix in the social circles I shall be enjoying.'

At the insult to Senara, Adam swung out at his cousin, slamming his fist into his jaw. Etienne reeled backward crashing against the railing of the quarter-deck. When he recovered his balance, he rubbed his jaw, his black eyes narrowed with hatred.

'You'll regret laying a hand on me, cousin. I needed your ship to escape from France and had it been possible for me to get away and leave you rotting in a French prison I would have happily done so. I do not need your family and the limited connections they would offer me.'

Etienne swung away and marched to his quarters.

Long Tom looked up at Adam. 'If you are wise, you will stay away from your cousin, Adam. He will cause trouble. He hates you.'

'There is no love lost between us. I vowed to kill him for the way he abandoned his mother and Lisette. He is a traitor to his family and his homeland. He deserves to die. The day will come when we cross swords and he will answer for his treachery. Honour demands it.'

Long Tom did not try to dissuade Adam. A true gentleman lived and even died by the code of honour, which governed their society.

The Loveday Trials

Kate Tremayne

CORNWALL: 1793
As the Lovedays' finances recover from near ruin, it is clear their trials are far from over.

Adam, returning to Trevowan with Senara – now his wife – and their baby son, finds himself at loggerheads with his father. Edward refuses to accept his son's choice of bride, and as a result Adam finds it impossible to continue working in the family shipyard. To support his wife and child, he works as an English agent in a France still in the grip of the Terror, whilst Senara strives to be accepted by the Lovedays.

Adam's brother St John, meanwhile, is in trouble again. His involvement in the murky world of smuggling has made him some dangerous enemies – not least the corrupt and evil Thadeous Lanyon – and when Thadeous is found murdered, St John is arrested. If found guilty, he will be hanged. Can the Lovedays pull together as they have done before? Or will these new trials finally tear them apart?

Don't miss *Adam Loveday* and *The Loveday Fortunes*, the first two books in this compelling series:

'Thrilling family saga . . . leaves the reader breathless for the next book in the series' *Historical Novels Review*

'Guaranteed to appeal to those who have been entranced by *Poldark*' *Sussex Life*

0 7472 6412 0

headline

The Loveday Fortunes

Kate Tremayne

Cornwall: 1791. As the civil unrest in France gathers force, ripples of conflict are also reaching across the Channel, for the Loveday family are fighting their own private battles. Charles Mercer – Edward Loveday's brother-in-law – has been found dead, the reputation of his eminent bank in tatters. Charles has left the Lovedays facing emotional trauma and financial ruin.

But risk comes as second nature to the Lovedays. Adam finds refuge from the pressures of keeping the family boat-yard solvent in the arms of gypsy-bred Senara – whom he is determined to marry despite his father's threats of dis-inheritance. And his twin, St John, angry at having to curb his spending, throws his hand in with the Sawle brothers – the notorious smugglers who rule Penuran by intimidation and violence.

As changing fortunes strain a family already buckling with internal tensions, each one of the Lovedays must sacrifice personal ambition and unite like never before to overcome such a crisis. But to some of them sacrifice does not come easy . . .

Packed with drama, tensions and passion, *The Loveday Fortune* – the second book in the Loveday series – is a totally unputdownable read.

'A thrilling family saga . . . leaves the reader breathless for the next book' *Historical Novels Review*

'Guaranteed to appeal to those who have been entranced by *Poldark*' Sussex Life

0 7472 6411 2

headline

Now you can buy any of these other bestselling
Headline books from your bookshop or
direct from the publisher.

FREE P&P AND UK DELIVERY
(Overseas and Ireland £3.50 per book)

Vale Valhalla	Joy Chambers	£5.99
The Journal of Mrs Pepys	Sara George	£6.99
The Last Great Dance on Earth	Sandra Gulland	£6.99
Killigrew and the Incorrigibles	Jonathan Lunn	£5.99
Virgin	Robin Maxwell	£6.99
The One Thing More	Anne Perry	£5.99
A History of Insects	Yvonne Roberts	£6.99
The Eagle's Conquest	Simon Scarrow	£5.99
The Kindly Ones	Caroline Stickland	£5.99
The Seventh Son	Reay Tannahill	£6.99
Bone House	Betsy Tobin	£6.99
The Loveday Trials	Kate Tremayne	£6.99
The Passion of Artemisia	Susan Vreeland	£6.99

TO ORDER SIMPLY CALL THIS NUMBER

01235 400 414

or visit our website: www.madaboutbooks.com

Prices and availability subject to change without notice.